THE OBSCURITY IN WISHING

USA TODAY BESTSELLING AUTHOR

M.L. PHILPITT

AUTHOR'S NOTE

The Obscurity in Wishing is book 6 of The Fractured Ever Afters series. This reads as a standalone but for complete background on the characters' lives and how we've gotten to Yasmine and Caladin's story, you can start for free with book 1, The Hunt in Elusion.

This book has content some people may find triggering. You can read the content warning list on the last page.

This book uses Canadian spelling. This means words will have U's in them, "re", or double LL's. (colour vs color, centre vs center, signalling vs signaling, etc.) These are not typos.

PLAYLIST

“Nowhere To Go” by Bad Omens
“I’m Not Okay” by Citizen Soldier
“I Didn’t Ask For This” by Beth Crowley
“Nightmares” by Ellise
“Make Hate to Me” by Citizen Soldier
“Dangerous State of Mind” by Chri$tian Gate$
“Glad You Came” by The Wanted
“The Death of Peace of Mind” by Bad Omens
“A Drop in the Ocean” by Ron Pope
“Speechless” by Naomi Scott
“Lilith” by Ellise
“A Whole New World” by Lea Salonga & Brade Kane
“War of Hearts” by Ruelle
“Meet Me on the Battlefield” by SVRCINA
“Another Life” by Motionless In White
“Walk Through Fire” by Zayde Wolfe & Ruelle
“Awake and Alive” by Skillet

For those fighting through the restraints that try to keep you down.
Take control. Don't let them win.

I hate my cousin.

If it wasn't for Erico, my pain-in-the-ass older cousin and Boss of the *Famiglia*, I wouldn't be in some random city called White Rock, British Columbia, Canada. *Canada.* The place where "eh" is attached to every statement. Their government must control what they all drink because it seems like every second person carries a red takeout coffee cup. Best of all: there's been three instances in which people have accidentally bumped into one another, where *both parties* apologized.

What is wrong with these people? The frosty temperatures must numb their senses.

Out of every eligible woman in New York, my cousin married a mute woman from Montreal, a large city on the opposite side of this damn country. Essentially, he's brought these Canadian-isms straight into our lives. *Moron.*

As long as she doesn't influence me into saying "eh." It's too country for my city self.

Although, little Ariella is probably the best thing that's ever happened to my cousin. He may not realize it, but the changes he's undergone since they wed have been noticeable to me and our soldiers. He's less cranky, less of the rigid robot his parents trained him to be. With Ariella, it's like he woke up and realized he's his own man.

In some ways, I'm grateful to her.

Which is why I'm sitting in this fucking town, completing the task Erico gave me. *For her*.

I spin my cell phone in my hand to scan over the electronic note I've been adding to since arriving in this pitiful small town three days ago. It's a schedule pertaining to the woman Ariella's asking me to track down—what I've been able to learn anyway. After checking the time in the upper left corner of the screen and scanning for the associated time on the schedule, I'm satisfied I'm where I need to be, provided her daily routine continues.

Then I swipe to my photos app to study the picture of my target again.

Yasmine De Falco is fucking gorgeous in an ethereal way that doesn't even seem real. A curtain of night-black hair falls to waist-length, which seems like entirely too much work to maintain. Imagining her with shorter hair, though, is nearly impossible. Her skin is a light tan, as though she spends a lot of time outdoors, and her eyes are a matching warm brown. Captured through a zoomed-in lens within the photo, I bet they're stunning in real life. A woman's eyes are her most attractive feature in my opinion. They're so expressive, indicating how much pleasure or pain they can go through, which emotions she's hiding.

Before flying out here on the *Famiglia*'s private jet, Erico caught me up on Yasmine's history. Daughter to Stefano De Falco, who created a fake mob within Montreal to target their enemies, the Corsetti organization. Stefano's second wife came with two daughters, who were once Yasmine's stepsisters, but now are referred to as Della Corsetti, of the very same Corsettis, and Ariella Rossi, the queen to the *Famiglia* and the very organization I've been bred within. Della and Ariella have a complicated history with Yasmine, but Ariella, more than her sister, hence the request for me to find Yasmine and bring her home. Still in Montreal, Yasmine's older sister, and girlfriend to the Corsetti enforcer, Rozelyn, is also making similar demands to ensure her sister is safe.

Needless to say, if it wasn't for Erico drawing me a fucking map, I'd be very confused over who's related to Yasmine.

Because if it wasn't complicated enough, Stefano De Falco wasn't only the leader of a mob, he's a soldier—or whatever—of some weird, secret society who refers to themselves as the Seven, based right here in White Rock, British Columbia. When Stefano's plans exploded, he fled Montreal with Yasmine and left Rozelyn in the city as a distraction to occupy the Corsettis. Except now, Stefano's dead, killed by the Corsettis after being handed over by the very people he worked for, but Yasmine's never returned home to Montreal.

Three days ago, I arrived by the *Famiglia* plane, booked a hotel on the edge of the town, and hunkered down to observe from afar and concoct a plan. Given all the information the Corsettis provided, and the size of this small but elite town, it was easy to find her.

Getting to her is my second issue.

While the town may be small, it's obviously the Seven's headquarters, built specifically to hide them. Based on the opposite end of town is a massive school: a university designed like a castle. After two days of observing, she doesn't leave the building in the evenings, so I presume she's being kept on-campus, which makes getting to her even more of a challenge.

Whatever the Seven still wants with Yasmine, they're hiding her within their centre of operations.

But the past two days, she did leave for a couple hours, coming to this very mall I'm presently occupying a bench in. Day one, she got her nails done. Day two, clothes shopping. Wonder what today will bring and why this routine if she's, as the Corsettis and Ariella believes, being held captive.

For a moment, she seemed fine and I nearly reported back to Erico that Ariella and Rozelyn were making something out of nothing; that Yasmine clearly found a better life here after her father dragged her away. But something in my gut wasn't sitting right and said otherwise, so I kept watching, studying her behaviours and emotions from afar.

When getting her nails done, she looked more miserable than someone facing death does. Reluctantly sliding over each of her hands to the nail tech, her sneer almost messing up her beautiful face. All of that enforced by the thug who shadowed her every move, leaning against the nail salon's entrance.

I tracked them back to the school that day. Once out of the vehicle, the thug grabbed her arm and basically pushed her through the doorway, but the final flash of her expression is what secured me to remain.

Desolateness.

The time on my phone, comparing to her couple days of routine, means hopefully it'll be three-for-three and she'll appear soon. Today, I have to figure out a way to talk with her. In public, here, it'll be easier to get to her, but once she's locked inside the school, not so much. Not without knowing precisely what I'm walking into.

"Can you *not* walk so close to me? 'Kay, thanks."

Even without looking up, I *know* it's her, even if I've yet to hear her talk. In the expressions I've caught so far, she's obviously packed full of an attitude I'd otherwise appreciate. After being abandoned by her father and kept away from her sister, she makes her fierceness apparent, right down to her tone. Icy, edgy...sexy. A fighter's spirit lodged within her body.

This is gonna be fun. Ariella will get my thanks when I return with her stepsister, simply because for once, my target will be an enjoyable task. Most of the men Erico sends me after fight back, they curse, they hit, but no one will be like Yasmine.

Yasmine and her thug comes into view and for a second, I stop breathing. The past two days, she's come to the mall in dresses, but today, she's casual, and while I wonder why the change, I'm too busy staring to care. Tight jeans that hug her ass, running shoes, and dark hair bound up in a messy bun atop her head, all covered by a black, baggy hoodie with what I presume is the university's crest over the chest.

Her shoulders are hunched, her pace slow, her shadow walking much too close. He's dressed head-to-toe in black, like he's really trying to hammer home the bodyguard concept.

The two of them pass by, neither looking in my direction. After another dozen feet, I stand and trail them. Yasmine's small figure eventually halts by the entranceway of a candle shop.

"Keep going." He shoves into her back so roughly, she stumbles, but ignores him to stop by a large display table at the shop's front. Based on the thug's tight jaw and obvious huff, he's pissed, and her rebellion brings a smirk to my face.

The shopkeeper rushes over to assist the potential customer so I wander nearer, keeping my head down to scan the surrounding area. There's a bend in the mall up ahead, which I walk toward, hoping to use the angled wall for a better vantage point. Her guard glances me as I pass and looks away after a second, clearly deeming I'm no threat to whatever fucked-up orders he's following by Yasmine's side.

Big mistake, buddy.

At the bend, I press against the wall beside the doorway to

the female washroom, and pull out my phone, feigning a social media addiction while I observe the trio. The shop owner is gesturing for Yasmine to follow her deeper into the store, but Yasmine glances away and down the mall's strip, in my direction.

The role of Erico's Consigliere is an element of my job. Tracking people is extra because I'm good at it. But with both those roles, studying people's behaviours is a required skill. Determining why people do what they do, how they think, and what motivates them. So while the shopkeeper is gesturing to Yasmine, she's studying the mall. Up and down the stretch, toward her bodyguard, and repeat.

She's going to run.

Her feet inch backward and I realize, her outfit choice is purposeful. She planned this.

I rub at the side of my face, feeling my own half-smile. At least she has some sense to attempt escaping, which only makes my job easier. She'll want to be saved and I'm happy to be the one to do that.

She picks up the same candle she first touched, studying it intently. Then, in a flash, she pockets it, spins on her heel, and takes off in my direction.

"Shit," I mumble.

Chaos breaks out, the shop owner screaming in her direction. Some mallgoers pause walking and shopping to determine the source of the drama, some sipping from those red takeout cups as they observe the show. Her bodyguard's attention flicks back and forth between his escapee and the elderly woman, who looks like she's about to throwdown over a stolen candle. He chooses the owner, likely threatening her silence.

Works for me.

Yasmine's five feet away from me...three...I tuck my phone in my back pocket and prepare for her arrival. The second she's turning the mall's bend, I wrap an arm around her waist, my other hand covering her mouth as I spin us into the room at my back—the female washroom. She screams into my palm, warming my skin with her fear.

Once inside, I press her against the shut door and pin her there, hand still covering her mouth while I flick the lock shut. She screeches again into my skin, eyes widening until all I see is the brown iris darkening with terror, and fist after fist lands in my gut, my chest, making me grunt. She's weak, and it's like being hit by a child, but her fighting attempt surprises me.

I stop her easily with my body, pressing my chest to hers as I shake my head and shush her. "You're not in danger."

She's shorter than me, only reaching my shoulder, and the scent of jasmine and lavender is strong, filling my senses until it's all I smell. Her soft curves hug my body, more when she wiggles her shoulders, trying to free herself.

"Stop," I command again. "If this is you trying to fight, I have to say, *piccola tigre*, it's a bit pathetic."

Not sure where the name came from, but *little tiger* is my first thought if I had to describe her. A fighter but cautious and guarded, like the animal. Beautiful and majestic but feared by so many.

Her eyes narrow, drawing my attention to the warm colour I've so far only seen in the photo Erico gave me. Soft, chocolate, with specks of green. The emotion buried in them is what makes my heart skip a beat. Fear, but curiosity too.

"I'm here to help," I continue before she has more reason to fight me. "If I lower my hand, don't scream. Believe me, I'm the better option than fucktard out there."

She nods her head, so after searching her expression for a lie, I slowly lower my hand. Her breaths come out heavier after her run, as well as the flurried commotion getting into the bathroom. They blow over my neck as she tilts her head to look at my face.

"Qu'est-ce qui ne va pas chez toi, espèce de psychopathe?"

Her words are fluid, smooth, and almost sexy, that they make me pause. I assume they're spoken in French, given where she's from. Certainly nothing I understand.

"What?"

She makes a snarling sound that's more cute than fearful and shoves her arms into my chest, demanding I back up. "I *said*, what the fuck is wrong with you, you psycho? Since you started spitting out new languages, I thought that's the acceptable thing to do."

Feisty. She's cute, like a kitten. With huge teeth to eat her victims and claws that'll shred me. It's decided: the tiger nickname is suitable.

She rolls her eyes at my lack of a response. "Who *are* you?"

Instead of answering that, I explain, "I'm here because Ariella is worried about you."

She blinks, all signs of her battle fading off, her tanned skin flushing paler. "Ariella? Is she—are they—?"

"Hey!" Her numerous questions get cut off by her bodyguard's heavy thump to the door, jiggling the lock and rocking her forward and into me. One of those red cup carrying Canadians probably ratted her location out.

"Fuck," she curses, widened gaze going for the door handle. Getting found isn't an issue now. With Yasmine in my possession, it means I'm winning, but we need to get out of here.

I flick my leather coat aside and reach for my holster, retrieving my Glock. I cock it beneath her stunned expression and gesture the barrel at her, indicating for her to step aside. I doubt this is the first time she's seen a gun though, given her background.

Since she doesn't move, I nudge her myself, placing her at

my back so I'm between her and the bodyguard still throwing his weight at the door. A public washroom's door probably isn't built very strong, which means we don't have long before he manages to break it down.

"Who the hell *are* you?"

Throwing a smirk over my shoulder, I finally introduce myself. "Name's Caladin Rossi, from the New York *Famiglia*."

2

YASMINE

The New York *Famiglia*.

Why me?

Why again?

Why does my life continue to throw curveball after curveball without giving me a chance to catch any of them? Whoever I pissed off in another life, I despise them.

At this point, I'm not even surprised to hear who this stranger claims to be because everything I've learned over the past few weeks has me nearly ready to commit myself to a hospital psych ward, simply to escape it all. I'd do it too, if it wasn't for my predicament called captivity. I'm surviving—*am I?*—a desolate situation I have no way out of. A maze I'm lost in without directions.

This guy, this Caladin Rossi, claims he's here because of Ariella but that makes no sense. I've been lied to more than once in the past month and he's likely another liar meant to push me over. Somehow, he probably learned her name and this is some ploy to fuck me over.

For what purpose...I don't know. Can I even guess at this

point?

I mean, the New York mafia? Recent events unveiled what my father's spent my entire life hiding from me and Rozelyn, but New York was never mentioned at any time.

Although, his slight accent now makes sense.

Caladin lifts the gun in one hand and reaches for the lock with his other. That'll open the door to Derek, my asshole guard that *he's* stuck on me to ensure I don't escape. While I'm in support of Caladin shooting him, there's an entire group waiting in the parking lot for us. Caladin would have to fight all of them, and then he'd die and I'd be at square one.

I ran because...I don't know. Escape is so far-fetched, but I had to try. Had to make a point to *him* that he can only hold me for so long. That I'd be returning to my old life one way or the other, even if the entire thing was a giant lie fabricated by my father. I'm already in hell so the chance of escaping is worth it, but I hadn't counted on this new player to enter the messed-up game of *fuck Yasmine's life over*.

There's also the fact that Caladin might not even be the best option to save me. Hell, the idea that I need saving at all churns my stomach, but my options are quite limited.

He did mention Ariella though...so maybe he's not lying.

And his stance is wide, protective, keeping me behind him while he could very well be shot down by Derek first. That has to mean something.

Derek bangs on the door again and everything is in slow motion. Caladin reaching for the switch. My frazzled thoughts trying to pick the safest person for me.

If Caladin wins this showdown, we'll lose at every mall entrance.

If Caladin's here to capture me, then I'm in the same place as my current situation, but with a different handler.

If this is a test by *him*, then he's predicting I'll side with Caladin and freedom will be yanked away regardless.

I wish I had a fucking better life. Dad, I hate you. I hope wherever you are, you're paying for what you did to me.

When the gun clicks, I shove around his protective barrier and place myself at the door, palms up in defence. Caladin falters, annoyance covering his expression, but he lowers his gun.

"Move."

Always commanded. By everyone in my life, I've been the girl who's forced to follow instructions. Left in the dark by Dad, and even my own sister. By Ariella, who had ample opportunity to admit what she suspected about my father's role in the accident that injured her and killed her mother.

"You can't kill him," I whisper. "If you do, there's five more outside waiting who'll take you down."

He blinks. "What are you talking about?"

"It's not only him. As much as I want to believe you, we won't make it out of this mall. Or the town. You're one against an army. Trust me."

He scoffs. "I'll take them all down. Trust *me*."

"Here maybe, but there's eyes everywhere. If you're really who you claim to be, then go home and get your soldiers for backup."

Of the numerous follow-up questions I expect, he asks none of them. Instead, he reaches for me, his touch soft and hard all at the same time. Two fingers grasp my chin, controlling my face, but not painfully. More like a suggestion to go with his movements. His eyes flick over my face, pinching with every pass.

"You're genuinely frightened," he concludes after a minute. "I see it in your eyes."

"Obviously. You think I tried to run away for the exercise?"

He smirks, breaking the sudden and serious tension filling the tiny space between our bodies. "I like you, Yasmine. But for this to work, you need to tell me who's keeping you captive."

I look away at the stalls behind him. This stranger correctly presumed half my situation after a brief study. If I'm obvious to him, why am I not to anyone else? Why is no one helping me?

Pressing my lips together, I bob my head in a single nod. An admittance of truth without directly saying it, even while I plea with everything in the world that this isn't some cruel trap. That Caladin is truly here to help.

"Who in the Seven is trapping you?"

Everything inside my body tightens. My core, my heart. It might be the way he asked that, or it could be the protective edge to his words. But I tighten with hope. Hope and surprise that he's aware of what's going on here, and while I have so many of my own questions now, the dim light of hope shines brighter with every breath.

Maybe he *can* save me.

But I've seen the proof around the academy. It's not only me imprisoned here, it's everyone. But it doesn't change the fact there's a legion of men stationed in the shadows, always watching me. The army at the boarders. *He* outlined every reason I'd never be able to escape White Rock.

"It doesn't matter," I answer, pulling my face away from his hold. "All you'll do is get us killed. I mean it when I say it'll take more than one person to get me out of here. You'll need backup."

It feels fucked up to be placing this level of trust in a stranger, but Dad sealed my fate when he walked away from me. My options are captivity with Caladin, who'll hopefully bring me to Rozelyn, or staying here and probably dying within the year. At the very least, I'll want to, to escape permanently.

"Let me go out there," I urge, pressing my palm to his gun.

"Go home, bring men, and then come back." *Or don't and my hope will die when you go.*

"You underestimate me." But he's smirking rather than being annoyed and even clicks his gun back into its holster on his hip. "I'll follow your lead, but why run from me—your chance at escape?"

"Because it's only a chance to die," I answer gravelly. "If you really are here to save me, now isn't the time. Not here." In truth, I don't know where would be the ideal place and time. The mall is a good location, but he can't fight against everyone in the parking lot. And by the time he finds men to fight, I'll be back inside the school and that place is a fortress.

Derek pounds on the door again, stopping every moment or so, likely not to draw the attention of strangers walking by.

"I'll tell him I had to pee."

Caladin cocks his head. "You'll lie for a stranger."

"If you're who you claim to be, then I need you breathing and alive, so yeah, I'll lie." And pray Derek doesn't see right through me or opt to go exploring on his own. "Stay behind the door."

Surprisingly, he listens and moves to the corner as I turn for the door, inhale a sharp breath, and prepare to face what this evening will bring. What crime I'll pay for running. I might not have escaped, but tossing a final look toward the mobster beside me proved some benefit came out of my attempt.

I flick the lock open when he promises, "I'll be seeing you soon, *piccola tigre.*"

I think it's Italian, but I'm not sure. Either way, his statement passes over my head.

With a final breath, I pull open the door, covering Caladin behind it, and glaring at the mountain of a man who looms over me, his lip pulled up in an angry snarl. Which I've come to realize is his typical expression at any time of the day.

"I'm done, I'm done, let's go." Pushing into his chest, I leave the bathroom, urging him away from the door and Caladin.

Derek glances over my head, so I shove him again, forcing his attention elsewhere. "Who's in there with you?"

"Nobody, let's go."

With eyes as slitted as a snake's, he grabs hold of my upper arm and jerks me away from the bathroom door. I hide my small relieved breath, even as he reaches inside my pocket and yanks out the blue candle that served as a distractor. "Don't fucking take off like that again."

"Would you believe I had to pee?"

He doesn't respond, which means he doesn't, which also means *he'll* be hearing about this later, not that I expected anything different when I took off. An hour ago, the concept of his wrath had me shaking with fear, but now there's hope. I'll endure his punishment.

I'll hang on a bit longer.

That is my vow, my protection.

Go through Hell today to survive tomorrow.

～

An hour later, I'm shoved through the door of *his* apartment, which is actually the entire upper floor of the university's staff wing, since so many of them live on-campus. They can opt to take one of the dorm-like apartments on the seven floors of this tower below us.

From Dad's minuscule explanation, my captor controls the university and any business here in the province while six of his comrades and co-leaders are all over the rest of the country. He never fully explained what these seven men do, and his descriptions of them were vague.

"Dangerous men who control everything in the country. Every. Thing. Yasmine, listen when I say, these people are not to be fucked with."

"And the school?"

"A place to train their sons who'll eventually take their position, like they did to their fathers, their fathers for their grandfathers, and so on."

With Derek's firm shove, I stumble, catching myself on the entranceway table. Derek reaches in and slams the door shut behind me, cutting off my only path of light. The rest of the place is dark, hiding the monster within. I can't flick on the light, though. Learned yesterday, *he* gets upset when I do.

The hand swings to the underside of my head before I even notice him move. One second, he was down the hall, and somehow, his silent steps took him right by my side. To hitting me. My head jerks back, unprepared for the attack. I roll my jaw, biting down on the numerous things I'd like to say. To do in retaliation.

But on the first day spent with him, I swore at him and punched him in the face. He pinned me to the door and smacked me so hard, I had a headache for hours following.

So this time, I only meet his fuming stare as he reaches by my shoulder and flicks the switch in the down position. The overhead light turns off, leaving me in the dim sunlight peeking from the living room, giving me barely enough of a glow to fully see him.

"Lights. Off. Only I'll decide when they go on."

I think he enjoys making a point, lording his power over me, and keeps the place in darkness to kill many of my senses.

Each day, I learn a bit more what *not* to do. I'd enjoy fighting him...if I could. Dad never taught me to fight, said it wasn't my role as a mafia daughter—a lie so scoffable now. I'm weak, and every attempt is useless against his strength. More so, every attempt delivers pain, so until I have an out, I'll get beat bloody, trying to save myself if I continue trying.

Better dead than having this life.

A truth becoming more and more prevalent. But today gave me hope and Caladin may prove to be my saving grace.

After kicking off my shoes, because it's what he expects, I slowly venture to the foyer, having memorized the route by now. Given how clean this place always is, there's never anything I'd trip over so I'm not worried about that.

In the doorway of the living room, I pause. Sunlight seeps from the curtain's edges, lighting him up enough I can make out his snake-like grin, goatee, and receding hairline. He sits in a recliner, rocking gently as he meets my stare.

Jasper.

Also known as: asshole, creep, my captor, and monster—within the safe confines of my mind at least.

For a long five seconds, we're in a standoff until he lifts his right hand from the armrest and crooks two fingers, indicating for me to approach.

Gritting my teeth, I do, using the strip of sunlight as my runway, and stop only a few inches away, hands forming fists by my side. I bite down on my tongue so hard, trying to ground myself until he's satisfied with whatever show this is.

"Nice time at the mall?" His voice grates on my nerves. It's slow, malicious, and I swear, he practices it.

"Peachy."

A lie. Wood being shoved beneath my fingernails would be better than going along with his stupid shopping trips. If it wasn't for me running away, I was supposed to purchase new makeup since, apparently, he disapproves of my regular brands. I'd think that one of the Seven would have other things to do than worry about a woman's preferences. Yesterday, he forced me to stock the closet with clothing he finds more appropriate, and the day before that, he made me a nail appointment, like I'm some doll he's entertaining himself with. And why he isn't having me complete all this in one trip rather than separate ones has me ready to lose my fucking mind.

Closer, I study who my father abandoned me to with no explanation. Cast out by the rest, by even my father, and claimed by this disgusting man.

"You're done, Stefano. We're ending this today. You've had numerous chances. And as for your daughter," the man with a snake-like face peers at me with way too much interest, "well, you know as well as I do, we own her."

Own me? No one fucking owns me! I whip around to face my father, who's tied to a chair a few feet away. They haven't tied me, but the large person behind me is the deadly threat of what'd come if I tried to run, reinforced by the gun loose in his grip.

"D-Dad?"

For the first time since dragging me from home, school, Rozelyn, and the life I believed we had, there's remorse in his desolate gaze. "Sorry, Yasmine."

The snake-like man shoves off the table and turns toward me, until I reluctantly look from my father to him. He grasps my chin and rotates my head, studying my face. I stare at the ceiling over his shoulder.

"Well," he says after a moment, releasing me to return to my father's side, "at least you did one thing right, De Falco. Marrying an Italian woman served you well. Your daughter is a beauty."

Then he turns his hungry gaze back on me and I shrink back, suspecting I'll soon despise what's to come, if his final words are a hint.

Jasper readjusts until his knees spread open wider. One arm remains on the chair's side, the other resting on his lap, fingers tapping his pants' inner seam. He's a very tall man, easily towering two feet over me, and sitting doesn't change that fact. There's a sick appreciation glistening in his dark eyes, which makes me want to puke, but now I'm also thankful for the baggy clothing I've chosen to wear. His mouth slowly spreads into a smirk as he studies me and he wipes his mouth, pausing to scratch his beard, staring at me more intently than a fifty-year-old man should.

Using the hand on his lap, he indicates for me to sit. With a deep breath I aim to hide and pressed lips, I do, knowing the consequences of refusing, even if that's all I long to do. I perch on his knee, knowing this is the farthest I can get from him. The first time he demanded me to sit on his lap, I refused. So he dragged me by my hair until I sat on his lap, tears burning down my face, with the true realization of what my life has become.

Jasper's hand clamps down on my upper thigh, creeping much too close for comfort, but I'm thankful for the protection of my jeans. With his grip, he slides me until my hip touches his stomach.

"What are you wearing?" He pinches my hoodie, his slim features slipping into a sneer. "Was the shopping trip yesterday not indicative of what I expect you to dress in?"

"Sorry," I mutter, not meaning it at all. "I assumed they were for classes."

"You have a uniform for that."

A couple years ago, I *finally* convinced Dad to allow me to go get a degree. Being only a few semesters from completion, Dad yanking me away from Montreal was the worst timing possible. Jasper enrolled me here, but I think it's more so he can track me during the day than his desire to support my educational dream.

"Sorry. Forgot. Haven't been to class yet, remember?"

He makes a noise in the back of his throat and thankfully drops the matter of my clothing. "You'll begin tomorrow. I have your schedule all set aside. Out of the goodness of my heart, I've gotten you into the Psychology program, so you can pick up right where you left off."

"Wonderful." I shoot him a sugary smile. Not being forced into a whole other program is a win, but this...this is also so far from being a win. All my classes were approved by him, no doubt. As dean of this place, he's deciding everything.

"Well," he releases my hoodie, "be sure to dress more appropriately in the evenings. You're being watched, and as my future wife, people will judge us."

Future wife.

Once the room begins clearing out, there's only four people left in here: me, Dad, the snake-like man I've learned is named Jasper, and a soldier poised by the door.

Jasper strides toward me and drops to a knee in front of where I'm seated on a chair beside Dad. It'd be romantic if he were literally anyone else. His finger strokes my cheek softly but I still turn my head away. His touch may be placid, but the fierce look in his eyes is not. This is merely to lure me in.

"She's lovely. So much of her mother in her," he says to Dad. "You will make a beautiful wife."

Wife. Wife! No one mentioned that! I glare at him, then Dad, confused, frazzled, praying I misheard Jasper.

But Dad's eyes pinch and he shies away. "Sorry, Yasmine, but it's true."

"Why?"

Nothing.

I look back to Jasper, who's leaning back on his haunches, smirking at my misery. "Tell me what is going on! No, I'm not marrying you, you old psycho fuck!"

The smirk hesitates, a gleam sharpening his eyes, but I don't care. He can do anything to me, and I don't care. Not now. He slaps his knees as he lifts to his feet and paces away, ignoring my screeches.

He stops in front of Dad. "Say goodbye. Five minutes. Do not say shit about it, De Falco, or we'll make this even more painful on you."

Then he strides away, only the guard remaining behind to ensure his orders are followed.

Jasper enjoys consistently reminding me of what my life's become, what I'm trying to escape from. But every passing day brings me closer to the unknown date of when he'll drag me in front of a judge or a priest.

Jasper's slim fingers stroke the back of my neck, beneath my messy bun. I tense and shiver in disgust, hating how he feels my responsiveness. I've always been overly sensitive, and with the right guy, it can make sex more pleasurable. But this isn't that.

His fingers walk up the back of my neck until reaching my scalp, where he tugs the elastic from my hair and it tumbles down my back. "Unless you're exercising or cooking, your hair will be down."

It's the first time I've had my hair up since Jasper dragged me to his apartment; I do prefer it down, but given my planned attempt to run today, I wanted nothing in my way.

"Okay," I agree because it's the simpler option.

His hand comes down heavier in my hair, and then I'm suddenly arched backward, pain flittering over my scalp. The new angle puts his face in my neck, my back against his chest, and though I squirm, trying to slide off him, his other arm bands over my thighs, weighing me down and making his point known. When he speaks, I feel every single horrendous syllable against my skin.

"If you *ever* think of trying to escape again, I'll chain you to my fucking bed and you'll be reminded exactly who owns you. Understand?"

I nod, and the hold on my hair loosens, but he doesn't let me up. Instead, his nose skirts up and down my neck. I try to inch away but am pinned, meaning I have to finish feeling every pass of his breath.

"Mm," he hums. "You smell fucking delicious. There's a bet going with the others, you know. My determination to win is the only thing saving your ass from me fucking it. They bet me I wouldn't be able to resist your young cunt until the wedding."

It takes every deep breath the angle provides to prevent from throwing up. The thought of this man touching me *at all* makes the concept of jumping off the nearest balcony beyond appealing.

The hand on my thigh slides up, pressing against my core, and I'm thankful for my thick jeans. He doesn't stop there, though, and continues beneath my hoodie, brushing over my bare skin, until covering my bra-encased breast.

Oh, god. I twist, pulling against the hold he has me in, trying to beg him with my actions, my whimper, to release me. To not do *this.*

"That doesn't mean," his teeth scrapes my neck in his brief, weighted pause, "we can't play in other ways."

Despite everything he just said, I somehow win and he releases my hair and slides his hand from beneath my hoodie. With a tap on my hip, he motions for me to get off him and I've never obeyed an order quicker, rushing until there's a few feet of distance between us.

"Lucky for you," he calls out, "once I begin, I wouldn't be able to stop, so not touching you at all is safer for my bet."

Safer for both of us, you sick fuck.

"Go to bed. Be prepared to start classes tomorrow."

Without a final word, I rush from the room, using the darkness as my guide to the guest bedroom he's put me up in. Separate from his own thankfully because the thought of Jasper anywhere near me makes puking extremely likely.

Once inside the bare room with nothing more than a bed,

closet, and a bathroom, I lean against the door. If only there was a dresser I could push in front of it, ensuring he remains out. That probably wouldn't stop him, but still, I'd feel better about the protection.

I'd like to say in here, I'm safe, but who fucking knows.

If Caladin Rossi is who he truly claims to be, then he needs to come through quickly.

CALADIN

In front of the mirror, I finish knotting the green tie around my neck before tossing the black blazer overtop, convincing myself this is simply a Halloween costume. Close enough; I'll be pretending to be a student to get inside the academy to find Yasmine. I begin doing up the blazer's buttons before giving up after the second, and leaving it parted. It's tight and uncomfortable, worse than the suits I'm not a fan of wearing either.

My cousin's laughter booms from where he's observing through a video call on my phone propped up against the mirror. "You really think you'll pull off masking as a student?" Erico asks, his face a deep red, considering he's been laughing since the moment I called him twenty minutes ago with updates. "You're twenty-six, for fuck's sake."

"Yasmine is too."

"Yasmine's stuck. She's not a great example."

"People go to school later in life, Erico. Besides," I reach into my wallet, pulling out the newest plastic addition and bring it into the focus of the video call, "picked this up last night."

My student ID with the nicest picture I managed to pose for in the two-second warning the receptionist gave me after signing the enrollment papers. It took a bit of cash to skip through their regular enrollment process, and them taking a bribe at all is disturbing. The receptionist didn't recognize my name, but I bet someone here will.

"Was enrolling under your actual name smart?" Erico's humour slips into a frown. My cousin's skepticism is strong and his disapproval apparent by that cranky, displeased expression he gets. Reminds me so much of my uncle, his father, it's scary sometimes. A fact I'm holding onto until the day he pisses me off because Erico's newest ambition is to be everything his father isn't.

"Whoever's in charge of Yasmine is probably an important man, considering the bodyguard following her. Whatever fuckery's happening will take the big guns. Literally." I lift the edge of my blazer, revealing the gun tucked in my waistband. Fake student or not, I refuse to go anywhere without my weapon. "A fake name would discount me as yet another student."

"That's the idea. Before you drag down the *Famiglia*."

I throw him a scathing look as I finish gathering my items, shoving my wallet in my back pocket and grabbing the small backpack I picked up this morning alongside the new laptop. Gotta look the part and all.

"Have more faith, cuz. I'd never do anything to jeopardize us, you know that. If I play just another student, it'll take forever to get Yasmine out of here. Like she said at the mall, and everything the Corsettis told us about this place, it's stupid to grab her and run. Even if I succeeded, ten bucks says they have that airport watched so they'd track us right to New York anyway. My way, nothing's hidden. I'll walk right in as a Rossi and once word makes it to whoever's imprisoning Yasmine that someone from the *Famiglia* is in their territory, I'll gain an audience. And then I'll make a deal for Yasmine's freedom. Simple."

After yesterday, I realized the sooner I attract the asshole's attention, the sooner I can free her.

Erico's brows spike. "A deal?"

I shrug. "If that's what it takes, which I suspect it will. Reality is, the guy had a bodyguard on her, and a few more outside. After meeting her, I trailed them, and she was correct. One posted at every entrance. Neither of us were getting out without a fight."

"You're telling me you can't fight one guy?"

"I can't fight an army alone when they show up at the airport after tracking us. She's scared, Erico. I saw it in her eyes. She's putting on a brave face, but it's fake. Whoever we're dealing with isn't some lowly guy."

"Not just someone of the society then, but likely one of the Seven." He sighs, leaning back in his chair and farther from his laptop's camera. "I get it, I do, but this seems risky. What happens when they learn the *Famiglia* has stake in Yasmine's well-being?"

Again I shrug. "Problem for another day. You're listing too many what-ifs. I promise I won't blow the organization up. Besides, even *if* they were pissed and tried to start something, we have the Corsettis on our side."

Erico's expression pinches. "The Seven also made a deal with them. Nico didn't explain what, but if the Seven feels threatened, they could call on them too."

I roll my eyes. "Think it through. Nico would do anything to make Della happy, and Della would be quite displeased if Ariella or Yasmine were in danger. The Corsettis not siding with us would put them in danger. With Corsetti's sister-in-law wearing your ring, we're untouchable."

"Well," he concedes after a moment, "true. Good luck then. Text or call me later so I know they haven't killed you. And enjoy your classes. Get straight A's and all that." He grins cheekily.

"Fuck off."

I end the video call with a tap to the large red button, tuck the phone in my back pocket, and take a final glance at myself before leaving my hotel room to go to...school.

Fucking university of all places.

Ariella owes me huge for this, but Erico: even bigger. Why? Simply because I can hold him to stricter standards than I can her.

School fucking *sucks*. How do fresh-out-of-high-school kids do it? Stress is a constant emotion clinging to the lecture halls until, somehow, *I* was getting wrapped up into it too, and I'm not even here to get the grades.

Intel from the Corsettis through Yasmine's older sister, Rozelyn, revealed that Yasmine's working on a bachelor's degree, majoring in psychology—or was at her Montreal school anyway—so I took a chance and got myself into the same program. Given the small list of course options, it's a gamble and hope that, eventually, Yasmine and I end up in the same electives.

After two, it hasn't happened yet.

My first class, abnormal psychology with today's lecture about personality disorders, went right over my head. The few interesting facts I managed to obtain seem relevant to life as a mobster. There's definitely some assholes with undiagnosed personality disorders that I've dealt with.

After this ordeal, perhaps I'll start diagnosing them before they die. For fun.

The second course was something about clinical psychology. *Something* being key because if I thought personality disorders were confusing, it was kindergarten-level learning compared to clinical.

In the first course, I even took notes, further playing the part, but it was too much to keep up with so by the midway point, I gave up and ignored the curious stares of the fellow students around me.

They're basically kids and worth little of my time. Spoiled, rotten kids made obvious by the way they tout themselves, the jewellery decorating their necks, wrists, and fingers, and the side-eyed glares they throw my way as though they feel their territory is being threatened.

The lecture hall chairs are a fate worse than death and I'll be telling Erico to get some for the warehouses. Perfect torture devices. After an hour in one, the body's so numb and uncomfortable, they're truly agonizing.

Class three is forensic psychology and for once, it's a course that sounds half interesting. Anything forensics-related could teach me how cops think. Not that the *Famiglia* doesn't already have them in our pockets, but still, could be valuable one day.

Upon entering, my eyes sweep the room, searching for anyone closely resembling Yasmine, like I did in the previous two classes. Those came up empty, but this time, there's victory seated in a row midway down the hall, the second chair of the row.

Thank fuck, I'm not attending this castle of a school for nothing.

She's upright, notebook open on the tiny table that barely

counts as one, bolted to the chair. She's staring down at her lap, her nighttime-coloured hair falling on either side of her face. Her shoulders are curved inward, hunched and trying to hide.

Even her placement is specific, I bet. Not right at the end, but basically there, close to escape.

Works for me.

I stride down the stairs, ignoring the few new glances I receive. Without hesitation, I drop into the empty chair beside Yasmine, lowering my bag between my legs, and toss my arm over the back of her seat.

She jerks, her head turning so fast I'm hit with her jasmine smelling hair while wild eyes focus on me, widening. She glances behind her, then toward the professor setting up at the podium, and me again.

"You."

"Me."

"You're back." Another sweep of the room. "What the fuck are you doing here?"

"Same as you. Getting a degree." Playfully, I tap her shoulder, reminding her of the arm I have around the back of her chair, an almost intimate position. "Sit back before you draw attention."

"*Me?* What about you? This is the worst plan you could have come up with."

"Or the best." I turn my head until I'm speaking into the curve of her neck, right below her ear. "You were right about how protected this town is. The only way to get you out is through the person holding you captive. I want a meeting with your handler, and I get the idea he wouldn't ignore a *Famiglia* member in this place. And if you could bring me to whoever that is, it'd speed this up."

She leans away, but with my arm around her, I hold her in place. By now, if not soon, her professor should spot us, and will likely report about someone touching Yasmine, which means by the end of today, I'll get that meeting. A bit of touching, a bit of intimacy, and like a dog marking his property, he'll come barking. Hopefully.

"You can't," she whispers harshly and uses that feeble strength of hers to try to shoulder away. "Caladin, this is dangerous."

The professor calls the class to silence so he can begin what I'm sure will be yet another lecture I barely understand, but before granting the elderly man my attention, I lean closer to Yasmine's ear. So close that when I whisper, my lips touch the space right at the base of her lobe and she shivers, making me smile more.

"Danger fears me, not the other way around."

I release her in time to catch her eye roll. "My god, can you be any cockier?"

"Depends how much you can handle of my cock." *She ran into that one.*

Her pulse jumps and her mouth slips open a fraction. The grip she has on her pen weakens before she shakes her head and focuses on the lecture.

"I'm so fucked," she whispers, seemingly to herself. "You're gonna fail at saving me, aren't you?"

I slump deeper into my chair so with our height difference, my voice won't carry as far. "Considering I'm the only one here, *piccola tigre*, your choices are limited. Don't be picky."

Another eye roll. "And what the hell is with the nickname? Whatever language it is, I don't understand it."

"Italian. Translates to *little tiger*."

With a sneer, she looks from her empty notebook page to me. "Now I'm an animal? Lovely."

Under the professor's heavy stare, I take the opportunity and lean back toward her, blowing my breath over her nape and her cute schoolgirl uniform with my whispered explanation. "Tigers are cute. They're fierce with a sharp bite. The description is apt."

A complete five seconds pass before her shoulders droop and she mumbles, "Whatever." I'm ashamed at the lack of comeback this time. Her banter is half her charm.

While the professor drones on about...whatever he's lecturing on...Yasmine takes detailed notes like her life is dependent on it. A lot of effort considering I'm about to steal her away, but I don't comment. Given everything, maybe the method of note-taking is relaxing and grounding, and I'd be an asshole to take that away.

See? I did learn something in one of these psychology classes.

I watch her, wondering if *this* is the real version of her. One closer anyway than what I've thus far witnessed. Studious and a focused student, rapt on the lessons. The flip side of her has her running from her bodyguard, trusting a stranger's word without proof of ID, simply because she's desperate for escape. A fighting spirit because she recognizes when to fight and when to fold.

A woman who's had her life upturned but still battles for a semblance of control.

A woman I don't stop staring at for most of the class, and not because I'm trying to piss off the higher-ups in this place.

4

YASMINE

All day, he's been *here*. Like, somehow, other than my first two classes, he managed to get himself into every single one of mine. At the end of Forensic Psychology, he forced me to compare class schedules so at least I wasn't surprised when he trailed me from class to class.

During these walks, I made myself as small as possible because no matter the stupid-ass plan Caladin claims will work, *he's* not the one who has to return to Jasper later.

I want to believe him—I do. I *really* fucking do, but I'm scared. Reality is, if this fails, *I* pay the price. So I'm torn between wanting to go along with Caladin and wanting him gone and far away from me.

The buzz swirls around us, stifling as students and teachers alike stare. With it being my first day out of Jasper's rooms and Caladin's obvious domineering presence, we're quite the match.

Worse because Jasper did *something*. In my first two classes, I tried to speak to a few people, but they all turned away from me. And not expressions of disinterest, but pity. So now,

Caladin's throwing a giant red *fuck you* signal to everyone here, and he doesn't even realize it.

It's worse when he touches me. A redirection with his arm suddenly brushing my hip, his hand grazing mine—subtle, but they all make my stomach flip in ways I don't understand. Most likely, it's fear.

I'm so fucked.

Caladin is my best chance. My only chance. If escape from Jasper is possible, it'll be with Caladin, I know this. But when this goes south, Caladin loses his life and I'll spend the rest of mine—however long Jasper allows me have one—guilty for causing a stranger's death.

After another three classes, the end of the day arrives and I rush from the lecture hall, torn between wanting to hide and not returning to Jasper's cage. I'm barely out the door when Caladin's warm hand grasps my elbow and spins me in a quick movement, right into his chest. I swear, I feel every defined muscle in his abs.

Caladin is hot. Yesterday proved that. Caladin today, in a school uniform, doesn't look quite right, but he pulls it off better than anyone else here. I hate even thinking about him like that with everything going on, but can't help appreciating the dark-haired, sexy devil whose entire presence and focus is to help me.

Sometime during our fourth class, he grumbled and gave up on the tie entirely by undoing it. It remained around his neck like a rope, lining his unbuttoned blazer. His white dress shirt isn't tucked into his slacks, completing the *I don't care* guise.

When he dropped into the seat beside me earlier, I instantly had so many questions regarding how he got through the front door, and enrolled as a student to boot, but considering he's from the *Famiglia*, the truth isn't something I probably want. Dad may not have had dealings with them, but he's mentioned them in the past and titled them the most ruthless crime organization in North America—more than the Corsettis.

Caladin spins me around until my back hits the wall beside a bulletin board. Then he crowds me, stepping into the space between my legs, reminding me of yesterday in the woman's mall washroom. That was for protection, but this...I'm not entirely sure the purpose in this.

"Caladin," I murmur, eyes darting over the numerous people within Jasper's domain who'll report back to him. Many of them are already staring. "Caladin, back up right now." I push against his abs, but it's like trying to move a wall—useless and rigid. "Caladin." Ideally, he'll catch the desperation in my tone.

Apparently not. One palm rests by my head, keeping him upright as he leans into me, cheek brushing my own. He bends slightly, his nose skirting the edge of my jaw. Without meaning to, I shut my eyes, ignoring how my hands grow damp and my core clenches. He smells so good. *Feels* so good. But he's going to get us both killed.

"Caladin, please, stop."

With a look of almost concern, he meets my eyes, studying my face. He must find something because he actually listens by straightening, so I can suck in much-needed air.

"I'm making a statement," he explains in a low tone. "We have people's attention but where's your handler, Yasmine? If he won't come to me, then bring me to him."

And when Jasper slaughters Caladin, then all hope is gone. I want Caladin's help...but not at the expense of our safety. Even if remaining here is everything opposite of safe. Fear. Trauma. I don't know—pick a term, but the notion of bringing these two worlds together—of my hellish reality and the past and future I long for—terrifies me.

"I-I can't, I'm sorry. I don't know..." Without finishing, I duck beneath his arm and rush down the hallway, praying he knows what's good for him and won't follow. He lets me go and I reach the staircase at the end, knowing many floors above me is my cage.

Finally, I reach it with burning legs from the quick run, and head right for the bedroom Jasper's deemed as mine. I drop my bag by the door and rush to the window, leaning on the pane to stare outdoors. The university is a giant square, with a green, manicured square patch in the centre. When Dad dragged me here, I was struck by its beauty until finding the horrors within.

In the first couple days, I was forced to remain inside another set of rooms while Dad attended meetings I wasn't a part of. Sometimes, I sat outside the room and got to hear them yelling at one another, but nothing they said was decipherable.

Then there was that final meeting, of course. When, after Jasper revealed some bullshit about marriage, he left Dad and me alone, except for the bodyguard by the door.

Dad paces the room up and down, rubbing his palms over his face, now untied from the chair. "Sorry, honey, but this is your life. It's always been your life."

He sounds like he's giving up and that makes crying really tempting if I wasn't so confused. "I don't know whether to hate you or not."

His steps pause and he looks at me with that emotionless expression he often does. "Hate me, Yasmine. You're allowed to. You were an accident not meant to be born. Something I never planned on. And if Rozelyn didn't prove to be useful, I would have allowed her to remain lost when your mother revealed the secret pregnancy she had before we wed."

"What?" It's all I can manage. All I can say in response to my father's cruelty.

In the past week, I've learned who this man is. The drive to B.C. spent in near-silence after he finally admitted who he truly is, that our entire family was some façade for him. Nothing was real.

I was an accident because he never meant to remain in Montreal playing family mobster man as long as he had.

Mobster.

Monster.

Synonyms in my head.

"It's over, Yasmine. This is how it is."

And then he walks away, toward the guard. Just like that, he leaves me without a fight.

Dad murmurs something to the guard, who opens the door, but right before he goes, he turns to face me once more. "Final word of advice, daughter: protect yourself first. No one else matters more."

And then the door shuts and I'm alone.

That was the final time I saw Dad and in the weeks passing, I'm so confused how to feel about him. Pissed more than I've ever been. Still confused at how *this* became my life. Lost because he hasn't been in contact and I have no idea where he is or if he's even still alive. The single time I asked Jasper, he brushed me aside.

The apartment door slams shut and with a stifled breath, I push away from the window pane. Better to go out there and face him now than have him disrupt this room with abuse, destroying what's become my sanctuary.

He'll expect dinner prepared, like I'm some good, little housewife from the fifties. One day, I'll find poison and I swear to fucking Christ—

The bedroom door slams open with a crash I feel inside my bones, and long, quick strides bring him across the room. His clamp on my upper arm propels me closer to him before I'm shoved into an adjacent wall.

He makes the Corsettis I grew up hearing about, told to

fear, seem like gentle giants. Fantasy creatures who'll grant wishes and spread kindness. Jasper's the real monster. The one who hides beneath beds, slinks in the shadows, who devours their prey whole.

He drops my arm, but I'm not free. Instead, he grips me roughly, his large hand clamping on either cheek in a painful squeeze. With his weight on me, I can't move. Can't speak. Can't yell.

His teeth bare. "Why the fuck is the *Famiglia* here, Yasmine?"

He knows.

"What stake does New York have with *you?* Why is their Consigliere in *my* school, sniffing around *my* property?"

Is that who Caladin is? Given his last name, he's obviously one of the family, but his role is right up there. Advice-giver to their boss. Dad never had one, and now I understand why.

His grip tightens, thumb and forefinger pressing into my cheek. If he wants a reply, he's making it physically impossible to provide one. "Fucking answer me, you whore! Everyone here has explicit instructions not to go near you. Then I learn —have *seen* the pictures—of that *Famiglia* dog pawing at you."

As I presumed, he *did* do something to keep everyone from talking to me, making my entrapment here even lonelier. Now that Jasper knows about Caladin, I'm witnessing every smidgen of hope be snuffed out in his vicious glare.

Finally realizing I can't respond with the fish face he's painfully causing, he releases me roughly, throwing my head back into the wall with a small thump. And just when I'm about to respond, to say something that will appease him, his hand lifts again.

Quick as a whip, landing against my right cheek, instantly sending a shooting sting radiating up my face. By the time his actions can be comprehended, he grabs my face again, the pain worse this time.

He's close when he yells, his lips a fraction away from mine. An unpleasant scent wafts from his breath, but his hold too firm for me to turn away.

Always so weak. I hate this feeling.

"He's going to stay away from you while I determine how the *Famiglia* has broken into my territory. You be sure to tell him that too, that he better avoid you." His free hand grabs the edge of the pleated uniformed skirt before flapping the edge upwards, his hand diving beneath and cupping between my thighs. I shove into the wall, trying to escape but somehow, causing his touch to be even more apparent. "*This* is mine. Bought and paid for like a perfect little whore. Unless you want the Rossi kid to end up six-feet-under, he stays away. Starting *now*."

Jasper releases me. Then he's gone and the room rattles with the door being slammed shut. Thirty seconds later, the telltale crash of his anger comes from down the hall.

He can break his whole goddamn house for all I care, as long as it's not me he breaks. With heavy pants, I push off the wall and head into the attached bathroom, inspecting the red mark on my chin and cheek, stroking gently over the tender skin.

Caladin may be my escape, but I need to remain alive long enough to make that escape.

I need to be strong enough to help him rather than shy away.

But how does one face their captor when it's that very captor gripping the chain too tightly?

∽

Outside the lecture hall where my Criminal Psychology class occurs, Caladin's leaning against the wall, presumably waiting for me. In my first two classes, I'd been trying to come up with an explanation for yesterday. To plead for him to save me from my fate all while warning him away.

When he spots me, his eyes get brighter in a way I'd appreciate if he was another guy and this was another time. Caladin Rossi knows how to utilize that alluring gaze of his.

This hallway isn't the place to warn him about yesterday and class is starting soon. I'm sure Jasper will find another way to abuse me if he learns I was late to it, so ducking my head, I readjust my hair to curtain my face and conceal the red mark on my cheek. I'm barely by him when he's dragging me in front of him with a cocky smirk.

"Now, where do you think you're goi—" He stops, gaze stroking over the mark that makeup did little to cover. The dark marks of a blooming bruise on my chin and cheek.

For all the evilness I've witnessed in Jasper, Caladin beats him with a single look. His playfulness melts away, his fake student persona gone, replaced by a true *Famiglia* soldier. The Consigliere. Deadly and vicious but not scary. Not when that look is to protect *me*. An expression imbedded into him through his centuries-old family born and bred within death, destruction, and deception.

With two fingers beneath my chin, just shy of the bruise, he tilts my head until more of my hair falls to the side. More of that protectiveness grows, his eyes sharp, fingers still gentle, but the rest of him is tense.

This reaction is unnatural, especially considering he's only known me for a day, but regardless, my insides melt. At least now, he understands what his presence means. Why yesterday was the opposite of helpful.

When he finally speaks, every syllable is a venomous punch. A bite, a frostiness. If death had a sound, I'm listening to it.

"Motherfucker. I won't waste my fucking breath by asking who did this because I already know. This ends now."

His hand lowers, robbing me of his cooling, healing touch, and he drops his backpack to the ground with an uncaring thump while scanning the crowd. One guy passes, his slouch lazy, shaggy blond hair curtaining his eyes. His arm is tossed over a girl as they enter the lecture hall beside us. Caladin zeros in on him and sheds his blazer before I catch up to what's happening. He steps in front of me and I spot the gun he has tucked in a holster around his waist.

Caladin yanks the guy by his shirt, making his girlfriend screech and everyone around us pause. "You," he growls in his face. "You look like someone who'd piss me off." Without warning, without giving him an opportunity to block, Caladin slams his fist into the guy's face. A sickening crack, a scream—multiple screams—a yell. The guy tries to block the incoming second hit but fails.

After another punch that sends blood streaming down the guy's white school shirt, his head slumps to the side, apparently knocked out. Caladin releases him to drop to the floor, ensuring he'll wake with a sore body too. He faces me, breaths seething.

"Five...four..."

He's counting?

"...Three..."

Around the closest corner, a professor along with two campus security guards push students out of the way.

"Didn't even make it to one." Caladin grins, somehow finding amusement in the situation that has me ready to faint.

Violence. Even before Jasper, I've witnessed it. One of Dad's soldiers pissed him off once and I had the unfortunate chance of seeing him go apeshit on the man. Only for a moment before

Mom pulled me away. Violence is natural in the mafia, so Caladin's actions aren't anything new...but they are. The violence I've seen, have felt, has all been against me. No one's fought to protect me before, not even Dad.

The campus security guards grasp Caladin's upper arms, who surprisingly doesn't fight. One spots the gun he's not hiding and removes it from the holster, tucking it beneath his own arm.

"Any other weapons?"

"None."

I wonder if Caladin's lying.

The professor, a grey-haired hunched man, approaches, frowning at the scene. "Straight to the headmaster." His attention slides to me, and while I've never met this teacher before, he orders with conviction, "You too, Miss De Falco."

The security guards shove into Caladin's back, forcing him to walk, and as he passes me, he says with a cocky grin, "Finally gained the meeting I was hoping to get yesterday."

5

CALADIN

All bets were off when I saw the bruises.

He *touched* her. I'm not stupid. My actions yesterday did exactly as I planned and gained his attention. Only, it went down wrong. He took it out on her.

Fuck that.

There's never been a woman I've been protective over, but I've never *had* to be. Never wanted to. But fuck if I'll return her battered and bruised when I have this sudden inexplainable need to keep her safe.

Waiting isn't an option any longer after spotting the bruise on Yasmine's face. It made me murderous, makes me want to slaughter whoever dared darken her perfect skin. Who made her fierce attitude falter for distress.

Which is why, without argument, I stride in the direction the security guards maneuver me into, toward the *headmaster's* office. Of course, her captor runs the entire fucking school. Don't know how I didn't guess that. The kid I hit was simply because he looked like a douche and I needed to gain the correct kind of attention from the higher-ups in this place. A fight always does it.

Over the shoulders of the assholes who took my gun, I spot Yasmine trailing with her head low, using that dark hair of hers to hide. A professor is by her side. Another one came running from a nearby room to help the kid I beat up as I was getting led away from the scene.

After a few hallways, we finally reach an office area. Passing a sitting area, a few large desks, we head right to the far end, to a shut door with a wooden sign posted above it.

Headmaster.

A single knock and then a voice granting entry.

The professor mumbles, "Miss De Falco, you can wait right here."

Tightening my muscles, I pull on my handlers' hold, jerking us all to a stop, granting a look from them both. In truth, I could have broken their hold earlier, but there was no point when they were bringing me to where I'd been fighting to get to.

"She stays with me." I glare at the old man.

The door opens behind us and the hints of Yasmine's fear I've so far seen in small bits explodes when her face blanches white. She drops to the chairs indicated, obeying and becoming so instantly submissive, it sickens me.

"Is there an issue?" a new voice rings out. A smooth tone, one practiced in deception: a kind I'm all too familiar with.

I face the door, and the tall, skinny man stands there in a pressed suit. Snakelike features, right down to the slitted eyes that bounce over each of us. Beneath his thin goatee, he smiles, as though aiming for friendly but mixing it up with malicious.

"Mr. Rossi, so nice to meet you finally."

"If you know who I am, you'll understand why I don't trust

any of you assholes. She's not to be left unattended." I tip my head toward Yasmine.

"Oh, but she won't be." He waves his hand toward the campus security guards who release me and move to stand against the far wall. "They'll be here. She's not going anywhere."

Arguing about where Yasmine waits is pointless when I have the man I need. She won't be going anywhere for the time being, and if I pull this off right, she won't be going anywhere else that isn't with me.

Seeing no further argument, the headmaster steps aside and gestures for me to follow with a gracious tilt of his head. For now, we're both playing nice. Erico would be so proud of my restraint when the thought of stabbing one of the headmaster's fancy, metal pens resting on his desk into his neck is becoming really fucking appealing.

"Please sit," he orders in a commanding tone, one used on all his minions no doubt.

Making my point, I lean against the nearest wall and purposely avoid the large, wingback leather chairs situated in front of the ornate desk. Beside me is some fake plant. Fake as the rest of this bullshit.

"Very well." He drops into his own seat, his hands melding together on the desk's surface. "Mr. Rossi, why is the *Famiglia* in my territory?"

"Why are assholes abusing women?"

His brows spike all while his mouth curves downwards in a contradictory expression. "Straight to it then? All right. I'm not abusing what I own."

"You don't own her."

"Come now," he coos, "we both know men do own women. Your entire institution is built upon it, as is ours. Women are a means to an end. Unions, heirs...pleasure."

A rumble bursts in my chest, but I keep it contained—for now. After this, she better tell me he hasn't fucking sexually assaulted her or else I'll blow this fucktard's dick off.

"What's your name?" I ask instead. *So I know what to mark on the gravestone I'll be having carved, all so I can piss on it.*

"Jasper."

Three seconds pass.

"A last name go with that?"

"None you get to know."

Whatever. "All right, Jasper, since you gave me your name, I'll answer your original question, though I'm sure you're able to guess by now. I'm here to collect Yasmine De Falco."

"Oh." He leans back in his chair and rocks slowly, his head ticking to the side. "That so? She's not exactly yours to collect."

"She has a family back home waiting for her."

"Her useless sister, Rozelyn, in Montreal. Yes, I'm aware. Yet, it's a New Yorker here in the Corsettis' stead. We're well aware of the union between Nico Corsetti's sister-in-law and your cousin."

My tongue stabs the inside of my mouth, considering his words. Our marriages aren't kept private for reason, but the fact someone from another country cares about the *Famiglia*'s actions is unsettling.

As if responding to my silent thoughts, he adds, "We make it our mission to know all of what's happening with our enemies. And allies."

Meaning us and the Corsettis. "Shame," I mutter. "Because we don't have the same energy to care about you."

"Because you were only made aware of us recently."

Shrugging, I continue, "If you know so much, then you know exactly why I'm here for Yasmine. Also, if your goons could return my gun, that'd be great because it's my favourite one. Then I'll take it and her and we'll be out of your hair by sundown. I realize her father caused your organization a lot of chaos, but it's not Yasmine's job to pay the price of his crimes."

He stares for a beat, his eyes wrinkling in the corners, until he barks out a single laugh and opens his desk drawer. From it, he brings out a sheet of paper. "Oh, but I can make her do whatever I want because she is truly mine."

Chills snake my spine and even without looking at the document, I know it'll make this entire situation worse.

"Come read for yourself." When I finally do make it to his desk, picking up the document between pinched fingers and a glare he better relive in his nightmares, he continues, "You know all about arranged marriages. We are Stefano De Falco's true home, and his intention was to always return. When he accidentally impregnated his wife, he saw this as a way to pay back the Seven. From the moment of Yasmine's birth, he signed her over to me."

Sure enough, what's in my hand is a marriage contract, dated twenty-six years ago. *Fuck.* A marriage to him.

"Under the circumstances, his return took longer than expected, but regardless of his death, Yasmine De Falco is rightfully the Seven's. Mine, anyway. Once she completes her degree —a nicety on my part to occupy her while I get things settled— she'll bear my ring, my name, and one day," he throws a wolfish grin, "perhaps even my child."

Only when I'm dead and six feet under will he touch her.

Contracts are finicky and if there's one thing I've learned within the *Famiglia,* it's that there is often a better deal than the previous one made. Contracts and backdoor deals only go so far when there's other offers. Regardless of how gorgeous Yasmine is, a man like Jasper chases power.

I drop the contract back onto his desk with a flick of my fingers. "What'll it take to break that?"

He smiles his snake grin, telling me I've guessed correctly. "What makes you think she isn't what I truly wish for?"

"Because a sick fuck like you can get anyone to sell their daughter to you. You're one of the Seven, after all. Don't you all claim to be untouchable and shit. Yasmine, the daughter of a traitor, can't be your best offer."

"Maybe. Maybe not. But my job now consists of making a point to her family name. Yasmine will pay for her father's crimes by spreading her legs. The Corsettis got their revenge by killing Stefano. We're getting ours through her marriage to me."

At my side, my hands curl into fists and I replace the kid's face I hit earlier with Jasper's. His attention skips to my hands, and his smirk deepens.

"If she's making you jealous after only a day, you must understand my own eagerness to claim her."

"Or I just don't like the idea of old men raping young women. Because we both know, she wouldn't be with you willingly."

He waves his hand, as though sexual assault is nothing to him. "Such strong words coming from a man claiming to want to make a deal."

"The *Famiglia* doesn't play well with others."

His brow ticks. "Clearly. Right down to sending their Consigliere into my midst." His eyes flick down my school uniform, sans blazer. "You don't pull off being a student very well, Mr. Rossi."

"Wasn't supposed to. A means to gain your attention."

"You have it." His hands spread wide, palms up. "So what can I do for you?"

This conversation is going in circles and I'm seconds away from allowing my fists to make my point. It'd be a much more mob-approved method. Leaning over his desk, getting into his face, I stab my finger into the contract. "What can I offer you that'll break this? Money?"

"We have money. Lots of it." He scoffs and shoots back, "Why do you care so much about her?"

"Is that your offer?"

He chuckles. "Humour me as a sign of good faith before we strike a deal."

Not *if*. Which means there is something he wants. "Like I said before, she has people who care for her back home. As for why I'm here, this is my job. I hunt people and I'm very fucking good at it so be careful how much you piss me off."

He accepts my threat with a slow blink. "The only thing worth that woman's cunt is an alliance with the *Famiglia*."

Erico's going to kill me...I rear back, studying his expression for a lie. "What does an alliance look like?"

"Same deal as the Corsettis. We'd consider a treaty with the most powerful mafia family in the United States a great arrangement. If we have need of your army, you will offer your men to us. If we have needs within U.S. grounds, we will call upon you."

"We don't rule the entire United States." Just half.

"An issue for another day."

Erico is going to slaughter me, but he never stated *how* I'd be getting Yasmine home, just to get her. Consider this my wedding present to Ariella.

"De—"

"Not quite," he cuts me off with a palm up. "There's still the matter of Stefano's punishment. Yasmine's happiness."

Where the fuck are you going with this? "She had no hand in committing her father's crimes." According to Rozelyn, Yasmine was totally in the dark about their true background.

"We both know the power behind a family name, Rossi.

How one can be held to their family's standards, or pay for their family's crimes, simply for bearing that name." He pauses, letting the weight of his statements sink in. "I'll give you a hint about how we run things here with the Seven: marriages are as good as contracts, the same as your world. We're speaking the same language as the *Famiglia*, only a different dialect, so you see the issue."

"Draw up a contract then if you feel we won't hold up our side."

"I plan to, but it's not enough. We need something more… binding." His gaze lowers to the contract between us and I know what he's about to say even before he suggests it. "The only way I will release Yasmine to you is if she becomes your wife."

The name I bear and the job I do both deem one day I'll be forced into a marriage. Given that my cousin only took over as *Famiglia* Boss with his own marriage to Ariella, weeks ago, I'm surprised my uncle, the previous head, hadn't forced me into anything yet. It only means, eventually Erico will call on me. It's the way it goes.

Marriage holds no interest for me. It'll be a task as part of my job and my wife will live separately. Hell, I don't even plan on having children. Nothing that'll risk me caring for her. Caring for a woman only hurts in the end. Allowing her to love me would break her.

So while a marriage is in my future, not like *this*. Not forced. Not to the woman I'm here to save.

"No deal. My offer is: I walk away with Yasmine *today* and you gain an alliance with the *Famiglia*. Nothing more, nothing less."

His slow smile contradicts my own irritation. He's too calm in all this. "No. This is a two-fold transaction. Yasmine's paying for her father's crimes with her happiness one way or the other. It's marriage to me or you, non-negotiable. You pick." He pauses, aware he has me exactly where he wants. "Of course, you'll take her for yourself, which is fine. But for you both to walk out of here today, an alliance with the *Famiglia* is the price. Deal or no?"

There's numerous ways out of this and the *Famiglia's* lawyers will be all over it once I tell them. We can marry and divorce within the same day. Typically, the organization, being packed with traditionalists, despises the word *divorce*, but these aren't normal circumstances. We'll wed, I'll get her home, and then Erico can have the paperwork drawn up and she'll be free.

He takes my silence as doubt and continues, "The girl seeks freedom. You must have noticed. After all, why would she risk her own safety by allowing you to touch her?" He pauses again, that sneaky, sly grin returning. "I've seen the pictures. The way you look at her. You won't be able to release her either, so I do feel marriage to you is punishment enough."

"You don't know me very well then."

"If you agree, I'll have the contract drawn up right away and we'll have the ceremony later today with one of our ministers. You understand, I must see it for myself, to ensure its authenticity. Then you two can be right back on your plane for New York by nightfall."

Of course he wants to witness. I'd expect nothing less.

"And there will be an anti-divorce clause in there. You will not divorce her *ever* or she's mine again, and you've broken a contract with the Seven. It won't be a pretty battle."

That'll be worked on. Every clause has an out when you pay good enough lawyers. I glance at the door where she is. Erico's going to murder me. For agreeing to this. For coming home with Yasmine as my wife.

"Draw up the contract," I command, still staring at the door, imagining the woman behind it who's about to have her life controlled *again*. "Get it to me within the hour. My Boss and I will discuss it. If I agree, I'll return here at five for the ceremony."

6

YASMINE

Campus security hovers as I wait like some child while Jasper and Caladin speak about my future. Fear rattles my insides, making sitting still impossible, at having my fate decided by two men.

Much to the annoyance of the security guards, I stand after a few minutes to pace instead. At least, getting my energy out by some means is better than not. Up and down the hallway, pausing at the end to glance out the window overlooking the back of the university, and return, pausing by Jasper's office, debating whether to enter before completing another lap.

After what feels like forever but is only about twenty minutes, the door opens. First, Caladin exits, all previous cockiness from earlier gone, and that's what makes me the most scared. He glances from the ground to me, his expression sad as he approaches. An internal war swirls in his gaze and I want to ask him what happened, but he pauses, his hand gently stroking over the bruise. His jaw clicks and then he drops his hand and stalks off.

That's it? "Cala—" I stop because finishing will shatter my

heart more. That was it? Was that his goodbye? We lost and his look was an apology?

Jasper steps from the office too, his gaze locked on Caladin's back before he disappears around the corner. Based on Jasper's winning, malicious gaze, Caladin lost. I'm stuck. Back to the beginning, to fighting my own way out.

And I *will* fight. Somehow, someway. Jasper will kill me before he touches me again. That is the vow I make myself.

"Well, Yasmine, pack your bags. Consider this your final day of classes."

What? I think my stomach just dropped through the floor. He won? *We* won? But Caladin seemed sad, not victorious.

"You're letting me go?"

He tilts his head with a grin I've come to know all too well. Malicious and evil. "Rossi and I made a deal that'll satisfy all parties."

"A deal for what?" Dad's entire life was spent around deals gone wrong, so from recent events, I don't trust that term any longer.

"Well, he hasn't completely agreed yet, but," his eyes rake over me, "I expect he'll comply to my terms. So before repeating myself, if I were you, I'd go pack your things and be prepared to leave tonight. Return here at five."

He waves me away before disappearing, his door slammed shut in my face. It takes a full beat of my heart for his instructions to make their way to my brain. Before he changes his mind, I'll listen. There's nothing in *his* apartment I desire; everything's replaceable. Everything has a negative memory attached to it. They took all my personal effects when we arrived —laptop and cell phone.

I return to his place briefly, only to change out of the school uniform I'd be happy to see burn, but take nothing else and instead wander the university. My second day of classes here but also my last. Freedom is so near. So, so close, and yet so far. Six more hours until five o'clock, according to the clock.

I get to go home. Montreal. Rozelyn. Maybe Dad, and we can work through all this. I'll never forgive him but talking to him is a start. All of this will be a horrible nightmare. A blip in my life.

As I wander, I keep my eyes peeled for Caladin, though I doubt I'd find him in the halls. Eventually, I head outside to the grassy quad, where I claim a free bench beneath a leafy tree. At least, it'll serve as a lookout.

~

At five, I return to Jasper's office with dread heavy in my stomach. Both he and Caladin haven't explained what the deal they made is, or why I have to come back at this time.

Lingering in the doorway, stopping me short of breath, is Caladin. His back to me but still, he makes me pause. When I met him, he was dressed casually, like any mall-goer with a hidden, dangerous streak. The second time, he posed as a student and wore pressed slacks and the school's blazer. But this time... this is a *Famiglia* soldier. The Consigliere, a position of respect and power. Dressed impeccably in a dark suit that's fitted well.

He turns with my approach. Dark eyes rake me up and down before he enters the office without speaking. I follow, stopping by the entrance when spotting Jasper speaking with another man. Also dressed in a suit but he's no one I recognize.

Jasper breaks away from the conversation when I enter. "Oh, good, everyone's here so we can begin."

Begin?

The stranger smiles kindly my way, but it does little to calm the storm whipping my insides. He moves toward Jasper's desk and shuffles through a couple sheets of paper. I glance to Caladin, seeking clarification, but his glare is unblinking on Jasper.

"I want five minutes alone with her."

Jasper's smirk turns mocking. "Is that really appropriate? We understand your kind's behaviours."

Caladin's eyes narrow and he repeats, "Five minutes so she's not blindsided."

Jasper stares for a beat, and then glances at me before gesturing for the other man to leave the room. "Whatever. No more than five. Not that this conversation will change anything for either of you."

The moment we're alone, Caladin sighs, and all sign of the *Famiglia* man evaporates into someone who looks too exhausted for life.

I wander closer. "What's going on? This morning, Jasper mentioned a deal you agreed to."

He scoffs. "A fucking deal, all right. A rigid, tight-ass, unbreakable one." He steps away and heads for Jasper's desk, reaching into a drawer I'm surprised is unlocked. From it, he returns holding a document. "Do you know exactly why Jasper took you in?"

"Not that I enjoy reliving that day, but no. Dad wouldn't say. No one would. Jasper just keeps claiming he owns me."

Caladin laughs once, humourlessly, and shoves the document into my hand. "Your father fucking sold you, Yasmine. Look at the date on that contract. One day after your birth."

My eyes drop to the bottom of the document, skipping right by the large strip of writing and signatures, to the date. It's exactly as he said.

"Wh-what is this?"

"A contract. Signed by both your father and Jasper, which states you are his as of your twenty-fifth birthday."

All his talk of owning me was true...by Dad's hand too. I'm not sad. I'm fucking *pissed*. Red, fiery rage that has the contract crinkling in my hands. Raising me in a fake life wasn't enough for Dad? He *sold me* to some old guy.

"But I'm twenty-six," is the only point I make.

"As of six months ago. I don't know why he was waiting, but I guess your father dragging you out here with him wasn't a complete coincidence."

The paper—the *contract*—slips from my grip, heavier and more weighted than I could have ever imagined a sheet of paper being. To learn, this entire time, Dad's been planning on shipping me here...

He's an asshole and a traitor to his own family. He once claimed I was a love child between him and Mom, but this whole time, he was planning to ship me back here—to his *real* family. The people he felt true loyalty toward. He allowed me to work on a degree, to plan a future all while he laughed behind my back because it'd never come true.

I hope he's dead.

A thought that should shock me. After all, despite recent actions and revelations, he raised me. He loved me since my birth.

But did he? This isn't love. Love isn't lying to your family, selling them off, abandoning your other daughter to your enemies.

Dad has no love. Not for me, not for Rozelyn, certainly not for Della, Ariella, or their mother. Maybe not even for my own.

"Why?"

Caladin shrugs as though it's not his life blowing up. "Unions are a big deal. While I don't always agree with them, your father obviously thought it best to marry you to the people he felt the biggest connection to. His family—you—in Montreal was all designed for his plans, but here," he gestures to the office, "the Seven holds his true loyalties. By blood, the Seven are your people."

These people will *never* be mine.

"Then what is this?" Tone spiking, I glance around Jasper's office, to the door he and the stranger left from, a heaviness settling on me. So heavy, my emotions are clustered and weighted, confusion controlling everything. White spots decorate my eyes, even my vision betraying the control over myself I truly don't have.

Caladin takes two strides and then he's all I see. His form fills my vision, his hand tilting my face to his. An apology lies in his depths, churning my insides.

But then he releases me altogether and reaches for one of the documents on Jasper's desk. The words are blurry, unfocused, but it seems similar to the last contract I held.

No...

My eyes drop to the bottom, reading Jasper's signature, as well as Caladin's elaborate scribbles.

*No...*My breaths come out shallow.

The date. Today's date.

"No."

He lowers the contract back to the desk and takes my face again, this time a palm on each cheek. A tender position if I wasn't numb to the feeling.

"Like I said, unions are important, and the price of breaking yours was the *Famiglia*. But Jasper would only release you if we got married." His thumbs stroke over my cheek bones, thawing out my skin. Reminding me I'm still present. "*Piccola tigre*, I'm sorry. My lawyers looked over the contract he drew up, figuring there's some loophole out of this, but it's tight. Anything we do to break it backfires and would send you right back here. I even reached out to Nico Corsetti for support, hoping his lawyers would understand Canadian laws better than mine do, but they too said there's nothing."

"Wait." In my head, I replay his speech. He spoke so quickly, words stopped making sense after the first. "We're stuck?"

"Yeah," he responds, his voice thicker than normal. He ducks his head. "Yasmine, I swear, I tried to look for ways out of this. I figured we'd wed, get you home, and then divorce, and move this whole day behind us both. If we do, Jasper has contractual rights to you. It'll be a war to keep you safe."

"Contractual. I'll run."

His face pinches. "And I'd help you but we'd be under fire."

He's accepted this clearly. He's accepted this and I'm supposed to as well? "*Married*, Caladin. I'm not—we're not—you're going to marry *me*?"

With a downturned smile, he shrugs. "Marriage was always in my future, Yasmine. At least this way, you get to come home."

"To New York." That's not home. Home is Montreal. Home is with my sister.

"Yeah..." He scrapes the bottom of his lip. "I'm sorry."

"I'm forced to marry you then. To what—become a Made Man's wife?"

"Isn't that the future you always presumed you'd have, when you thought your father had a real mafia organization under him?"

Maybe. Dad didn't really talk about my future in that regard. Now, I see why.

"It's me or Jasper. I don't know how to save you otherwise. At least this way, we're in the clear. The Seven won't hunt us."

"You sound so okay with this."

He drops his hands limply to his sides and turns away. At

the last second, I catch that sad expression returning. "I've had all afternoon to come to terms with it. Now, you need to. You marry me, and you're free. I bring you back to New York. Everything else, we'll figure out in time."

Figure out. *Figure out* an entire marriage? I'd sputter in shock and disbelief if I wasn't so numb.

For so long, I've gone along with whatever everyone else wanted. The *only* reason I enrolled in university, which Dad claimed I'd never use, was because I begged him. Because I wanted to feel *normal*. To be with other people my age. For so long, he expected me to sit around all day and do nothing.

Every decision in my life's been made for me. Dad hid the truth of who he is, who our family was to him, from me. He kept me in the dark like some princess who couldn't handle the truth.

Then *he* dragged me from Montreal, the only home I've known. Forced me away from Rozelyn, from my memories of Mom, our house—everything. All to come here and survive through whatever hell the Seven immediately deemed we were worthy of.

And now, even the man who's come to save me has claimed control of my life.

"You know," I finally manage, "everyone's always decided everything for me. Glad to know you're lumped into that category too."

"Yeah, well, welcome to my life," he replies, just as the door opens again and Jasper and the other man returns. Caladin steps closer, his suit brushing my bare arm.

We'll be husband and wife soon. Which means, he's bound to have expectations of me. Ones I have no desire in keeping.

"I'm sure you're eager to start your lives together." Jasper speaks directly to me.

But it's Caladin who responds. "Very." His arm bands

around my waist, pulling me to his side and I gasp low, startled, as the two guys end in this faceoff, both glaring at one another until the third breaks through—literally steps between them and toward Jasper's desk.

"Miss De Falco, my name is Pastor Norman. I'll be here to oversee the union."

A pastor. Seriously?

"Thanks," I say because what else am I supposed to?

He tugs another sheet from the small stack and retrieves a pen from his front pocket. "Mr. Rossi has already informed me you'd like to get this over with quickly, so we'll skip all the formalities and get right to it."

Yasmine is stiff in my arms, not that I blame her. She turns to face the pastor and her blouse rises up an inch, her bare skin meeting my arm. I use the opportunity to stroke her skin, to calm her, but her shoulders tense more.

Already a disaster, and it's only going to get worse from here. Hell, the disaster began hours ago, on the video call with Erico and our lawyers.

"Say that again," my cousin demands, rubbing a hand over his hair. "So I heard you correctly. You're going to marry her, to free her."

"Unless anyone here finds me a way out of it, yeah. They're fucking good, Erico. Fighting ends in death, possibly mine, or worse, they'll chase us to New York and we'll have that war you don't want. At least this way, everyone wins."

"Until they call on the Famiglia for support over whoever the fuck knows. I'm displeased. I don't want you agreeing to this."

"We'll deal with that when we have to."

"Or we return later and kill him," Erico offers. "Start knocking down each of the seven assholes. Problem solved."

"Maybe a far-off possibility. Besides, Ariella's gonna smile so fucking large when her friend walks through the door. You'll benefit from it."

He frowns. "Still, fuck, Caladin. When I sent you out there, I didn't think you'd be returning with her as your bride."

Neither did I. Since this call began with our lawyers saying the contract is tight-knit, we're fucked. Like it or not, I'm coming home with Yasmine as my wife, in an unbreakable deal.

"Eventually you would have married me off. Wouldn't you consider being linked to some psychotic secret society in Canada worthy? Who knows, maybe we'll get stock in red cups."

"What?" My cousin blinks, confused, but quickly shakes it off. "Never mind. Sure, eventually, but we're in a good place right now, so I wasn't planning on pushing anything."

"Well," I shrug, "now we're in a better place. It is what it is."

Erico's mouth flattens and he leans away from the camera, crossing his arms. "See you soon, I suppose. Nice work...all things considered. Coming from someone who recently married his wife because of an arrangement, if you want it to work, learn who she is. What she needs. Open up to her. Be a partner. Given Yasmine's shit history, and the fact she's about to be forced into a wedding, give her time. That's the biggest thing."

I'm already disagreeing with all his relationship advice with a shake of my head, even shocked he's giving it. He knows my stance on the ordeal. He understands. So many drunken conversations were spent on the topic.

"This is nothing more than a way to bring her home. You know why I'd never fall in love."

A few seconds pass of us staring at one another before he blinks. "What's her take on this?"

"Guess we'll see."

The pastor holds up a silver pen, which Yasmine takes after a long hesitation. She stares at it, rolling it between two fingers before leaning over and scribbling where the pastor indicates to.

Without glancing my way, she all but throws the pen at me and crosses the room. Her signature is messy. The exact marks where the pen dig in deeper is apparent by the darkened dots, her slight pauses.

Positioning the pen above the line with my name typed beneath it, I do the same. *Caladin Rossi.* Signing away my freedom, my single life...my life. From here on out, we're a partnership, at least by the *Famiglia*'s perspective. She'll live in my space, she'll have access to all the finer things that come along with being a mobster's wife. She'll be safe and protected and will want for nothing.

Lies. My stomach churns as I drop the pen onto the desk. *She'll long for freedom one day.* Her freedom from me, from marriage, from *us*.

Pastor Norman adds his signature as the witness before slipping it into a waiting folder. "Very well, we're done. Congratulations, Mr. and Mrs. Rossi."

Yasmine chokes. And I bite back my own cough. A fucking missus with my name. Damn.

Jasper takes the pastor's place, smiling like an evil cat. "Congratulations are in order for you both. Stay for a drink?"

With the bullshit ceremony over, I grasp Yasmine's wrist and tug her to my side, keeping her close. She's mine now to protect from this asshole, which means he's unable to touch her.

She's mine.

Jesus...

"Thanks, but no. We'll be heading to the airport."

Jasper makes a face I give no attention to, and drag my... wife...past him. We make it to the door when he speaks. "Rossi,

I'll be watching. And, Yasmine, in case you're wondering, there's numerous reasons your father wanted you here with the Seven. You think we're the villains, but you've yet to meet true ones. You will soon, now that you've married one. One day, you might come crawling back and I look forward to when you do."

"Only when you're six feet under," I shoot back, my hands forming fists, but I push my new bride through the door, slamming it behind me with a final glare. *"Stronzo."* Ushering Yasmine along, I'm eager to get out of this damn school, off the grounds, and back to the plane. "Let's get out of here before someone else pisses me off."

Before the bullshit ceremony, I texted my pilot to begin preparations for takeoff, so when the taxi drops us off at the private terminal in Vancouver International Airport, the stairs are lowered, and he's speaking with airport staff, going over the final steps.

Yasmine hasn't spoken the entire trip over. Hell, she barely seems present. Shock isn't something I'm unfamiliar with, though. She needs the space and time to wrap her head around her new reality. She allows me to lead her up the stairs and inside, so that's something.

The *Famiglia* private plane is well-stocked with couches as well as a bedroom at the back. I lead her toward the nearest black, leather couch, and nudge her down into the cushions, right as the middle-aged flight attendant, Aggie, is offering us both drinks. I thank her with a wave off, entirely focused on Yasmine.

My knees land with a gentle thud on the hard carpet as I kneel in front of her and cup her face, trying to snag her attention. Instead of saying, thinking, and doing all things I need to,

I simply stare. Christ, she's beautiful. I'd thought it the second Erico handed me her photo and instructed me to track her down. The dark mark on her cheek burns warm beneath my palm, a reminder of what exactly got us here.

Finally, her eyes meet mine and they sparkle with some recognition, but she looks sad. Resigned. With her single blink, I feel an emotion I've hardly ever had before meeting this woman.

Guilt.

The emotion is backed by the gold ring in my pocket, which now feels heavier with the regret she'll have to wear it. Like it or not, this is a real, contracted marriage and by *Famiglia* standards, she's my wife—forced or not. Which means bearing a ring worthy of her status as a Consigliere's wife.

The pilot's voice comes over the intercom. "Mr. Rossi, takeoff in two."

"You know," she murmurs, her voice rougher than earlier, "last night, I wished for a way out of there. But now, I feel just as trapped."

In some ways, more.

"We can talk through the details later."

While my thumbs stroke over her bruise, searching for a reply that won't make her hate me more, she angles her face away with a harsh sneer. "We'll talk now. All anyone's ever done is hide shit from me. Protect me. I'm not the helpless woman you all think I am."

"Never said you were." Nonetheless, I drop onto the couch adjacent hers and settle in, kicking one leg up over the other as the plane's engines begin whirling. "What do you want to talk about?"

She waves her hand between us exaggeratedly. "This. Us. It affects you too. You found yourself with a wife all of a sudden."

"And you're freed from a madman. 'Thank you' should be the only words from your pretty, little mouth."

She blanches, and yeah, I'm an asshole. They're not the finest words I could have used, but in the end, this is real and dealing with it now will prevent dragging the pain on.

"Dick."

I shrug because I am. But I won't be the worst she'll encounter in New York.

The plane's takeoff speed shifts into a tilt and then we're in the air, beginning the six-hour flight to New York.

It's gonna be a long flight if this is the next six hours of my life.

She crosses her arms. "What's expected of me then?"

I'd known this question was coming eventually, and prepared for it. "We're strangers, Yasmine, and though unions have occurred on less meetings than we've been lucky to have, we're not going to pretend to be something we're not. For most of your life, you believed you were from a mafia organization, so I assume you understand how marriages work in them. That marriage in this life isn't for love, but power and connections."

Her tongue runs over her teeth before asking, "And physically?"

"Nothing." My fingers fiddle with a stray string on my slacks, and that's what I focus on. "In public, at *Famiglia* events, we'll have to arrive as a couple. Pretend to be one for their sake. Eventually, there will be social events my position mandates me to attend, but behind closed doors, roommates only." I pause, looking at her to search for her feelings on that, but her expression remains blank. "I'm not ready for a wife. Erico keeps me busy so I don't have the time for a relationship. There's a reason I was single, and it's by choice. The *Famiglia* is packed of traditionalists, so to appease their nosy asses, we'll live together for one year. After that, I'll move you out to an apartment or a house in the Hamptons—your choice. You'll want for nothing, you'll be protected, you won't need to work or fear anything."

She looks out the windows beside her, eyes drawn for a moment. She looks sad again. Resigned. Guilt returns stronger, even though it's a misplaced feeling. That plan is the best I can come up with to save everyone. When we return, the *Famiglia* would wonder why I immediately dropped my new wife off elsewhere and spent no time with her, so dealing with Yasmine's misery is easier than dealing with their nagging.

She sighs heavily, the sound of heartbreak covering the plane's walls. "Fine. Guess I don't have a choice, do I?" she asks bitterly.

I say nothing, my silence responding for me.

At this point, she's already upset, so while we're on the topic, I reach into my pocket and pull out the black, velvet jewellery box before tossing it onto her lap. "That's for you."

Her throat moves and she glances from me to it, then back again before pinching the lid slowly open, taking in the slim, gold wedding band with a single large diamond.

After our lawyers stated the contract was iron-clad and there was nothing I could do to get out of it, I went ring shopping. Seems ridiculous when thinking about it, but it helped me better come to terms with the situation. It was the first nice one I found, opting to purchase it rather than have one custommade like what Erico did for Ariella. That would mean I care about it too much. Buying a matching simple, gold band for myself was also a bit of a reality check.

While she's studying hers, I slip mine on, circling it once until my hand gets used to the weight. Not sure it ever will. The physical symbol of the signature I signed onto the contract earlier. Of my freedom gone. Because no matter how much of the *not married* game we play, these small gold pieces prove otherwise.

I have a wife. She has a husband.

Yasmine Rossi.

I swallow.

"It's beautiful," she murmurs in a voice so low, I almost don't hear her over the whirling jets. "But if we're not acting married, do I have to—"

"You're my wife. You'll wear my ring. For show."

"No more than a business deal?"

"Exactly."

She slips it onto her left hand, holding it up in the air, gazing at it. Something passes in her expression.

Curiosity.

Blinking, she shakes her head and lowers her hand into her lap, fisting it, which only draws my attention to the ring.

"Looks nice," I say.

"Thanks."

While she stares out the window, I stare at her. Despite the situation, this is the most ideal marriage for me. She doesn't want me, I don't want her—simple. Love matches can remain being for Erico and Ariella. And my parents.

Even at ten, I picked up on my parents happiness and love for one another. They were the idols of the emotion. Compared to Erico and his emotionless upbringing, I once considered myself lucky. I was raised until I was ten in a blissful household with two parents who loved me as much as they adored each other. As an ignorant ten-year-old, I once claimed to wanting a marriage exactly like theirs.

They were an arranged marriage, as most are in the *Famiglia*. Mother was one of two daughters of a Florida politician. Her older sister was engaged to Father, but at the wedding ceremony, fled, and Mother was forced to take her sister's place.

It worked out and in only a few months, they quickly fell in love and had me.

I swallow, still unable to look away from Yasmine. If Mother was alive, she'd take Yasmine in. Both she and Father would praise me for making the decision I had today, and Mother would ensure Yasmine got settled in her new life. She'd become a mom to her—because that's who Mother was. Unfailing in her kindness.

But that future can never play out because they're dead. Their love for one another killed them.

It's why lines will never blur between Yasmine and me. Why we won't even have sex. Casual sex might work other times, but does it remain casual with one's own wife? Definitions become frazzled and it's not worth it.

I blink, trying to come up with any other topic to think about. Anything else to keep my mind off this.

"Is there anyone from your past we need to worry about?"

She blinks, turning away from the clouds below us. "What?"

"Men. From your past. Jealous exes. Bitchy best friends. Before your father took you from Montreal, you were living a regular-ish life, so is there anyone waiting around for you, other than your sister, that I should be aware of? Old boyfriends perhaps. Can't protect you if I don't know."

She rolls her eyes. "No one to worry about."

That sounds like a brush-off. I lean forward, elbows on my knees. "Which means there is."

"Nope," she counters again. "Left everyone I once hung out with behind and since I'm not returning home, there's no point in looking into the past. They all assume I'm still in B.C. so get off the topic."

I lean back, smirking. Liar, she is not. "All right," I murmur in a disbelieving tone.

She sneers over her shoulder. "Anyone *I* should worry about?"

"It's cute you're concerning yourself with me. If you want, I'll send over a list of every woman I've slept with and you can review it for the psychopaths."

She makes a loud, huffing sound. "God, you're irritating. Is this what the next few years will be like?"

"Few?" I repeat with a laugh. "*Piccola tigre*, try forever."

8

YASMINE

I knew that.

There's no way out of this marriage that doesn't land me back in B.C. But it doesn't mean I've accepted that *this*, that New York and Caladin Rossi are my forever. He's saying in a year he'll move me out into a home of my own. That home can be in Montreal, with Rozelyn, and he can summon me whenever he needs. Therefore, yeah, a few years is still an apt statement.

This can't be my future, that's for certain. My gaze drops to the wedding ring he bought for me. Pretty and large, heavy as fuck, being that I'm unused to jewellery on my hands. Another woman would adore this ring, I'm sure, but me, not so much. The design for one, but also what it symbolizes.

Entrapment.

For fucking once, I'd like to make my own decisions.

I think back to Caladin's question regarding people in my past, and there was one. One who *I* chose, right beneath my father's nose. Dad never learned, and I never even told Rozelyn about all the times he'd sneak into my bedroom or he'd fuck me in the back of one of Dad's cars after picking me up from school. The entire affair was a giant middle finger to my father.

Gene Lampel was one of my father's soldiers. A year older than me, I used him as much as he used me. It began with flirting two years ago, and eventually, he took my virginity in a night of passionless sex that did the job. After that, it got a bit better, and we only fucked once in a while, but it served a purpose for us both. Nothing was special, or even personal, which is why my new, nosy husband doesn't need to know about him. Gene remained behind in Montreal after we fled, and I'll never see him again, which I don't care about either. He won't be my final sexual encounter.

Sex.

I look across the plane again to Caladin, who's playing with a loose string on his clothing.

Caladin's offering a romance-free marriage, and this, I'm all for. But at some point, I'll either need to buy a battery-operated boyfriend or...something. No sex for the next few decades sounds like a fate worse than death. I assume if I'm moved out and we're living separate lives, that means we're both free to do what we want, with who. Right?

An issue for another day, I think, as the plane rocks slightly with turbulence.

At first glance, there's a lot of similarities between New York and Montreal, so at least there's that. By similarities, I mean they're both huge cities with many tall skyscrapers, and traffic backed-up forever. The very traffic we're presently stuck in, and the exact many tall skyscrapers I'm scanning as we pass them.

In the driver's seat, Caladin looks very much at home. His

fingers drill on the console, his other elbow positioned on the door. His knees are spread as wide as the sports car allows for, his right leg moving every few minutes when traffic allows us to drive forward a couple feet. I hate how fucking hot he looks driving. The suit, the rumpled hair, his eased position, it all fits the sports car.

Couldn't guess the kind of car this is, but I did spot a gold bull on the hood if that means anything. It's black and uber low to the ground, all cut lines with a pointed nose. It moves fast, speeding away from the private airfield quickly, only to get stopped in traffic.

Caladin claims it's a forty-minute drive from the airport to his condo, but that he'd do it in thirty, thanks to the car's speeds. With the traffic, seems like it'll be an hour, or longer, but I lean against the comfortable leather seat and wait it out.

While we drive, I watch out the windows, at the city with enough people that I convince myself it's home. Cars everywhere, honking, noises, yelling from pedestrians. A bluster of commotion.

Comforting chaos.

One hour exactly later—a point I feel like making if only I'd speak to him—Caladin pulls into the dark underground lot beneath a tall building. He claims we're in a neighbourhood in New York called Manhattan.

"No mansion?"

"Too small for you?" Caladin side-eyes me as the car purrs, parking in the spot by the elevator. There's few cars down here, only a handful, and they all look very pricey. It dredges up a question.

But I instead answer in a haughty tone, "I do prefer my cages larger."

Caladin climbs out of the low car with little issue but I scramble. He comes around the front to help me, but I ignore the offered hand, getting out myself. He backs away with a shrug and pursed lips that say *suit yourself* and walks toward the elevator.

"There's very few cars down here."

He glances over his shoulder. "This is the parking level only my cousin and I park in. The *Famiglia* owns the building. My cousin, the organization's Boss, owns the top floor and I have the one beneath him. This," he gestures to the far wall with at least five vehicles parked, "is all ours. Erico enjoys racing so he keeps quite the collection here and at the Rossi mansion. The other residents park at a lot below us."

"Got it." *Fuck, my head hurts.*

Because already, this isn't like Dad. When he told me what he'd done, I almost didn't believe that we weren't a real organization, but it made sense the more I thought about it. Mafia families, like the Corsettis, have history. Aunts, uncles, cousins, grandparents—family lines existing for decades. A hold on their territory due to years of fearmongering. Power from the connections of their criminal activities. Mansions and properties owned for as long as they've been there.

We didn't have that. None of that. As a child, Dad said he moved into Montreal to steal Corsettis' hold, which I suppose was some of the truth, but I never looked twice at the fact we were so different than them.

Standing in a parking garage, surrounded by the handful of cars, in a building that Caladin's family owns—presumably one of many—I suspect it's only the beginning.

Caladin taps a button to call the elevator and the metal doors open immediately. I file in with him, pressing against the far wall and observe as he types a code on the screen and then a floor number. The elevator slides right up the shaft without stopping.

When the small box dings, he leads me from it and toward

the only door on this floor, right across from the elevator. The carpet is a deep red, soft beneath my feet. The walls a beige, and even his door a dark oak. It's pretty.

As he unlocks his door, he murmurs, "I'll get you a key made so you can come and go."

The door clicks open and he steps aside, pushing it with one hand, gesturing for me to enter first with his other. I do without hesitation, curious of what my life's been subjected to.

"Holy shit."

The first thing I notice is the wall of windows directly across from me—*far* from me due to the vast size of the condo. The large balcony beyond the windows overlooking a gorgeous skyline. Blue, with a defined line of grey of the city's smog, but still lovely. The other tall buildings surround us, but it's the cerulean blue between each one claiming my attention. Gazing at skylines has always been my favourite activity. No matter where in the world you are, everyone looks at the same sky. The same atmosphere, the same gasses. But the colours change based on weather, time of day, or other factors, and it's nice to know, no matter what bullshit occurs during the day, the sky will darken; nighttime will fall. The day will end and another will begin. Nighttime skies are my favourite with the stars twinkling, lighting up in small, bright dots over the deep blue.

The skyline view alone makes me enter this stranger's home, but it's the rest that keeps me here. Decorator, he is not, since all the white walls look depressingly plain—all except one. The living room beside the large windows boasts a beige padded couch and a huge flatscreen hanging on the wall. Bigger than Dad had. Ideal for watching horror movies in the dark, moonlight casting through beside me.

What are you doing? Why are you seeing this place as pleasant when it's only a cage?

Ignoring my inner voice, I continue forward. Into the large

foyer, the kitchen to my left. All silver appliances and white countertops. Large for an apartment. The dining room table made for six people, a low chandelier dangling above. I look right, down the hallway, spotting doors farther down.

"This is pretty," I admit.

"Not what you expected?" His voice sounds closer now.

I shake my head. "I expected a mess. Clothes strewn everywhere, dirty dishes piled in the sink. That kinda stuff."

He chuckles. "You're gonna be a load of fun to live with if you assume everything about anything. But if it's a mess you want, you should see the bedroom."

Why would I look at his when being brought to mine is all I want?

"Is it always this clean?" I ask skeptically, scanning over the shiny kitchen again.

"You asking if I had it specifically cleaned before I left for my job and returned from Canada with a wife I never expected having to entertain? Nope, can't say I did. Can't tell the future though it'd be a mighty fuckin' useful skill."

I throw him a scathing look so he can see me rolling my eyes. "Dick."

"You asked!" His palms rise in submission as he steps around me, much closer than I'd prefer. His scent washes over me, clouding my mind and making it difficult to focus as he heads for a slim door by the front entrance and opens it, gesturing to the few coats, umbrellas, and shoes in there. "Closet-y things." Then he heads down the hallway, toward the single door, which I find odd a place this large only has one.

At the entrance, I pause at the large room with a king-sized bed in the centre. A bedspread not quite black, but like a very deep plum covers it, multiple pillows by the head. Hardwood floors, and another balcony outside the glass doors. Against the right wall is an opened door, white ceramic peeking from the edge, and I presume it's the bathroom.

But it's the door to my right, he taps on. "I'll make room in the closet for your stuff."

Um. "Why? I'll be in another bedroom."

His knowing smirk is slow building, enticing a lump in my throat with every heavy beat of my heart. "Did you see this second bedroom at all in the hallway we just walked down? If you did, please let me know because I could have been using it this entire time, and I'd feel like an idiot."

There's no... "We're not sharing this room."

He drops his body against the closet door, ankles and arms crossing. "Well, I'm not sleeping on my own couch, so yeah, we are."

My stomach feels hollow. "But you said we'd be roommates only."

He shrugs, smirking. "And we will be. Literal *room*mates. Mates sharing a room."

He thinks he's funny when he's anything but. "You're a dick! You totally had me believing I'd have my own room."

"Not my fault you assumed. Really gotta stop that. It's unappealing."

Oh, if only I had something to throw at his head... The bed behind me looms, now a threat. We'll be sharing that. Which means, we'll be *sleeping beside one another*. That's not what roommates do. Not ones in a non-romantic situation.

Worse: he'll see what no one else does. When at night, sleep is tough if the room isn't set up right. When the nightmares keep me awake and I stare at the ceiling all night.

"But the bed," is all I can weakly murmur. "We'll be sharing it."

"Yes."

"How do I know you won't touch me?" The question slips

out in stupid wonder, in a question I regret immediately, hands flinging up to cover my mouth. I regret them the moment I ask it because deep down, I *know* that's not who he is. He's a stranger, but he's not Jasper. He doesn't have my instincts rising. He feels safe.

In a deadly, heavy silence, Caladin shoves off the closet door, all bits of previous humour long gone for pure rage. No, not rage. Not anything. No emotion as his arms drop to his sides and he strides toward me with paced steps, the same way a tiger would stalk its prey. He might call me a little tiger, but right now, I'm not the hunter.

I step back, and his jaw clenches. Earlier, I knew he wouldn't hurt me...but now is something else. Caladin's too much of a stranger to be certain if he would act on rage or not.

Going against all my instincts, I stop after a single step and let him tower over me, his hair skirting the top of my head as he bends down. He tilts his head until his lips hover over mine. If I were to lift onto my toes, we'd be kissing. Instead, I hold my breath, unable to fathom anything but surviving.

"I promise on my vows to the *Famiglia*, I will not touch you until you ask me to. Lucky for you, Erico sends me on a lot of jobs, so you'll be alone often. I'm sorry to inconvenience your life so much."

Before I can formulate my own response, he spins on his heel and heads for the door. He's by the doorway when I find my voice. "W-where are you going?"

"Out. It's our wedding night, after all, so excuse me while I go get wasted," he replies without turning around. His back is stiff, shoulders rigid, and I know how badly I've fucked up. How he's so different than the laidback man I've so far known. "Make yourself at home. Pick any side of the bed and have a good night."

9
CALADIN

The benefit of being who I am is that after one phone call to a *Famiglia* owned club, it got cleared out within the hour. Erico might be irritated over the lost business, but he owes me at least this much; a place I can be alone and down as much alcohol as my body allows for since I no longer have the pleasure of an empty condo to wallow in.

My second phone call was made to Erico. The least the fucker can do is leave his wife's pussy long enough to sit with me. Drive me home when I'm too far gone to do it myself. To hear how much I've fucked my life up by marring a woman who'd believe I'd *touch* her all because we're sleeping in the same bed.

I know she didn't mean it, not really. The apology darkened her otherwise gorgeous eyes the moment the words left her mouth, but it doesn't change the fact that she said them. If the thought wasn't initially there, she wouldn't have asked.

I'm already three shots in and my head feels light. I'm reclined on a couch on the club's VIP balcony—a bad idea I'm realizing now, since I'll have to somehow get down the stairs later—but I roll my neck until seeing the hand clutching my drink. The gold band taunting me with everything I am now. Everything I'll have to deal with. A home that isn't only mine now. This morning, I woke in B.C. expecting to finally convince her to bring me to the Seven. Now, I'm a fucking husband.

"One day, you'll find a nice girl to love as much as I love your mother, Caladin."

"Fuck you." I chug another gulp, using the alcohol to burn the childhood memory of my father's words. "Fuck you and fuck off."

"You invited me here and I left Ariella to come, so no, I'm not fucking off as you so rudely demand." My cousin drops into the couch across from me and reaches for one of the three dozen shot glasses I had delivered earlier. "Ariella's in a pleasant mood because of you and you've interrupted a great night, so this better be worth it."

I hold up the now-empty glass in my hand in a toast. "Cheers to you, man. At least someone's getting laid on *my* wedding night."

"You would be too if you stayed home."

Now, *that's* laughable. I wouldn't be. Maybe ass-fucked with a metal pole *by* her if I even looked in her direction. "She'd rather chop off my dick than ride it."

He shakes his head. "There's an image I didn't need. Love your cheery disposition."

"Fuck off." My glare asks *you serious right now?* I lean forward for another shot—this one vodka, and it burns my throat. "I need you to send me away on another job. One that'll take a while. Preferably weeks." Or months. Hell, even years.

Erico, the fucking asshole, grins as he rubs a palm over his chin. "Country's calm. Everything's covered and there's nothing for you to do besides stay here and get to know your new wife."

"In a marriage neither of us want. Trust me, she'll be thrilled if I leave."

"Will she?" His brow arches in challenge. "Might seem that way, but women can hide a lot of pain. Ariella buried so many deep longings because she assumed I'd break her heart. You never know what Yasmine truly wants until she begins opening up to you."

I'm not you. Another shot. My head's getting so heavy now and if I was upright at all, I'm not any longer.

"Difference is, Ariella wanted a husband. Happiness. A good marriage. Yasmine wanted escape and all I did was offer her another cage." The somber thought has me tipping another shot down my throat. "We're not having a happy union, cuz. In a year, I'm moving her out. She can do whatever she wants. *Who*ever she wants."

"In your one-bedroom condo?" Erico checks, amusement tinging his tone.

My one-bedroom condo with the one bed. Maybe, I'll get two in there so she doesn't think I'll *touch* her without her permission.

I get it. I do. I really do. After everything Nico Corsetti told us about her family, what her father did, it's bound to fuck with her. Yasmine doesn't know who to trust anymore as she's dragged from person to person: her father to the Seven to me. From place to place: Montreal to White Rock to New York City.

But I'm drunk. And alcohol elevates my anger. So rationality no longer exists.

All it does is highlight how wrong we are for one another. She's not in a place to trust and I don't have the desire to make the effort.

"Caladin," my cousin prompts.

"Yeah," I reply, barely recalling what I'm even agreeing to.

"*You're* going to let her fuck around with others."

I huff. "Erico, just stop. I haven't had five fucking minutes to wrap my head around what all this means. No doubt, news has already travelled through the *Famiglia*, which means we need to be prepared for that. I went from doing a job to having a roommate bearing my last name. Yasmine's life has been changed so many fuckin' times, and right now, I don't know what to do about any of it."

Erico's silent through my drunken seething, and I wonder how much of it even made sense until he nods slowly, taking in my rambles. "All right. Well, considering your consumption," he gestures to the empty glasses on the low table between us, "don't decide anything tonight."

I lean forward—which takes *way* too much effort—and grab another one. "Workin' on it."

He sighs, watching me with judgemental eyes that remind me of his father's. "I never wanted a marriage either. Ariella was a task for my role and nothing more, but when I allowed myself to feel something, it was right. Caladin, being married isn't the end of the world."

Telling him to stop is on the edge of my tongue, but instead I mutter, "Yes, you and your perfect marriage. Doesn't work well when mine wants out. Besides, you know my own feelings on it."

"So this will be your life now?" He waves his hand up and down my body. "Practically passed out in a club. Which was stupid of you to empty out on a Saturday night. That's thousands of dollars of missed revenue."

"Consider it a wedding present from you to me." I press my mouth together in what I think and hope is a grin. "Any word about the Bratva?"

It was only a week ago that Erico shot and killed Ursin Volkov, the Bratva's Boss, after he tried to kidnap Ariella. I arrived to help just as the fight ended. Erico's obsession with Ariella prevented Ursin from living for his attempt, but he did release Ursin's daughter, Vanessa, to return to Russia. In time, I'm sure they'll rebuild and will want revenge.

He shakes his head. "Nothing. Good job on the topic switch."

"You're awfully invested in my relationship."

His lips press together. "Well, it's my fault you're in it."

My arms toss in the air, dramatic from the liquor. "At least you're finally getting it. Fine, you wanna talk about this. Let's talk about the fact she basically thinks I'll rape her. Ever been told that by a woman? No. Guess what: it fuckin' hurts."

He flinches. "She had a lot happen to her in a short amount of time. She's scared, Cal. Don't be the villain in her story. She's had enough of those."

And then he reaches forward to grab only his second shot, leaving his heavy words lingering in the air. I *know* he's correct. Know I shouldn't be a complete ass to her. I was telling the truth when I said we'd be roommates. Who knows, perhaps even friends in time.

But a friendship opens to other things. Things I couldn't bear to do to her.

It's more humane *not* to love her, and not to let her love me in return.

Love destroys.

Much later, I stumble into my condo, slamming the door shut behind me. I've had who knows how many drinks but at this point, who cares? Yasmine already thinks I'm scum, so let's add drunken frat boy to her list.

The club's couch was really fucking inviting, but my irritating cousin dragged me by the back of my suit jacket and drove me home, making me wonder why I invited the killjoy along in the first place.

"Don't leave her alone on your wedding night, even if all you two do is sleep. Trust me on this," was his advice when he shoved me out of the elevator.

Stellar advice from the man who did precisely the same thing to Ariella. He disappeared to Vegas the same night and stayed away from New York for days. He did it, but it's too much for me to demand he send me off somewhere?

Hypocrite.

I glare at my shut door, knowing he's long gone. Probably heading home to his beloved wife.

I eye the couch, contemplating passing out there, but I turn toward the bedroom regardless. Amidst the heavy amount of alcohol consumed, my head continued to be plagued by pretty dark eyes and luscious nightshade hair. She's gorgeous, certainly, but it's everything else accompanying her appearance that I don't need.

At the doorway, I pause at the sight of Yasmine in my bed. She's perched on the farthest edge, her back to the door. Her hair is free over the pillow she's claimed on the left side while the duvet's tugged up to her middle, her arm untucked.

Her breaths are steady, though I have no idea how. The curtain's been pulled open wide, all that moonlight entering. If it didn't take every muscle in my legs to even make it this far in my condo, I'd cross the room and shut it. Fuck, I despise any form of light during the night. Not that I can't sleep through it, but it's never as good.

I turn for the attached bathroom, noting the door's practically shut, cracked open about two inches. And the light's been left on. An accident, I presume. Inside, I splash water on my face, noting how there's none of Yasmine's products in here, which means she'll need to tell me what she prefers.

On my way out, my finger hovers over the light switch, but even through the drunken fog, pieces fall into place. I look at the drawn-open curtains again. Maybe...

Nah, my head's not clear enough for this.

But instead of flicking the light off, I leave it on and close the door again, cracking it an inch so a bit of light seeps through before unsteadily walking to my closet, shedding my clothing in the centre. I'll get the private shopper who stocked Erico's closet for Ariella in here tomorrow. After tossing on shorts, I head to bed.

Even though she's far from me, by the edge, the bed seems smaller with her in it. But not small enough to feel cramped. Rather...pleasant.

God, I'm so fuckin' drunk to be thinking like this.

In the shadows of the room, her figure moves, and dare I say it, she somehow gets *closer* to the bed's edge, inching to the side, informing me she's awake.

Of course, you are. All this light. No one could sleep through this.

"Do that again and you'll fall off."

Her shoulders stiffen, but she doesn't respond, likely pretending to still be asleep.

"Whatever. Fall off the bed then. See if I care."

I *don't* care. She never moves. I remain on my back, watching and waiting for her shape to make a better choice. Can't have her falling off the bed her first night here. She'll somehow find a way to blame me. So I can't turn away until proving to her I'm not some asshole her head's designed me as.

I do the very thing I told myself I wouldn't and slide toward her, an arm wrapping her middle. With a slight and low grunt, I drag her over the bed with me. Her hair ends up in my face, so all I'm smelling is her fucking addictive flowery, jasmine scent. Even drunk, it wakes my body up, a hardening thrum coasting through me.

I release her before drunk me gets anymore horrible ideas and return to my side, even rolling until our backs face each other.

My side. Well, isn't that laughable.

There's an ache now. One she satisfied during the short breath I held her close to me.

Once again, I'm too drunk for rational thinking.

"Thanks." Her quiet mumble arises from behind me. "I guess."

"No problem." I shut my eyes, assuming that'll be the end of our conversation.

"You were gone a while."

"Yep. Does it matter?"

It takes counting to five by the time she responds. "Guess not."

It does or she wouldn't be asking. Maybe it's jealousy but that's stupid to assume, all things considering.

"Good night," I tell her, ending the conversation.

"Night, Caladin."

Fuck my cock for jumping at the soft way she murmurs my name. Soft but throaty. A tone I long for more of.

I need sleep. To end this day, these thoughts, this everything. To wake in B.C. and this to be all a damn nightmare.

But I remain awake longer than I wish. It's easy to blame the bathroom light or the moonlight glow, but the truth is, as the time ticks away on my phone's screen, I *can't* and it has everything to do with the body beside me. This isn't the first time I've shared a bed with a woman, but my god, does it feel different knowing she'll be here every night. She owns my last name, my ring, and eventually will be expected to one day bear my—

The thought cuts out before I allow it to finish because it won't happen. Can't even think about *that* or why my drunken thoughts went there.

Close your eyes. Block everything out.

My eyes shut but still, I don't sleep. Not until I finally hear her breathing even out. But before I pass out, a thought flits through my mind.

Was she waiting up for me?

10

YASMINE

For all the shit of my life, denying Caladin's mattress is easily the comfiest bed I've ever slept on would be an utter lie.

When I wake, I expect to find his cocky grin and watchful eyes, but instead, I'm alone. Patting his side of the bed, it feels cool, which means he's been gone for a while. With that, I roll from bed and make my side of the bed, clearly dividing the two halves.

Oh my god, there's a "his" side and a "my" side.

Scowling, I stomp away from the bed and into the bathroom where I eye the shower, wanting one. Wanting one, but having no soap to use other than his male-scented one.

No soap.

Very few clothes to my name.

No cell phone.

In fact, after peeing, I hightail it out of the bedroom, in search of my new *husband*. He claimed I'll want for nothing. Well, there's a few things I require, including a cell phone to call

Rozelyn because half a day here is already a day too long without contact.

Once I open the bedroom door, I don't manage a step before I'm blocked by a pile of items. On the very top: a black credit card with a sticky note attached to it: *Whatever you want, you buy.* Beneath the card is clothing, and I rifle through the jeans and teal blouse, wondering how he knew my sizes.

Beneath all that is the single item I abandon all the rest for. A cell phone. A way to call Rozelyn and end the nightmare our father created. There's no password so it unlocks with a tap of the screen.

The first thing I notice is the few contacts already programmed in.

His own—of course.

Ariella Rossi—a name that'll take a moment to get used to.

Rozelyn De Falco—the name I need.

I tap her name, eagerly awaiting her to answer, not caring how ridiculous this whole scene could look. Me grasping a cell phone, kneeling on the ground in a doorway.

"Hello?" My sister's throaty voice comes through the speaker, robbing me of all breath. It's only been a few weeks, but it feels like a lifetime, so by the time my voice finally works again, it's more of a gasp.

"Rozelyn. It's me."

"Yasmine?" Her voice spikes, repeating, "Yasmine? Oh, my god! I was told Caladin found you but he didn't...holy fuck, Yas!"

Weeks and weeks of fear and agony wash away in that single statement. With the relief in her tone. Nothing else matters. Not what's happening. Not being forced to live in New York, married to a Made Man. Not about Dad and all the chaos he bred.

Nothing but her.

"Rozelyn," I repeat. A weakness trembles through my body and I fall backwards onto my ass, my hands clutching the phone to my ear like it'll never be close enough. "Roz, hearing your voice…"

"Are you okay?" she demands. Then there's shuffling in the background, and voices, and then a door closing. "Where are you?"

"New York, and I don't know," I answer her in opposite order, but truthfully. Am I okay? I'm alive but my life's been flipped upside down.

She curses. "That makes sense. Nico mentioned when Caladin found you, you'd return there first."

"We're—" I stop, wondering if now's the time to admit everything, when it doesn't even make sense in my head. "I don't know when I'll get to come back to Canada."

"Maybe after you see Ariella, since she's the one who put all this in motion?"

As much as I'd enjoy seeing Ariella again, Rozelyn's my priority. Besides, apparently I'm stuck here for the rest of my life so I'll have ample opportunity to visit Ariella.

"Where are you now?" I counter-ask. "The Corsettis… you're safe?" Dad told me some of what he's been having Rozelyn do, and I felt sick. And scared that the Corsettis would punish her for our father's decisions. I'd hope Della would protect her, but I also couldn't blame our ex-stepsister for turning her back on Rozelyn.

"I'm fine, Yas, better than fine even." She pauses and I know her well enough to imagine her running a hand through her long hair. "Look, we have a lot to catch up on, and over the phone isn't the best."

"Dad."

"Yeah, him too." I can all but hear the frown in her tone,

which hits me right in the heart like a dagger. Uncertain what the answers I want from her are: what his outcome was.

"I'll be right there." I roll back to my knees, scooping up the clothing Caladin left behind. Whatever Caladin's "rules" are, I'm seeing my damn sister.

Take away freedom and marry me—fine.

Keep me away from family—less fine.

With my clothes, his note and the credit card catch my eye. He instructed me to buy what I want; therefore, I'll be ordering a taxi.

"Wait, does Caladin know you're about to take off?"

"No and it's none of his business." The marriage licence we signed would beg to differ, but that's another day's issue.

"Um."

"What?" I bark into the phone after tossing it onto the bed, setting it to speakerphone. "I want to see you, Roz. We're both free now."

Free-ish at least.

"I do too," she replies slowly, like she's not believing her own words, "but the fact is New York is who saved you, so you should be playing by their rules. Don't do anything that'll end with you cut up into pieces and tossed in a garbage bin."

"Gruesome and gross." But I pause from dressing, reflecting on her words. Caladin's so far been easy, I guess—as easy as a husband after a day can be. What *would* he do to return home and find me gone? Surely, he'd understand I want to see my sister. "Whatever," I mumble, more to myself and finish dressing.

"Do you even still have your ID?"

"Yes." Thankfully. One of the few personal articles I *do* still have that I was sure to grab from Jasper's apartment was my wallet and passport. Dad was wise enough to have me take them in case *"we needed to leave the country."*

"Well...all right then. I guess I'll see you soon." She speaks slow, uncertain, but I hang up before she dwells too long on the what-ifs.

I grab my small bag with all my possessions, slip the new cell in my jeans pocket alongside Caladin's fancy credit card and rush down the hallway of the empty condo and out the front door.

The elevator brings me straight to the ground floor, luckily not stopping on any of the other floors, and once I'm outside, I feel free. That much closer to my sister. The late morning sunlight and stifling New York air hits me once I reach the sidewalk. It's noticeably thicker than Montreal's air.

A taxi passes, so I rush to the edge of the sidewalk, waving my arms like a maniac until another yellow car pulls over. Taxis in Montreal are usually whatever the driver owns, but I appreciate the ease of finding the bright yellow cars.

A middle-aged man with a receding hairline stops by the curb and I get into the back, waving the black credit card to indicate I have means to pay. "Airport please."

He drives away from Caladin's condo and I fall back against the cloth seat with a deep, contented sigh.

Life will soon make sense once again.

~

I'd like to say John F. Kennedy International Airport is larger than Montreal Trudeau, but I wouldn't know since Dad never brought me anywhere that'd require flight. What Caladin isn't aware of is the flight from B.C. to here was my first time in the air.

Paying and exiting the taxi is thrilling because every step brings me closer to Rozelyn. By mid-afternoon, Caladin will go back to the condo and find me gone. By then, I'll be safe in

Montreal and when he undoubtedly drags me home, it'll be okay because I'll have seen Rozelyn again.

The inside of the airport is *packed.* People criss-cross everywhere, rushing to airline counters for tickets and bags. Children yelling, people talking loudly about flight times, food, and anything else travellers discuss. It's pure chaos but I love it.

At the far end, I spot a recognized Canadian airline's counter and make that my direction. By the time I'm nearing the back of the short line, a large body cuts in front of me, not at all excusing themselves with the slightest of decent manners. Anger swirls until I'm about to shove them out of my way.

"Hey—" The remainder of my argument gets stuck at the sight of my husband, muscled arms crossing over his chest, his glare heavier than the bag on my shoulder. "What..." My question trails off because I already know the answer to *what are you doing here?* He's here for me. Found me. Already—somehow tracked me within the hour since I climbed into the taxi.

With a deep-set frown, he drags me from the line, eyes roving the area. I dig my heels into the smooth ground, aware I'm battling a literal killer. A Made Man who'd have no qualms in doing whatever he wants with me. Still, I try, nails scratching at his hold until he releases me.

"Calad—" The rest of his name is lost in a small screech as he leans down, one arm wrapping around my knees, the other at my back to steady me, and I'm tossed over his shoulder like a sack. "Caladin!"

Beneath a few curious glances, he stomps away from the terminal and out the front entrance, down the stretch by a few cars, and then drops me to my feet, pushing me against the building.

"What?" He growls, his hand scraping through his hair until I'd believe the strands could be yanked out. "You have zero right to bitch. You realize what could fucking happen to you?

You're a *Famiglia* wife now, and I know that means nothing to you, but here's your damn lesson. We have enemies who'd fucking *love* to get their hands on you, simply to get to us. You can't go trying to leave the country unprotected!"

His face is flushed, his jaw tight. Another man, I'd believe was concerned about me but that isn't us. Isn't this. His anger doesn't come from fear but rather pure rage that I disobeyed him.

"How'd you know where I was?"

"Raj." He gestures to a shiny black SUV parked a few vehicles away. It stands out from all the other travellers' vehicles simply by the suited man leaning on the passenger door. "When you left the building, I got a call. He tracked you here. Not that it was difficult to guess where you'd be headed."

I stare at the man wearing sunglasses, pretending like he isn't observing. Then my husband. And back, realization hitting me. He was having me watched by a— "You got me a fucking bodyguard?"

Furious eyes roll, doing nothing to lower the harshness in his actions. I swear, he vibrates, like a bomb seconds from exploding. His fingers drag through the sides of his hair again, ending with fists that pull on the strands.

"Did you *not* listen when I said you're part of the *Famiglia*? Yasmine, we are not some game, no matter what you think. We're not a fake mafia like the one your father created. We have enemies—many of them. A war's probably brewing half a world away as I speak. So yes, you have a bodyguard. For *your* comfort, I had him stay outside the building, but you pull shit like this again, he'll be stationed inside the condo." He stops, seething breaths blowing a minty scent over my face, but it doesn't lull me. "Let's fucking go." He reaches for my arm again.

I yank away, avoiding him altogether, and shove into his chest. I hear him, I do. A family organization this old would come with history and enemies, but it doesn't change my situation.

"No. Caladin, I'm going to Montreal."

He laughs once and still grabs my arm, shoving me in the direction of the vehicle. With every step he takes, I stumble back one.

"I'm going to see my sister," I try again. "You can't keep me from her."

He laughs again, this time with even less humour. "Wanna bet, Yasmine? You're my *wife*, and if I fucking wanted to, I could keep you locked in a goddamned cage. Lucky for you," his eyes rake over me in the same manner one would when looking at garbage, "I have no such desires. But you continue to believe this," he taps my ring, "is some sort of game, I will. This is our reality now, so deal with it."

Toward the end, his tone held what I'd like to believe is regret, so I use that. Over the bustling around us, I whisper, "She's my sister. I need to see her. *Please.*"

His jaw ticks.

"I'll run again."

"You do, and I'll track you. Forget who I am already? This," he gestures to the airport behind us, "this was child's play to find you."

That wasn't a yes or a no on me visiting, but the argument seems to be over for now. If I have a chance of winning, it's not here and now. It's when Caladin has a second to cool off. Just like Dad growing up. He was always angry, but once given a few hours to ease his mood, then he was pleasant.

So I allow him to direct me toward the SUV and my new bodyguard, Raj. Only instead of that vehicle, he leads me to the smaller one parked in front: his black sports car.

To Raj, he commands, "Head back to the condo. I'll take her from here."

He gestures for me to get in before walking to his own side. I glance at the airport again, and then Caladin's daring expression before I drop into the low, leather seat. Once inside, Caladin follows. When I expect a cocky, satisfied expression from him, he looks drawn. Upset almost, but that can't be it.

In a move too smooth, and dare I think it, too hot, he shifts the car into another gear and takes off quickly, the purr and rumble comforting beneath me.

After thirty minutes of tense silence, he speaks. Bites his words out, like he has no desire to say them. "I'm normally not an asshole, Yasmine. At least, I try not to be; I leave that for Erico, but you can't pull shit like that again. If I didn't have Raj on you, if I returned home later and found you gone, I'd be genuinely frightened something bad happened."

Doubt that.

His eyes shift to me, masked of emotions. "When I said I require very little from this marriage, it was the truth. We might have to live together for now, to share the same bed, but that's as far as our interactions have to go. You're free to do whatever you'd like, to keep your days full, as long as Raj accompanies you. For the most part, work will keep me out of your way."

Well, now *I* feel like an idiot. Guilt. That heavy emotion I haven't had much opportunity through the course of my life to feel. Dad never let me do anything that warranted a situation in which feeling guilty was appropriate. But I do now, and I hate it.

Caladin flew all the way out west *for me.*

He gave up being single *for me.*

A part of his home *for me.*

A chance of his own happiness *for me.*

To save me. To get me away from a madman who'd probably have raped me by now.

All he wants is for me to follow a couple of rules. To remain within the bounds of this form of captivity. It should be no different than living back with Dad, months ago. Should be simple and reasonable even…but I'm tired.

"I'm sorry," I mumble back. "But I'm not really free to do whatever I want, am I? Or else you wouldn't have stopped me from boarding a plane."

After a long beat of silence, he murmurs, "No, you're not. I'm sorry for the shit cards you were dealt."

As the vehicle pulls onto an off-ramp, I realize I have no idea where we're headed. He told Raj to head to the condo, but I didn't expect to be travelling with Caladin. I suppose it was to finish having this conversation in private rather than screaming at each other outside an airport.

"You can't keep me from my sister forever."

"Wasn't planning on it. When Raj phoned that you were taking off, I was in the middle of a video meeting with Erico and Nico Corsetti because your sister and her boyfriend will be flying up tomorrow for a one-day visit. I know you love and miss your sister more than anything, and I wouldn't keep her from you. If they weren't coming here, then we would have flown up there."

Oh. I sink into the rich leather. This time it's not only guilt; it's shame. I can't feel bad for trying to claim my own future but that list of things Caladin's done for me since we met is growing still. I'm the asshole who didn't give him a chance to explain.

"Where are we going?" I ask after another few minutes of silence.

"Rossi mansion. You're going to see Ariella."

11

CALADIN

While Ariella and Yasmine reunite in the backyard, I head to Erico's office, interrupting him from whatever document has snagged his attention for the time being. Without glancing up, he gestures at a glass waiting by the corner of his desk, half full with an amber liquid.

"Figured that'd be in order. Get her before she boarded?" Erico finally slides his work aside.

"As she was lining up to buy a ticket." Glass in hand, I drop into one of his chairs, the liquid sloshing dangerously close to the glass's edge. "Fuck, man, what do I do?" My head falls back, staring at the ceiling instead.

"You can talk to her. Show her you're not a complete dick. We both know why she ran, and you'd do the same in her position."

"I know." With a heavy groan, I lift my head again. "We're going to spend our lives at one another's throats. Somehow, I get the sense that eventually living alone won't change anything."

"Move her out sooner," he suggests, dragging his own glass toward him. It only has a sip left.

"The Seven probably somehow has eyes in our damn territory, which I don't even want to think about, but until things settle, I'd rather play by their rules. Besides, you know the rest of the *Famiglia* will want to meet her, and admitting I've shipped her away so soon looks bad on us all."

He tips his head, staring at me with pursed lips. "Isn't that interesting," he murmurs after a second. "You thought something through."

Flipping him off, I say, "You didn't make me your Consigliere for my good looks."

"No, no, I didn't. Look," he waves toward my slumped form, "what I do know is this can't keep up. A year of you coming in here every day, complaining about your marriage, will make me want to put a gun to *my* head."

"Your sympathy is astounding." I grunt. "Send me away then."

"Told you," he replies in the most non-apologetic tone I've ever heard, "there's nothing for you to do, nowhere for you to go. Clubs can use another round of checks this week. That'll occupy some of your time."

"Maybe seeing her sister will help too." I rub my hand over my face, but the sudden tiredness doesn't go away. "Worst part is, I *get* it. Like you said, we know why she ran, and yeah, you're right, I'd probably do the same. But she didn't even give me a fuckin' chance. Woke up, took off. No note, no call. If I didn't have someone on her, she'd probably have made it by the time I even realized she left. I told her she can't do that because of who she is now. Between your parents and the Bratva and the Seven, who the fuck knows how many would use her to take a shot, but that's only half the truth." Words now rambling, the rant unable to stop, I scramble in the chair a bit more upright.

"Three days ago, I could be the scum of the earth in her mind and I wouldn't give two fucks. But I gave up *everything* for her. My home, my life, my name. Every-fucking-thing I've ran from, and you know how she repays me? By acting like I've destroyed her life. That I'm not trying to give parts of it *back* to her. She'll never return to the way things were, not completely, but she's so selfishly deep down the denial hole, it's fucked. Even *if* I allowed her to return to Montreal, does she honestly think her life would go back to normal? She'd go back to her family home with her sister and all would be fucking dandy? No. But she acts like I'm throwing her in a tiny box and tossing away the key when all I've been doing for a week is living *for her*. Since the moment I left to find her, it's all been *her!* Not even a fuckin' thank you..."

My rant dies off, my body tense and on the seat's edge. My grip nearly painful around my drink. The thick glass prevents it from being crushed and imbedded into my palm.

"You done?" Erico asks after a moment, smirking behind his hand. "That was the most emotion I've seen from you in a long time. I take it all back."

"Take what back?" I ask, voice low, still trying to make sense of my entire rant.

"Ariella, knowing Yasmine's personality, believes you two will fall in love. We have a bet going. She thinks in six months, you'll love her. I bet against her because I know you and your avoidance of the feeling. Said you'd spend the next six months at each other's throats instead." He pauses, fingers tapping along his desk. "But now, I take it back. I think both. You two will spend six months fighting, but once you actually *talk* and she thinks you're not a monster, and she gets to visit with her sister, you might actually find common ground."

I stare at him for a beat, searching for the joke. Because

there *must* be a joke somewhere in that comment. Nothing. Not a damn sign of one and I chuckle. First calming down with a heady swig until the cup is empty, and then laughing more.

"That's the best thing I've heard all year. But if you want to win the bet with your wife, I'd stick to your first assumption."

He shrugs, rocking back in his seat, his eyes twinkling with a knowing light. "We'll see."

"No, I'm telling you right now, there is no *seeing*. There's only what *is*. She thinks I'm a monster. Yet, she's acting like the bitchy villain, but again, I can't even fuckin' fault her."

"Sounds like you are," he replies dryly. "You really want to start up again?" When I don't respond with anything but a glower, he shrugs. "Surprised you're not seeing this as a good thing. Having a woman who won't love you is your dream girl."

"Yeah, but this is different." She's making our union easy so far. She'll never love me because she's too busy hating me. "I'm angry. That's all. I don't deserve her treatment."

"You don't," he agrees. "Deal with her or separate your lives. Don't know what other advice I have for you. But the sooner the *Famiglia* meets her, the quicker that requirement is over. Right now, your union is sudden but shiny news for the heads. We'll throw a gathering so they get to see her."

"Oh, she'll *love* that. Can't wait. Sounds like the worst idea in the world."

He grins. "Then I've just ensured my win."

"You'll win. I'll be sure to show her I'm a street rat in a fancy suit before I'm a prince."

Hours later, we're back in the car. Yasmine's stiff as fuck beside me, hardly saying more than three words since I retrieved her from Ariella's music room, where she was being shown the piano. Yasmine was smiling and nodding at the silent woman's messages, and when I stood in the doorway watching them, it slowly hit me.

The difference, and the way it had my heart clenching.

Her smile. When unguarded, she's stunning. So at peace.

If I bought her something meaningful, would she smile like that for me?

That thought can fuck right off. A pretty smile isn't worth the emotions associated with a happy marriage.

Her sullen look as we drive back into the city is a bit of a gut punch, reminding me of my conversation with Erico. There needs to be a middle ground between us before we both go insane. I don't need her to love me, just not despise my presence.

My stomach grumbles, reminding me of the last time I ate, and wondering—and doubting—that she ate anything before running away from the condo this morning.

"Hungry?"

Just as I ask, her own grumbles in response, and she giggles. A feminine sound that has my feet pressing down on the brake a bit jerkier than I should. It's the alcohol from Erico's office I blame for these fleeting thoughts.

"Guess so," she answers. "According to my stomach anyway."

"Ever have pizza from New York?" While doubtful, there's a world of facts I don't know about her.

"I mean, I've had New York style pizza. Does that count?"

I throw her a mock scathing look that doubles as a mirror check as I take a street toward Little Italy, where my favourite pizza joint is located. Even Erico's parents loved the place, so the owners partnered with the *Famiglia*, earning protection in exchange of profit.

"That New York style pizza you Canadians oddly enjoy is *not* the authentic taste of heaven. Your senses won't know pleasure until it's tasted the exact combination of sauce, dough, and cheese you're about to consume. Then you can thank me."

She giggles again, and I never would have thought pizza would be the thing to thaw her frozen heart. "All right. I take what I said back."

The car falls silent again, and I hate it. Hate that I hate it.

"Speaking of food, what *is* the obsession with those red takeout cups Canadians all seem to carry? I sat in that mall, and I swear, every second person had one. Also, the apologies...fuck, if I downed a shot for every one I heard, I'd be wasted within the first five minutes."

Her peals of laughter fill the car, complete with snorts, and wiping of mist decorating her eyes, and I find myself smiling back. A lightness I dislike blooms. My internal systems confused over which is better: her joy and amusement or her distaste of me. Boundaries, after all.

Still, I chuckle in response as I park my Lamborghini in front of the restaurant. It's the classic Italian place, complete with a faded red awning, a checkered curtain and a large front window that could use a washing.

"Those red cups you speak of," she finally manages, "is a national chain. Serves good coffee. And food. But they're most known for their coffee. So popular, you'd find one on nearly every street corner. As for the apology thing, *that* you're exaggerating. We're not that bad."

"Um, you weren't there to hear them all."

"No, but I spent all twenty-six years of my life there. I know how we function. It's not that bad. *Nous ne nous excusons pas tant que ça.*"

I stare at her, waiting for the translation, trying my best to use humour so I don't consider the smoothness of her language. "Don't speak alien. Repeat that in a language I understand."

"My point exactly. French is one of two languages in Canada. I know more about my home than you do."

Smartass. I climb from my car and come to her side by the time she unbuckles, and help her out. She takes my offered hand after a cautious minute but drops it as soon as she's upright. I lead her toward the entrance and pull open the metal door handle for her to step inside.

Immediately, the owner's wife, an old Italian woman, spots us from where she's wiping a menu behind the counter. Her work gets abandoned as she rushes toward me.

"Ciao, Signore Rossi!"

I step around Yasmine to give Rosetta a one-armed hug because if I don't initiate, she'll tackle me.

In a heavy Italian accent, she switches to broken English to say, "Boy, why you not tell us you were coming?"

I release the older woman with a shrug. "Wasn't in the plans until ten minutes ago."

She swats my chest affectionately, an action no one else is allowed to do and survive. "That gave you ten minutes to call."

"Couldn't. Was too busy with my newest lady."

Rosetta turns her hawk-like gaze onto Yasmine, who visibly shifts beneath the scrutiny. Rosetta breaks away to approach, offering her hand. "You're a pretty one." She shakes Yasmine's hand, spotting the ring immediately.

Blocking her verbal lashing before she incorrectly assumes what I'm doing with a married woman, I lift my own left hand, crooking the fourth finger. "Rosetta, meet my wife, Yasmine."

Rosetta's mouth slips open, but she quickly composes herself. *"Signora Rossi,* forgive me."

Yasmine smiles and pats the back of Rosetta's hand. "We'll blame Caladin for his atrocious introduction."

Rosetta bursts into a loud rumbustious laughter, only she'd be able to make endearing. "I like this one," she tells me, hiking a thumb over her shoulder. "We'll make you two the best pizza ever."

"You better. Yasmine hasn't eaten genuine New York pizza, so of course we had to come to the best place. Found her in chilly Canada, where they live on coffee that comes in red cups and this weird concoction involving fries. Between us, I think we can change her opinion of America simply with one of your husband's pizzas."

Rosetta claps her hands together. "Of course, of course! Staying or going?"

I glance to Yasmine, leaving it up to her. I'd prefer to stay here, because the less time we're alone in the condo, the better it'll be.

She shrugs and scans the clean but old-styled Italian restaurant. "Let's eat in."

Rosetta claps her hands again and bustles to the back. "Sit, *Signore*."

Yasmine's observing her exit with a curious expression she quickly shifts my way. Like she's thinking about something, and while I doubt she'd tell me, I ask regardless.

She shrugs the expression off with a long blink. "Nothing. Just...clearly she knows you well."

"Basically grew up here," I explain, heading for the booth farthest from the door. She climbs in first, claiming the spot against the wall, which leaves me available to fight if I need to. Never know who'll stumble upon us in a neighbourhood like this one.

"You don't only enjoy the food here then," she, for once, correctly assumes.

"Nope." I lean back against the booth and kick my feet onto the chair across from me, settling in.

"You're sweet with her. Different."

"Different, or just someone you haven't met yet?" Against the booth's backing, I roll my head until she's in sight again.

"I guess there's many parts of you I haven't met."

12

YASMINE

Caladin falls silent after my point, staring around the restaurant, so I take the chance to do the same.

It's a classic Italian place in every way, right down to the black and white tiles, the red checkered curtains, the images of what I assume are Italian landscapes, and the yelling from the back room as two naturally loud people work together.

It's in the silence of my head, I also replay my visit with Ariella. Caladin led me to where she was swimming in the backyard, and every step through the beautiful mansion and toward her was one more step I wanted to take the opposite way.

Visiting Ariella against my father's wishes, when she was trapped by his cruelty, was one thing. A place for me to remind myself I'm not the bitch Rozelyn made me pretend to be. And that Ariella wasn't alone. But seeing her when we're both away from the past, when she's *married* to the *Famiglia*'s boss is something entirely different. I never voiced these worries to Caladin, simply tossed on a fake cheery disposition and allowed him to believe I was doing what was right.

It was an awkward meeting, both of us not naturally outgoing. But finally after a moment of silence, she hugged me. It was that hug that changed things. That made me feel, just for a moment, okay. I might be forced away from Rozelyn and wed to a stranger, but I still had Ariella.

Our silent conversation was mainly catch-up, which meant a lot of typing on her phone. She told me everything that led to her own marriage, but always skipped over the parts about my sister or father. When I asked, she told me to wait until seeing Rozelyn, which only made what I suspect—that he's dead—more concrete.

Rosetta comes out from the back room with a wine bottle and two glasses, which breaks my concentration. She rests them both on the table and explains, in broken English, "Must celebrate marriage," before taking off again.

Caladin chuckles and pours the wine before sliding me over one glass. I take it, sipping slowly, pleased when the flavour is more sweet than bitter.

"Italian seems like a language I'd never hear," I muse, filling the silence. "Growing up with only French and English, they're all I know."

He looks at me over his glass. "Makes sense. New York has a fairly large Italian community and much less French. Personally, I don't know anyone who really speaks it, nor do I even understand it."

"*Heureusement pour moi.*"

His tongue dabs at the corner of his lips, drawing attention to the building smirk. "Case in point. If you're not careful, I'll start saying things you don't understand either."

"Battle of the languages."

He winks. "*Sì.*"

"Yes." I roll my eyes. "Everyone knows that."

"*I tuoi capelli sono come mezzanotte.*"

It flows so smoothly through his lips, I momentarily forget all my other worries and annoyances. Images of him talking like that...while doing other activities...invade my traitorous mind. Another and much larger swig of wine burns them away.

"What'd you say?"

His eyes flick from my face to my hair, staying there, making me conscious enough to want to reach up and touch it. "Your hair is like midnight." His throat moves with his swallow before taking another sip and looking away. "It's one of the first things I noticed about you."

Thankfully, Rosetta bringing out a large pizza, with wisps of steam rising from it, fills where I should be replying. Which is good because the compliment seems like a lot for me right now. This is the same man I'm currently angry at; my insides shouldn't be heated by a simple compliment.

Don't be mad at Caladin. I asked him to get you, Ariella's phone had read to me earlier today.

I'm grateful...but angry. Without a way to release the emotion, at the notion I can't decide anything for myself. Confused, I suppose, would be a more apt description.

Rosetta rests the very large pizza in front of us and lowers two plates. My stomach immediately growls, mouth salivating at the sight and scent of food. Ariella offered a snack, but I turned her down, not in the mood to do something as normal as eat.

"Enjoy, yeah." Rosetta takes off again, as a phone rings in the back.

Caladin leans forward to grab two pre-sliced pieces and drags one to each plate. More cheese than I'd ever known to fit on a pizza drips from the edges, the pepperoni perfectly rounded and crisp. Somehow I sense it'll be delicious even before my first bite, and when I take one, I've officially died and gone to heaven.

I don't hide my groan, chewing slowly to savour every single fragment of flavour that bursts inside my mouth. Fuck him for being correct. Canada truly doesn't have pizza like *this*.

"Damn," he murmurs after a moment.

I open my eyes as embarrassment heats my cheeks. I was so involved in the food, I'd forgotten he was even here. Caladin's watching me, his own pizza slice curling in his large hand. Heated eyes are on my mouth, but before I have a chance to ask, he shakes his head and begins eating.

He returns to staring out the front window and I tell myself that he's ensuring his fancy car remains safe and untouched and isn't avoiding me. Not that I blame him.

Even without Ariella's explanation, I know I did a shitty thing this morning. Desperation for normality, for my family, might have been the driving force, but considering he didn't toss me in some cell and throw away the key, I never gave him a chance to be nice. Just selfishly assumed and took off.

Dad would be proud.

"Protect yourself first. No one else matters more."

The idea of doing what he feels morally okay churns my stomach against the tasty pizza. This is the same man who threw his newborn daughter into an arranged marriage with a man double her age. His moral compass is broken.

But I'm like him. Selfish. Today was a sign of that. I put myself and my wants first. Caladin's situation didn't matter when it was my own happiness on the line.

Still, I don't like feeling like this.

"Good, right?" His question pulls me away from my musings. "Told you, New York pizza will set new expectations."

"Good thing I'll get to eat it for the rest of my life then." It comes out more bitter than intended, but it's the truth.

We both eat in silence, and eventually, he offers me a second slice, which I take since one has done nothing to satiate my hunger. Before continuing to eat, though, his distracted motions tell me he's about to speak. The way his thumb and forefinger rub together, his other hand clenched in his lap. His concrete stare with the outdoors that tells me he's thinking hard about something.

I finally begin on my second slice, and I'm halfway through when he finally speaks what's on his mind. "If you could have any three wishes granted, what would they be? Other than seeing your sister and going home to Montreal."

Three wishes.

So laughable the way my mind blanks. All my life, I've wished for things. For the newest toy, the prettiest dress, and other silly childhood desires. As I was older: to go to school and get away from Dad's constraints. To be nice to my stepsisters, who I never had an issue with. To not be lied to my entire life. Simple things one shouldn't even have to wish for.

But now that he's asking, I don't know. One is easy to list, but the other two, I couldn't guess what my heart truly desires.

"I don't know," I murmur. "I mean, I have one, but not three."

"Think on them. Let me know when you have the others."

I lower my food, brushing the crumbs onto my napkin as though it'll help me focus better. "Is this your indirect way of saying you'll get me what I want?"

I expect him to smirk, but with a serious expression, he faces me. "Materialistic shit doesn't count. You're a *Famiglia* wife. Anything you want, you can have with a snap of your fingers. New house—done. New car—done."

Uncomfortable weight settles in my stomach. I still hadn't fully considered what he's explaining. The *Famiglia* isn't like my life was with Dad. They're a decades-old organization. Old Money.

...and I'm a wife of one of the members. So far, I've been so concerned with, and rightly so, chasing my past, that the heavy ring on my left hand has lost all its meaning.

"Things you truly desire. Stuff money can't buy, that I can —that I'll *try* to get you."

"Why?" is the first demand flitting through my head. "What does it matter to you?"

With a clamped jaw and the same expression from the airport earlier, he taps my ring. "Call it a wedding present. What's your first wish?"

After spotting what might be hurt, I almost don't want to. It takes clearing my head with a sip of wine, finding bravado to admit it.

"Freedom."

His expression remains masked.

"My entire life, everything's been decided for me. Dad was overly-protective, but I realize now, he was controlling the narrative, which makes everything worse. Being lied to my entire life. Not being trusted with the truth. Losing Mom young felt like I'd lost control, unable to stop an illness from robbing her from our lives. No one decided that, least of all me. When Della and Ariella came into our lives, Rozelyn demanded I not be friendly to them. Personally, *I* had nothing against them, but what's a younger sister to do other than listen to her older, wiser one?" I shrug, pursing my lips in a downward, soft smile. "Even then, Roz hid so much from me. Why did *she* decide what I could know or not know? After years of begging, Dad let me get a degree and for the first time ever, I felt free. Like I made a decision for myself and it felt fucking amazing."

I recall the moment he granted me it. When I asked him over and over and over and he finally conceded with so many rules, it made my head spin, but I didn't care. For the first time ever, I was released from the silk ropes he had around my life. Pretty and decorative in design, but still constraining.

"But then he yanked it all away," I continue. "Forced me into a vehicle and out of Quebec. I had an essay due that day, but he didn't care. One second, I'm crying and hugging Rozelyn goodbye, so fucking confused why I was going and she was staying. Why Dad had so many of his men travel with us, and so many remain behind. Why we were leaving home so abruptly and heading across the country." I pause for another sip, needing the break to stabilize my voice, and Caladin patiently watches, his mask still up. "In the car ride, he confessed everything, and then suddenly, we're tossed in a room and he's disappearing to meetings. My life was torn from me, flipped, and redesigned all before I could catch my breath. And *then*," I lift my gaze to his, "you enter, intent to save me, robbing me of another decision. At twenty-six, I'm tired of having everything decided for me. Do you realize how...how..." I search for the best description, "how *confining* it is to have never made a decision for yourself? To be seen as the younger sister, the weaker daughter, the innocent one, and have every fucking thing robbed from you?" My voice is rising now, but it won't lower, no matter the subtle, deep breaths I manage. "Suddenly, I'm purchased by you, dragged to New York. New country, new home, only this time, with no way out. Forced to make this my home. So yeah, every decision in my life has been made by someone else, and it's sickening. I'm so damn tired, and my ultimate longing—my first wish—is for freedom. To make my own choices. Go where I want to go. Live where I want to live. And love who I want to love."

Because, while unsaid earlier, my marriage to Caladin might have saved me, but it also stole away future possibilities. Of a decision I could eventually make. Of a love I discover myself. A guy I meet, date, fall in love with, and eventually marry. The fairy-tale ending that'll never be lived, being trapped in his chains and branded by his ring.

But life isn't always fair, and I learned that early on.

Dad might have told me to put myself above all others, but that's not who *I* am, even if today had been full of mistakes implying otherwise. And when Caladin's jaw ticks, the only sign he's even listening, I know it's not only my life that's changed. Not only my future stolen.

My hand inches toward him, to touch him, to show him my feelings, but I pull back at the last moment, second-guessing every action. "But you're dealing with the same, and I *am* sorry, Caladin." He blinks, finally looking toward me, his eyes so dark, it's like there's no colour at all anymore. "Truly sorry for today and how I've been acting. I'm trying to not be the bitch life's made me so great at being. That's not who I am deep down, and one day, hopefully, you'll see that. While I'm whining about freedom lost, you're living it too. Completing a job for Ariella ended with me attached to you, and now, you're sharing your condo and dealing with whatever having a wife means in your world. Having to chase me down when I stupidly run off instead of doing your job. You also got future opportunities stolen. You tried to get out of the contract for yourself as much as me." I pause my rambles, hoping something in them is conveying what I want it to. "And for today, I'm sorry. It wasn't fair to take off like that, to not even talk to you. You told me yesterday you're not expecting anything, that we'll be room-mates, and I know for a fact, that's a kindness you didn't have to give." Another pause. A deep breath. A final apology while my nerves cling to the hope he accepts it. "I really am sorry, Caladin. For how I've been, for stealing your life, and for not thanking you. Truly...*thank you* for saving me."

There's that silence that always seems to occur after a lot is said and everyone in the conversation is simply trying to *breathe*. To make sense of what was said, to reflect and think up a suitable response.

Yeah.

Caladin stares. A question swirling in his eyes, his own desires etched on his face, but I can't make them out. Can't understand his own language. The skin between his brows ripple, his head tipping half an inch. His full lips part the slightest before shutting together again, and he licks his bottom one. It curls beneath his teeth and then he tries to speak again.

Meanwhile, my nerves are beyond frayed. Our entire relationship is a giant living experience of *like it or not*. I might not be enjoying this, but we're in it. He might not accept my apology, but he's stuck with me. And as much as I want to look away, to hide, to bring my legs up and curl into myself, I force myself still, and that's what makes the nerves worse. Torn up in tiny pieces and fluttered to the tabletop, over our food, for him to brush aside or tape back together.

Just when I think he might respond, when he inhales, Rosetta returns from the back, a bluster of smiles and cheers with an older man beside her. Caladin immediately switches roles and stands to shake the man's hand, before introducing me. So I do what I always am forced to.

Smile and play the role.

Finally, we're back in my car and I'm driving home after Rosetta tried to send us with dessert after dessert option. She and her husband couldn't have interrupted at a worse time and it took every ounce of restraint not to yank Yasmine away so we could continue the conversation.

Freedom.

An imaginary notion in the mob world. There is no such thing as freedom. Not for Erico who has to lead, not for me or the capos of each branch, not for the wives, or for the soldiers. No one is completely free in this world.

But I get it. I do. I understand her emotions, even relate on one level.

Freedom is fleeting. Given and taken away so quickly, exactly like happiness. For some, the two link together. My parents' freedom of living was stolen much too soon, robbing my happiness away.

Yasmine feels a loss of control as every decision has been made for her. How to treat her stepsisters, what she was told about her own family, where she lives, who she was given to. And this marriage.

"And love who I want to love."

I did that. By giving her freedom, I trapped her. Stole away possible relationships. A man who'd be worthy of her love, who she'd want to love in return. Instead, I forced myself onto her and she'll never know that kind of emotion. Not from me.

It's not safe for either of us.

My grip is tight on the steering wheel, the response that's been formulating in my head for the past thirty minutes right *there* ever since she apologized. With Erico this morning, her lack of gratitude pissed me off, but now that she's given it…I almost don't want it. We might be in the same spot, but we're not really. Very different ends of the same spectrum.

There'll be no romance for me. Not with another, not with her. Whoever bore my ring would be the same in my mind. For her, though, it's not. She had the chance of falling in love when I never wanted it.

"I'm sorry for your shitty past," I murmur at the next red light, "and I'm sorry you're not free now."

"At least I'm used to it."

If she said that bitterly, it'd be okay. But the sad, broken tone does something to my insides, to my guilt.

Tears it up. Makes me *feel* something.

I don't know how to react other than a shifting in my seat, my hands clenching and unclenching the wheel in a repetitive motion. Three times later, and I'm finally able to put proper words to my traitorous thoughts.

"I'll get your degree transferred to a school here. Do some research, let me know which one you'd like to attend, and I'll see to it. In a few months, I'll get you your own place. A house, a condo—your choice. I'll buy a mansion in the Hamptons so you're near Ariella, if you'd like. We'll only see each other for

Famiglia events. Your life will be completely separate. We don't have to have children, unless you want them. And if you find —" I stop, lick my lips, gaze narrowing on the brake lights of the car in front of us. If not them, the numerous buildings around us. Anything but her. "If you find someone else you want to be with, whether long-term or only for a night, be discreet so it doesn't come down on both of us."

Infidelity from women in the *Famiglia* is treason, according to the traditionalist capos. But Erico's debating replacing many of them if they cause an uproar after his recent banishment of his parents, so maybe this will be one more tick against them, if they were to find out.

I'll blame the guilt of this situation, of making the deal without even mentioning it to her first and getting her own take. She feels trapped and wishes for freedom. To a point, I can grant it. Divorce isn't possible but the contract never said anything about loyalty to one another.

If she loves someone else, it'll mean she isn't falling in love with me. Us coming together for events will be two strangers meeting one another time and time again. And those only occur once every few months. Perhaps less now, without my aunt running the show.

"Okay," is all she replies with. A barely-there whisper, packed with a greater question she doesn't ask, nor do I want to answer. "Same for you, I guess...right?"

"Yeah," I murmur, skipping over the true answer.

I'll never love a woman. I'll never allow myself to be loved.

Growing up, I watched my parents love one another so fucking much. They were the visual definition for the term. But they died together in a shooting. Whoever was behind it targeted my father. Mother shouldn't have been there; she should have been home with ten-year-old me, but they barely stood to be away from one another, so she joined him. By doing so, she signed her death warrant. I lost both parents that day.

Love leads to death. Like my father, a bullet can always take me out and there's no guarantee of safety in my world. If Yasmine or even another woman loved me, if I allowed myself to feel it in return, what would happen if they joined me on a job, even one as safe as inspecting one of our businesses, and something happened? What happens when loving me gets her killed?

What happens if I survive and she dies and I'm forced to live without her?

It's easier not to care for another person.

If they only had the kind of relationship Erico's parents had, Mother would be alive. She wouldn't have loved him enough to join him. I wish I could blame her for going, blame him for taking her, but I can't when all my early memories are of them smiling at one another.

Neither of us says anything more and finally, we pull up to my condo. I don't park in the underground lot, but behind Raj's SUV by the curb because I'm not staying. It's only four. Going home now means we'll be together for the rest of the night when I plan on spending my every free minute outside the house and only being there to sleep.

I gesture toward Raj in the SUV. "It's early if you wanted to go shopping with the card I've left. Buy whatever. I know you need stuff. Or do it another day, but with your sister coming tomorrow, thought you'd want to today. Your choice." I keep my gaze forward.

In my peripheral vision, I catch her nodding once. "You're not coming?"

"Other things to do. I'll come home after you're asleep."

She nods again, hesitates, and then finally stands from the car, Raj now hovering a bit closer. She leans down after shutting the door to look at me through the window. "Thanks for the late lunch, I guess, and for letting me visit Ariella."

Then she turns to Raj and they share a few words before she's climbing into the back of the SUV. I wait for them to drive off before I do too, heading in the opposite direction.

~

The leather of the punching bag moves and groans with hit after hit from my taped hands. It sways before returning for a larger beating, and with a determined stride, I throw my body into it harder, telling myself I'm merely practicing.

This is where I feel most alive. Where I'm able to work out stress and forget whatever shit's in my head. The gym and our underground fighting ring, where I really work out steam against my opponents. They're a better challenge than the punching bags in this place.

While Erico street races, I fight in the *Famiglia*-ran underground fighting ring. It's been since before Erico's wedding that I've fought in one because he had me running on job after job, hunting fuckers from Ariella's past, and then off to B.C. Now that I'm home and my condo's become somewhere to avoid, I'll reach out to the ringleader soon because a fight sounds really fucking appealing.

My body *craves* it. The adrenaline. The release. The victory.

"Don't hold back." My cousin's voice comes nearer, his steps echoing through the silent gym. He parks himself beside me, watching my repetitive punching.

"Shouldn't you be at home with your doting wife?"

"Say that a bit saltier." He sounds amused when I'm anything but. He steps forward to lean against the punching bag, blocking my use of it, even if one firm punch will take them both down.

Whatever. The tape on my hands need adjusting and I could use a healthy drink of water. I turn away and toward the benches along the nearest wall. "You have two minutes to say what's on your mind," I tell him. "By the time I've finished fixing the tape."

"How'd things go after you left my place?"

I blow out a quiet breath, debating how much truth to admit. Erico's like a brother to me, being that I've lived with him since I was ten after his parents took me in. More so, he's my boss. And the most trusted fucker in my life.

"Went to Rosetta's for food, got talking, asked her what she wants in life." With the tape adjusted, I return to the bags. "She told me freedom."

"From marriage."

Rubbing a hand over my hair, another breath releases. No matter how many of them, they're doing little to ease me. "From everything. Me, this life. Woman's never made a decision for herself. Our marriage was the final straw. She lost the choice in her own romantic life."

He scoffs. "There was never a choice. In her mind, her father was a mob boss. She must have believed an arranged marriage was always in her future."

I shrug because she didn't indicate so. With her father's deal, she was likely raised under the assumption of having a choice. "Either way, I gave her an out. If she wants, she can have an affair. As long as it's discreet, I'll look away."

And then like I hadn't just dropped the truth of my wife's presumed future infidelity, I head for the punching bag beside him, making fists and sending one right into the leather.

Erico's disapproval emits from him in waves. I hear it in his tone even before he speaks. "Fucking Christ, man, if that got out…There's already so much instability in the family after the situation with my parents. Do you really want people knowing their Consigliere is allowing his wife to cheat?"

I glare after another swift punch. "That's your problem. You sent me to save her. I saved her. Now you deal with the consequences. It's none of their business." My arms drop, my punches ending. "Look, you didn't see her face. We talked; you should be happy since this was your stellar advice earlier. This is the best I can do for her. To free her as much as this marriage allows me to."

After a bated breath, he asks, "What about you?"

I have no fucking idea.

The thought of another woman, even for a night, can't even formulate in my head. Like, since Yasmine's come into my life only days ago, my dick won't look elsewhere. It's confused what to feel, how to act, but you know what? Me fucking too.

"I see."

"Do you?" I say slightly mocking as I face the bag again.

He strides forward to grasp the leather, even pushing it away from my trajectory as he stands in my way. "You're pushing her away so you never have a chance to love her."

"I'm releasing her." I head for another bag.

He follows, stepping in front of me again. "You're hiding. You're self-sabotaging."

Annoyance builds, a protective wall to keep him away from the truth. "There is no sabotage," I deny, a near-yell. "She doesn't want *me*. Me or this marriage. I'm fucking helping her!"

"You are allowed to love a woman!" he yells back, nostrils flaring. "Caladin, consider what she can mean for you and your future. You need to put the past aside. This isn't what your parents would want for you."

He knows.

He fucking *knows* not to mention them.

Instead of the bag, I whirl on him, taped fists shoving into his chest to make him unsteady. For as good of a fighter he is, I'm better, and I catch him off guard. An arm comes up to swipe at me, a firm warning look not stopping my advance.

"Fuck off. You're pissed because you know I'm right." He shoves me away, angling himself toward the door.

Good. Leave. I push him, urging him farther in that direction. "I'm pissed because you won't stay out of my business. What does it matter what happens behind the closed doors of my marriage? I didn't butt into yours."

He pauses walking, palms up as he considers my words. "Fine. You're right. But maybe that's because I fucking care about you, cuz. Ever think about that? Seeing you miserable for the rest of your life isn't what I want for you and neither would they."

Again...My teeth press together, rage slicing at my insides.

"Last warning, Erico. Fuck off. Misery makes for good company, haven't you heard? Unlike you, I don't need a woman to love me, so no misery here."

He shakes his head slowly, mouth opening with a response. But then it shuts, his hands drop, and he spins on his heel and heads out the front doors, leaving the warehouse-turned-*Famiglia*-gym and me alone.

I turn to punch the bag behind me while seething over his mock counselling session for hours after he goes.

14

YASMINE

Until Raj took me shopping, I didn't comprehend the weight of being a *Famiglia* wife. Raj pulled up to some ritzy store Caladin recommended he take me to, opened my door, and even assisted me to step out.

And then the staff immediately rushed over, offered a flute of champagne, and stated they were "so excited" for my arrival, which had obviously been previously set up by Caladin.

It was like that in every store after. All three of them.

On the way back to the condo, with a trunk filled with shopping bags holding everything required to start my life over, I call up to the front, "How does everyone know who I am already?"

"The Rossis own the city, miss."

The name on my credit card certainly didn't help. Every time I handed it over, I was faced with it. Yasmine Rossi. Because marrying me wasn't enough, I also had my identity taken from me.

You're being silly, my inner voice chides. Maybe I am since a changed last name is a common practice in marriage and there's no way he'd want the tainted De Falco name in his orga-nization.

Hell, did *I* even want my last name still? It's an ongoing reminder of all the pain, of Dad's lies and his real identify, of not being with my sister, and of Mom.

The trip would be considered good if it wasn't for the slith-ering down my spine the entire evening. At first, I thought it was the store, but by the time we reached the second, the sensa-tion followed. A prickling on the back of my neck, like I was being watched. It didn't go away when we left the ornate shop and stood on the busy sidewalk. I studied the crowds rushing around us, much to Raj's irritation because he wanted me in the safe SUV sooner, but I was looking for...for something. For something *off*. In the third store, my attention was only half on the clerk because I felt insane, constantly studying out the front windows, every rack, willing the feeling to leave me alone.

Raj parks in the underground lot right by the elevator and immediately helps me from the vehicle before I even move an inch. With a sigh, I tell him, "I *can* get out of a car, you know."

His lips quirk. "I'm sure you can, Mrs. Rossi. It's habit, I'm afraid."

"Yasmine's fine."

His eyes pinch in the corners, his mouth pressing together because I've probably asked him to go against years of training. "If you wish," he finally concedes. "Yasmine."

"Thank you."

I head for the trunk, only for him to block my way, waving me toward the elevator. "I'll grab the bags."

He does while I keep the elevator doors open, and once up to Caladin's floor, he unloads them in the doorway. He offers the bedroom, but I wave him off from further doing my work for me.

Despite my upbringing with household staff, Dad still had

Rozelyn and me do a lot of our own stuff, such as opening doors. His staff was much smaller than what the Corsettis' and Rossis' are.

Once Raj leaves, I unload the bags, cut off tags, and put the items away. It feels weird to basically be officially moving in now, but weirder, since all this stuff isn't even mine. Not really. Once Caladin's closet's half full with my new clothing and some of the bathroom counter is consumed by my products, there's no hiding my presence now.

Stuck. Free and not free, after our latest conversation.

He's offered me an opening to be with other men, if I want. The problem is...I don't know what I want. That wasn't where the conversation was supposed to go. My point was that I no longer had the option in the future to date and fall in love. Not that I was seeking to now.

Confused? Yeah, me too. Everything about this whole thing is fucked. Despite the lies, I'd kill to return to the day before I helped Della get dressed for Nico Corsetti's party. That was the start of the end.

It's eight now; shopping consumed four hours of my day and though there's barely any daylight left, I turn away from the living room and head to the bedroom. Today's been a lot, tomorrow will be more, and I've yet to sit on Caladin's couch. Not sure I ever can.

You'll have to adapt eventually.

Eventually...not today.

In the bathroom, with all the new soap I purchased, I take a proper hot shower, listening for a door opening and shutting. Despite the thirty-minute shower, the condo remains empty.

And when I dress in one of my new pyjama sets, some red, silk shorts and tank, I'm still alone. He never indicated when he'd be back, and I shouldn't care.

I keep the bathroom light on but shut the door two-thirds

of the way. The curtain is still drawn from last night. He didn't reset all my work, so hopefully he doesn't tonight either.

Sleep avoids me when the room is in complete darkness. It's been like that for years.

Like usual, Mommy kisses me on the forehead, gives me a final hug goodnight, and then switches on my nightlights. Two of them. One by my bed, and one by the door. She says it's to keep the monsters away at night and since I don't want to be eaten, I like that she does.

She did the same last night, and she'll do the same tomorrow.

Growing up with two nightlights on, my body became conditioned to sleeping like that, and even as a teenager, she'd come in to say night and would flick them on. It was our routine; how it was. Even when she was getting sick and I insisted she didn't need to, she was adamant to continue.

And then one day, she didn't come to turn them on.

After a week of darkness—literal and metaphorical—I stopped sleeping. Was a zombie, up all night. Sleeping in Rozelyn's room helped for the weeks afterwards, but she enjoyed the pitch-dark so I never lasted too long.

Eventually, I had to start turning on my own lights.

Caladin is already gone when I wake and the bed shows no sign of him using it. I don't allow myself to consider where he slept as I get ready for the day. Soon, I stop thinking about him entirely, other than being annoyed that he never offered me to accompany him in retrieving Rozelyn from the airport.

After I'm ready, I wait.

I open my phone and find Caladin's pre-programmed number, nearly messaging him for an update but opt not to.

Then I click on Rozelyn's name and send a text, but considering she doesn't answer, she's likely still in the air. So I sit...and wait.

Until almost two hours later, the door opens and I leap to my feet from where I was anxiously perched on the couch. Caladin steps inside, his eyes sweeping the apartment until finding me, a smirk at my obvious excitement expanding his expression. I stand on my toes and try to peek around him but see no one there.

Caladin shuts the door, his hands making a calming motion like I'm some animal. "She's out there. I'm a text away if you need anything, or Raj is if you two want to leave. I'll be gone for the day, so you two can be alone, and back this evening to return her to her plane."

One day isn't enough, but it's what I need right now. When I nod, he turns for the door, opens it, and leaves without another word. The door remains open and my feet get heavy with anticipation.

And then everything's okay.

All the weeks without her, the near hell with Jasper and the Seven, Dad's lies, my marriage, it all melts away when Rozelyn runs into the condo and slams into me, almost knocking me sideways. Her signature sweet-scented hair fills my nose, my eyes squeezing shut as my arms tighten around her neck.

For the first time since I was forced to leave her behind, I *breathe.*

There's so much to ask, so much to update her on, so much to explain, but the surreal emotions block my voice. Weigh down my muscles until hugging her is the only possible action.

In a calming motion, in the only way an older sister can manage, she strokes my hair, making a soothing sound. "God, Yasmine, you have no idea how relieved I am to see you again. It's been a hell of a few weeks."

"Yeah," I agree.

She pulls back and cups my face, holding me tenderly as her foot kicks the door shut. Then she studies the condo around me, coming to rest on the ring on my left hand, like she knew exactly where to look. "I'll start, but I'm extremely curious to know how all this happened."

I lead her to the beige couch and sit, keeping both her hands in mine, our knees touching. While the joy I'm experiencing can't possibly be overshadowed whatsoever, she makes it falter with her frown. Her apologetic gaze as she looks from me to the floor and licks her lips.

It's her tells. The same way she acted around anyone after Mom passed.

Grief.

"Yasmine, I don't know what Dad explained to you, but there's a lot we need to go over. And I can't have this conversation without first admitting...Dad's dead."

I knew that.

I *felt* that.

It doesn't stop the wave from crashing over me. The tears alongside the confusion. Since the moment he tore my life up, admitted what he did to Rozelyn, to Della, to their mother, I've prayed for him to die. When he left me in Jasper's clutches, *still* not disclosing the true reason I was there, I realized life without him is fine. He'd done enough damage that my future didn't need to be wrecked further.

But he's still Dad. For better or worse, he raised me. Lies don't exist when the other party isn't aware of the truth, so for a long time, the shadows encompassing our life was my reality. It felt like sunlight. I didn't know better. Existing in the beliefs I was fed.

"I think I knew that." I squeeze my fist together in my sister's lap. "I assumed the Corsettis wouldn't keep him alive."

She looks away. Up to the ceiling light and then her feet. "There's a lot more though."

And then she launches into a story leaving me sick, horrified, and like I can't get to a toilet fast enough to throw up yesterday's pizza. Except to do so would involve standing and my body isn't allowing that.

Dad continued to feed me lies. He told me half-truths, admitting that Rozelyn was staying to distract the Corsettis because she was the older sibling.

Nothing of what she tells me. Nothing about the physical, emotional, and mental abuse from him. From him to her *and* Mom. How did I never notice the bruises? Was I that stupid, that naïve? All the reasons she advised me away from a relationship with Della and Ariella was because she *knew* he was a bad man. That marrying their mother was a ploy, but she couldn't guess how it'd end.

The sickening part is how long it's been going on as she recounts *everything*, dating all the way back to high school, to when she did a one-year stint in a public school. She was insane for wanting away from our lovely private school. She was so miserable in the days following Dad demanding she go back to the private one. I assumed it was because we were losing Mom that week too. She said, almost as painful as the abuse, was being taken from who she found back then.

Then she walks to the door and waves in someone from the hallway, introducing me to Flynn Rhodes, and launches into their entire history while he sits in a chair across from us.

I *hate* our father.

Not only for my own reasons, or for the abuse and Rozelyn's past, but even the recent weeks. To drugging Aurora Corsetti, but she countered it with explaining her own planning. How she used Dad's plots to get inside the Corsetti household and help them bring down Dad.

She might have been his "chosen" daughter, but it came with a steep price. Della was a tool, Ariella the consequence, and Rozelyn the weapon.

And then she ends her story by recounting the torture the Corsettis exacted on him, and I wish I'd flinch...but I don't. Simply listen mutely, nodding every so often, until the ending. Whispered words, tinged with guilt but no regret.

"I'm the one who pulled the trigger. I killed our father."

She pulled the trigger in the moment, but really, she killed him long before that. By working with the Corsettis, she signed his death warrant.

I don't blame her for it.

I *can't.*

Dad might have shown me one version, but she experienced the monster within. Once, I might have been horrified over her actions, but I'm not the same woman who got dragged away from Montreal. In my time away, light has become dark, everything I thought I knew, a lie.

Which is why I embrace her and tell her the words she needs to hear from me, to release the uncertainty wavering in her voice.

"You did what you had to. It's okay."

After I battled the waves of grief that hit me all at once, she filled in any gaps of her story that related to Flynn. Years later, these two finding one another again, somehow, is actually magical. Like she had her own wishes, thought one up, and it got granted. After everything Dad's done, at least his actions gave her back Flynn—unknown to him initially, of course.

Afterwards, I ask Raj to order us pizza from the same place

Caladin took me yesterday, and Rozelyn and Flynn both share a very contented groan with the first bite.

"Told you," I mumble around my own mouthful. "Good stuff. Better than all the 'authentic' stuff we have up there. Probably the only benefit to living in New York."

"Can't say that." Flynn speaks up from where he sits beside my sister. He's a man of very few words, I've noticed, but watches my sister with a devotion I've never in my life seen a person have toward another. "You haven't explored enough."

They're seated together on the couch while I took the chair across from them, giving them space to be together. She's pressed so tight into his side, no light is between their bodies. While he watches her with devotion, she stares at him like he hangs the moon in the sky. It hurts—that my sister was able to choose her happy ending, but I'm also pleased for her, considering all she's gone through.

"Still," I grumble, resting my now-empty plate on the edge of the table. "Name me three positives about this whole situation. Go ahead, I'll wait."

Rozelyn glances at Flynn and shares some unspoken conversation. "For one, you're not trapped in B.C., married to some old fucktard because of Dad. Two: you live in a penthouse condo, married into the most powerful mafia family of North America—sorry, Nico, but it's true." She glances out the floor-to-ceiling windows a few feet away, as though speaking to him in Montreal directly. "And three: I've seen pictures of Caladin Rossi." She whistles, earning an irritated grunt from Flynn. "You could do worse."

I flip her off. "Looks aren't everything."

She shrugs, clearly not getting my point. "No, but in this case, they're a start. Do you deny he's hot?"

"Far from. But I don't *know* him, so he's not exactly my number one choice in husband."

Rozelyn lowers her plate to the table and leans closer, her hands dangling between her legs, which tells me I'm about to get a sisterly talk. "So *get to know him*. Yasmine, I understand the entire situation sucks. Did I beg Nico to help find you an out? Sure have, but he claims the contract's iron-clad. I'd much rather have you home with me than living here, but this is how it has to go. Caladin isn't a danger to you, and the Corsettis have accepted me. You have Ariella here. She's alone too, without Della. You have a *sister* here. There's not only me."

And she has Della is her unspoken statement.

"As for your husband," Rozelyn continues, leaning back against Flynn again, "you really want to live in a loveless marriage forever? You didn't choose him, but work with what you're given."

Easy for her to say. *She* had a choice. Hell, Flynn was the only man she's ever loved. She got a second-chance with her one.

"We'll become friends eventually, I'm sure. It'll be fine." I shrug her off.

Her expression pinches, her doubt obvious. "What happens when you get lonely? When *he* gets lonely? Friends-with-bene-fits then?"

"Oh," I wave her off, thankful to have an actual response, "he's covered that already. We're free to be with others, discreetly."

Her frown deepens into a low curse. "Yasmine, you're a *Famiglia* wife now. The organization will put you on a pedestal simply because you're married to their Consigliere. Be careful managing this."

"It'll be fine," I tell her.

Even when I'm not certain.

15

CALADIN

My day is spent inside the hallways of a university Erico recommended because the dean is eager to make good with the *Famiglia*; therefore, he's basically tripping over himself to appease me. Seated across from me, he's simultaneously tapping away at his keyboard and talking on his office phone. The mingle of noises is enough to distract my mind from Yasmine.

Wondering about how she is this second. Being with her sister again is bound to be relieving, but perhaps strange too. Corsetti reports stated it was her sister who killed their father, so when that's revealed, Yasmine's going to be affected in some way.

When the dean finishes his call, he reassures me with little beads of sweat all over his forehead that it's all been taken care of. So I leave and continue my day, doing all I need to, at one point lingering in a bar to avoid the condo longer. But when the sun begins lowering behind the tall buildings, it's time to steal Yasmine's familiarity away again.

I return to the condo and hesitate outside the door, trying

to give the sisters a bit more time before being forced to separate them. Earlier, I texted Erico, wondering if we had room for another enforcer in our ranks so I can offer Flynn a job with us, but he said not to. That Flynn's too embedded in the Corsetti organization to ever leave.

Without knocking, I enter my home, and then immediately regret my abrupt entrance. Three sets of eyes find me lingering awkwardly in the doorway. *Awkwardly* like I don't live here or something.

Flynn and Rozelyn are seated together on the couch, but it's Yasmine who holds my attention. Cross-legged on a chair across from them, she's smiling—genuinely smiling—and for a moment, I forget how to breathe. Have I ever seen her smile in such a way? Not even with Ariella. Seeing her sister has given her *life*, and the urge to do anything she'd ask hits me. Anything to keep her smiling like that.

But the moment she spots me entering, her smile fades out, like someone flicked a switch. And I hate how I obviously make her so miserable.

"Good day?" I probe the silence.

Yasmine gives me a barely-there tight smile and nods before staring at the empty pizza box on the table between them. Raj mentioned she asked him to call in an order from Rosetta's, and it's odd how her meal choice had me smiling when he told me.

"Quick day," Rozelyn speaks up with a grim look as Flynn stands, hovering by Rozelyn's side. Her eyes track him but ask me, "Assume it's home time?"

Yasmine's staring the opposite direction, like avoiding looking at me will make a difference. "Yeah," I answer, "I'll be in the hall. Give you two a minute to say goodbye."

A moment after I close the door, it's opening, Flynn stepping out. He looks me up and down before shifting his stance closer to the elevator. "Thanks for this."

"I'd be no better than their father if I didn't allow Yasmine to see her sister again. They were split up due to a shit situation. Neither of them needs to live with those consequences."

He nods once. "Nico also wanted me to pass along how generous marrying her to save her was."

"Wasn't for him."

"Still."

When the door opens again, it's Rozelyn, wiping at her reddened cheeks. "I'm ready. Yasmine's not coming."

I didn't think she would.

A few hours later, after dropping Flynn and Rozelyn at the Corsetti jet—and after Rozelyn's strict warning against hurting Yasmine—I return to the condo where Yasmine's seated on the same chair. This time, it's turned and she's gazing at the nighttime New York skyline. When I shut the door, her shoulders stiffen.

I approach with the folder I grabbed from my car on the way up, shifting it from hand to hand, wondering if she'll hate me for this too. I did tell her she can choose her own school, which was the intention, but then Erico mentioned this place, and the dean already wanting to work with us, so it was an easy in.

"It's pretty here," she murmurs still without turning. "Your skyline is busier than Montreal's. Taller skyrises, and more of them."

From behind her chair, I study the same image she is and see nothing pretty about it. It's unimportant and unimpressive. One I know so well, being born and raised here.

"At least there's one positive to living here."

"And that pizza." In her reflection, half her mouth pulls into a half-smirk.

"That too." I slide the folder in front of her face, blocking her view until she takes it. "Look inside."

She hesitates. "What is it?"

"Look inside."

She obeys after another second and opens it to spot the acceptance letter the dean printed on formality. We both know it was useless; she was in either way. Although, he was impressed with her grades and said had she applied normally, during admissions, she'd be accepted regardless.

Her head whips up, silky hair brushing my hand. "I never applied."

"Now you don't have to." I come around the other side, leaning against the window to see her. "Had a few strings pulled. Also discovered the Seven never transferred your file from your Montreal school, which means you were technically still a student there. The dean had it officially moved over, and you're in the same degree program, with most of the same courses you were taking in Montreal. Your credits have been dealt with and you're still on track to graduate in another semester. Finish this current one by Christmas, do one more in the new year, and you'll be done."

With my every word, her expression softens until my own stomach is becoming churned butter. Her muscles untense, the fight leaving her. All except her hand, which grips the folder like a lifeline. A lifeline *I've* given her. I try to ignore the way that makes me feel.

"Second page is your new schedule. You start tomorrow, if you want. Or the next day. Whatever you want. Raj has a copy too because he'll be accompanying you. Your professors are being made aware that he'll be in the back of all your lecture halls. That is as much distance as I'll allow, sorry." I shove away from the window, having nothing more to say. I've done my job as a forced-upon husband and there's nothing left.

I make it to the door, to leave again so she's alone for the evening, when the chair scrapes backwards, and over the noise is a soft and whispered, "Thanks, Caladin. This means a lot."

I pause, hand on the knob, and say, "You're welcome" all while focusing on the breath coming and going through my lungs. It takes three inhales before I look over my shoulder, spotting her by the window, folder clutched in her hands in front of her. She looks smaller like this, more hesitant.

"Where are you going?" Her eyes somehow darken.

Nowhere. "Out."

She looks at the floor between us, pressing her lips together. "Got it."

She doesn't, and before she incorrectly assumes—which I know she's wonderful at doing—I add, "To the *Famiglia* gym to train. I prefer the evening since it's emptier than the morning."

"Oh." Is that relief I hear in her tone?

"I'll be back long after you go to bed."

Because I'll guarantee I am. She'll have less reason to hate me if I'm never around.

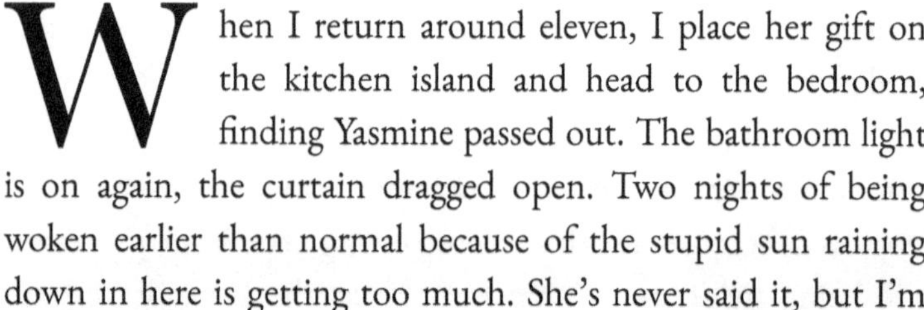

When I return around eleven, I place her gift on the kitchen island and head to the bedroom, finding Yasmine passed out. The bathroom light is on again, the curtain dragged open. Two nights of being woken earlier than normal because of the stupid sun raining down in here is getting too much. She's never said it, but I'm guessing the bathroom light means something. But the curtains...balance. I'll deal with a light but not the fiery rays of hell waking me up.

So I shut the curtain and slip into bed, having a fucking peaceful sleep *finally*.

Until less than an hour later, she whimpers. Facing away from me, she jerks in her sleep, the blanket sliding down her form. I stay still, watching in the shadows as she moves in her sleep, makes another noise, settles for a second, and then repeats it.

This hadn't happened the past two nights, which means the difference is all in the curtain. With a huff, I open it again. Being just past midnight, the light from outdoors isn't much, but a streak of moonlight falls over her sleeping face.

She sighs and settles almost instantly, and I stand there, gripping the curtain, caught between being so fucking irritated and pleased, my own sanity is shredding.

I'm not only losing the life I've grown used to, I'm losing my home. My sleep. Everything I'm doing is *for her*. For a woman who wants nothing to do with me. Maybe I need to say fuck it all and get her shipped out sooner than later. Let her hate me from afar so I can return to being comfortable in my own house and she'll never grow to feel anything good for me. It's the best path.

But then, as I stand there, staring at her sleeping form, I imagine her *not* there. Not in this house. After only two days, she's consumed it. Every time I enter, all I smell is jasmine—her. The scent that lingers around her. If she goes, so does the scent unless I'm some pathetic fucker who buys jasmine-scented candles and shit to fill this space with.

Since she hasn't made another disturbed noise, I release the curtain and stride back to bed. But not my side, not at first. Instead, I stop by her head, studying her upturned lips slightly parted with breath. Her hair covering half her pillow. The blanket still halfway down her waist, so I pull it up, knowing she prefers it covering her shoulder. That's how it is when she wakes every day.

And then I fall to my knees when I should be returning to my side of the bed. Has there been a second since meeting Yasmine that I've completely studied her with the same intensity I had the photo Erico gave me alongside the job to search for her?

No. And before she wakes up and returns to her hatred, I want at least this. While asleep, unaware to who's above her, my thumb strokes those lips, following an invisible line over her cheek. Skin so fucking soft, it's nearly unreal. It'll likely be the final time I get to touch her, so I don't rush it.

When I had her in my arms, pinned to the wall of the Seven's school, it was solely to create drama, but I noticed then, how right she felt in my arms. Perfect size, perfect height, perfect feel. She was nothing more than a job, though, so the thought was fleeting and was left at that.

But *she's* not fleeting. What I believed then and what I'm staring at now isn't at all fleeting. She's mine to touch, to care for...to love.

I rip my hand away because no, she's not mine.

Tomorrow, she'll start school again and it'll fill her days. Classes, new friends...guys for her to choose someone better. I'll be the annoyance she returns home to. The stranger she shares a bed with while she flies free.

It's best for her and me.

"You need to put the past aside." My cousin's annoying voice bugs me even now.

Impossible when the past could very well repeat in the future.

～

When Hell's rays light up my room, I wake with a groan. Five a.m., like yesterday and the day before. If she needs the curtain open, I might have to take to sleeping in the living room. As fast as the idea forms, I'm questioning myself. Wasn't it only five hours ago that I was annoyed how much she's changing my life? Not sleeping in my bed only allows her to win this *take Caladin's life over* game we're both stupidly playing.

With a groan, I try to move, eyes opening. If I'm up, may as well do something useful. Relaxing isn't for me. Being sedentary for long is boring. But as I go to move, something has my arm pinned to the bed.

I blink into the morning glow, finally registering exactly how I've woken. The scent of jasmine invades my nostrils, making my traitorous cock twitch in my shorts. Strands of black tickle my shoulder, my chest, and with my movement, she reacts, her hand curling into my abs, nails scraping at the skin.

Some fucking how, Yasmine ended up in my arms while we slept. My shoulder as her pillow, my arm loose around her hips, hand on the skin between her tank and her tiny sleep shorts. Her knee is pulled up, resting right over my leg, brushing my morning wood.

Fucking Christ. She went from the edge of the bed to being tangled with me. To prevent a fight, I should attempt to slide away now. Let her sleep and disappear like this never happened. Like she isn't on top of me, my cock making its own feelings apparent.

But instead, I let my head fall to the pillow and stare at the ceiling for the same reason I touched her yesterday. Which is what exactly? Wish I knew.

She makes a noise and her knee shifts an inch, making my cock even more painfully hard. Good god, at some point we'll either need to fuck or I'll need to do the same thing I've allowed her to do and find someone else.

She moves again and her head falls back. I stroke her lips again, like I had last night. She's beautiful asleep. Peaceful. Likely dreaming of a world where she was home with her sister.

I need to let her go, but yet, I remain still, watching the way sleep makes her calm for once, knowing once she wakes, it won't be this again.

Like she heard my own thoughts, her eyes slowly blink open. She arches her back in a stretch, her breasts rising from her tank and I'm asshole enough not to look away.

And then she spots me.

Her eyes go wide. She stiffens. Glances down, catching her in my arms. Stares at me again. In a flash, she rolls nearly into a crouching position, sleepy eyes still clearing as I push to sit up, watching with slight amusement at her pointless defence.

"What the fuck, Caladin?"

If it wasn't for my cock needing to calm the hell down, I'd leave and skip over the fight she's all but salivating for, but standing now and letting her see it will worsen her mood. Although, as her lips pull up, her face wrinkling with distaste, she reminds me of the girl I found in B.C., so it's tempting. She was fiery and cute. The wife I've had for the past few days has been fearful and distant.

"Why the hell were you holding me?"

Yep, cute. "Relax. You probably rolled into me." Or I brought her to me. Can't say who's at fault.

With a final sneer, she ends the argument much sooner than I expected her to and rolls from bed. Her sleep shorts ride up, revealing the curve of her ass, and all the work my dick's been doing to calm down is gone. Back to square one.

She stalks to the bathroom door and slams it shut with an extra loud bang I know is for my benefit. To be spiteful, she'll probably be in there for a while too, so I go to the closet instead and dress in a suit for the day. Erico and I will be going over the *Famiglia's* finances when our accountant sends over the documentation. The distance and thinking about my coming day is good for my body so by the time I return to the bedroom, my dick's calmed down.

Yasmine exits the bathroom at the same time, the previous anger completely gone. She scans me up and down. "Heading out?"

"Meeting with Erico."

She bobs her head. "That's your job, right?" She pauses, her cheeks flushing a cute shade of pink, her hands knotting in front of her. "I mean...Dad never had a Consigliere, so I don't really know what the job consists of."

She's showing an interest in the very organization she believes ruined her life. Totally opposite from the woman who woke up yelling, and I answer slowly, carefully. "Yeah, we work closely with one another. I'm his right-hand man basically. Advisor. Most trusted."

"And he's your cousin?"

I nod, wondering where she's going with this. Her curiosity is new but slightly alarming. It also reminds me of her apology from the other night. She's being genuine.

"Yes."

"Got it. Well, have a good day then, I guess. I'm headed to class later."

"You too," I reply amicably and head for the bathroom the same time she goes to the closet.

16

YASMINE

This feels right.

If there's a single thing in this new reality that's at all similar to my old one, it's this. Sitting in a lecture hall, my new laptop—one I found on the kitchen island after Caladin left this morning—being filled with typed notes. For a second, it's like Dad never robbed me of my life.

Attending classes under Jasper's watch wasn't at all the same. A sword was held over my head. A threat for every second passing.

But this place reminds me of my school in Montreal, except for the conversations I've had with all my professors at the start of each class: *"If you can't make it to class due to your husband's job, please take the time you need and you won't be penalized in any way."*

Meaning, *we won't be fucking with the Famiglia.*

The first time was intimidating. The second, I shrugged it off and thanked them. At this point, I'm understanding it's how it'll be, and it's fine. As long as no one stops me from going to class, I don't care.

The other main difference is Raj in the background. When we first arrived, I was gritting my teeth, but he's been quite easy to ignore. He remains in the first seat of the very top row in every lecture hall, right by the door. Dressed in jeans, a Henley, and converse, he blends in with every other student here. Even equipped with a notebook I wonder if he's pretending to use at all.

Between classes, he remains nearby, always two feet behind me. Closer than I'd prefer, but I get it. And once we get to the next course's room, he melts into the background.

In my third class, I settle into a seat in the middle row, a few seats in from the aisle. After setting up my laptop, I glance over my left shoulder, spotting Raj seated by the hall's door. He meets my gaze, nods once, and then looks away, which I appreciate.

More people join me in the row as the classroom begins filling up, and a large guy sits beside me, his muscled arm taking up his arm rest and some of mine. I shift, casting him a glare, and reposition myself.

Then he reaches over and drops a folded-up piece of paper on my lap. I don't move, staring at it for a long while before peeking toward the guy. His eyes remain locked on the front of the room, where the professor is setting up his presentation.

With shaky fingers, I unfold the paper, while pretending to be listening as the professor calls the class to attention. If Raj can tell I'm not focused in the same way I have been in my other classes, I suspect this will come back to Caladin, who then could rob me of this chance at finishing my degree.

There's a washroom right around the corner. Go there after class. —Gene

My stomach drops.

Gene.

As in, *Gene.* There's no fucking way.

The same guy who worked for my father, who was one of the soldiers left behind when he took me from Montreal. Honestly, until Caladin was asking about people from my past, I hadn't thought about him at all. Since our connection was casual, sex only when one of us needed it, there was never an emotional entanglement.

How did he find me? He should be in Quebec still. At the very least, *maybe* in White Rock, mingling with the Seven, assuming he's caught up to meet Dad. Dad never explained why some soldiers remained behind with Rozelyn, and I never asked.

I whip my gaze to the student beside me. He mumbles, "Sorry. Was paid to give you that."

"By who? What'd he look like?" I'm sure I sound desperate, my fingers knotting in the paper, crumpling the note.

He shrugs. "I don't know. Large. Scary as fuck. Tats up his neck."

Fuck. Not very descriptive, but it must be Gene, based on the details. Which means, this isn't some game.

How he found me is the question. The last time we fucked was long before the drama with Della began. I got busy with school, and then everything with the Corsettis began and he was doing extra rounds. All of Dad's guys were, even if I didn't understand why at the time.

Blood rushes through my ears, making the lecture impossible to pay attention to. My mind is whirling, every fear and possibility making the psychology subject unheard. This is insane and I should tell Raj, so he can inform Caladin, but a part of me wants to figure out what Gene wants on my own.

In the longest lecture known to man, simply because my anxiety can't take sitting around and waiting, it finally finishes.

Gene's messenger gives me a brief head nod before rushing away, likely thinking I'll demand more from him.

Raj is waiting by the end of his row until I catch up. He steps from the lecture hall first, scanning the surroundings before allowing me out. I angle toward the right, where the bathrooms are.

"Bathroom before we head home," I explain and he falls into a few steps behind me.

My every step is weighted. Every pace feels impossible until we're finally by the bathrooms. Until I hesitate by the female washroom, trying to decide how horrible of an idea this is. Gene wouldn't have me killed...right? Our past, his loyalty for my father, it all must mean something.

Before giving Raj time to question my hesitation, I push open the heavy door and step inside, shutting it with my back. My heart beats so quickly, it feels like it'll burst from my chest. I press one hand to it, willing my anxiety to decrease, to not end up having a heart attack at the young age of twenty-six.

No other woman is in here, but I have a feeling Gene's made it so—somehow. Neither is he, though, and I want to call out, but my lips are frozen. I scan the stalls, waiting, biding my time until finally, the last stall opens and a person steps from it.

Quick strides take him to my side before my eyes fully register. Fear spikes and though I should keep my eyes open and alert, they squeeze shut, praying this isn't my end. That my stupidity hasn't led me to my death. I angle away, like that'll change anything.

This is it. This is where I die.

Gene presses his large body to mine and I'm yanked back to the numerous times he'd pin me to my bedroom door, like he got a thrill of us being so close to the hallway and the possibility of getting caught. He reaches by me and flicks the bathroom lock shut. Then he backs away and my rapidly beating heart slows enough my eyes are able to open, to look him fully up and down.

In all the time I've known Gene, he's always been dressed in his soldier uniform of a leather jacket, black tee, cargo pants, and boots. Always equipped with a few weapons he'd remove and rest on my bedroom's floor so he never accidentally hurt me. He was always polite. Literal boredom and Dad's protectiveness brought us together. Even the first time, when he took my virginity, it was nothing special. He never hurt me. Sex never felt mind-blowing, the way I've heard others talk about it, but it filled the gaps.

This isn't the soldier I knew. Dressed in a hoodie, the hood pulled up over his head, and dirty jeans, like he's trying to fit in with the student body here. Maybe he'd succeed if it wasn't for the bloodshot eyes. They're...maniacal. Crazy, making my heartbeat quicken again.

Is he on something?

"Gene," I finally manage. "H-how—"

"Your father told me where you two were headed. I trailed you guys to B.C. at his request."

Through the fear, a flicker of uncertainty blooms. If that was the case, then why wouldn't he have been one of the guys who travelled with us?

"He told me I could continue to guard you, even after your marriage to Jasper."

Wait, so a soldier knew about my future before I even did? Nothing's making sense.

"Come with me." He reaches a hand toward me. "Your marriage to the *Famiglia* was never your father's wishes for you. I'll get you out. We can leave."

I stare at his offered hand. Once, even two days ago, I might have considered this, but the Seven is written all over this so I press into the door at my back, willing myself to be sucked through it. He's offering me an escape from Caladin, the husband I don't want, but right now, instinct says it's Caladin's arms I need to be running into.

But his hand twitches again. Eyes I once enjoyed looking at rapidly blink, crazed in his attempts. Like a dangerous animal, I ask in a quiet voice, "W-where would we go?"

"Back to the Seven. It's all your father wanted for you."

Gene isn't here to save me at all. He's continuing my father's bidding. "No, Gene, Jasper was abusing me. That's not..." I hold my hand up so he can see the ring. "Things have changed."

In a blink, he rushes at me, covering my body with his own. A heavy hand slaps into the door above my head, his head over-hanging mine and it takes everything not to shut my eyes and hide.

I have enough sense to push my hands into his chest, though it does nothing. Once, he respected if I wanted distance, but no longer. I'm not strong enough to fight...I'm fucked. But I still don't believe he'd hurt me, since he's only acting like this under the belief he has to. If I calm him down, make him see sense, I'll get out fine.

"This marriage is fake." He snarls. "This isn't you. You belong with the people who care about you."

No one cares about me. That's how this world is—how my life is. Dad didn't, and certainly not the Seven. Rozelyn is the only one. Ariella out of some trauma bond we found ourselves in. Caladin because he has to, to a point.

I shake my head, trying to meet his eyes so he sees what's in mine. Fear. The recognition of his own reflection; the stranger glaring down at me who seems seconds away from breaking something.

Possibly me.

I need out of here.

I push against him again, throwing my shoulders into the door for momentum, but all I do is make them sting with pain. Still, I try, but he doesn't flinch at all. Doesn't even notice. I'd huff in frustration if my breath worked.

Steeling my voice, breathing through the anxiety rattling my insides, I command, "You need to back up before I scream." One loud shout will bring Raj in here.

I hope.

"You do that, and his death is on your conscious."

My stomach drops and my nerves ice over because he doesn't need to define *his*. He knows I have someone out there. He knew which classroom to find me in. Where I was sitting.

"Have you been stalking me?" The feeling shopping the other evening. The sensation of being watched. Oh... "When I was shopping the other night, you were there." It's not even a question anymore.

"Of course I have," he replies in a tone like I've insulted him for even questioning it. "I needed to see how protected you are, but when I trailed you here this morning, it was too perfect. So public. So many dumbasses who'll happily take a bribe."

Fuck. "Gene, I don't know what deals you made with my father but we're in the past."

He rolls his eyes mockingly. "Oh, don't think this is some grandeur of love, Yasmine. It's a coincidence, our history, that's all. Your father appreciates my loyalty and ensured you'd be safe."

Were you loyal when you fucked his daughter? I shoot back in my head.

"B.C. wasn't safe," I say carefully. "The Seven are shady, Gene. With my father dead, you're free. Do what you want. Don't spend more of your life on me." I force a small smile, hoping that'll bring him down again. "I'm fine. Happy with this outcome."

"I *am* doing what I want," he counters, his words slow and paced. Arms creep up around me, pinning me to him, removing me from the door, which felt safer than he is. "I've met Jasper. They're the winners. The Seven is powerful, exactly what your legacy can be. You're a part of them by blood."

"No," I whisper, shaking my head, still trying to make him understand. "There's a deal, Gene. I'm wed to a Rossi now. They can't touch me. Jasper should have told you that."

He barks out a humourless laugh. "Is that what your new husband's telling you? They *can* touch you, Yasmine. There's only one fucking reason Jasper allowed you to go and that's to eventually *use* you."

My swallow is rough, and I peek over his shoulder, searching for an escape. Hopefully, with the length of time I've been gone, Raj will start questioning. He'll come in here. Somehow, considering the door's been locked. I'll be okay. That's what I tell myself while I continue calming him down.

Ignoring his statement, I repeat, "You have to let me go, Gene. They'll—"

He punches the wall, pulling a small screech from my throat. "They'll do *nothing*, Yasmine. I'm here to protect you and there's nothing your husband will do to stop that. On your father's orders, you belong to the Seven."

He's crazy. There's nothing I can say that'll change whatever he's cooked up in his head.

"Yasmine!" Raj's loud bellow comes from the other side of the door, a fist banging soon following. The handle jiggles and both our attentions fall to the locked door.

Gene slowly brings a finger up to his mouth in a shushing motion. Then he lifts the edge of his jacket to show me a gun. The silent threat: *say shit and he's dead.*

"You're going to act like nothing's wrong. Do not breathe

one word about me. In a week, I'll return you back to your rightful place. Where you should have always been."

He releases me and backs away, disappearing back into the stall he hid in before. Although Raj is still banging on the door, trying to get it unlocked, and I'm free, I can't move. I'm numb, frozen. Gene thinks he'd save me by returning me to the monsters my father built our fake lives around.

No.

If only I was stronger. If only I knew how to fight. Could have escaped Gene's hold rather than be pinned by him. I need a shower now. To wash him off me, to forget this happened.

"Mrs. Rossi!"

I flip the switch and move away from the door as Raj throws it open, his hand at his hip, prepared to take out his gun if needed. His eyes scan me first, checking if I'm okay, and then glances around the empty bathroom. The stall Gene disappeared into is still open, his feet off the ground, suggesting he's likely perched on the toilet.

A hand comes down on my shoulder, drawing attention to my heaving breaths. "Mrs. Rossi, what happened?"

"N-nothing. Let's go."

He blocks my way. "Yasmine, you're shaking."

Am I?

I look down, catching the slight quiver in my hand. *Huh, guess I am.*

"What happened?" he demands again.

I should tell him. He and Caladin can find Gene and end this before anything happens, but not here. Not while Gene can overhear and it'll end with a fight I won't be certain Raj will win.

"A spider," I lie. "It was nothing, I swear." Fisting my hands, I lock them by my side so the shakes slow. "I want to go home."

And for once, I don't mean Montreal.

17

CALADIN

"This weekend," Erico reaffirms. "Think she'll be ready?" He tosses his phone aside after inviting business partners, organization heads, and distant family members to the gathering Ariella planned.

"She'll hate it," I say with conviction. "But it has to happen."

His own was a disaster. When Ariella was formally introduced as Erico's wife, his father, my uncle, was insistent to end the arrangement and for Erico to instead marry Vanessa Volkov, the daughter of the Bratva's then-leader. After dragging Erico off to argue over it, his mother and Vanessa went on the attack. Until silent, little Ariella proved she's not someone to fuck with when slapping Vanessa.

With Yasmine's spite, I imagine if anyone said shit to her this weekend, I'd be breaking up a full-on physical fight.

"Will she behave or be spiteful?"

"Dude, she's not a dog. Besides, her mother was from an Italian mob. I'm sure Yasmine was raised to be polite at events."

After a chug of his drink, he asks, "When are you breaking the news to her?"

"Not sure, but—" My phone rings, ending my response when Raj's name flashes on the screen. If he's calling, it's likely about Yasmine, so I answer right away. She should be having her first day of classes today. University is...simple. Boring. Away from the crime life, so I can't imagine anything overly exciting would be happening that he needs to update me on.

"Sir," Raj's voice comes through right away, "I think something happened with Mrs. Rossi." And then he runs down the entire situation with Yasmine and the bathroom and her refusal to talk about it.

"Where are you now?" I demand, getting to my feet. After a quick wave to my cousin, in which I don't explain my abrupt departure, I rush from the club's office, heading toward the outdoors.

"Hallway outside your place. She's inside."

"Good. Stay 'til I'm there."

The club's somewhat close and traffic is lighter at this time of day—if there's a time for light traffic in New York—so I get there within twenty minutes. Raj is where he told me he was, so I dismiss him with a grateful nod.

Being powerless is my greatest fear. Not being able to control the situation. The Seven already had a hand up, and whatever she dealt with today is too soon after I took her from them. This protective nature is strange and new, but it quickens my steps toward the bedroom after finding an empty living room.

Was this how my father felt every time something bad happened with my mother? The drive to *fix*, even when not understanding the issue. He loved Mother, though, so his drive was deadly.

As I approach, I hear the slosh of water, but it doesn't

register until I'm standing in the bathroom doorway, mind blanking at the sight. My breath stalls. My heart hammers quicker and then not at all. All previous concerns to help— gone with her slow breaths.

Yasmine's in a bubble bath, facing the door. Her long hair is swept up in a messy bun, loose tendrils clinging to the side of her face and neck. Her head is tipped back against the tiled wall, her eyes shut, not paying my entrance attention. The angle makes her neck longer and though I'm aware I should walk away now, my gaze follows the line of her body, down her neck and to her—The water is just low enough her breasts are half out of the water. Water laps at her nipples, the same way my mouth longs to.

God, she's fucking gorgeous. My wife is sexy.

Like *ridiculously* gorgeous.

I wouldn't doubt she can hear the blood rushing from my head to my cock, so when her eyes open, it's not a complete surprise. For me. For her, her dark gaze widens before flicking over her surroundings. With cheeks growing redder, she dips deeper into the water, hiding her nipples from me, and cups the bubbles to shield her body.

It's too late to change what I've already seen, and the image of Yasmine, relaxed and wet, will live in my head forever.

"Sorry, I didn't hear you come in."

And fuck me, her throaty voice makes me painfully hard. Imagining her like this, spread out on our bed, bath water staining the blankets, as I take those nipples into my mouth and drive her to the brink. I wonder how quickly she'd come. How sensitive she truly is. If she'd be interested in me playing with her body the way I crave.

"Caladin?"

Am I staring? Yeah…I am, and it's only her questioning tone that reluctantly pulls me from my deep thoughts. Stuffing my hands into my pockets helps loosen my pants, giving my cock a chance to calm down, and I drop against the doorframe, pretending to be blasé.

"What happened today?"

The hint of her smile immediately drops into a flat mouth. "Nothing."

"Bullshit. Raj snitched, so stop lying. What had you so freaked out about the women's bathroom?"

"Nothing." Her chin lifts a fraction, daring me to fight her. Lucky for her, I'm the best fighter in New York and her defiance isn't a deterrent. It's a fucking thrill that has me crossing the room.

With every step, she leans into the tub's backing, as though escape is possible in her position. Using the bubbles to cover her naked body becomes forgotten, second to wariness as she angles away. It's not far enough, doesn't keep her from my reach as I sit on the tub's edge and lean over with one hand bracing the tile above her head.

"What do you care?" she asks before I can demand another answer.

"You're seriously asking that? You're my fucking *wife*, Yasmine, in case you've forgotten, and you're mine—"

"To protect," she interrupts, sneering and assuming.

That was what I was going to say, yes, but I alter my statement, making a larger point. Before I stop myself, I pinch her chin between my thumb and forefinger, forcing her face up to mine.

"Mine. You're *mine*. My wife, Yasmine. Mine to protect, yes, and that is why I care."

She tries to pull away, but my grip is too firm, so without escape, she argues through a narrowed glare. "Right. Forgot how you people are."

"How am I, in your words?"

"You only care about ownership. No reason other than this." She lifts her left hand from the water, twirling her ring with her thumb.

"That's all that matters," I tell her truthfully, searching her eyes. Searching for other possible reasons she's hoping I'd care. But her walls remain up, and I have no desire to break them down.

Her gaze drops to my lips before she looks away entirely, her tanned skin flashing darker with whatever secrets are buried in her head. I take the opportunity to scan her body, catching her budded nipples beneath the hot water, telling me what she'd never openly admit.

Attraction. Desire. Lust.

My position over her would make it so easy to taste, to devour, to—

I release her and stand from the tub, pacing away. With my back to her, she's unable to see the hand I rub over my face, willing my senses to calm the fuck down and remember everything that'll never be between us.

When I face her again, she's readjusted, bubbles covering her chest again. A pointless barrier at this point.

"What happened at school?" I repeat the earlier question, bringing us back to the reason I've interrupted her bath.

She dips her head, staring into the water.

"You're obviously hiding something, Yasmine. What is it?"

"Not here." She looks up finally. "Let me get out of the bath, and we'll talk."

With a dip of my head, I accept that and leave, even closing the door on my way out because I will not manage witnessing her climb from the tub.

Back in the bedroom, I head straight for the closet to strip from the suit, dropping the clothes in the centre of the floor and leaving them there. With two hands, I rub at my face, willing my thoughts to calm, to ease the throb in my dick.

For fuck's sake, get laid. That's all this is. My wife is a sexy woman, and it's been too long since I've fucked anyone, so lust and logic are confused. Find someone else, and I'll be able to return to seeing Yasmine as merely a roommate.

As though I've called her, she appears in the doorway, a deep blue, fluffy towel wrapped around her. Water slides down her legs, collecting at her feet. Her hair's still bound up, those wet strands clinging to her neck. I long to pull them away, to tuck them behind her ear and bare her neck for my mouth. The neck's a sensitive location for many women, and I long for her moans. Bet she'd be fucking responsive.

She pauses, skimming my body, which is bare besides my boxers. "Oh, um, sorry." She turns away. "I'll wait for you to finish."

By the time I'm dressed in a pair of shorts and a plain tee, I'm scowling at how we're treating the shared spaces. It's fucking stupid. We *live* together, so there's bound to be instances we will see one another's bodies.

"It's free."

She scampers by me, returning moments later in a baggy shirt and tiny shorts, spotting me seated on the edge of our bed. She's nibbling on her bottom lip, worried, which tells me there's something to be worried about. My muscles tense the same way they do before a fight.

"What happened today?" I try for what feels like the umpteenth time.

"Can I make a second wish?"

She didn't answer my question, but she also didn't ignore me completely. Consider my intrigue the reason I ask, "Which is?"

"Can you teach me self-defence?"

Her wish isn't random and it takes fisting the blanket to keep me seated and continue a civil conversation. Her reasoning for wanting to learn how to fight obviously ties into today.

"That's why you have Raj."

She shakes her head. "I get that, but if I'm alone..." As though realizing what she's said, she trails off, tongue dabbing at her bottom lip.

"Like today?" Unable to function sitting any longer, I push to my feet but somehow maintain distance.

"Will you? Teach me to defend myself? Please, Caladin."

I was already going to grant her this, but it's that *please* that breaks me. The breathless hopefulness that has my chest burning. Bodyguard or not, if she wants to learn how to fight, there's nothing wrong with that.

Maybe if Mother knew how to fight, she'd be alive.

A disruptive thought, because no hand-to-hand combat training would have won against a flying bullet, but the unwelcome pondering still filters through the spaces in my brain.

Still an uninviting thought that has me agreeing. Because if my men can't be by her side, if I'm not there to protect her, then yeah. Fuck yeah, I want her to protect herself. She won't lose her life because she couldn't hit back. Over my dead body. *Famiglia* women are never trained in combat, but Yasmine will change that. We'll create a trend.

She blinks and unhidden sorrow fills her expression because she's incorrectly assuming I'll deny her wish. I reflect on what she's told me in the past, her first wish. Wanting to control her own life, and her request is simply that—another method of taking control. To fight as she wants or needs to. To remain alive is the ultimate way of controlling one's life.

"Yeah," I murmur. "Yeah, I'll teach you some things. You're right; it'll be good for you to learn."

She takes a step closer, her tongue continuing to dab

nervously at her bottom lip. "Do you remember when you asked about guys from my past and I shrugged you off?"

"Yes." Why do I get the sense I won't like where this is headed?

"There was only ever one," she continues slowly, pacing out each word. "He was one of my father's soldiers, new-ish, hired a few months prior when we started fucking around. I was twenty-four at the time, and bored. He was always around when I was home and we became friends, I guess." She wrinkles her nose. "Closest term anyway. One day, flirting turned into more, and we ended up fucking around a couple times. He didn't want to get in trouble with my father and I wanted nothing serious, so it was casual."

My hands form fists by my side, questioning why I'm even reacting at all.

"He stayed behind when Dad dragged me away. Well...he found me. Today. At school." She pauses, rolling her lips together, shifting from foot to foot, studying my own tense reaction as I study her in return. "I-I didn't know he even knew where I was. I haven't thought about him in months, but Dad told him where we were headed. That he can continue to work for him. Guess he went to the Seven and learned about us. Then...came here. He's claiming the Seven still has rights to me."

Over my dead body.

She gestures toward her ring. "I tried to explain that marriage to you was a deal made with *them* and they're fine with it. That they don't own me, but...I don't know..." She glances at her feet. "He's different than the guy I knew. Like, insane. Wasn't listening to me."

I might not want a wife. Might be planning to send her on her own in a few months, to grant her the ultimate distance between us, but this, this won't fucking happen. He *won't* touch her. Won't even try to steal her away from me or else I'll rain hell down on his ass. He won't know the meaning of death until I have him torn in burnt pieces, twenty feet beneath me. I don't have to love her to keep her safe. Hell, I don't have to have any feelings toward her at all, to be planning this fucker's painful, slow death.

"His name?" I demand when the pissed-off red fog clouding my head dissipates enough for rational questions to form.

"Gene. Gene Lampel." Her tongue drags over her top teeth before she continues, every word another punch I'll deliver to him when we find the fucker. "He had someone deliver a note, and I should have mentioned it to Raj, but I had to know for certain. He trapped me in the bathroom. Wouldn't let me go when I begged him to. Wouldn't back away when I pushed him away. I was weak and—" Her eyes flash to me, a strength in there I've never seen before. Determination. And that's a strength on its own. "I wasn't trying to hide this. I'm not stupid. I was scared Raj would get hurt if I said anything right there, and I realize how dumb that is because Gene would have been cornered. And now, we don't know where he is, so I am sorry for that." She pauses, her rapid stream of consciousness coming to an end. "Somehow he snuck his way into the U.S. and found me and is determined to return me to the Seven."

"That'll never happen as long as I'm breathing."

She smiles, and it almost seems relieved. Genuine.

I don't know how to feel about that. That she trusts me enough to not only tell me but be pleased for the safety I'll ensure she has.

"That's why I want to learn to fight. Maybe if I had a bit of strength and skill, I could have gotten away from him."

I nod because it makes sense, even if I don't like it one bit.

Not that she wants to learn, but that she feels the need to. "Did you yell for Raj?"

"I did, but Gene had the door locked. Said if I told you or him, he'd kill you, but that sounds like a pretty empty threat."

It's very empty because if one washed-up, obsessed bodyguard even looks in her direction again, he won't see me coming before I have his life in my unrelenting grip.

My feet take me to her side before I realize what I'm doing. My finger tipping her chin up before I comprehend I'm touching her *again*. "You did good today. Thank you for telling me that. I can't help you if you keep secrets. If he seeks you out again, tell me, but I vow it won't come to that."

Wariness flashes through her eyes. "You're not going to prevent me from going to classes, are you?" Her voice spikes. "Because, Caladin, today felt *good*. Don't keep me chained in here. Please."

The thought did cross my mind, but even before her plea, I decided one fucker won't take away the bit of freedom I'm allowed to give her. Especially now, with how she's looking at me. Finishing her degree is meaningful for her, and nothing will be stopping that.

"Don't worry, I won't. But I will be stationing more men around. They'll be undercover, guarding the building's exterior. With his name, we'll begin searching for him, and I'll ensure my guys know what he looks like so, if he tries to approach you again, they'll catch him. I'll be letting the dean know about the criminal stalking his students too."

My thumb strokes her soft cheek before I release her altogether, even when I don't want to. I reach for my phone to message Erico and begin the search.

She speaks again, her voice soft. "Thank you. Guess you're not so bad after all." Then she treads from the bedroom, her latest statement rolling over and over in my head.

It was her way of saying, *this marriage isn't so bad.*
At least, that's what I convince myself.
And then I wonder why I even care.

163

18

YASMINE

Thump...thump...thump... The knife drops onto the cutting board in a steady rhythm, slicing the vegetables as it does. I try to focus on it rather than the earlier conversation with Caladin. He had this look in his eyes... Not maniacal and crazed like Gene's form of protection but gentle and possessive. It made me want to step into his arms and *allow* myself his protection.

After a few minutes of me prepping supper, Caladin claimed the barstool across from me, keeping silent company. It's strange to see him here since normally he does everything to avoid me.

He's not watching, but is spending all his time on his phone, fingers moving rapidly over the screen.

"I'm getting that fucker found whether he likes it or not," he announces suddenly, setting the phone aside. By now, I've moved to the stove to heat a skillet, so his immediate question becomes, "You cook?"

"Hung out with our chef often as a teen. I picked up a few things."

"Huh." Skin between his eyes furrows, his mind nearly visibly leaving this condo, and then he's back to his cell phone while I return to cooking.

After another few minutes of silence, only the crackle of oil mingling with frying vegetables, I ask, "When do we begin training?"

I almost can't believe he granted me that wish. That he's entertaining training a woman to fight. Dad would never. He had this concept of femininity he shoved onto Mom and me. Once, I believed Rozelyn fell into that category too, but after her story, apparently not. She learned to fight, but only for his selfish use.

Caladin makes a thinking noise. "Um, tomorrow? After your classes."

"That'd be good."

"It's a plan then," he says and my stomach heats to a temperature having nothing to do with the stove's flames. As I turn for the chicken I already had sliced, he adds, "And this weekend, the *Famiglia* is getting together for a party. So you can meet everyone."

I pause, goopy chicken lumped in my palms. "Excuse me?" It shouldn't be surprising. Being the Consigliere's wife was bound to catch up at some point.

"It's time. People will want to meet its newest member. You and Ariella can go shopping later this week, if you'd like, and get a dress for it."

The downside of not thinking ahead and purchasing something suitable the other day is now I have to go out again. Although, it'll be good to spend time with Ariella doing an activity neither of us imagined we'd ever be experiencing together.

Besides, this is the price of my freedom. Marriage to Caladin means acting the part.

"Is it at their mansion?"

"A third-party location. Erico doesn't like when everyone descends upon the house. Interrupts the peaceful little bubble he and Ariella have created." He rolls his eyes like it's the most ridiculous concept.

My gaze sweeps the condo. They have a larger bubble than what we do. Does this even constitute as having a bubble? We're two people stuck together. Roommates.

Married roommates.

Married roommates who stand in bathrooms and gaze at their wife in bathtubs with expressions that made my insides clench in desire. The way he watched me...he looked *hungry*. Like he was interested.

I miss physical touch.

When he was leaning over me, it was pure power and authority, and then throwing out words like *mine*, every determined bone in my body melted with those four, little letters and I wanted to be his. His in every single way. His to touch, to fuck. To have him sink inside me and claim me as his wife in all the official ways.

I study his mouth, imagining it against mine. We've never even kissed yet.

Yet?

Never. There won't be a moment, making *yet* irrelevant.

Right?

"Yasmine, the pan's hot enough by now."

Right. Cooking. Fuck.

With the pile of cut meat still in hand, I turn and drop it into the sizzling, hot pan before he can comment on my obvious mental vacation.

"Okay," I finally answer his previous point about the party, realizing I've yet to. "Sounds thrilling." It's everything but.

Dressing up, putting on a show for his family that we're some happily, wed couple is fucked up in a cruel way.

"It'll be quick. One dance, to appease everyone and then we'll be home free."

A first dance. Like a wedding reception.

"Can you dance?" he asks.

"Can *you* dance?"

"Please," he scoffs, "I was forced into lessons by Erico's mother."

Not his own? I know nothing about him and he's never even mentioned his parents. My in-laws technically.

I brush aside the prickling on the back of my neck by telling myself Erico's mother was involved because Caladin was probably put through the same lessons his cousin was.

"Good. Me too. At least we won't look completely ridiculous."

He's silent as I finish cooking, and then offers to help me dish the two plates, but I deny his assistance then too. At the island, I take the bar stool beside him and we eat together like a couple. It's strange to have him here. Odder to be cooking for him. Weird to spend time like this.

After we finish, he single handily cleans up and waves away my offer to help. "You cooked, I'll clean," he announces.

Once the whole place is spotless and there's nothing else to occupy either of us, we're at an impasse. Caladin stares at the couch, and then me, and once again, we're stuck. Forced to be around one another, but no idea how to be. He leaves so often in the evening, but now I wonder if he leaves because I'm here. Because he'd rather not be around the woman he's forced to be around the rest of his life.

"I have to study," I mumble, giving him the out he's looking for.

Still, he heads for the door. "I'll be back later." Like I'm not used to this routine by now. He doesn't tell me where he's going, and I don't ask. Whatever understanding we came to today is gone, replaced by the distance we both want that's brought on by the evening. It feels like we're back to square one again.

Not sure if that's good or not.

Reviewing notes fills my hours, mainly because I'm barely paying attention. It also keeps me up longer than I normally would be. Close to eleven now, but he's still not back, so I head to bed, keeping the bathroom light on and the curtain open. He hasn't asked or even altered my sleeping preferences yet, and I hope he never does because then I don't have to explain how pathetic I am to still need a nightlight at twenty-six.

Past midnight, he returns. Showers and gets into bed and I hide the fact I'm awake. He leaves the bathroom light on after his shower and doesn't touch the curtain, which I'm thankful for. I hate myself for sniffing the air, searching for any sign of liquor, drugs, or perfume—something to indicate where he was.

When I find nothing, I squeeze my eyes shut and sleep.

~

"One more."

Last night, I had a dream. A nightmare, actually. It was unfortunately very similar to the present: me on my back, sweaty and panting, while Caladin is over me. Only, it wasn't in *these* circumstances, where I'm now second-guessing the wish I made yesterday.

"You're fucking kidding me, right?"

Caladin grins playfully from where he's standing above me. Hands on his hips, looking way too at ease. A slight sweat runs down the front of his shirt, but it's sexy and quite unlike the disgusting mess my body is. I'll hand it to him; he's been doing move for move alongside me. He's a great encourager, but I hadn't expected *this*.

It began with a stretch. A light jog on the treadmill. A warm-up, he claimed, which had me realizing how utterly out of shape I am, but I was ready for training either way.

When I think training, I assumed he'd teach me to punch.

Not this.

Not hell.

"Not at all," he answers. "With every passing second you don't, I'm adding one more to the amount you'll need to do."

"That's the most unfair punishment," I argue between breaths so heavy they sound like I'm dying.

He shoots me a heated look that finds its way right down to my core. "Do this, and I won't punish you in other ways."

"You're an ass."

"Three more, *piccola tigre*."

I'll admit, it's that nickname that gets me moving. In a fucked-up way, I've missed it. With all the awkwardness between us the past couple days, he hasn't referred to me by it. Not that I blame him. And after yesterday, I wasn't certain if he'd stick to his deal, but after classes, Raj brought me home. Within the hour, Caladin arrived and he brought me to the *Famiglia* gym, where at least another dozen guys are working out. They all watched us enter. One almost dropped a weight. Since then, he's back to the guy I first met in B.C. The one, I now realize, I missed.

Grunting, I place my hands by my head, and arch off the mat, curling my spine to bring my body into a sit-up position. My abs screech because they feel bruised from the number of these fucking torturous moves he's made me do so far. Pure determination to meet his challenge drives me to finish.

From above me, Caladin watches and counts, smiling in a

way I would think could be pride, and that's what brings me all the way up again, and then slowly and oh so agonizingly down to the mat. The moment my spine touches the padding, my body drops, arms and legs splayed with exhaustion. It can't do this anymore—determination or not.

"Done. Dick."

He grins. "Two more, remember."

"Ha. No." I stick my tongue out at him because lifting my hand to shoot him the finger requires too much energy.

"You wanted this."

"No, I want to learn to fight. Not whatever tortuous boot camp you're putting me through. Is this supposed to get me to *not* want to learn?"

"Not at all. I like the wish you made. If I didn't, I wouldn't have agreed."

Except my wish was to learn how to protect myself, not workout. It started with a warm up, but then he decided push-ups (I think I managed a single one), light weight lifting (it wasn't light), and sit-ups (my abs are dead). My wish was *not* to exercise my body into a grave.

Caladin's been a champ and has done every single move with me. Except, when I struggled to do more than three sit-ups, he was managing them without issue and finished his twenty by the time I did six. My arms nearly gave out, even getting onto my hands and knees for a push-up, and he pumped three regular ones in the time it took me to position myself.

Show-off.

It's been an impressive show nonetheless that had me realizing exactly how in lust I am for my husband. It was incredibly sexy to watch him workout. Enough, I paid all the other hot men around us no attention.

When we entered, they might have been shocked to see me there, but it was like being faced with a shark. We're scared of them, but they also fear humans. The men were surprised and made it known but entering a massive gym with a bunch of large men working out like bodybuilders...well, I can only be so strong. After the initial surprise wore off, they stopped staring and returned to their own exercising. They've allowed me to die in peace beneath Caladin's grin, which was very generous of them.

Caladin stretches a hand down for me to take. I do, but even lifting my arm requires more work than I have in me. He lifts my limp body weight like I'm nothing—which might be the case—and I sway into his chest.

His very hard chest.

I step back with a brush over the strands of hair that have long been pulled from my ponytail.

"Like I explained earlier, you're too out of shape to learn anything right now."

I roll my eyes. "Isn't self-defence all about poking out eyes, kneeing men in the balls, that kind of thing?"

"Sure, and I'm positive you can lift a knee." His brows lift with his point. "But yesterday, you didn't attempt that. Your instinct was to shove and use your arms, so we'll build upon that. Why train new instincts into you when we can capitalize on the ones you have?"

I suck on my teeth. *I guess...* "Well, I get needing to be in better shape, but I don't even know what fighting looks like. Fight me now. I'll obviously lose, but it'll give me an idea of what to prepare for."

He purses his lips in consideration. "I can have you pinned to the mat in three seconds."

Why did my lust-raddled brain hear another connotation in his words?

"Prove it. I dare you."

He grins. "Happily. Right after I piss." He steps by me,

gesturing to the fridge in the far corner. "Get water. Relax your muscles for a few minutes. I'll be back." He strides away with a cocky gait. The walk of a winner.

He will win, that I have little doubt of. But three seconds; maybe I can manage to stay on my feet for four.

"Here."

The voice pulls my attention away from Caladin's retreating back, and toward another a taller guy who's come up beside me. Smiling kindly beneath shaggy hair, which he pushes away from his striking, blue eyes, he hands me a chilled, sealed water bottle.

"Looks like you need it."

"Thanks." I take it, twisting the cap and immediately sucking down large gulps, groaning as the icy water heals me from the inside. "God, that feels amazing. Certainly better than Caladin's hell."

"I'm proficient at making women feel good." He smirks, taking a sip of his own cold bottle.

I pause. Fuck, I need to have sex soon. Everything anyone says now, my brain is twisting into another kind of statement.

"That so?"

"Very much so." He throws out his hand. "Wanted to introduce myself to the newest Rossi. Name's Elias."

I take his in a quick shake. "Thanks. I'm—"

"Yasmine," Elias fills in quickly, his sapphire eyes sparkling in the gym's lighting. "Yeah, Mrs. Rossi. Everyone here knows who you are."

"Then you'd also know to only call me Yasmine."

With a tip of his head and a cute, playful grin, he replies, "Your wish is my command."

19
CALADIN

When I return to the main part of the gym, I'm excited. Excited to have my hands on my wife, to pin her to the mat beneath me, to make my point that she needs to get stronger before properly teaching her to fight.

But when I broach the entranceway, she's not where I last left her on the mats, nor is she by the fridge where I recommended her to go. She's off to the side, by the punching bags, talking to one of the men. He has his hands on her, curling her hand into a fist, teaching her the proper technique.

That's *my* job. After all, she's mine and these fuckers know better. When I told her she can look outside the marriage, I didn't mean my soldiers. That's just...no...not where I have to fucking *see* it.

No matter the number of breaths I take in that second, the jealousy doesn't taper off.

Jealousy?

Yeah, actually, I decide. Fucking jealousy. Green tinges my vision as her hair falls to the side, her flirty grin so fucking impactful against Elias. How do I know? Because the sight of her now, hair in a high ponytail, sports bra and workout leggings, and a fucking smile robs me of breath, so I know it's affecting him too. She's too sexy to ignore.

"Elias has a death wish," Jonas, one of my other soldiers, approaches, nodding toward the duo. "It's downright disrespectful. He wouldn't do that to Erico's wife."

"Elias will get what's coming to him soon," I state with menace. "There's a reason I've been having her workout before learning fighting techniques."

"Yeah, speaking of, it was quite the surprise when you two showed up. She must be the first woman to step foot in here?"

"She asked to learn to fight, to protect herself. I see nothing wrong with that."

He holds his hands up. "I get it. Makes sense. Even with bodyguards around her, one can never be too safe. It's admirable, sir."

Not that I was seeking his approval, but I grunt, accepting it regardless.

He steps away, heading back to the rowing machine he was just using. "Better get over there soon. Looks like he's entertaining himself with your wife."

I shove a hand into Jonas as he passes, knocking him unsteady. "*My wife* is going to find herself on her back in *two* seconds rather than the three I bet her."

"And that is a show I will be watching," he calls out as I stride across the gym.

A few of the other guys quickly glance our way before returning to their own workout. More attention garners by the time I reach the duo, not that I care. Let them all watch and witness the point I'm about to make.

My arm loops Yasmine's waist and I draw her to my side, sparking a small gasp as she first, weakly, pushes into my arm, and then glances up, her fight ending when she realizes who's holding her.

My glare locks on my soldier, whose face is a shade whiter than normal, like he couldn't have guessed this would be my response. "I told you," I say to her, but keep my stare on him, "we're not at this stage yet."

She flips her hair, whacking me in the face with her ponytail, that scent of jasmine filling my nose again. "Yeah, well, *Elias* was nice enough to teach me."

"*Elias* needs to remember his fucking place," I seethe, this time completely to him. My heavy glare has him backing up, palms in the air. I'm not finished with him yet, but I won't do this in front of her, so I tug her away, releasing her when we're back on the mats. "Come on. You wanted a demonstration of fighting. You'll get it."

By now, we've gained the crowd of men. Most have ended their workouts to openly observe, but I don't care. This won't take long.

I position her in the centre of the mat, bringing her arms up and kicking her feet apart, causing her to wobble. Once she's in the fighting stance, I say, "Try to land a hit on me. Be sure to move as you need to, to avoid getting caught."

Her mouth flattens, her eyes determined, and I'll admit, it's cute. Certainly a look I'm coming to appreciate. Reminds me of her in the mall, the first time we met. So determined to make an escape on her own.

Then I circle her like a predator, and my wise, little prey, my *tigre*, keeps one foot locked while the other's used to spin. In some forests, the tiger *is* the predator. But the circle of life says there's always a larger predator. For tigers, it's man.

Man versus beast.

And I'm the man.

"Gonna attack sometime today?" she taunts, but there's a

quiver in her tone, indicating she's aware when I do, she's fucked.

I complete another circle, catching Elias' pained look in the crowd, and Jonas' amused one. Then I focus on her again.

"Ready?"

"And waiting."

One more circle. With my every step, more of her protective barriers will increase. Then it'll be more fun winning.

Her throat moves with her swallow. She tracks me, not blinking. Her fists waver, tightening and untightening as she shifts, waiting for me to make my move.

Between her next inhale and exhale, I lunge.

With an arm around her hips and head, as not to injure her, I have her flipped before her next breath. She swings out once, but I block her and stretch a leg out to trip her, dropping her gently to the mat.

She's panting, her breasts rising and falling with her rapid breaths from her pathetic attempt. I'm on my hands and knees, crouched over her, putting us in a very intimate position. I feel her breaths against my neck, her eyes flickering first in wariness...and then something else.

Something about her in this position, sweaty, reminds me of my dream from last night that had me waking this morning with a painfully hard dick. Only jacking off in the bathroom like some virginal teenager eased me.

"I win."

"That was more than three seconds. You circled me for a while."

"From the moment of my lunge to getting you on your back was two seconds."

Her eyes narrow into cute, little slits. "That took you no effort."

"Told you. Would now be the time to admit I'm the *Famiglia's* top fighter in our ring?"

Her brows spike. "Oh, and he's humble too."

"No reason to deny the truth. But this is why we need to build some muscle onto you. My *piccola tigre* needs to be a *forte tigre*."

"A strong tiger," she correctly translates and then explains, "Similar word in French."

Not sure why, but I admit, "I like when you speak French."

"Je suis sur le dos, exactement là où tu as dit que je serais."

God, I'd be hard from hearing that alone, if it wasn't for pure will and focus. The roll of the other language on her tongue. The fluidity she speaks it, no different than her English, is poetic. "Translation?"

"I'm on my back, exactly where you said I'd be."

I laugh and it feels fucking good to do so. *"Sì. Mi stai mettendo delle idee in testa."*

She tips her head. "Now we're in some kind of language game."

"Yeah. You're putting ideas in my head, is what I said."

"What ideas?"

What ideas could I *not* be having? Yasmine on her back, strands of her hair freed from her ponytail after the afternoon of working out. Sweat coats her body, her breaths heavy, breasts rising. I want this exact image, sans clothing, and in my bed.

I *want* her.

Distance and limits be damned.

Instead of responding, I balance on my right hand to use my other to stroke her cheek, completely ignoring the crowd, or if they're even still observing. I'm too enamoured by her this second to check, or to even care. Starting at the base of her chin and following the column, her pulse jumps beneath my thumb.

Her pulse first, and then her breath.

"Sensitive?"

"Yeah," she replies a bit breathless, almost like she doesn't want to admit it. "That feels good."

My finger follows the trail to the tops of her breasts before I stop touching her entirely, positioning myself on both hands again. Only this time, I bend my arms until I'm in a half-push-up position, knees framing her thighs.

"Did you know sweat releases sexual pheromones that call to your partner?"

"Oh, yeah? So do I find a partner then to work them out on?" She grins cheekily, drawing upon all previous conversations about our marriage.

My response should be a yes. It should be to get off her, having made my point about her training. Instead, I dip my head and trail my tongue up her skin. Beginning at the dip between her breasts and following an invisible line straight up her chest to her neck and ending at her pulse, flicking once.

"Tasty, little pheromones."

Her lips part, eyes growing darker with lust. I have no idea what she sees in mine, but it must be something if my hardening cock has anything to say. The need to lower myself, to show her the effects she's having on me is so fucking tempting. For now, I return to her pulse and trace her chin, marking her with my scent like an animal in front of all my men. Maybe now, they understand not to go the fuck near something that's mine.

And then I lick over her lips and everything. Fucking. Alters.

My brain chemistry.

My sanity.

My logic that yells I shouldn't be doing this. To not get physical with her, knowing there's only one fucking way this will end, and I'll be on a fast-track to Hell when I can't stop it.

But then her tongue peeks out between her lips, licking right over my claiming mark and I lose it.

Control.

Myself.

Everything.

I cup her neck, holding her steady and lick her lips. First with my tongue, and then my lips as I do the single-handedly stupidest thing of my life and kiss my wife. I kiss her, I devour her...

...I lose myself.

She lets out a surprised gasp, then a moan and parts her lips, kissing me back. Her nails skate up my arms, marking me with her own claiming scratches I enjoy way too much. The effect of this kiss is visceral, and I hate every fucking second of it. Addiction satiates in my bones, ensuring I'll keep begging for more. One taste leads into another, and another, until I'm unsure how I'll ever be able to stop tasting her.

To not kiss her again after today.

To not allow myself to go *there* with her.

Stop. You need to pull away.

I kiss her harder, my tongue battling my head for domination within the confines of her mouth.

End this before you get hurt and lose her.

I kiss her harder, *keeping* her. There will be no losing if I never let her go.

Don't be them.

I freeze and pull back, lifting myself off her completely and so abruptly something similar to hurt flashes over her expression. With it, I end the kiss that could have easily become more. My death, her death. Our destruction.

She's panting again, this time for a whole other reason. Her eyes skate over my face, but I look away, tightening mine shut before she discovers what she's looking for.

My desire. My need to have her. To finish what was started here.

Fuck.

I glance over the crowd of men who, most of which have gone back to working out, granting us the privacy the gym certainly doesn't allow for. Elias is watching from over by the punching bags, and I don't know why, but it pisses me off. Like *he's* annoyed by me kissing my own goddamn wife.

Christ, my wife. I finally kissed my wife.

"I won," I proclaim again, voice gruffer than earlier. "But that didn't give you a good idea about fighting, did it?" Before she can answer, I push to my knees, then my feet and reach down to help her up. Once she's standing, I scan the crowd, even though I've already picked my victim earlier. More like, he picked me as his attacker.

I point to Elias. "You. Come here now."

He won't say no because my position is one of authority, and though it's one I don't use often, it's useful today. He approaches with a grim expression, aware of what's about to go down even before reaching the mat. His expression is pleading, apologetic, but with a grin every man in here should recognize, I point toward Yasmine's spot.

"Right there. Yasmine, off the mat. You're going to watch a real fight."

"Mr. Rossi—"

"Oh, now you've remembered my role," I cut him off. "Just in time for you to be useful. Fight me, Elias. Let's show my wife what true defence looks like. Try to block my hits."

That's the only warning I provide before launching myself at him, throwing a fist immediately toward his face. With Yasmine, I was cautious of where my arms went, so to not truly harm her, but with Elias, none of that matters. He'll defend himself or he'll be injured.

The fucker's quick though, and dodges my hit, bending his knees and rolling to the side as I spin on my heel and throw myself at him again. In passing, people approach again, observing the show. Somewhere behind me, I feel Yasmine watching, and would kill to know what's in her head.

Elias blocks me again, but this isn't feeding my rage the same way it should, so I demand, "Try to get a hit on me. First to land a punch wins."

"Sir—" His protest cuts off as my leg swings out to take him down. He's protesting because he's aware of what everyone else in here—other than Yasmine—is. As the *Famiglia*'s underground champion, he has no true chance of winning. Not if I truly try.

He remains upright, but my second attempt at tripping takes him down. He lands with a loud thump to the blue mats, and in the two seconds I have before he finds his footing, I search for Yasmine.

She's not watching the fight, but staring at me, her mouth flat and arms crossed over her chest. She looks pissed but that's a concern for later.

Before Elias gets to his feet, I throw myself at him, an elbow jamming in the space between his neck and his shoulder, making him cry out with pain. It's more of a distractor though, and he realizes it one second too late as the moment he goes to block, my punch makes it through, landing with a crack on his nose.

A trickle of blood soon follows and while it's tempting to hit him again, numerous eyes are on me. One punch, as per the deal, is to demonstrate a real fight to Yasmine. Another, people will claim I'm pissed and jealous, and I'm not.

I'm *not*. I can't be.

I shove off him, jerking my chin toward the change rooms

and remember my true role to these men. "Good fight. You're strong at defence. Go clean up."

Before he follows my direction, his look conveys he understands the meaning behind that fight: *Don't touch her again.*

"And that," I mock bow to my wife, "is a fight. Tripping, pressure points, punching, all in combination. This is why we'll get you a bit more fit and turn you into a fighter."

She doesn't blink, nor does that pissed-off expression change. Instead, she steps by me. "I'm hungry and sore and want to leave."

20

YASMINE

Damn right, I'm angry. Irate. Pissed. Heated. Pick a term and stick it to me, because any will work.

That wasn't displaying a real fight. Not for my benefit. That was pure jealousy. That was entrapment in ways worse than I already am. That was Caladin breaking his own deal.

Out of all the men he chose in that gym, he picked the *one* who'd spoken to me. Elias wasn't even flirting! He provided water and when I asked about the punching bags, he was teaching me how to make a proper fist. Nothing beyond that, but the moment Caladin returned from the bathroom, he acted possessed.

I don't talk to him until we're in his car. Hell, I'm not even planning on speaking until we're safely in his condo.

"What has you suddenly in a bad mood?" he asks the moment his car rumbles beneath my ass.

"You can't be that dumb." I throw a *you're kidding me?* glare his way.

"Enlighten me." He backs up from his parking spot by the gym's door. "We have a bit until we're home. That's more than enough time for you to get it out."

At least it means it won't fester the entire drive. "You told me to be discreet if I wanted to look for sex outside the marriage, but how could I ever, if you react like *that*?"

In a tone too calm and deadly to be easing, he asks, "Like what?"

"That." I point to the gym beside us. "You specifically chose Elias to make a point."

He stomps on the brake before we even make it from the parking lot, all so he can twist and look at me. "And what was that point, *wife*?"

"That!" I screech, gesturing toward him. "That, right there. You saw a man talking to me and your possessive nature took over, even when you claimed it wouldn't."

I swear neither of us are breathing, both remaining silent until the other breaks. His eyes flick over my shoulder, toward the gym, and he mutters, "You're right, we should wait until we're home to have this conversation. I won't be able to drive and focus."

"Then let's have it right here."

Still staring at the gym, he says, "No," with finality. "No, because when my men start leaving, I'd rather they not see us arguing."

He throws the car back into drive and exits the parking lot. Two minutes into the drive, I'm tempted to talk, just to spite him, but it'll go nowhere, so I stick to my silent fuming and try *not* to relive everything that happened in the gym.

He kissed me.

We kissed.

My lips still tingle, and it takes a whole lot of focus not to touch my mouth so he doesn't know I'm thinking about it. Hell, it's only the swell of anger that replaces the sensation all together. Did he kiss me because he wanted to or was that another show for his guys?

The moment he parks in his underground parking lot, I'm out of the vehicle and pressing the elevator button, demanding it come to us. Thankfully, it opens instantly, being already downstairs, and I lean against the farthest corner while he stretches out in the opposite.

Once we're inside the condo, I whirl, finally ready for this conversation. But the second my mouth opens, my next point ready, he barrels down on me, backing me up, so close, if I breathe too hard, our chests would touch.

"To answer your latest point, I said you could look outside the marriage. *Not my men.* That's the opposite of discreet."

Scoffing, I cross my arms. "Please. Elias was being kind. It was nothing more than that. Besides, I'm not mad that it was *him* you fought. I'm mad that you were angry at all."

His hands come up to grip his hair, but he drops them before he can, hands curling in frustration. "You...you're maddening, you know that?"

Oh, but I'm not done. "If you reacted like that to your own guy, how will you be if you learn I've fucked someone from school?"

The look in Caladin's eyes when he was going for Elias at the gym was downright terrifying, but this—this is death. What I saw on his face was *nothing* compared to what's there now.

"You clearly have no idea what a man looks like when he wants a woman. Elias wasn't simply being kind to you. If I gave him the chance, he'd happily be sinking his dick into you right now."

"Ugh, can you not be so crass?" I step back, seeking space,

but he doesn't give it. Step for step, until I'm trapped against the wall. Where I've made my first mistake when he presses against me, lifting his arms to prop them above my head and leans in closer. "Also, maybe *I* didn't want Elias. Ever think of that? *Also*," my finger jabs into his chest, shoving my final point into a place he'll feel it, "I do know what a man looks like when he wants a woman because it's the exact expression you had before you kissed me. *You* kissed *me*."

His jaw locks and my hand is knocked away to be trapped in one of his above my head, his other thumb dragging against my bottom lip. "I might have started it, *piccola tigre*, but you can't deny kissing me back."

I can't because I did. Because in that single kiss, it felt *right*. Righter than I'd ever be willing to admit. Like a part of me came alive beneath his touch. I wanted him to continue, audience be damned, to kiss down my body and discover every sensitive spot on me.

"See?" He smirks.

I jerk away from his thumb, yanking on my arms, which don't budge from his unrelenting grip. "Fine, I can't deny kissing you back, but it doesn't change the fact that you were jealous."

Another tick of his jaw. His tell. Which is why I know even before he speaks, his smooth tone will be a cover-up for his true feelings. "How can I be jealous over someone I own?"

"Back on that, huh? Thought we weren't going to have that kind of marriage. Gotta make up your mind, Caladin, because I can't keep up."

His thumb traps my chin, forcing my head still. "You don't have to keep up because that's not your job. You seem to forget what the ring around your finger truly means and maybe one day, I'll wake up sick of this pathetic cat-and-mouse roommate game we're playing. Maybe one day, I'll remind us both who rightfully owns your body." He smirks, and I hate it. It's nothing like the Caladin I know. He's being cruel as a cover-up. He continues, his thumb pressing against my bottom lip again, completely disregarding the fact I don't want him to touch me. In a softer tone that eases a fraction of my anger, he murmurs, "Our deal hasn't changed. You do what you want, but my men will not touch you. It's basic respect. You're their boss, and they know that, so unless they're taking a bullet for you, they have no reason to be near you." His finger does another sweep over my lip and it's gentler, reminding me of earlier. Awakening every desire and every reason I'm mad at him.

"Don't be another disappointment in my life and rob me of that freedom you've agreed to grant me." It's whispered but hits him with the impact I need it to. He stills before dropping his hands entirely and giving me space to breathe.

His mouth opens and shuts three times before he finally speaks, but I don't think it's originally what he wanted to say. "I have a meeting with Erico. I'll be back late."

Then he's gone.

Later, in bed, with my phone resting on my stomach, my sister's voice fills the air, which feels more electrifying since the argument with Caladin. Everything about me is more charged since earlier. The three hours passing since he ran off have changed nothing.

"Um, yeah, that sounds exactly like he was jealous. But do you not remember what I said? You're stuck in this marriage, Yas, so stop acting like it'll randomly end one day. It's not temporary, so embrace it. Clearly, there's something between you two."

"It's called dislike."

"Or sexual tension."

"No," I immediately deny. There's nothing between us. Not that.

"Then *please*, describe that kiss again."

I groan. "Why'd I tell you in the first place?"

"Oh, because it's your best, and I quote, kiss you've ever had. What'd you say? Altered your brain chemistry." She snaps her fingers. "Yeah, that."

"Fuck off before I throw my phone across the room to shut you up. It was so much easier to argue with you when we were together. But don't you agree with me at all, Roz? Like, he lost his shit on the single guy who spoke to me. That's not the actions of a man who'll let me do whatever."

"Maybe it's a sign you shouldn't *be* doing whatever. Also, don't forget his role. He's right. Stay away from his men because it'll end badly for everyone involved. Besides, you're so worried about something you haven't even acted on yet. Any interest in anyone else?"

Answering her carefully because I don't know where she's going with this, I say, "No."

"Have you looked?"

Shit. I close my eyes, hating my own admittance. "No."

"No, huh? That could have easily been a 'not yet.' Admit it, you *want* to be physical with him."

Deny. Maybe if my sister didn't know me so well.

"We both made the agreement for distance so we can be with who we want to."

"Yes, and why is that? You're obviously both running from something. You don't want to actually fall in love with your husband, so you think distance is the answer. All the other men you know have been asshole disappointments who've controlled your life, so you're lumping him into the same category."

"He *is* in the same category," I counter, throat burning because it's not the complete truth and I know it. "He married me, taking away that choice."

Rozelyn continues like I haven't spoken. "But I wonder why he doesn't want the marriage. Bad experiences with love? A player and he doesn't want to be stuck to a single woman? I wonder..."

"From what I know, he hasn't slept with anyone since finding me, so I doubt it's the second one." But my sister's curiosity *does* have me wondering why Caladin granted my first wish in the way he had.

Then why be jealous today? The two paths don't intersect.

I groan, rubbing my hands against my forehead. "I don't know, nothing makes sense. At this point, all I can think about is this weekend."

"What's happening this weekend?"

"A party. Guess the *Famiglia* wants to get to know me formally, thus the event."

She barks out laughter. "That's hilarious. Good luck. I have no words of wisdom. Definitely the benefit of being with an enforcer. We get to skip all the political, family stuff."

"No advice at all then?"

"None. Have fun? Buy a nice dress? I don't know; I'm trying over here. Send me a picture when you're all done up. Don't be a bitch to Caladin or else you'll make it worse on him in front of the organization."

"Wasn't planning on it. He said we'll have one dance, to appease the crowd, and that'll be it. Then it's just meeting everyone."

"It'll be over before you know it. Get drunk." She pauses, and I hear voices in the background. "Oh, hey, I gotta go."

Click.

Even my sister abandons me. Lovely.

I put the phone to sleep before tossing it onto the charger on the nightstand and sliding beneath the blankets, adopting my usual position of being on the edge of the bed, farthest from him.

Sleep takes me immediately, exhausted from the workout.

21

CALADIN

There is no meeting with Erico. Instead, I head to one of our bars, get drunk, and pass out in the security room. Hours later, I wake with a hangover and crawl into bed at two in the morning.

At two-fifteen, I drag Yasmine into my arms, falling asleep with my head buried in jasmine.

At five, I let her go, to prevent another argument.

It's the next day, after a painfully silent drive from Manhattan to the Hamptons so Yasmine can join Ariella dress shopping, I unload on my cousin.

His response: a deep belly laugh that has me reaching for the glass of bourbon he slid me earlier.

"Fuck off." I take a large swig, swirling the liquid inside my mouth.

"Hey, I hadn't said anything but you certainly did. Actions speak louder than words and all that, and cuz, hate to say it, but you made your feelings very known to all the men there."

Feelings. That's too large of a word to use in this case.

"It was about disrespect. Elias is lucky to still have a job." *And his limbs.* "If it was Ariella, you would have flown off the handle."

"Sure would have," he easily agrees. "I was jealous over Sebastian. It was how I knew I was in trouble. Take that as a lesson. If you were truly into your whole 'don't fall in love' plan, you're in for a world of pain."

I scowl. "'Kay, we're not all like you though. Just because you fell in love with your wife doesn't mean I will. I need distance, Erico. After the party, I'll fly to Vegas, check things out there. Make sure none of the capos are pocketing anything behind our backs." Anything to get away. "I'll fuck, fight, and sleep out whatever's inside me and I'll return and be fine again. All will be well."

Over the rim of his glass, he gives me a look that speaks to the years of growing up like brothers. The look that says he sees right through me. Whatever he's finding, I'd hope he'd share so I can become un-transparent.

"Avoiding won't help."

"I'm not ready to be a husband. There's nothing more than that."

He stares at me for a beat before leaning forward, his tone dropping lower despite us being alone in his office. "I have news for you: you're already a husband. Don't fuck this up more than you already are."

"Fuck what up?" I grit, my fingers tightening around the glass in my hand. "There's nothing to fuck up."

"Says the man who felt the need to remind our soldiers who Yasmine is to them."

We're talking in circles. Slamming my glass down a bit harder than I mean to, I lean over. "Again, it's a respect thing. Whatever happens behind closed doors between Yasmine and me is secret. If she has side flings, the deal is to be discreet. You know our family would rip me apart for allowing my wife to sleep with other men. That's all. I was preventing talk amongst the ranks."

He chuckles, a sound grating on my already-fragile nerves. "By beating one of them up. You could have dragged her away from the gym and left it at that."

"And allow Elias to be smug and think he can openly flirt with my woman—*my wife?*"

My cousin's smile is slow and thought-out. "Your woman. All right, Caladin. I'm done arguing, considering it's your life. But when Yasmine gives up on your cranky ass and finds someone else to sleep with, please warn me before you kill the poor unsuspecting fool so I can do damage control where needed."

"That won't happen," I grumble, taking back my glass. I press my back into the chair, leaning as far away from him—and the uncomfortable truth in his statements. "It won't because I won't give two fucks."

"Even when she comes home to *your* bed smelling like *him.*"

I...hadn't thought of that. What happens when Yasmine walks through the door, her skin dewy with being freshly fucked, her hair mussed, and a smile I hadn't placed there?

I hate it.

Hate the feelings that image gives me. The uncomfortable knot in the base of my stomach but the murderous rage to go hunt the imaginary man.

I wipe my hand over my face, begging my mental state to do better. "It's whatever. Moving on...the shit I had dug up on Gene Lampel is limited. Can't find his background, or his current location. I have half the city on lookout for him."

Since I only explained minimal details the other day, I launch into everything Yasmine told me about him. I want his sorry excuse for an existence to come to a close before anything that'd potentially harm her comes from his presence.

But Erico's only response is another head shake. "Interesting that something threatening your wife is less important than your obvious jealousy. The threat, that can be handled... but you can't get your emotions under control and it's why it was the first topic you got off your chest."

"Fuck off." For the second time, I slide him my glass and get to my feet. "You're a big help, cuz. I'll be back when they're done shopping."

I exit his office quickly, denying everything about his final statement. The plan was to unload both issues on him, and sure, yeah, the gym was mentioned first. Why? Because...

...I can't come up with an exact reason. It was heavier on my mind. Something Erico, as Boss, should be aware of. That his men were acting out of line by openly flirting with a Consigliere's wife. I could have killed Elias and no one would have blinked at me, as per my rights.

I didn't because he didn't truly deserve it and if Yasmine was pissed about the fighting, she would have been downright ferocious about murder. *La mia piccola tigre feroce.*

I'd love to see that. She has a spark, but it needs to be unleashed. Freed from the bounds everyone in her life has tied around her. Freed to the world, to explore.

I want to do that for her.

Fuck, what am I saying?

Instead of turning toward the main lobby, I find myself walking the opposite way, past his office again, past Ariella's music room, and to the very end. Toward the painting I used to look at often because it was like having them around still. At ten, I could pretend we still lived in the same house like a happy family.

Four people, two couples. Standing in the back right is

Erico's father, my uncle. He's raised me since I was ten, and while I used to have a ton of respect for the man who finished my training, he had little claim on the man I've become. Seated in front of him is his wife, Erico's mother. My aunt's calculating smile looks evil, something I've never noticed until now. They both do, actually, making recent events less surprising.

But they're not why I'm here, and while I'll always love my aunt and uncle, and respect the *Famiglia*'s ex-leadership and the people who took me in, one act can truly change a person's emotions, and that's what happened in recent weeks. What they did to Erico and Ariella wasn't what family does.

My attention is owned by the couple beside them. In a similar position, the man standing while a woman is seated in front of him. Unlike Erico's parents, the look in his eyes is kind and the woman's smile is genuine. Like she's glad to have the portrait taken.

I reach up to stroke the bottom of the image, hung high, my fingers only brushing the base of the frame.

Mother and Father.

The familiar sharp pain of grief stabs me in the heart. My mother's smile—the same smile she'd always give me when I ran into her arms; when I rode my bike until it was dark and she had the guards dragging me back inside. I wonder what she'd do now, meeting Yasmine as my forced-upon wife.

She'd love her.

Yasmine's fighting spirit is similar to the mother I remember. There'd be moments Father did or said something to piss her off and she wouldn't let it go for anything. She'd argue until she made her point, and then they'd laugh it off like the fight didn't happen.

A different ending than what Yasmine and I had yesterday.

Mother would empathize with Yasmine, because she too was in a marriage deal—as is so many of us in the mob. Mother was a stand-in for her older sister, after her sister ran away from the wedding ceremony to my father. Similar to how Ariella took Aurora Corsetti's place in the deal with Erico. Mother would love both women, wouldn't have done what my aunt did to Ariella.

My gaze travels up the length of her to the man at her back, his hand lightly resting on her shoulder. Possessive but caring. A touch informing the world that the woman seated in front of him is *his* but not in a heavy or malicious way. Nothing to remind Mother of the fact.

Their love shines through, but it's a reminder of every reason why I can't be a regular husband to Yasmine. They loved one another so much that she went with him into danger. If she hadn't, she'd be alive today. Father would be gone, but a part of him would live on through her. I wouldn't have been sent to Erico's parents.

She'd be alive to see the sacrifice I made when I saved Yasmine from the Seven. I bet she'd praise me for it too. Then call me an idiot for not loving her instantly. If she was still alive, would I allow myself to be in this marriage completely? I wouldn't have this...this trauma hanging over me that deems what loving another person can result in.

A heavy hand rests on my shoulder, ripping me from the past, and toward my cousin who steps up behind me. He studies the portrait too, scanning both couples.

"Figured you'd be here. You always are when you have a lot of thoughts."

Shifting the focus from me to him, I gesture toward his own parents. "Still no word?"

"No. Thankfully."

Not that his reasoning isn't good, but sometimes it hurts knowing he sent away the family he still *does* have when I don't have that option. Then glancing at his tight expression, pinched lips and narrowed eyes, I'm relieved it's not an easy choice for him. Erico wasn't raised with a deep love like I was. His parents were unemotional, breeding him for the exact role he's found himself in. But in the end, they're still his family.

"They'd love her, you know," he declares suddenly. "Your parents. Yasmine. They'd be proud of what you did for her."

"I know."

"I tried to say this the other day but didn't go about it the best, and I'm sorry." His hand slides from my shoulder. "It was an unfortunate accident, Caladin. Love might have brought your parents together that day, but think about everything else it also did for them. Created you, gave you a happy childhood. You grew up witnessing their devotion for one another, with the opportunity to learn from it. The years they had together were filled with love. Do you really want to get taken out without having that same emotion greet you every single day leading up to your final moments?" He pauses, heavy words settling in. "The devil himself will have to drag me to Hell before I willingly leave Ariella's side, but when that time comes, it'll be okay because I got to experience that emotion with her. The devotion and care. A shortened lifetime with her is better than a lifetime without her. When the grief passes, she'll be okay. She'll find a way to go on, and that's all I'd want for her."

"That's you, Erico." I turn away from my parents, from his parents, and from him. "Not me. A little bit of happiness to endure a lifetime of pain and heartache isn't worth it. I won't do that to her, or to myself."

I make it down the hall before he speaks again. "You talk like you're certain you'll die early. You really planning on spending an entire lifetime, living to old age, all with these barriers between you and her?"

Before turning, I answer, "They didn't know they were

going to die. It takes one freak moment. A bullet, a car accident, a fire. Anything can happen."

"Then you'll live your life in fear of losing her without allowing yourself to experience what you two can be."

So be it.

I walk away.

22

YASMINE

There's two other women in the small boutique that Erico's private shopper brought us to, and they're loud, squealing over the numerous, lavish gowns and laughing with the shop's employees. It's the total opposite demeanour of Ariella and me. I've been allowing the private shopper, Lia, to lead.

As we move around the store, Ariella's eyes get wider and wider, reminding me of the day she and Della came into my family's lives, when they entered Dad's mansion for the first time with pure joy and amazement in their expressions. They and their mother had been living in a small, rented apartment before Dad burst into their lives.

Right up until the accident, Ariella remained in the shadows, watching from afar, never quite adapting, even as new and expensive clothing brands filled her closet, courtesy of my father. I appreciated that about her because she reminded me of myself.

"What about this one?" Lia pulls on a silver dress the three of us pass by. It's slimming, which is something I did tell her I preferred. "It'll look great with your colouring."

She points out a few more dresses for me, and then works on Ariella, and we both only nod, taking her advice since she has so much more knowledge about this stuff than us.

Of the three dresses, she's suggested, I like them all but skip over the silver to instead try on a plain black one with long, draping sleeves that mingle with the waterfall train. The neck cuts into a V, but not too low. It's slimming and beautiful in an ethereal, fantasy gown kind of way.

Lia *oob*s and *aw*s and Ariella gives me a thumbs up before I try on the second one. This one, a light teal, with a low dipping back but straight neckline that connects to the off-shoulder straps. The bodice is a tight silk with cut outs framing my side. More skin than the black dress but in a way that's sexy. It's slimmer too, less of a train, falling straight to the floor with a slit going partially up my right leg, ensuring an easier time walking.

This is the one.

And when I exit the changing room, the expression on both their faces agree with me. Ariella stands, her hand stroking over the gown's silk as she grins, nodding. She quickly types on her phone and then shows me the screen.

CALADIN WILL LOVE THIS ONE.

I scowl, but not at her kind words. More at the thought of him and his approval when I'm only choosing this for me.

She laughs and pulls her phone back to type a new sentence:

NEVER MIND THEN. WELL, I LOVE THIS ONE.

I beam. "Better." And to Lia, I state, "This one for sure."

She claps her hands together, smiling with glee. "Perfect choice. The black was stunning but this one..." She whistles.

"Mr. Rossi is a lucky man and his heart will restart when he sees you in it."

A sigh works at my throat. Somehow, it's always about him. Ariella doesn't miss my look and with another laugh, she enters the changing room. Now it's her turn to try on the handful of Lia's suggestions.

She exits first in a forest green dress, which really makes her bold hair pop. She mentioned earlier Erico enjoying that colour most too.

Then it's a red one, which only clashes with her hair, so that quickly goes into the discard pile. A pink one follows with the same fate. But when Ariella next comes out in a simple V-cut sparkling dress that's somewhere between a blue and a silver, *I* feel like I've swallowed my tongue and I'm not even attracted to the woman.

"Damn." I stand, pacing around her to scan the simple back with straps that criss-cross over her shoulders. "You're going to show me up." Not that I mind. If she takes all the attention, no one will care about me and I can slip into the background.

She smiles and twirls to study herself in the mirror, her hands skating down her sides. With every second passing, her grin grows and grows and I'm struck with how *happy* she looks. Despite the arranged marriage—even if she's the one who volunteered for it—she embraced it. She's embrac*ing* being the wife to a mob boss with all the poise I could only dream of. When she goes home later, she'll tell Erico about her shopping trip, who's so in love with her, that he'll anticipate tomorrow night.

She's happy. And I think a part of me is jealous. If my clenched teeth are any indication.

Not that I want that with Caladin; I don't. I think.

I don't know what I want anymore and it hits me then. While standing in an expensive boutique's changing room, with my life having been altered in every possible way over the past few months, I'm not *unhappy*. But I'm also not happy and have no idea what it'll take to make me so.

To Lia, she mouths, *This one*, so Lia gathers up all the dresses we both discarded and returns them to the staff lingering nearby. Once we're both dressed in our regular clothes, Lia takes our chosen dresses to the counter with two black credit cards—Erico's and Caladin's.

"Go have fun now." She waves us out the door. "These will be on your husbands' accounts, and I'll have them dropped off by this afternoon along with some shoes I believe will go well with each of these."

Husbands. I glance at Ariella, wondering how she took to Lia's statement, but Ariella's already turning for the door, where both her bodyguard and Raj wait for us. Inside the condo, it's easy to pretend we're merely roommates. Or at school, where the *Famiglia* doesn't exist.

So if it's striking when Lia states it, what's going to happen tomorrow when I'm in front everyone?

Raj and Ariella's bodyguard, who I finally learn is named Jack, accompany us to a cute coffee shop down the road from the dress store. They each take a table, one by the entrance and one close to us, sipping on bottles of water and looking entirely out of place amongst the quaint décor, studying students, and artsy writers who are all furiously working on their laptops.

The mocha I've ordered is hot and steamy, and I lick the foam, willing it to cool down faster. I need coffee in my system and soon, to help calm my rattled nerves, leftover from yesterday.

My phone vibrates on the table, garnering my attention. Caladin?

I glance back up, trying to convince myself I'm *not* upset that it's not Caladin. "Basically."

I hesitate, uncertain how much to tell her. The connection we've had so far, when she was in the medical centre seemed different. Both of us clinging to some form of companionship away from our sisters. Unspoken agreements that our friendship—if it could be called that—would be downplayed. Like it didn't even exist. Dad would have killed me if he knew I was sneaking off to see her. Rozelyn too, maybe.

Now, we're both wed to mobsters within the same organization, living in the same city, away from our older sisters. It's strange that of all people, that between Della and her, it's Ariella who ended up in New York too. Like deep down, years ago, I formed a bond with her because my instincts sensed it'd lead to this moment.

"Caladin and I kissed."

She stares, tipping her head and mouthing, *And?*

"It was our first one." Lowering my voice so no one can hear, I explain, "Since this marriage was sprung on us both, and we both don't want it, so we haven't done...that. Or anything."

Her brows furrow until realization settles and she makes an O with her mouth as she types.

> With Erico, he didn't think he wanted a marriage either because his parents were his example. But then he came to want ME and learned how to be a husband, just like I learned to trust.

Her situation is vastly different than mine and there's a list of reasons why but her mention of their relationship provides an out, so I ask, "Tell me about how you and Erico ended up getting to where you are."

She types on her phone for a *long* time before handing it to me. Every single word is packed with an emotion I could only imagine how she'd verbally tell me. She disclosed her infertility and the challenges associated, but it seems like she found a good man in a world full of evil. Even with Erico not wanting to spend time with his wife and not planning on a regular marriage, he fell for her.

What would happen if I gave Caladin a shot?

Resting the phone on the table beside my mocha, I take a small sip, composing my insides until I manage a calm and rational response. "It's nice you found your happy ending in a place, with a person, you didn't think you could. Insane looking back and offering yourself in place of Aurora. Della must have been livid."

She wrinkles her nose and giggles, shaking her head and then wagging her hand back and forth. There's a lot of response in her actions and I wait for her typed explanation.

ARIELLA

> It was a fight at first. She thought I was certifiably insane for doing so. But eventually respected my decision. Erico loves me, so she's good with it now.

I bet. All Della ever wanted was to do right by her sister. In many ways, Rozelyn and Della are the same because most of Rozelyn's actions were to keep Dad away from me.

ARIELLA

You should come over tomorrow. Let's get ready together.

There's a tinge of hope in her expression. A gentle lip bite as her teeth scrape over the bottom one. A mending of what could be between us with a bit of effort to remain in the present and not the past.

"I'd love that."

23

CALADIN

My fingers work at the tie again, readjusting it while I shift from foot to foot. Fix my sleeves, check my buttons and—

"Will you fucking stop?" Erico's hand lands on my shoulder, causing me to flinch. "You're making *me* anxious."

I scowl and shoulder him off. "I hate dressing up, that's all."

"Uh huh. You mean, in a suit similar to the one you wear every other day? Sure it has nothing to do with Yasmine about to come down those stairs?"

I glance at the staircase leading toward Erico and Ariella's room, where she and Yasmine are getting ready for the forced event. Guess their shopping trip yesterday went so well, Ariella invited her over to get ready together. Yasmine and I drove from Manhattan to the Hamptons and will be headed to the country club, only minutes away, in separate vehicles from Erico and Ariella, so we can escape on our own terms.

"And what do you think will happen?" I glare, daring him to speak the words I presume he will.

He chuckles, leaning against the staircase post as he glances at the time listed on his phone. "Well, seeing her all done up changes shit."

"Maybe for you."

This is oddly similar to a few weeks ago when Erico's parents insisted the organization meet Ariella formally. I drove over with them and witnessed Erico choke on his own spit when Ariella came down the staircase. He was already a goner for her, giving me endless ammo to torment him with.

This time, we're standing in the same place, only now waiting for two women instead of one. I sigh at how changed my life's become in a short span of time.

Slow steps echo through the house and Ariella appears at the top of the stairs, beaming in a sparkly blue-silver dress that reminds me of a waterfall.

Erico pushes off the railing and exactly like the last time, he's watching her as though he's seconds away from dropping to his knees to worship her. Fool's completely besotted.

"Damn, *la mia sirena*, you're beautiful."

With a snort, I lean against the far wall and cross my arms as I wait for her to finish walking down. If she's ready, presumably Yasmine will be soon too.

As soon as Erico has his arms around his wife, she finds me by the wall, her eyes promising mischief. This woman's betting I'll fall in love with Yasmine in time, so no doubt, she pulled out every damn stop upstairs. Unfortunately for her, she has no idea she's running in a race she's already lost.

When steps echo again, I lock my gaze on the bottom step, fighting the urge to look up. To make my point to the couple who's staring at me, both with identical *aha* expressions. Ariella, I can ignore because she's too pretty to hit, but my cousin's fair game. Hell, maybe he'll get two. One for each of them.

One, two, three, four, five. I sigh. I look up.

All that shit people say about the ground falling away... yeah, I'm not steady, even leaning against the wall. I want to stand straight, to get a better view, but fuck if I'm stuck. Stuck and unable to move as every part of my body goes numb with electricity. Heavy and weighted as the absolute fucking realization smacks me in the face.

Yasmine descending the marble staircase in a teal dress, a colour bolder than I've yet to ever see her in. I wish I could describe it in detail, but words aren't working. It's just... gorgeous. *She's* gorgeous. Her long black hair is twisted on top of her head in some sort of fancy braid I'm assuming Ariella had a part in creating.

"Fucking Christ."

I don't realize I've spoken, or that I've finally shoved off the wall, or that I've even approached the staircase until my cousin speaks. "Yasmine, you look lovely. Doesn't she, Caladin?"

Lovely is too nice of a word for what is going through my head. Too tame.

Yasmine reaches the bottom step, which makes her a bit taller than me. She's studying me with the same intensity as I am her, but there's an uncertainty in her gaze. A vulnerability which has no place. She's hoping I'll speak, but I can't with my tongue knotted in the back of my throat.

My hands feel fucking sweaty. *Sweaty.* What is wrong with me?

"Wow."

Hey, I spoke.

"Wow yourself." She smiles, relieved. "You clean up nice."

I swallow, lick my lips, blink. Anything to wake up my senses. There's never been a time, a woman, who's made me lose all functionality.

For once, Erico helps by sending a sharp swat to my chest as he takes Ariella's arm in his and starts walking away. "We'll be in our car. Come out when you're ready. Good to know how close I am to losing the bet."

With him gone, Yasmine steps down beside me, taking the place Erico last was. She smiles again before trailing them, and right when my brain had a fucking shot at working again, the back of her dress comes into view.

It's low. Like ungodly low. Like men will stare at her low and I will—

Do nothing, remember. Nothing. She's free. We put on a show tonight and then she can do whatever, whoever, she wants.

No.

"Coming?" She glances over her shoulder, her red-painted lips pulled into a small smirk, like my little tiger, my goddess, she knows exactly the effect she's having on me.

Before she's too far, I reach for her, pulling her by her elbow. She spins right into my chest with a small gasp. Her heels put her only an inch below me, and I hate how easy she'd be to kiss.

How much I *want* to again.

"Yasmine, wow."

"You said that already."

"It's the only thing I can. Damn, *piccola tigre*, you're a vision in this dress."

"Just in the dress, huh?"

She's joking. Making light of the situation, and I need to play along for both our sakes. She's beautiful, sure, but this is nothing more than her in jeans. She's the same woman she was this morning. Yesterday.

"Basically," I reply, taking advantage of her lightheartedness, but the lie burns my throat. It's not only the dress. She's simply less ignorable in it. "We should go." I offer my arm and she takes it. "We'll meet anyone important. There will be music and food.

We'll snack, dance if they force us too, and then head home. Sound good?"

"Sounds perfect."

Outside, Erico and Ariella are in their car, talking to each other, but when he spots us exiting the mansion, he waves and points down the road, indicating they're going to start driving. Somehow, I get the sense he's ensuring Yasmine has no one else but me when we arrive, so she can't cling to Ariella for escape.

I lead her to my car, opening the passenger door and helping her into the low vehicle. Her hand is warm—warmer than usual, and I hate noticing it. By the time I'm seated, I'm willing this night to end.

"Will we be meeting your parents there finally?" she asks in a quiet voice, like she somehow knows the answer already but needs the confirmation.

Her question was bound to come up eventually. Without the emotional entanglement between us, it's been easy to pretend we're truly only roommates, but nothing changes the diamond ring on her finger. That she's my wife, and with that, comes the introduction to the in-laws. Which means, it's fair she's wondering.

"Dead."

"Oh. I'm sorry."

"Don't be. No different than yours, right?" I flinch at my own crassness, backpedalling. "Sorry. Meant we're in the same situation."

From my peripheral vision, I catch her watching me. "When did it happen?"

"When I was ten. My parents went everywhere together. Did everything. My father had business one day, and Mother went with him, as she often did. The club was attacked. They were both shot."

My hands tighten around the wheel. I've recounted the

story so many times, it doesn't hurt anymore. It's factual; something unable to be changed, but it's a welcome reminder of what *not* to do with Yasmine. Needed after I almost lost myself in the mansion.

For her own protection, we can't become my parents. Addicted to one another to the point death is inevitable.

"That's really sad, Caladin, I'm sorry. At least they loved one another. That's uncommon in this life, right?"

Instead of answering, I glance toward her. Her hands are pinching the material of her gown, and she's staring down at her lap with a strange expression. "Yeah," I finally say, driving the car around the next corner. "Guess it is."

"What happened to you after?"

"Erico's parents took me in. My aunt and uncle raised me. It was different than my own parents, my old life, but I appreciate what they did. It made Erico and I closer, like brothers. Already, we were spending a lot of time together, but that forged the bond even greater. Wasn't the same, but having him helped."

Thankfully, the venue comes into view, ending this conversation, and I park behind Erico's black sports car. It has a name even I can't pronounce because mister racer enjoys all the fancy cars.

"Ready?" I ask, knowing full well I'm not.

"Do I have a choice?"

Touché. I get out of the car and walk around to help her. She gives me her hand, lifting herself from the low car until she's standing close to me. Her breasts a breath away from touching my chest. So close, the dusting of colour framing her eyes becomes bolder. Black and teal blended together as a subtle nod to the dress.

"Ariella really did a number on you," I tell her without thinking, contradicting every reminder I gave myself on the drive.

She touches her hair. "Yeah, took way too long, but she's good."

"It was well worth the wait." It's the truth, and I'd be cruel to tell her a lie.

The moment we enter the venue, people are on us. Thankfully, Erico manages to keep most of the attention, people sucking up to their boss, but a few slip by. Distant uncles and other businessmen we're partnered with. People I don't care for until finally, I spot someone I would like around; a staff member balancing a silver tray of champagne flutes.

Happily, I take two, pressing one into Yasmine's waiting hand. "Trust me. You'll want this. It'll make this bullshit quick and painless." Well, quick*er*, but I skip that tidbit.

The next hour consists of cycling through the room, introducing Yasmine to everyone. Most act surprised, considering the marriage happened without a ceremony they were present for. The details remain at a minimum, which is Erico's choice. He doesn't want the capos aware of the Seven.

When someone demands a second ceremony they can all attend, Yasmine stiffens, so I leave it as a mere "maybe," with every intention for that to be a definitive "no."

"Please don't force me down the aisle," she says harshly beneath her breath. "It'll seem so real then."

In another world, that would hurt.

"I won't," I promise because the thought of living this farce of a marriage yet again sounds painful on another level.

Finally our cycle ends with Erico and Ariella, who break away from the couple they're speaking to. Yasmine subtly separates herself from me and moves closer to Ariella, her head down like I can't notice.

One of our distant uncles shoves into the group, placing himself between Yasmine and me. He staggers, an obscene scent of whisky pouring off him. His large meaty hand goes for

Yasmine's waist, who tries to disentangle herself, shooting a panicked look toward me. Immediately, I slide between them, pushing my drunken uncle away, taking Yasmine myself.

"Sorry," I say smoothly, "but I don't share."

He cackles. "Of course not, my boy." The same meaty hand slaps me on the back. "Since you've deprived us of a wedding, how 'bout a first dance?" He gestures to the centre of the room, and people nearby who overheard his suggestion begins chanting, "Dance! Dance! Dance!"

Yasmine's face whitens, her teeth scraping over her bottom lip. I could probably get us out of this. After all, Erico got married in Montreal with only the Corsettis and myself in attendance, and no one bothered them.

Instead, I offer my palm to her and the crowd's encouragement shifts into full cheers. Even Erico joins in, winking as Yasmine places her hand in mine and lifts her chin, the anxiety melting off her in waves.

"It'd be my pleasure," she murmurs.

The crowd parts for us, and then a song starts. Some traditional wedding song because clearly the family is making their point. In the centre of the room, with one hand on her hip, fingers fiddling with the edge of the dress's low backing and her heated skin, the other wrapped around her other hand, I move, spinning her into a traditional dance.

Her brow hikes. "He dances."

"Told you I do."

"Why didn't you argue with him?" She nods over my shoulder. "You could have easily gotten us out of this."

"Yes." No point in lying. With my hand on her back, I propel her closer, deleting any space between us. "But consider me old-fashioned and agreeing with them. It's criminal we've never had a first dance and since this event is the start of so many more, this is simply one of many we'll end up doing."

That part's a half-lie because after Erico was born, pretty sure his parents never danced together again.

She lets the subject go with another pass of the floor. Movement makes her slim dress flare just a little and I find myself up to the challenge, making our twirls faster. At one point, I swear I also catch the hint of her smile.

A part of me wants to make it grow as much as another part wants to destroy it. Destroy the lightness before it can fester and taunt me with horrendous ideas.

Toward the end of the song, as though my family fucking despises me, they begin another chant. "Kiss! Kiss! Kiss! Kiss! Kiss! Kiss! Kiss!"

I groan, smirking. "Fuckin' drunk Italians. They're incorrigible."

I'm sure Yasmine will pull away and not allow this farce to continue, so colour me fucking surprised when she doesn't. When, for the second time this evening, the ground falls away. "For the show."

With her permission, I bring us to a stop in the centre of the room and drop my hands, instead cupping her face. Her dark eyes expand as I move in, hesitating at the last second, giving her an out I have no desire to grant. The single wish I'll deny her because I'm a selfish fucker who desires her and despises what she can be for me.

It's meant to be the brush of lips, a barely-there kiss to appease my family, but the moment I taste her, feel her, my plan alters. Everything inside me releases, unleashing pent-up frustrations and desires I'm battling.

She was correct about the kiss in the gym. It was me making a point, mixed with a bit of my own cravings. The distance between us has been great, but call it curiosity. I had to know, even once, what she tasted like. Felt like. Kissed like.

That was the gym, though. This...this isn't me making a point to anyone but my family. To appease them.

At least, that's what I tell myself.

Our kiss deepens, her lips parting, tongue meeting mine, and then, like that somehow woke her up, she jerks her mouth away, breaking the kiss. She pants in the half-inch between us, eyes darkening in confusion. Her hands drop from my shoulders, angling away for escape.

Before anyone spots her distress, I stretch my arms out dramatically and face the crowd. "There. Now you can all fuck off."

As soon as we're near Erico and Ariella, she's dragging Ariella off into the direction of the bathrooms. Ariella glances back with a sheepish look.

Erico glances from them, to the room's centre, then to me. "Well. That was some show."

"A show is all it was."

"*Right.*" He drags the word out. "I'm really enjoying this denial thing you're doing, cuz."

"Fuck off." I stalk toward the bar for a drink stronger than champagne, chugging it in the time Yasmine's hiding. When she returns, we're fucking leaving. We did our jobs, showed our faces. Gave them a dance *and* a kiss. Now they can leave us alone.

I'm two shots in when I sense her. Some-fucking-how, I know it's her in that damn ethereal dress before her hand brushes along my back as she sidles up beside me.

"Careful now. Keep doing that and I'll be the one driving us home."

When did her voice become so sexy? And why, when she says home, do I enjoy the way it sounds?

Why am I staring at my wife like if I look away, I'll never get this opportunity again?

"Let's go." I wrap my hand around hers to drag her from the room. A few people call out, but until we're safely outside, I don't stop.

"You're in a sour mood," she mutters as we climb into my car.

"Just tired. Ready to end this day."

"You and me both."

24
YASMINE

We don't speak for the rest of the drive. The entire two hours from the Hamptons. Normally, a three-hour drive, but his heavy foot got us home in record time. Whatever got into Caladin, I want nothing to do with it.

So when we finally enter his condo, I kick off the heels, my feet thankful for the reprieve, and immediately start toward the bedroom to end this day. Three steps in, his fingers wrap my wrist and he tugs me back to his side. An argument bubbles but is popped the second I catch his expression. He's...sad, almost. I didn't think Caladin could even show this emotion.

"Before you go to bed, can we talk?"

Even if I wanted to, I can't deny that request. Not with his despondent tone. I head for the couch instead of the bedroom. He doesn't follow; instead, he goes to the kitchen and pulls out two glasses and a bottle of something amber.

He hands me one, but I don't sip it. When I expect him to sit, he instead stands across from me, staring into his own glass.

"It's been clear from the beginning neither of us wanted

this arrangement. You feel trapped, this being yet another thing out of your control. You were robbed of choosing your own partner." His eyes flash up from his glass, but only to take a lengthy swig that looks more pained than comforting. "When I told you, you could find someone outside this marriage to spend your nights with—" Another chug, emptying two-thirds of the glass, and he does so with his mouth barely screwing up from the taste. "I skipped over my reasoning. My parents were so in love, Yasmine. Look up the word in the dictionary, and I swear you'd find a picture of them. They were addicted to one another. In the car, I explained she did everything with him—that's why. One day, it went badly. If she didn't love him so much...if she didn't insist on going with him, I'd still have a mother."

My grip grows weak and tighter around the glass all at the same time as his buried pain rises. It's heavy, his shoulders lowering, his earlier smile fading to a point, it's difficult to imagine it ever returning.

"At ten-years-old, I was an orphan. As I got older and learned that marriage would be eventually in my future, I vowed not to love my wife."

Oh. I sense where this is going, even before his next breath.

"It's not fair to either of us if my job gets you killed because of our emotions. And if there's a child—" He stops, licks his lips, blinks. "I mean, luckily, I'm not Erico. An heir isn't mandatory, but if *you* wanted a child one day, and we...just so you could get pregnant, well...if there's a child, they don't deserve the same fate I had, losing us both. And that is why I'm fine with the distance between us. Why I don't *want* there to be anything in this union."

But the kiss is the point I want to make. Not tonight's, but the one from the gym. That wasn't from pressure; that was all us. All him. A momentary lapse of judgement.

I feel for him though. I truly do, as someone who lost a parent. *Two, technically.* But Mom when I was younger. Not as young as he was, and I still had Dad's love to fall back on...but to a point, I understand. It makes me appreciate Caladin more, and my guilt eases. Guilt for taking him away from his duty as a husband, when in truth, that was his plan the entire time.

"That makes sense," I manage when I realize he's waiting for a response. "Thanks for telling me that. So friends, I guess?" We've had a similar conversation before, but this time seems... *more.* A greater understanding of each of our reasonings, versus in the beginning when my hatred, anger, and annoyance ruled, and I didn't consider his own feelings at all.

"Friends," he agrees with a sad smile. His eyes scan my face and then down my body, landing for a second on my chest and following the line of my dress. My body grows hot when I think I spot regret, and then he repeats, "Friends."

I rest my unfinished drink on the table and stand, wiping my suddenly damp hands on the expensive dress. With a tip of my head and a murmur, I explain, "I'm going to shower and go to bed. Class in the morning. Night."

"Night." His dejected voice follows me down the hallway.

Once safely in the bedroom—our bedroom—I shut the door and lean on it. Something shifted between us tonight, but I can't figure out what. Can't determine if it's a good or bad thing.

Only that it's a thing.

~

I toss and turn. Toss and turn again, and Caladin still hasn't come to bed. It's well past midnight. I wonder why he hasn't, and why I'm still up. The curtain's drawn, the bathroom light on, so it's not that.

No, it's the feeling of being lost. Of mixed desires. Of a confusion I don't understand.

I haven't heard him leave the condo, but maybe he had. I roll to my feet and pace out of the room to check—*only* to check.

He's seated where I left him, completely in the dark. His suit is more rumpled than before, his tie half undone. His legs are spread and his head tipped back against the back of the couch. In his hand is an empty glass, balanced on his knee. The bottle from earlier half-empty on the table in front of him.

I take a step forward, the hardwood cracking beneath my feet, and Caladin's upright in a second, his hand reaching for his hip where I presume his weapon to be.

"Yasmine?" His voice is thick with sleep.

"Yeah, just me." I shift into the strip of moonlight, so he can see me better. "Can't sleep. Realized you never came to bed."

"I'm right here."

"I see that." I tip forward onto my toes, feeling very awkward all of a sudden. Seriously, what did I expect from coming out here? "Well, I guess I'll head off again."

"Wait," he calls. "Come sit."

After a long look to the cushion beside him, I do, bringing my bare legs beneath me, curling my arms around them. I'm not cold, but I'm also not warm.

Caladin notices—because he always notices—and he leans forward to remove his coat. He hands the warm article to me, his heat and scent clinging to the fine material. Made worse when I drape it over my body and practically hug it.

"Thanks."

"No problem."

It's silent and I drop my head to the couch, gazing at him as he stares straight at the TV. Words evade me, and I'm unsure how to act, but it's comfortable like this.

After a few moments of quiet, he asks, "What's keeping you up?"

"Not sure. Busy mind."

"Is being out here helping?"

Actually...yes. "A bit," I answer. "I need sleep because of classes tomorrow, but some part of me doesn't want to."

He shifts slightly, rubbing his palms on his thighs. "How's that going, by the way? I can't find anything on Gene—his location, nothing—but I've been told no one's seen him. But other than what happened the other day, do you like it? The school?" Hope tinges his tone, making my stomach flip. Despite everything, he's *trying* to not make this experience completely shitty.

I nod into the couch. "Being in class again feels right. The campus is pretty. Almost easy to forget I'm in New York." At some point, I think I'd like to explore my new home, but I'd rather someone guide me around because they want to. Caladin would do it out of obligation. Raj would because he's paid to. Ariella's too new to the city herself and already stated she's barely been outside Erico's property.

Turns out, I need a friend.

"That's good," he says in a tone that makes me think he's being truthful. "It's good you're finding some happiness here, even if..." He trails off, a nakedness in his gaze. After a throat clear, he repeats, "Even if," and never expands.

"Yeah," I agree, filling the space with a response that only makes half-sense.

My gaze scans the room, the large flatscreen across from us, and then to the mobster beside me. I wonder when the last time the TV was on, if he's ever here in the evening to enjoy it. At home, before Dad's chaos, watching movies was one of my favourite pastimes. While my friends enjoyed clubbing, I preferred a night in.

Something about that concept of freedom, I suppose.

Hitting the clubs isn't freedom. It's another form of entrapment. Forced to dress a certain way, act a certain way, go out with the goal of fun, but that's not my definition of fun. Fun is exploring. Learning. New experiences. Sure, movies aren't the best way to go about it, but the imaginary fantasy worlds producers invent are close enough. Or documentaries revealing facts. Movies taking place in different countries and cultures. In many ways, the fiction on screen is the most adventure my life would ever allow for. I dreamed of being able to get away from it all and explore, like the characters on TV do.

"Do you have the controller?"

"You mean the remote?"

I roll my eyes, reaching my palm toward him. "You know what I mean. Give it."

He does, and the room bathes in a glow from the TV. I flick through the familiar TV apps until finding what I'm searching for, and then put on a classic horror movie. The movie loads right as the villain slices one of the victims' necks. With the comforting sight of gore, I settle deeper into his warm jacket and do the most unwise thing ever before classes, and stay up later, watching movies.

Caladin's eyes are on me, and after a moment of him staring, I finally meet his gaze, amused. "What?"

"A horror movie, Yasmine? You don't seem like the type."

"There's a lot you don't know about me."

"Fair. Seems you were destined for this life then."

I look away from the screaming and cold-blooded murder again. "What do you mean?"

He gestures toward the screen. "Murder, blood...you realize who you married, right?"

I roll my eyes. "No offence, but you're, like, the least scary mobster I've met."

"There's a lot you don't know about me." He tosses my own words back at me and I can't help but chuckle.

"You once said you're good at tracking. Tell me about that."

He shrugs. "Not much to tell. Just good at hunting people, which makes this Gene situation more unsettling. It's why I was sent for you."

"So, I could very well be wed to someone else then." If someone else had showed up in White Rock, they would have made the deal. I'd have a different husband.

Don't think I'd enjoy that.

A deep rumble fills the room, which he coughs away, readjusting like he wasn't just making noise. "Probably not. The Seven made the deal because of my position. If another soldier was sent, he'd probably be dead."

"So sure of yourself." I smirk. "Now, stop talking and enjoy the movie." When I burrow in deeper into the couch, his coat slips off my shoulder. Moving my arm to fix it will mean having to readjust everything, so I either deal with the patch of chill or—

Caladin fixes his coat, covering my entire chest with his scent and warmth.

"Thanks."

"No problem." He faces the screen again. The characters are now hiding in a basement, catching their breath while the murderer stomps over the floor above them. Big mistake on their part. "You know, I can't recall the last time I sat down and watched a movie."

He didn't just say that. "Blasphemy! You better be joking."

"Not at all. I prefer to stay busy. This," he gestures between us and then to his living room, "isn't normal. I bought the TV because the room felt incomplete without one, but honestly, I barely sit around this place at all."

The fact he's constantly on the move being his norm eases

me a bit. His obvious absence in the evenings isn't because of me. Or, at least, solely because of my presence.

"Well, that might be the worst news I've ever heard. We'll have to make movie nights a thing. I'll show you all my favourites."

He's silent for three beats of my heart until murmuring, "I'd like that."

Did we...*wait, what just happened?* So soon after we both gained a new understanding of one another and why we shouldn't hang out past the required times.

"I mean," I backtrack, "when you're free. That's what roommates do. Sometimes, they hang out."

"Of course." His gaze slides away from the screaming on the TV and to me, a smirk pulling at the corner of his lips. "It's a plan."

We settle into a comfortable silence, me buried in his coat and between couch cushions, him inches away, both of us watching the gore on the screen. We look ridiculous from the outside, me in pyjamas, him still in his suit.

After another twenty of screaming, he suddenly speaks. "Can I ask you something and you tell the truth?"

"Sure."

"What's with the lights on when you sleep?"

My eyes slam shut, momentarily hiding the truth. Fuck, he noticed. Then again, I'd be stupid if I thought he wouldn't have.

"Picked up on it the first day," he continues. "By the third, I shut the curtain before I went to bed, but within minutes, you were flailing in bed. Once I opened it again, you calmed."

Given everything he's admitted, I want to be open with him. There's no one else in the world who's aware, other than Rozelyn, and since she's only partially in my life now, I *want* another trusted person. Want that person to be him.

"As long as you don't laugh."

He marks an X over his heart. "On my vows, I promise I won't."

"When I was a kid, my mother always turned on my night-lights before sleep. Kept the monsters away. Not sure why, but it was like that even as a teenager. When other people grew out of nightlights, I never did. It continued right up until she—" On the screen, a victim is stabbed repeatedly and I pull upon the vicious sight to kill the thick emotion. "One day, there was no one to turn on the lights. I don't think it's a fear of the dark, but I can't sleep without light in the room. It reminds me of...her."

Caladin's silent for a moment and while I want to look at him, I don't. Can't. He probably thinks of me as some pathetic person who can't sleep like an adult should. If that's what he's thinking, I'd rather not know.

"That's meaningful, Yasmine. Truly. A pattern only you two shared living on."

I watch the side of his face, checking for the lie. If he is, he's hiding it well.

"Thanks. Does it bother you?"

"Not at all."

His cheek twitches. A lie. But I love that he's hiding it from me. That he'll give up his own comfort for my trauma.

Maybe now...maybe it's time to try. To shut a curtain but leave the bathroom light on. A compromise so he can sleep better.

"Don't ever change that," he continues. "Not unless you want to, and you're ready. There's worst things in the world than sleeping with lights on as an adult. It's fine."

Oh my fucking heart.

We return to not talking. Eventually, the movie fades, and I assume it's ending. But no...it's still on, but the edges are fuzzy. My head feels heavier than before...

Until it doesn't. Until the couch is replaced for something harder and a chill coasts over my body with the missing coat. Gone but then replaced by something hotter.

I blink through the darkness. Caladin's holding me. My head's on his arm, his other beneath my legs. There's a rocking sensation telling me we're walking.

"What...?"

"You fell asleep. It's okay. Go back to sleep. I'm bringing you to bed."

With his command, I do. My eyes flutter shut until the soft bed greets my back, my head on the pillow, his arms being tugged away. He covers me with the duvet and I want to open my eyes. Want to look up at him and watch him, but everything feels so heavy.

Exhaustion is making it so difficult. Difficult and altering, because as Caladin moves away, I swear his fingers linger on my cheek. My collarbone.

He murmurs something I don't catch.

Something that sounds like, "I really wish I could love you, Yasmine."

But no...impossible. Dreamland's already tugged me beneath the darkness, and that's all that was.

25
CALADIN

In the late afternoon of the next day, I'm in the centre of the living room, dressed in only shorts, positioned on my hands and feet, pushing repetitively against the floor when the door opens.

To look at her would involve admitting why I'm here in the first place when I shouldn't be home yet. I should be *far* away from her after last night.

I *liked* the downtime with her. There's very few instances I get to relax and it's certainly nothing I actively try to do, but last night could be the beginning of an addition I'll need to one day purge my body of. When she fell asleep, I'll admit to staring at her for longer than I should have before finally switching off the TV and carrying her to bed before having the most restless sleep of my life.

I remained awake for too long, wondering what my parents were like after they were married. Did they jump into their duties or fight the attraction initially?

After the party, I spent the entire drive back to Manhattan reflecting over them, over us. Telling her about my parents was never in the cards, but after two kisses, I had to stop whatever *this* could be before it got too deep. Before I accidentally hurt her in other ways. Explaining the reasons would be fairer to both of us.

"You're here," she states, but there's another question in her tone: *Why?*

I'm surprised by this too but after being unable to focus on shit today, and with Erico's annoying taunts, I gave up. One of the bartenders was updating me on the week's business and everything he said went right over my head.

According to Erico, I was also pissing him off with my constant pacing. There's a solution for that and it's one I've avoided since bringing Yasmine to New York. An easy healing solution for the energy thrumming in my veins, and once released, I'll be back to my regular, easy self.

Instead of hiding in the gym every night, burning my body past the point of what's healthy, I have a fight set up tonight. Can't fucking wait. The adrenaline will be useful.

"Jesus," she curses, finally gaining my attention. My push-ups slow until I drop to my knees, ending my workout, and reach for a water bottle nearby.

She stares down from a few feet away, an expensive large purse clutched in her hand. She's in a cute sundress that seems too summery for the cool fall temperatures, but what do I know about women's clothing? She looks every bit the rich wife mingled with the focused college student.

I look away, scowling at myself for even noticing these things. "What?"

"You're...here. And," she waves her hand in my direction, "here. And—"

"So you've said."

Her gaze lands on my chest, her expression softening and

right when I have a snide remark prepared, she shakes her head. "Do you do anything other than workout?"

"Nope," I answer as she moves deeper into the condo, dropping her bag on the island. "Prepping for a fight tonight."

She pauses. "A fight? Like...what they show in movies?"

"You don't remember when I mentioned it the first time we went to the gym together? The *Famiglia* has an underground ring, and well, it's fun."

Her lips purse. "To the death or...?"

"Not usually." But sometimes.

"And you have one later today?"

I nod.

"Can I come?"

She wants to see a fight? *Her?* Considering she's the same woman who requested self-defence lessons, this isn't a complete stretch, but still. Underground fighting is dirty. No rules. A lot of chaos. A lot of betting and a ravenous crowd begging for entertainment. It's a dangerous place, one I normally wouldn't consider bringing her to. Not with her fucking doe eyes and jasmine scent that'll lure any man in. Her safety will distract me.

She can remain on the VIP balcony, set aside for the richest of fuckers. With a few soldiers, she'll be safe. Considering where we are, people would know better than to fuck with her, but I wouldn't risk it.

I must take too long to answer because she frowns and turns back around. "Got it. Sorry for asking."

"No, wait." I push to my feet, ready to physically stop her if I have to. "I was thinking over the logistics. You can come."

She smirks over her shoulder, adopting the playful attitude I've come to see as her shield. "Worried about me now? That's sweet. You'd be free if I died."

I get it's a joke, but a flash goes through my head, imagining her dead on the ground. The dirty ground, a pool of blood seeping from her body, her jasmine scent dissipating…*No. Never.* Not as long as I live.

"Don't joke that like." I wipe a hand down my face and turn away, hiding how rattled the thought makes me. How much I despise being affected at all. "We'll leave in a few hours."

"Sounds good. When do we get back to my training?"

Thankful for the topic switch, I turn to reply. "Get changed. We can go right now, if you're up for it."

Fuck me, how her expression brightens. It's the simple things that make her pleased, which makes *not* going out of my way to make her happy a challenge. "You sure you can? Don't want you tired before your big fight."

"Please," I scoff, "all you'll be doing is giving me a warm-up."

"Because the push-ups I walked in on weren't enough?"

"Just get changed."

~

After an intense—for her—workout session, I'm warmed up and she's dead in the passenger seat. Back in the same sundress because she insisted on showering and changing in the gym, replacing her sweaty workout outfit for something cleaner. I almost begged her to remain in the gym clothes rather than this thing showing off her thighs.

Where we're going, men are thirsty for pain, rage, and violence. And Yasmine, my little tiger, looks way too fucking innocent thrown into the mix.

"You will stick by me. You'll be on the VIP balcony away from the pit with soldiers for protection. Yasmine, I swear to fuck, if you even think about moving an inch from where I drop you, you will regret it." My eyes cut to her, to show her how serious I am.

"Careful there, Caladin. You sound like you care."

I shift, hating that she's right. "It's not exactly a place full of sunshine and rainbows. This is for your safety, therefore, let me keep you safe."

I park behind the warehouse-slash-rave *Famiglia*-owned building on the outskirts of Brooklyn. Beside us are two of my soldiers' vehicles, which I recognize. Jonas, because I trust him, and another. Not Elias, the fucker. I debated Raj, but since he's with her all day and will be tomorrow, he needs his rest to remain sharp.

Once parked, I drag her inside and down the single staircase until reaching the Y. A man stands guard at one entrance, and a blast of shouts and cheers come from the other. He nods to me as I pass, leading her toward the VIP balcony.

"Head down, don't make eye contact."

Thankfully with the discreet entrance, we avoid the chaos below. While there's other fights happening tonight, I'm the main attraction. It's a fact. The *Famiglia* Consigliere fighting always draws a crowd and ups the bets.

I take the first doorway and walk down a short curve until reaching the section overlooking the large pit below, where the crowd is already rowdy. Staff collect large-sum bets as cash is flashed around, but up here, there's only two others—the men I've ensured would be.

Yasmine's staring below with no apparent signs of fear. Why do I like her interest so much? She has the hint of a smile, and I wonder if she'll still be smiling by the end of the night.

"Sir," the soldier closest to us greets. His gaze settles on Yasmine by my side, her attention still on the crowd. "And ma'am."

That draws her attention, jolting at the two soldiers.

"Thomas." I point to the first, and then, "Jonas." I place her between them, in the centre of the balcony and stare meaningful at her, not speaking until I've garnered her complete attention. "Stay. I mean it. Down there, they'll rip you apart. Even when the fight's over, I'll come get you myself."

She nods, pressing her lips together before glancing over my shoulder. "Is it wrong to say this is kinda fun?"

I groan. Why is this woman so fucking perfect? "Not at all. If you stomach tonight, maybe you can come more often. Take notes. You might learn something." I release her to flick her nose playfully. "If I win, what's my prize?"

"If?" She latches onto the single word, her brow lifting a fraction. "You doubt yourself, Rossi?"

"Oh, I'll win, but I'm trying to be humble." Besides, nothing's certain and there's never been someone to distract me before. Sometimes Erico accompanies me, but I'm not worried about his safety. "I ask again: what do I get for winning?"

"Anything you want."

Her innocence seeps out in that statement because if I was another man, wanting other things from his wife, there's a million things I could demand. A flash of Yasmine naked, bound in our bed, tied by her wrists and ankles as I drip hot wax—

My eyes flick to her full lips. I can't want this...her. I shouldn't want anything to do with her, especially considering we're at such a good place, but fucking Christ, all I can do is recall yesterday. Her flavour, her scent, it'd be a fucking prize for winning.

I touch her cheek before sharing a long look with my men. "If there's a hair on her head gone..." The threat remains unfinished, but the threat's implied of what'll happen if some crazy fucker from below manages to sneak up here and go near her. "Wish me luck, *piccola tigre*," I say in parting.

"*Bonne chance!*"

For her, I will win, and I'll make tonight my greatest show ever.

~

Three fights later, which I've remained on the edges for, it's finally my turn. My fight's the final of the night. The encore everyone's been anticipating.

From the shadows, I follow the ring leader into the cement room's centre as he announces my name to the deafening crowd. Over the whoops and screams, I seek her out. She waves and grins, so eager. My entire body tingles at seeing her up there *for me*, her cheers the only ones mattering.

Focus. Fuck, she will be a distraction I need to forget about.

The announcer calls my opponent's name, and I refix the tape around my fists and retie my shorts, ensuring nothing's too tight or restricting. The crowd grows louder when another guy, one larger than me, enters the space, a mean grin ruining his face.

He's not someone I recognize, which means, new blood. New blood stupid enough to test the *Famiglia* champion. That's okay, though. Means there's a better show for the crowd, and Yasmine will really get her time's worth.

"Rossi." He growls, approaching. "Can't wait to tear you the fuck apart."

I don't reply because the whole trash-talking thing is a waste of time.

The announcer glances between us, reciting rules he's done millions of times, and I've heard thousands. "No weapons. First knocked out wins. You die, well, then you die."

I won't hit hard enough to kill him. Not tonight. Not unless he does something to piss me off. Not in front of Yasmine because she doesn't need to see that shit.

The fucker follows my gaze, his lip curling alongside his hungry expression. "Nice catch, Rossi. She the winner's prize? Because lemme tell you, I could really use a sweet thing like that riding my cock tonight."

Red covers my vision. It's not even jealousy. It's anger that *he* thinks she's available for his pleasure. She'll be going home with one man tonight—me.

"Move your eyes or you lose them."

Surprisingly, he does, grinning at me. "Jealous, lover boy? Lemme guess, that's your wife? News travelled that some bitch finally strapped you down."

The announcer is devouring every verbal lashing, dollar signs within his gaze. "Good luck, boys." Then his arm drops and he bounces out of the way as we crash together.

My opponent's larger than me, but his movements are messy. He reaches for my upper arms so I duck, shoving a fist into his abs. He grunts and releases me, attempting to spin from my hold, but my shoulder rams into his gut, knocking him to the ground instead. He lands on the cement with a thud and I throw my body down, fists and elbows, with the intent to weaken him wherever and however I can. He rolls quickly though, landing a punch to my ribs I'll likely feel tomorrow.

As he lunges again, I do too. The pain on my side is worse than I thought but not touching it hides a weakness he'd be too pleased to take advantage of. Adrenaline courses through me and I throw myself at him, fist into the underside of his jaw.

It lands with a crack and a roar, causing him to spin, his leg swiping out to trip me. I see it coming, but too late, and the cement ground and my back battle through incredible pain shooting up my spine.

Fuck.

He lunges again, but I kick his thighs, forcing him back a

foot so I can stand. He's actually a skilled competitor, tough, but I refuse to lose.

Not with my girl watching me.

My girl?

A fist lands on the side of my face and immediately, the taste of copper fills my mouth. Blood. Fucker made me bleed because I was too busy dissecting my latest thought.

Fucking knew she'd be a distraction!

The crowd is a feral energy, both sides cheering for both opponents. The bets are higher because so many people have seen me win already, but so many enjoy betting on the day they'll witness me lose.

That won't be today.

I charge, punching him again while moving to trip him, to confuse him. Thankfully, he does exactly as I hoped he would and blocks my punch all to end up on his back. Due to his size, he doesn't move quickly, and now he's getting tired, so before he can escape, I hit him in the face. The cheek, the mouth, the nose, until I see the familiar sight of blood, claiming I'm close to victory.

The crowd gets deafening as the viewers who bet on me winning approach their own financial victory. They're easy to tune out in favour of the win. But there's one voice—one shout —that pierces everything.

His blocks are slower with every hit, and after my next, I look at her. She's grinning as I bleed a man through pure abuse. Violence. She's gripping the railing, leaning so far over for a better view, I'd be concerned if it wasn't for Thomas' hands hovering, ready to catch her before her excitement takes her over the rails.

I blow her a kiss and return to my victory.

One final punch to make my point, and then I crouch so he can hear me over the shouting. "That's what you get for believing you'd be inside my wife's pussy. You're not good enough for the likes of her."

Before the ring leader declares me as the winner, I seal his loss with a wad of spit to the middle of his face. Staff drag my opponent to his feet and away, his swollen eye and blood-filled face glaring as he slumps with their support.

People swarm, the excitement of touching the victor, taking over. Some curse over their financial losses, most are screaming with the thrills. I shove through them all with one goal in mind, and before I disappear into the shadows, I meet her eyes.

My traitorous heart clenches.

26

YASMINE

Sometime between the first hit and the third, I realized Caladin didn't trap me. Not completely. He might have taken a lot of choice away, but did I even have a future? Truly? Dad signed that away a long time ago.

Caladin might have moved me to the U.S. and away from the only home I'd ever known, but Dad did that first. Besides, is New York really that different than Montreal, minus not having Rozelyn? Technology keeps me connected with her.

In many ways, Caladin freed me from the binds restraining me. Binds I didn't even realize were tied around me. Because of him, I'm back in school. He's given me the freedom to just *be*. Has willingly been training me to defend myself. He's...a nice guy. Not the mobster or even a monster. Not cold-hearted or an asshole.

Another man wouldn't have allowed me to be here. This is freedom in a form I never expected to find. *This*, what I'm witnessing, is something I didn't know to search for. The feeling of not worrying about my actions, of not wondering who'll make the decision for me.

To be free is to have experiences and this...this is a fucking experience. A bloodthirsty, ravenous experience. When I asked to accompany him, it was mere curiosity, and when we arrived and I saw the living, breathing chaos below, I believed I made a mistake. That whatever I was about to witness would have me running for the hills.

The first two fights were a bit nerve-wracking. They were so rough and tough to watch, but every time I looked away, it was only for a second before my attention, unable to help itself, was back on the vicious fight.

I like it here. A place where humanity lets themselves go. Unleashes the anger, the hatred, the thrills onto one another.

And then it was Caladin's fight and he emerged from the room's edges without fear. Lights skimmed over his bare abs, the tape on his hand, the shorts and shoes his only articles of clothing. He seemed completely relaxed, like he's done this over and over.

When the fight started, I forgot how to breathe. At first, out of fear he'd be injured, but then because he stole my breath with every hit, every carefully dodged movement. Like a well-orches-trated dance, I was enamoured by every step. Him in the gym is *nothing* compared to the pure force, the power I was witnessing.

I don't even remember when I started yelling, or leaning over the railing. At some point, one of Caladin's men got closer, which probably meant I was leaning too far over the railing.

It was exhilarating. Thrilling.

Addicting.

Caladin is swarmed the second he's declared the winner. I want to be down there, cheering him on, but there'd be no chance of leaving this balcony with the two soldiers behind me. Luckily, he disappears toward the doorway quickly, so I push away from the railing, staring at the door, waiting for him to appear.

A moment later, he does, and nothing else is in my head other than glee as I rush at him and throw myself into his arms. Sweat and blood from his body dirty my dress but I don't care. Legs clamping his hips, arms wrapping his neck, I cling. His own tighten around my waist as he regains stability. Then, I wonder if he's injured, and I've just hurt him more.

Other than blood and sweat, he seems okay. I catalogued every hit he received, and study the side of his face since the bruise forming seems to be the worst.

"You won!" It's a dumb statement, but I have nothing else to say because I don't know what's expected. I reach up and stroke a hand through his damp hair, pushing strands away from his face.

His hold doesn't loosen, nor does he put me on my feet, but his hands drift dangerously close to a place they shouldn't be. Dark eyes scan my face, a strange look in his expression, which he quickly shakes away, throwing me one of his usual cocky grins.

"I had no doubt I would. Which means, I have a prize to collect." His eyes flick to my lips.

He did that earlier.

He wants to kiss me.

I want to kiss him.

A kiss doesn't mean love. A kiss means the energy coursing through the room is too electrifying to ignore.

I'm throwing every excuse at myself.

So I throw myself instead. Tumbling, freefalling, shattering into what might be a mistake. What could be the start of everything I'm running from.

With my hand on the back of his neck, I bring my mouth to his. Or, he kisses me, his hands shifting below my dress, cupping my ass through my panties. His touch feels fucking fantastic—better than anything I've ever felt.

The crowd below goes nuts. The guards behind us, easily ignorable.

My mouth parts, his tongue meets mine, and we battle for dominance. My legs tighten, practically climbing him, his bare abs are sweaty between my thighs and I imagine this in a whole other way.

He spins, shoving me against the cement wall behind us, using it to keep me balanced as he grips my thighs. He kisses me harder, hungrier—angrier.

I feel drunk. The room's energy, the adrenaline from his fight, the lust controlling my logical mind...whatever it is, I don't want this bubble to pop. Everything feels more sensitive when he touches me. Everything feels like more.

Pressing me harder into the wall, his hands weave between mine and he pins them above my head. His kiss drags down my neck, nipping the sensitive skin. The moment he licks my pulse, the moment I come alive, is also the moment reality crashes upon us.

All the boundaries we've placed—shattered—and we both pause. Me: my heart, my breath, my mind as I decide which direction to go. Him: as he pulls back, his eyes wide.

"F-fuck." His voice is thick with apology. "I'm sorry, Yasmine. I-I didn't mean. We were wrapped up in the— sorry."

"It's okay," I whisper, nodding, still deciding if I'm thanking him or not. "We got caught up in the moment."

"Yeah." With slow movements, he unwinds his fingers from mine, one at a time, and even slower, lowers my hands and then my legs to the ground. He maintains a hold on my waist as he redirects me to the door. "We should go."

Neither of us speak until the car. Neither of us know what to do. My lips feel swollen and I want to touch them, but he doesn't need to see the physical evidence of where my mind's at.

My leg muscles are so tightly wound, aching for more. For him to be between them.

Sex doesn't equal love, but I can also respect why he'd pull back. Why I should be grateful he did. If we add sex to the deal, and spend as much time together as we do, it's practically inevitable we'd...I don't even finish the thought.

My sister's words echo in my head. *"Would it be so bad to love your husband?"*

Even *if* I changed my mind, I'm only half the equation. For valid reasons, he craves distance too. It's not a question of desires anymore. It's pure logic. Even if I allowed myself to fall, I'd crash alone because he won't be following me. Therefore, going anywhere with Caladin will simply lead to heartbreak.

Back inside the condo, there's now an awkwardness that needs to fuck off before I go insane. While a part of me is tempted to scamper off and hide in the bedroom and pretend this thing didn't happen, it needs to be mentioned before it worsens.

"Movie?" I offer, half expecting him to say no and half wanting him to.

"Sure. Let me get cleaned up first."

He disappears toward the bedroom and only when I hear the shower do I follow, heading to the closet to get changed. My body is sore from my own workout earlier, and I have no idea how Caladin's still standing at this point.

When the shower turns off, I rush toward the living room again and start scouring through online movies, ensuring I'm away from the bedroom when he comes out, dripping with water, wrapped up in a towel—*For fuck's sake, get a hold of yourself.*

When he appears in the entranceway, my greeting is a forced smile, pretending there isn't a million and one concerns ravaging my brain. He crosses the room and drops onto the couch, his legs spreading lazily as he gazes at the few options I've bookmarked on the TV.

"Pick one?"

"A few. Figured you can make the final choice."

"I trust your judgement. Don't know about you, but I'm starving." He pulls out his phone. "I'll order something. Anything in particular?"

"I trust your judgement," I repeat his own words, enticing a chuckle I enjoy way too much. "Good fight, eh. You, um..." *Fuck that kiss for making this uncomfortable.*

That wasn't a kiss. That was everything.

"You enjoyed watching?"

"Loved it," I admit, my gaze falling to his fists, his bruised knuckles. "It was thrilling. Exciting. The way you won. The power of your hits. Can I come to another?"

"I don't do them often anymore, but yeah. I, um—" His tongue dabs the corner of his mouth; his hand scratching at the back of his neck. "I liked having you there."

We're silent again. Lost in thoughts. In wonder.

"Anyway." I choose the first movie of my bookmarked list. An action one rather than horror, and Caladin lowers his phone to the couch between us.

"Chinese food will be here in twenty."

"Great."

And this *is* great. I think. Great...but precarious.

Tonight began something. Our ending. We'll crash, burn, and will go up in smoke, or we'll explode into fireworks.

Not sure I want to be around to find out which it ends up being.

27

CALADIN

"Let me reiterate," my cousin starts in that annoying know-it-all-tone that grates on absolutely every single one of my nerves. Shreds them up into a neat, little pile. "You took Yasmine to the fighting ring."

"That is what I said, yes." Leaning back, I drum my fingers along the backing of the seat, waiting for him to finish whatever stupid point he's trying to make so we can move this meeting along.

"Last week."

"Also yes."

"And you two mauled each other after that?"

"Why do I tell you anything?" *Considering you make me relive it.*

"In the past week, you've hung out. Gone to the gym and trained together. Watched movies almost every night. Shared a bed. Meals."

"The sharing of the bed isn't a new fact, but yes, you're right on everything else."

Erico leans back, his grin expanding. "Caladin, fucking

admit it already. When will you realize you're falling for your wife?"

I scoff. "We're friends and nothing more. Coming to a mutual agreement and hanging more often means nothing. Roommates do this all the time. Friends of the opposite sex *are* a thing."

"Friends. Man, when will you two stop bullshitting each other?"

"Just because you couldn't handle not having a traditional marriage with *your* wife doesn't mean I can't. Leave it alone, Erico." My tone is final, a dare to my boss to continue his probing.

He leans forward in his desk. "I'm pointing all this out because I care about you. You're building these walls—hell, you both are. Anyone on the outside can see the only thing you two are missing is fucking."

"Is that wrong?"

He doesn't answer.

It's not wrong. If anything, it's given me ample space to think. The fight a week ago was intense, and we both got caught up in the moment. Both of us on edge from the lack of sex we've not been having.

After that one incident, we did fall into a routine, and I hate to admit it, but I love it. Before Yasmine, I'd barely be home most nights. Would remain at the gym or the bars until late enough for me to pass right out and do it all again. Anytime Erico or his father needed a job done, I'd be there. Every weapons trade. Every deal. It was all me. There was a comfort in staying busy. A routine I revelled in having. Always on the move, never sedentary.

Never having anyone to relax with. Relax *for*.

In the past week, two deals came up. One involving flying to Vegas, the other right here in the city.

I turned down both and sent others in my stead.

Instead of working late or exercising until my body is broken, I find myself rushing home. By then, Yasmine's back from classes and already completed whatever homework or studying she had. We get changed and head to the gym for a couple hours. Then we come home, cook together or order in, and settle down for a movie night.

I've become a man with a routine, and while discerning, there's comfort in it.

Yesterday, I went back to the condo earlier, having finished up a few meetings Erico booked for me, and arrived before she did. It was a farce that I had nothing better to do. The even bigger farce was pretending to watch whatever sports game was on rather than observing her.

The way she sat at the kitchen island, notebook and text-book framing the laptop her fingers rapidly typed on. A pen gripped between her teeth, her brows a deep dip. When I asked what she was working on, she mumbled about some mid-term paper and went right back to it. We skipped working out because she was so drained after her schoolwork. I ordered her pizza and we ended up starting a TV series she mentioned wanting to see, declaring it now as being "our" show.

It felt nice to care for her. To support her in ways beyond throwing a black credit card her way.

That was the moment I realized the next job to come up, I have to take.

I don't want to go and that's the very reason I need to. Ironic, that in the beginning, I begged Erico to get me away from the city for an extended period of time, and now, it's a fucking chore. Our meeting today's about a drug run three states over he wants me to oversee. It'll mean being away from Yasmine for a few days and breaking the pattern we've established.

"You still haven't given me an answer on the deal front," Erico says, his point aligning with my thoughts.

"You were the one who went on some tangent about my personal life. Yeah, I'll go."

"Even after your week of bliss?"

Because of my week of bliss.

I'm going because Erico's right. I'm one more night away from exploding. Mentally, emotionally, psychologically... sexually.

"I *need* the distance." I stare at him so he can see the meaning behind my words for himself. "You're fuckin' right. Getting away from her will be better."

Erico crosses his arms, his frown wiping away all amusement. "I should deny you because all you're doing is running from your problems. Fuck, it's not even problems you're running from, but the truth. Stay and face whatever's in your head."

"There's nothing in my head," I deny right away. "Nothing's changed."

Everything's changed. There's hanging out with my wife, and then there's a routine like we've created. Now, I need to un-create it and go our separate ways.

"I'll be on the *Famiglia* plane tomorrow by six a.m. Deal with it. Now, for the reason I actually came here." I hike one knee over the other, adopting an easy position, but all it does is hide the annoyance running through me. "Can't find shit on this Gene asshole."

"Nothing," he agrees because he's been helping my search too. "He's like a ghost. Contacted Nico Corsetti to see if they had anything useful on Stefano De Falco's household. Rozelyn's been a help as well. Said his behaviours are off."

"Yasmine basically said the same thing. I think that's why it threw her so much."

He centres his gaze on me. "She mention him since the incident?"

"No, thankfully. I want to say we could leave it alone now, that's it's a one-time thing, but we both know it's not. Until he's found, he's a threat and that won't stand."

With me gone three states over, he could come out of hiding again. Not that he'll get near her because every entrance into the condo will be staffed until I'm back, and even *if* he got through, his life would be very limited. He wouldn't make it far before I was burying his ass.

"I'm putting men at the condo in my absence. With me gone, he might come out. This could be the opening we need."

Erico tips his head. "Could be. Still not worth you leaving."

I scowl. "Whatever, man." Then I stand, grabbing my phone and keys and stride away. "Yasmine and I have plans to head to the gym later. I'll be teaching her actual fight moves today."

His laughter follows me out.

∾

If there's one thing for certain, it's that Yasmine's not only getting fitter, but stronger. To warm up, she punches one of the hanging bags, her hits controlled, firm, her arms steady.

There's a handful of guys here, as normal, but they've become so used to her presence now, they mainly ignore us after their initial greetings.

"Good," I comment. "Three more, and let's head to the mats."

Punch, punch, punch.

She might be hitting the bag, but the moment she steps back and grins, her hands coming up to wipe at stray hairs that came free from her braid, it feels like she's punching me in the gut.

She's so beautiful.

With a deep sigh, I lead her to the centre of the mats. This gains a few guys' attention, which I'm not sorry about. The more people witnessing her hold her own, the more they'll talk. The more people know not to fuck with her.

"Fists up."

In a stance way too adorable, she adopts the fighting position I taught her a while ago. Her feet shift a few inches apart, her arms up, fists in perfect, little balls.

La mia tigre è una combattente. My tiger is a fighter.

Ferocious.

Free.

Fierce.

"Good. Remember all that punching you did?" She nods, so I bring my own arms up, palms facing her. "Try to hit my hands."

With a smile indicating she believes this will be simple, she comes toward me. A few chuckles from the guys bounce over the room because they know what's about to happen.

After two large strides, she throws her body into it—impressive—and aims to land a fist on my right palm.

I slide out of the way, smirking.

With a grunt, she turns and rushes at me, another punch coming for my hands.

I duck, missing her punch.

"What the fuck?"

By now, she's coming at me faster. One arm, then the other. I continue to skip around her, arms still up on the slim chance she manages to hit.

"Caladin!"

More chuckles, and they draw her attention for the quickest

second, but it only increases her determination. With a growl, she lunges, but this time, instead of only her fists, she stretches her leg out, trying to trip me.

I see it, of course, and avoid the fall, but pride bursts through me. Without instruction, she did exactly as I wanted.

"What are you smiling about?" she demands, coming at me again.

This time, instead of avoiding, I remain still, arms up. As her knuckles brush my palm, I drop my hands, grasp her hips, and toss her to the mats, crouching over her as her breath concedes that she's lost, coming out in heavy pants.

"The fuck?" She shoves her hands into my abs, fingers dancing dangerously close to my waistband so before my dick loses focus, I stand, reaching a hand for her.

She takes it and—

—fucking surprises me. Instead of using my hand to help her up, her other cocks back and slams right into my chin. She's not strong enough for her hit to hurt, not with the force I'd like her to have one day, but I'll definitely feel it later. A few of the men even clap.

Rolling my jaw, I compliment her. "Nice one."

"You told me to punch your palms but didn't give me a chance."

"No, you asked to learn to fight. Fighting isn't all choreographed movements. If you want to learn, genuinely learn, then your instincts have to be on par. Noticed the more you missed, the quicker your attacks came? Even tried to trip me. When you technically lost," I gesture to the mat, "you still found a way to hit me. Instincts."

Her mouth opens and closes three times, like a fish before, with narrowed eyes, she yields. "Fine. I get the concept. Let's go again now that I know what to expect."

She doesn't...but she will soon.

With a partial, amused shrug, I pace back a few steps and lift my palms again. She immediately goes for the large attack, throwing her body and fists at me, but this time, I don't move and she lands the punch.

And then stops, her head tipping in a cute manner as she mentally works to determine why I never fought back. I let her consider for a second longer. A minute. Staring and when her arms begin lowering, deeming the fight over, I wrap an arm around her waist and flip her until she's on her back.

Her curse bounces over the room, booming over the others' laughter quickly following—mine included.

"You're an asshole, Caladin Rossi! Can you pick a direction?"

"Lesson number two: always remain primed to fight."

I reach to help her up and catch her small fist forming by her side. This time, I'm prepared to block and with the hold I cover her punch with, I spin her until her back's to my front and my head's in her neck, her scent of jasmine taunting me.

"Got you again."

She wiggles, but I'm holding too tightly, so all it does is rubs her ass against my dick. I arch away because another moment of that, and my desire for her won't remain hidden.

"Fight to be freed. Imagine if you were attacked and someone had you in this hold. What would you do?"

Her foot lifts, which it's wise to go for my balls, but I twist my hips, keeping my arms around her before she manages the full movement. What I don't see in time is the quick drop of her head, her teeth sinking into my skin.

Painfully hard, not holding back. I release her with a jerk, my arm stinging from the indents of teeth. The very teeth attached to the luscious mouth giving me a haughty grin.

"You asked for it, *piccolo tigre*."

I lunge.

28

YASMINE

Hours later, we're home and my entire body throbs. Back, hands, feet, boobs, head, thighs, arms—pick a spot. It's sore.

My back from being slammed onto the mats endless times.

My hands from the solid punches.

My feet from bouncing on the balls of them so much.

My boobs every time he pushed my front down.

My head from exhaustion and hunger.

My thighs from the extreme workout attached to fighting.

My arms from being used more they've ever been.

So much so, when Caladin shuts the door, I fall against the nearest wall, partially sliding down before his arms wrap my waist, tossing one arm over his broad shoulders, and he walks me down the hallway.

"No, no, none of that. Don't be passing out yet."

The fact I made it home without falling asleep in the car is amazing enough, but I doubt I'll make it any longer now that I'm home and able to relax.

"I think we went a bit too hard on you tonight." His warm breath ruffles strands of my hair. "Next time, a little less."

"It was fun though." I roll my neck to look at him, which puts my face entirely too close to his. So close, I'm able to see the individual specks of brown in his eyes. "As much as I hated it in the moment, I like your method. You're right; it made for a realistic fight rather than something sketched out."

He throws me a mocking look. "What, you're admitting I'm right?"

We make it to the bedroom and he walks me straight to the bathroom and drops me onto the toilet's shut lid before heading toward the bathtub. He switches on the two taps, and tests the temperatures before walking away.

"Undress. Relax in the hot water. I'll get you a snack and a cool drink. It'll do your body good."

He's gone before I can argue the fact that once I'm finished in the bath, I doubt I'll be awake for much longer. With strength my wobbly thighs certainly do not have, I stand and strip my clothes, which cling to me with sweat, and abandon them on the tiled floor.

As every inch of the hot water encompasses my exhausted body, I melt. Melt and relax and just sigh, sliding the rest of the way in. The water's hot enough to prickle at my sensitive skin, but it's secondary to the instant full body massage. *And he wants me to leave this thing?*

I don't know how long I remain in the tub, but by the time the water grows cooler and exhaustion becomes more prominent, I exit the bathroom with only a towel wrapped around myself with the intention of getting dressed—if I wasn't stopped by the sight of my husband.

Having exchanged his own workout clothes for pyjama pants, he's seated on the edge of the bed. The blankets are drawn down, the room's lights dimmed. A bowl of fruit rests on the table by my side of the bed, alongside a bottle of icy water and something else clear.

"What is this?"

"This is called care. And apology for bruising your body today." His crooked grin heats my insides. "Dress, but I'd recommend shorts and a tank."

I study the set-up again, trying to decipher his words, but for all Caladin's done, he's never led me astray. So I obey him and change in the precise clothes he instructed me to before returning to the bedroom where he's now standing.

"Lie down," he orders in a tone matching the dim lighting of this room. "On your stomach."

"What's happening?" I ask, trepidation making my sore nerves tighter even as I obey him. I stretch on my side of the bed, head on my soft pillow, arms sliding beneath it.

"Slide to the centre of the bed."

I do, bringing my pillow with me and positioning it closer to his, creating a nestle for my head between them. "I don't get what's happening."

Still, he doesn't respond. The bed dips, and I turn my head, catching his knees on either side of my hips. Weight settles me until he's crouched overtop me.

"I think a massage for your sore muscles is in order, no?"

"Y-you're massaging me?"

"No, the other man leaning over you is. Obviously, Yasmine. I thought my educated wife is smart in all things?"

I turn my head so he can hear my mumble. "Never said I was smart. You assume I am."

He chuckles and fuck, why does it sound deeper than usual? This entire experience is sensual for two roommates. His weight shifts as he reaches over to the bedside table. I don't turn my head to watch, but suddenly, his fingers are there, a green grape pinched between them.

"Open."

I part my lips and he slowly slips the grape in, moving away so I can chew on the chilled fruit as his weight shifts yet again, but this time, he returns with no fruit.

"In your defence," he continues, "I sat through your classes in B.C., and man, I was so fuckin' lost."

I'm about to comment, but then warmth skates my sides, and suddenly, my tank is being slid up my back. I shift and arch, moving so the shirt can better get out of his way. He reaches forward, his hands coming into view as he untucks my arms from beneath the pillow and reangles them to my side. I allow him to control my movements, placing my trust—my body—under this man's sinful spell.

"This is something else, Caladin," I comment, putting it out there how abnormal this is for roommates. "Elevating the roommate experience."

He makes a sound in his throat as his hands come to my back again, fingers dragging over my spine once before moving away altogether. I hear a cap of something opening and the nerves in my back prickle and tense, awaiting what's next.

"I strive to make every experience amazing. Besides, nothing in the rule book says I can't heal what I broke."

He's joking about my sore body, but I throw back my own quip. "Now I'm broken? Ouch."

He's silent and I assume he's shifting away from the topic. Until in a voice so low, it's practically a whisper, he replies, "You're far from broken, Yasmine. You're the most fucking resilient woman I know."

To cap off his statement, all my supposed resiliency fades away with the warm liquid pooling on my back. A line begins to drip down my side but two large, calloused hands are right there, sliding the oil over every inch, coating my back with it.

I moan. God this feels better than it should and he's barely touched me.

He hums. "Feel good?"

"Mhm."

His touch presses in harder, fingers working at the precise sore muscles, on the spots they most twinge. He massages my shoulders, skirts my blades, and draws a line down my spine until pressing his hands into my sides, my hips, moving upwards with his thumbs stroking the base of my back.

"Fuck, Caladin."

"Careful," he warns.

"'Bout what?" My question is mumbled, speech becoming difficult, but despite my efforts, he never answers.

After a few minutes of bliss, his oil-slick hands return to my shoulders and work their way down my arms, paying special attention to my biceps. Those took a beating today and immediately, every punch, every swing, every tug on the muscle becomes worth it.

"Feels so good."

"I know," he replies in that amused, cocky way he does, but I don't even have the effort to make a counter point.

After a few more minutes, he returns to my back and his knees inch their way down my sides. I'm about to complain until his hands trail behind, skipping over my ass, and to my upper thighs, explaining why he insisted on a tank top and shorts.

Up and down my thighs and lower legs, and then eventually my feet, my body feels so deep in bliss, so close to slumberland, and it's pure determination keeping me awake. Passing out will happen quickly, but I'd miss this—miss his touch—so I refuse to right now.

I moan again as his fingers brush the inside of my thighs, but this time, for an entirely other reason. Because along with exhaustion, his touch ignites my insides. I can't sleep, not only because I don't want to, but because with every muscle he eases, the surrounding nerves awaken. My core tightens, my fingers curling around the mattress sheet beneath me—anything to grip the instant lust. *That* isn't the point of this.

He's touching me everywhere now, this thumbs working at the muscles at the top of my thighs, and then between them. My legs slide apart, allowing him between them, and he rewards me by pushing against the muscle there.

Burying my head deeper into the pillow, I subtly bite the case, trying to taper down the moan. He's trying to help me with a problem he enticed. I should push him away now and thank him for the hot bath and relaxing massage, and be done with this before my mind becomes more and more entangled and forgets all the reasons we shouldn't.

What were those reasons anyway?

"Caladin." His name slips out in a moan, something certainly not meant to be spoken at all.

"Yasmine, you gotta stop or else I'll—"

"Yes?" *You'll what? Tell me.* I shift my head a fraction, not turning to face him though.

No answer. He returns to complete a pass on my upper body and then my arms, before shifting back to my legs again. My betraying body arches my core into the bed, seeking relief before I beg him to grant me it.

This needs to stop. We need to both back away.

"Fuck, Yasmine, stay still." His voice is strained, and when he shifts his own weight, I feel exactly why.

He's hard. His erection thick in his pants. He feels large, even covered up, even with the angle he holds himself.

"I-I think we should stop," he decides, a bit breathless than earlier, even while his touch continues up and down my legs.

"You're not yet," I point out after a moment, amused but also pleased he isn't.

"You haven't asked me to."

He's leaving it in my control. Every reason I had for not wanting this dissipates when his thumbs brush over the back of my knee, spreading the oil further.

Sex doesn't equal love, but I understand why we both placed those walls on one another.

Another moan. Another touch. The wall crumbles.

"Caladin..."

His thumbs stroke dangerously close to my core, the shorts now pulled up. He makes a noise in the back of his throat before pulling away entirely with a low curse. His weight shifts.

He's ending this.

I should allow him. After all, it's what we both want.

It doesn't explain why I'm twisting as much as I can, until I can see his face and pained expression. Why I beg.

"Caladin...please. You once said you wouldn't touch me until I asked. I'm asking."

Overtop me, he freezes. His gaze darts to the open window and back, the bed...me. His desire's there, but it's mixed with fear.

But then he looks between my legs and whatever fight he was mentally working through is eaten up by his *hunger*.

"Beg harder, *piccola tigre*. Show me that fighting spirit of yours. Convince me."

My knees shift, arching my back up in invitation as much as I can with him over my thighs. "*Please* touch me."

His thumb brushes along the wet spot between my legs, and he concedes with his next groan. "Fuck, baby, you're wet. Roll over."

I start to, but he quickly takes over, oil-slick hands grabbing my hips and flipping me onto my back in one quick movement, reminding me of earlier on the mats. He crouches over me, hands on either side of my head, legs framing my hips. He's panting, his hair more dishevelled than earlier, and I'm pleased to not be the only one affected.

"Yasmine, you're too much of a temptation. Are you sure?"

I rub my hand up his bare chest, over his abs. "It's only sex. We can do that and still not get close."

"You're going to be my fucking downfall," he whispers, his tone pained, expression pinching.

"What do you mean?"

"Do you trust me?" he asks instead.

My response is instant and without thought or debate. Despite everything… "Yeah."

"Shut your eyes."

I do, instantly, and his mouth slashes against mine. His kiss is angry, irate, annoyed we're doing this. Irritated but devouring, when he doesn't pull back and end this. He grasps my chin, holding me steady, kissing me until I'm as breathless as earlier during training.

"Keep your eyes closed," he commands in a whisper against my lips right before his mouth nips down my neck until reaching my tank. Another hesitation and then it's inched up my stomach, my breasts, until the condo's warm air brushes against my hard buds. "Damn." He groans. "I've been imagining this since the moment I walked in on you in the bath. These fuckin' pretty, little nipples begging for attention."

My eyes tighten, as does my core. I see why he's had me shut my eyes now. I can only imagine the way his gaze takes them in. The hunger. My own need to have his mouth on them.

The tank is pulled farther up and over my head but not off. Instead, he rests it over my shut eyes, using the material as a blindfold.

A pause. "Still trust me?"

"Yes."

"Thank god. I've had a dream of you exactly like this."

I've had a dream of being in this exact position.

Then he removes my shorts, my panties, baring me entirely to his heated gaze. I feel it stroke over every inch, lick between my legs, wrap my nipples, coat my stomach. There's something incredibly powerful being bare in front of my husband while being unable to see him. My legs fall open, chasing more of that power, but when I expect him to touch me, he doesn't.

There's no sounds. Nothing. I lie there and wait, my lips folding together. My thighs slowly shutting again. My hands inching closer to my side.

"Anxious?" he finally speaks, noticing all my subtle movements.

"Impatient."

"Good."

The bed shifts. There's a sound I can't make out, and then he's back, nestling between my legs. His arms come around me, and then I feel his hair brush my collarbone and—

Ice.

Pleasurable ice that makes me arch into him and shy away all at the same time.

A cold trail drifts down the centre of my chest, leaving me without air. As though being tossed into an icy shower or dunked in a pool, it's unexpected, robbing my breath while my lungs work harder to catch one.

"Caladin—" It's a gasp, a moan, and a beg all in one sound.

He chuckles, the heat of his breath mingling with the ice in his mouth as he nips down the centre of my chest. His watery trail heads for one breast, skirting over my nipple. My hands fist the blanket, clutching onto anything as the most extreme sensation follows.

Then he repeats with the other and continues his watery

trail to my stomach, ending there. As fast as my complaint is ready, he's back, nipping at my neck. His lips are soft, the ice cube hard, and he licks up my jawline, toward my mouth.

My lips part for the kiss, but instead, he nudges the ice cube inside my mouth. His tongue dabs at my bottom lip, imprinting his whispered explanation onto me. "You look like you needed to cool down."

My responding laugh is basically a choke as I readjust the half-melted ice cube in my mouth, sucking on it so it'll melt quicker. It nearly ends up in my throat with my next cough as Caladin's teeth take my right nipple, enticing a long moan.

His tongue is warm—so warm—so heated—the precise opposite temperature of the ice he just used. So opposite, it's striking. He does the same to my other nipple before lifting away again.

The same noise from last time. The same lean to the side, toward the nightstand. This time, I know he's retrieving more ice, so the shock is slightly less when he drops a cube on my lower stomach, controlling it with his mouth.

His hands find the inside of my thighs and he pulls them apart before trailing the ice over my mound and then—

"Fuck."

My clit. I lurch, cry out, my hands fisting into his hair, confused whether to push him away or force him to continue the pleasurable torture.

His tongue pokes out from beyond the ice, licking my slit with both a hot and cold sensation that confuses my senses and builds an impending orgasm. One that'll be different than any I've felt before.

"Caladin..."

And then he hits my centre, strokes the ice over it until my gasp is ungodly loud and pulls away, leaving me to catch my breath.

And again, dipping the ice just inside. I tense, chilled, relaxed in a way I've never been before. My brain, my nerves, everything in my body is confused and rattled with pleasure.

I grip his hair until he shakes me free, his hands brushing mine away. Mumbled around the ice, he instructs, "No."

His mouth lifts, and then his hands are on me, the ice cube rubbing chilling circles over my stomach, painting me with water. My body arches into his touch, chasing the sensation as his head dips again, hair brushing against my skin.

A cool tongue licks me, core to my clit before he latches on, pressure bringing me right to the edge. The cold of his mouth quickly fades with his natural heat. The orgasm is teetering, impossible to run from when he dips a finger inside me.

One hand wipes ice around my budded nipples, his tongue suctioning on the most sensitive place, and his finger wreaks ungodly noises from my throat. It's impossible not to *feel*. Not to explode.

It hits me like a giant wave. My insides clenching his finger, my orgasm harder than any experienced before. White spots fill my gaze, my breath working triple time to catch up.

The moment my breath evens out, his finger slowly pulls from my core, and his lips release my clit. He places a gentle kiss there, and then more up my body. His hands, one cool from the ice now melted, the other wet with me, massage my sides. He kisses the base of my neck and slides my tank off my head, granting me sight back.

His eyes search mine, the hint of a tentative, uncertain smile there, which I make certain by brushing strands of his hair away from his eyes, giving him a smile of my own.

"Holy fuck."

29

CALADIN

Holy fuck is right.

That was...I hadn't even orgasmed, and yet, I feel like I have. With her own, mine was an explosion of the mind. A realization of how fucked I truly am.

"It's only sex," is what she said to me. I agreed because yeah, fuck it. Casual sex is easy and both she and I are clearly worked up from weeks without fucking. It's natural after everything we found ourselves here.

Does casual sex even exist in marriage? Not very casual at that point.

When massaging her, I should have comprehended how totally fucked I was. Body slick with oil and a colour of sand on a hot summer's day, my dick woke up. My body demanded I stop avoiding the evitable.

Then she fucking pleaded and I was only so strong.

Her hands cup my face and she brings my head down to hers, placing a kiss on my mouth. An offer, and one I fucking want to take. To kiss her deeper. To show her all the ways that losing one's senses can add to the thrill of the act.

Fucking Christ, I want to.

Leaving tomorrow for the drug run will be beneficial because everything in my head's demanding I remain here with her, and that's the exact reason I shouldn't.

This isn't the start of sex.

This is the explosion of chemistry.

Of an addiction I'm already fighting to wean myself off of.

If this continues, it's inevitable. I'll grow addicted to my wife, feelings will bloom, and I will fall in love with her.

And like Mom, I'll lose her.

I won't handle someone's love all to end up destroying her.

When she pulls back with a secretive grin, it breaks me to do what I do. Fucking shatters me into becoming the bad guy. To be *that* man. But if she hates me, it'll make this easier.

I stare at the bed and then the wall above her head. Everywhere that isn't her while words formulate.

Her hands slide up my abs. "So once you catch your breath—"

"I'm leaving."

"What?" She blinks and her hands fall to the bed, like she can't bear to touch me any longer. I hate that.

I hate what I'm doing, but I'm on a ride I'm controlling, crashing it even while there's every reason to put on the brakes. A fight I'm inevitable to lose.

"Tonight," I tell her, my throat growing thicker. With the strength of every muscle, I lift off her altogether. "I have to go to Michigan for a couple days. Two or three. Flight leaves in a few hours, so I'm going to get ready and head over now."

Shock. Then fury. She stands from the bed, erecting herself in front of me. She has no idea the temptation she is, and my cock, unsatisfied after touching her, wants nothing more but to explore her further.

I turn away and stalk to the closet, anger coating my every step. Anger that I'm a moron and I know it.

She follows, hands slapping my back as her rage catches up. "The fuck, Caladin? You're running away. That's all this is."

Yes. I can't even lie to myself at this point.

Inside the closet, I continue ignoring her as I pack a duffel bag. "I'm doing my job, Yasmine. We might have been chilling in the evenings like a normal couple, but you forget my role. I have things I'm in charge of."

She slides in front of me, hands on her hip, placing herself between the bag and my clothing. "Convenient timing. What changed from *minutes* ago?"

I can't even put it into words, because I don't fully know what had.

I step around her and reach for the first items closest to me, stuffing them in before walking away and into the bathroom to get more things. She, of course, trails me.

"It's sex, Caladin. I'm positive you've had casual sex before. Probably a whole lot more than I have."

Casual sex was my forte before I met her. I did have a lot of it; it's simple. But nothing with Yasmine will ever be casual, no matter how hard we try. One of us *will* end up hurt, either by walls being erected around our hearts or when death forces us apart.

Once I'm packed, I face her again, *only* staring into her eyes. Not the curves I want to finish exploring or her pussy I'm dying for another taste of. Then I give her one truth: "It's not casual sex when it's with the woman who invades my every thought."

I walk away.

She doesn't follow.

～

The flight isn't slated to leave until late morning, and while tempting to call up the flight staff to leave sooner, their sleep doesn't need to be interrupted because I'm a shitty husband. So I head the three hours toward Erico's mansion, ignoring the fact I could have just crashed in his condo above mine. But that keeps me in the same building. One floor above Yasmine, where it'd be so easy to return to her, to beg forgiveness over my shitty behaviour. Way out here, it's far enough.

Having all the codes and keys to the mansion I once lived in, I enter the dark building, pausing to listen for any sounds indicating Erico or Ariella are awake, but it's silent.

After dropping my bag by the entrance, I head down the hall, through the foyer, past the living room with the giant fish tank and seating arrangement overlooking the ocean, and into the kitchen.

Erico keeps his alcohol in the same place my uncle had, and I take out a bottle of whisky and a glass, pouring a healthy amount, which I immediately start on.

"Why are you in my house?"

In the doorway, Erico leans, his arms crossed. His steps were silent, that of a trained killer. He's smirking in his dishevelled clothing and messy hair, implying *he* had a better night than I did.

I take another chug, downing the glass in one go. Instead of bothering with the refill, I sip directly from the glass bottle, much to his unamused glare. He pushes off the doorframe and approaches the counter, leaning on his forearms.

"And drinking my alcohol?"

"Sleeping here tonight. I'll take my old room. Leave for Michigan in the morning."

His eyes narrow. "Why do I get the sense this has something to do with your wife?"

"You're a smart one. That's why you're Boss."

Frowning, he reaches for the bottle, ripping it from my grasp before I manage another swig. Liquid sloshes before settling as he rests it in front of him, out of reach. So I grab a different bottle from the liquor cabinet. This one clear, and will ensure I don't remember much of tonight. Good ol' tequila.

He sighs. "What happened?"

"What didn't happen?"

"Not following." He reaches for the second bottle, but this time, I avoid, moving to lean against the fridge, my glare warning him to take no step farther.

"You should be thrilled, cuz. I did shit with my wife." *Holy fucking Christ, I sound like a fourteen-year-old virgin being exposed to girls for the first time.* Rubbing my hand over my face, I redefine my previous words into something that makes sense. "I had her in our bed, both of us willing to go further, while keeping it casual."

His gaze flicks to the bottle in my hand. "Yet, you're in my home, drinking my alcohol."

Throwing him a haughty smirk, I take another chug, the tequila burning my throat until I cough. Maybe drinking isn't the best idea.

"I needed away from her, Erico." Vulnerability burns through me and I open up, blaming the few chugs of alcohol for every unwilling syllable. "If I fuck her, what's the difference between us and another couple?" Before he can respond, I answer, "Nothing. That's the issue."

His mouth parts in an *Ah* expression and he pushes himself into a stance. "Look, I'm no psychologist, but I've seen this time and time again from you, Caladin. When things get tough, you run. You suck at facing your feelings. You did so after your parents' death, and you're doing it now. It's not fair to her."

None of this is fair. "She's aware of why I refuse to love her.

She's said numerous times, she doesn't want there to be an *us* either, so I'm saving us both the heartbreak."

"Sounds like you're only saving yourself the heartbreak. You're too scared to love her, and you believe, having sex with your wife will make you do exactly that."

Grumbling, I walk away from him and out the kitchen. "You should rethink that psychologist thing." Because he put my every emotion into words.

I *am* too scared to love her. For both her and me. If I loved her, only to lose her, I'd have to raze the earth, creating hell around me to be reunited again. If she lost me, then I'd spend an eternity in the afterlife regretting every kiss, giving her plea-sure all to rip it away. I'll destroy anyone who threatens her happiness—even myself. If we both die, all because of her love for me, then I'd hate myself for her death.

Erico follows, his steps echoing through the otherwise silent house. "You can't run forever, Caladin. She'll be here when you return. You'll have to face her."

That is true, but I planned for that.

Before disappearing around the corner and toward the stair-case that'll lead to teenage me's room, I say, "How I left tonight, I won't need to worry about anything. She'll hate me."

Michigan goes by in a blur. Meetings. The deal, which went off without a hitch. A single, unplanned fight I joined; not for the stakes but because it's new blood for me to smash. New blood for them to attempt to take me down, and fuck, if my victory made me *feel* something for the first time since I walked away from Yasmine.

By my final night in the city, I'm seated inside a bar, nursing my fourth beer and inventing new ways to convince Erico to keep me here for longer. Forever, perhaps.

Yasmine's safe. She has three men stationed in the building at all times, and Raj continues to send me insistent annoying updates about her days and evenings. I'd demand he stop if I wasn't clinging to his every update like a fucking addict craving their next fix. Even now, as I spin my phone around on the bar top, the latest update was from hours ago, when they got home.

She's been spending time at a coffee shop after her classes, and I long to know why. I could very well text her, but then she'd know I was keeping tabs on her, and that might end as an argument. It began right after I left apparently. Raj said it's a popular campus location, quite safe—no less safe than the rest of the university. She wanted to try the coffee there, and since I left three days ago, it's become her afternoon hang-out spot. She studies and works on her essays, and then goes home to eat dinner, where she remains for the rest of the night.

I urged him to take her to visit Ariella, but she declined.

She's had a single phone call with her sister, that he's aware of.

I hate myself for keeping track. For caring at all.

Yesterday, I could have been at gunpoint if the exchange went awry. My only thought then: Yasmine would be taken care of as a *Famiglia* widow. In time, Erico would release her to do what she wants: remain within the organization's care, remarry, or return to Montreal to her family.

It became every reason to ensure the deal went down fine.

"Another?"

I glance at the woman in front of me. She's different than the male bartender who was serving me earlier. Much prettier. Long, black hair that falls down her back, brushing the bottom of her beige crop top that's showing her tits off. A tattoo runs up the back of her hand and over her forearm, disappearing into that very top. She's not wearing a bra, based on the studs apparent through her top, and her smile promises more.

Dark eyes framed by smoke watch me, her smile spreading as she stretches a hand over the gloss top toward me, her sharp nails scraping at my wrist. "Or, *Mr. Rossi*, I can offer you something else." She leans forward, so her tits practically touch my hand. "Seems like you have a lot on your mind. I can help with that, if you want."

I stare at her, understanding in that second why she's so beautiful. In some ways, she reminds me of Yasmine. Different in many ways, but it's the hair. The long, black nighttime strands I long to wrap around my fist and show her all the ways I can bring her to orgasm.

Casual sex with a woman who reminds me of my wife. That should do it. It'll sate my cock so returning home won't be hellish.

But it's not what I want. Not *who* I want.

Even with the offer of sex in front of me, I deny myself.

Pulling my arm closer, I reply, "Just another beer, thanks."

30

YASMINE

Travelling caters to our desires.

Two days ago, one of my professors stated that in his lecture and something's never sat so well with me. For me, it's another form of claiming control over my life. Picking a place to go to, to explore the places *I* want to.

And yet, I've even been brought to a new city, in a country I've never before visited, and all I've seen is the inside of a condo, a private gym, and a university. Which is how, when I'd heard people mentioning a coffee shop on the edge of campus, I told Raj we had to go check it out after classes.

Is a coffee shop the equivalent of seeing the world, or even New York City? Not even close. But it's a start. It's better than going from class to Raj's SUV to home and doing it all again the next day.

I'm sitting here now, my laptop open, a small mocha to my right, but I'm not looking at my screen. I'm studying the ambiance, the vibe of this place. Every single day brings change, and I've only been here for two, so that's saying something.

There's the regulars, of course. The regular students and the staff working the counter, but it's never the same. The customers who come in and order vary. The conversations I overhear. The work I'm completing.

It's an internal change too. The building of distance. Of reminding myself of the deal my husband and I agreed upon at the start of our marriage to lead separate lives. Hanging out the past week, spending every evening together, had me forgetting, losing myself to the very thing neither of us want.

He made it apparent, even when I entertained the idea of giving our bodies what we both crave, what we were doing wrong.

So while this isn't exactly out-and-about in New York, it's not home. *His* home. Under *his* watch. Despite the fact that *his* man is still guarding me from across the shop, seated at a table by the entrance. He gets his daily water and pretends to be playing on his phone from the corner.

I sip my steaming mocha, which is slightly cooler than when I first ordered it. Instead of scalding my tongue, it's comfortably hot. As I lower the transparent mug back to the table and focus on my essay, a black figure fills the space across from me.

Shaggy blond hair tucked in a backwards cap, a baggy hoodie that looks almost double his size. He smiles at me, a dimple on his right cheek showing. A light splatter of freckles decorate the bridge of his nose and curl around his cheeks, drawing attention to the grassy green of his eyes.

"H-hey. You look familiar."

His grin grows and he takes that as a further invitation, dropping his phone onto the table behind my laptop and sliding his chair closer. "I'd hoped you would. We share PSYC 410. I sit behind you."

With a snap of my fingers, I see it. He's often seated before I am and every single day since my first, he's smiled at me. I always took it as being friendly but based on the hope sparking in his eyes now, I think I totally missed his reasonings.

"Right," I reply slowly, nodding, waiting for him to explain what brought him over here.

"I've been wanting to introduce myself for a while now," he says. "So when I saw you in here, I thought it was fate. You believe in fate, right?"

No. But I say, "Sure do," in a perky voice to avoid hurting his feelings. "What's your name again?" Lecture halls don't exactly provide much of a place for class-wide introductions so unless you're speaking to the person, you'd have no idea who they are.

"Parker. And you're Yasmine. Pretty name, by the way."

It disturbs me that he knows who I am, but I didn't know his name.

Over his shoulder, Raj is watching us and I throw him a subtle shake of his head so he knows I'm fine.

"Thanks," I reply, my attention sliding back to Parker. "So, your major's psychology?"

"Neuroscience, actually. Basically a mix of biology and psychology. It's challenging, but cool."

"Sounds busy." Thinking of how heavy psychology courses are, I couldn't imagine adding biology into the mix.

"It is," he agrees. "But not so much that I have no time for fun, such as introducing myself to the quiet girl who sits in front of me."

Smooth. For his effort, he earns a chuckle.

"So," he positions his elbows onto the table and leans closer, "tell me about you. You kinda randomly popped up one day."

"Pretty much." I tilt my laptop screen halfway down, welcoming the conversation in which I tell him what I'm allowed to: I'm new to New York, from Canada originally, and came due to family circumstances. It's close enough to the truth to be satisfactory.

"So, wait," he starts when I finish, his hand coming up to stop me from saying more, "you've been in New York for weeks and you *still* haven't gotten a tour."

"Yep."

"Well, I volunteer. If you'd like, of course. We can tour the city, show you all the major places. Experience it like a tourist would, because it's criminal you haven't seen the city."

Is this...he might be offering me the friendship I was hoping for. This is perfect. This gives me a person to talk to outside my husband. A reason to explore New York versus walking around it on my lonesome with Raj trailing me.

This is the start of a life that is mine and mine alone.

"I'd love that."

I reach for my mug, which has been nearly forgotten in the course of the conversation. But as I do, his gaze zeroes in on my hands, specifically my left one. They were tucked out of sight for the entirety of the conversation because I didn't think too much of it.

"Oh. I-I'm sorry, Yasmine." Scrambling, he gets to his feet, and while I can't believe I do, I reach for him. Reach for the only friendship I managed to find in this busy place, but he shies away. "I didn't realize you were married. Um, second thought, I think I'm busy. I'll see you in class instead." In his rush to escape, he nearly knocks over his own chair.

Slumping against the padded chair, I stare at my left hand, and more specifically, my wedding ring. I'd long forgotten about it, only ever removing it in the gym. It's so easily become part of my outfit, slipped onto my finger at every available moment. Something I was so adamant to fight him on wearing when not at Famiglia events has become a part of me, even if I don't want to admit it.

"Well," a new voice drawls. One so thick with a New York accent, but familiar for all the times I've heard it describing the newest horror movie he's watched. "That was pitiful. And a jackass move."

Oliver, the barista who works here takes Parker's seat. During my first visit, I complimented his forearm tattoo of Freddy and Jason, and we launched into a conversation over horror movie classics until another customer came in and he had to work. In the days following, he's always adding extra foam to my mug and throwing out small horror movie quips as he moves through the café to clean up after others.

I sigh, glancing at my ring again. "I get it, I guess. He was hoping for more. A married woman doesn't exactly scream *available for fucking*."

He sputters his laughter, which wipes the serious look from his face. "Still. Married or not, it's called being a good friend."

"Friendship wasn't on his mind," I respond with a shrug, trying to shove the entire situation away.

Oliver glares out the store's windows, in the direction Parker has long disappeared to. Then he crosses his arms and focuses on me again, jerking his chin toward his hand. "I am curious. What made you get married so early in life?"

"That's hard to answer."

Another person would pry, but Oliver simply shrugs and with pursed lips says, "All right. I guess when you know you know, right? I think I know, but there's no way I'm popping the question to Dylan until living together at least two years post-degree. See how real life alters us and our relationship."

"Smart," I reply quietly because a wave of self-deprecation gnaws at me. Oliver is the example of what I hoped to have one day.

Choice.

He got to *choose* his boyfriend and he's *choosing* when to propose.

"Well," he slaps his knees, readying to stand, "I should get back to work. But hey, if you're looking for a tour guide, I'm happy to be of service. Seriously, I'm prettier than that tool," he hikes his thumb toward the windows, "so I'm much better to look at. Born and raised New York—whole family is—so I can show you everything. The tourist traps and then the city as a New Yorker would. If you want. Dylan's working all weekend so it'll only be me. But bring your husband."

So much to reply there, but I start with, "Yeah, no, he won't be coming. But I'd love to take you up on the offer." Why was I looking for another friend when the natural conversations Oliver and I have been sharing over three days have been doing it for me? "I'm free tomorrow bright and early."

"Whoa now, not too early. Nine? I can bring you to the greatest bagel place you'll ever eat at in your life."

"Hm, Montreal's pretty known for their bagels too. You might need to do better than that."

Oliver laughs. "Challenge accepted, but I warn you, New York will win. Here—" He reaches across the small table for my phone and before I can properly react, he's positioning it in front of my face, which unlocks the screen, and then turns it to him. "I'm imputing my number and messaging me from it, so I have yours. That way we can meet up tomorrow." Then he stands and tucks his chair in but before returning to work, asks, "Why hasn't your husband taken you around yet?"

"It's complicated." Meaning I haven't asked him and wasn't sure I ever could or should.

"Got it. I get the sense a lot is with you." He takes a step away but *again* stops, this time coming closer to crouch and whisper, "Be sure to bring your bodyguard too, and before you ask, girl, it's obvious when two walk in within minutes of each other but arrive and leave in the same vehicle. He looks like a fucking army soldier about to slaughter us all, never orders anything, and glances at you constantly. But like, not in a *I like her* manner. More like a *no one go near her or I'll kill you* way." He shifts to glance Raj's way, whose eyes are sweeping subtly over us. "At least, he's pretty."

With a final wink, Oliver returns to work.

31

CALADIN

New York on a Saturday morning with a migraine, and still, my head is only on one thing.

My wife.

My car was left on the tarmac from takeoff the other day, so I'm able to hop right in and start toward home, eager to see her again. Two blocks away from the airfield, Raj texts. A bit early for an update, and when I see the picture attached to his message, I feel wrecked. Shattered.

My foot stomps on the brake pedal, slamming the car to a stop by the curb before better examining what he's sent me.

It's a picture of Yasmine and some guy eating bagels. Both are smiling. Eager in whatever conversation they're having.

I feel sick.

The image of the guy blurs as all focus falls on my wife. She looks happy and carefree.

For three days, I've despised the fact I'd have to face her again, while craving the moment I was finally able to. It's left my stomach in horrendous knots that even working didn't quell. Not the booze, the fights, the meetings.

Fact is, I have no fucking stance.

You have every stance. She's your wife.

The very wife I pushed away. Who I allowed to have her own life, away from me.

Change your mind.

She's doing the very thing I told her to do.

Claim her. Kill him.

I stare at the asshole smiling at my wife, imagining my fist in his face. Yasmine would be pissed but maybe that's what needs to happen for her to understand her role in this world.

But then you'll make your point, and you'll what—fuck her. Love her. Watch her die alongside you. Or die from heartbreak when you leave her behind.

As my thoughts battle, it's that last one sticking. She's doing the very thing I need her to do: move on. Perhaps then, my brain and dick will remember all our carefully erected walls and they'll leave her alone.

Still, I reply to the message, feeling like an outsider to my own body. Watching my own demise, able to stop myself, but not taking the step to.

ME

Where are you?

Raj immediately sends a pinned location, which the maps app shows to be only a twenty-minute drive from here.

RAJ

But they're nearly done. Cleaning up now to leave. Central Park after this.

ME

Stick close to her. That's an order, no matter what she tells you. Central Park is too dangerous.

Then I despise the asshole all over, simply for bringing her there. Truth is, Central Park is never completely safe, but it's certainly saf*er* during the daytime, when all vendors are out peddling, families taking walks, and joggers and bikers exercising. People use Central Park as a place to escape the chaos of the metropolitan area.

I pull my car back onto the road and drive to Central Park instead of home. It's huge, stretching over fifty blocks with numerous entrances into it, but I head to the North one.

ME

North entrance. 110th street. Use that one.

I park and get out, pacing a few feet into the grassy field, toward a row of trees. From here, there's a pond immediately to my left, which I imagine they might walk by, or if they go the opposite direction, they'll head down the bike path.

Either way, I'll be able to watch them. Being here, waiting them out, makes me feel like a fucking stalker.

A while later, the familiar black SUV pulls into the parking lot. Perhaps Raj spotted my car, maybe he didn't, but he parks on the opposite side, and with that act, he'll be getting a raise. Raj opens the back door to let Yasmine out, and I *hate* with a motherfucking passion the sensation that courses through me.

When Raj sent me the picture, it was taken at an angle where the table blocked her cute, white sundress. Large glasses are propped atop her head and she's taking in the park with the most amazed expression, one would think she's never seen nature before.

Given her family, maybe she hasn't.

The asshole I'm debating slaughtering comes around the other side and begins gesturing to things. Her smile grows bigger, and the tightness in my chest is replaced with fiery jealousy.

Why are they here?

Why do I *care?*

I need to go home and we'll continue whatever fucked-up blissfully wedded life we've found ourselves in.

But when Yasmine and fucktard approach the park's gates, they don't head toward the pond. They start down the bike path. He continues gesturing toward everything, and she's smiling and laughing in ways that make me want to take a bullet to a head. Mine or his, not sure which.

Raj falls into step behind them, maintaining a few feet of distance, but he glances over his shoulder, immediately finding me.

Great, so even my men know I'm a stalker now.

When they're far enough away, I leave the trees and turn for the park's entrance again. It's right there; a few dozen feet.

Yet, my steps take me in the direction they're walking. Somehow, my phone's back in my hand, and with the uncomfortable feeling gnawing at my insides, it's not ignorable. I won't be able to watch another second of this. My wife is finding another man with *my* ring on her finger and for all the claims I made, I won't allow it. Love—no. But infidelity—it ends now. We'll live a loveless, sexless marriage if we must, but she's doing it with *me* because I'm a selfish asshole where she's concerned.

With that out-of-body experience, the logical part of my brain is shaking his head at me. *You've fucking lost it.*

Maybe. Maybe I'm being stupid and irrational.

ME

I'm back in New York.

She pulls her phone from her small purse and reads the message. I swear if she puts that phone away and doesn't answer me, I might lose it.

More than I already am.

The responding vibration in my hand is the greatest sensation.

YASMINE

Welcome back.

ME

On my way home. Want to hit up the gym? Get back to training?

YASMINE

I'm not home right now. Out with a friend.

At least, she's telling the truth.

ME

When will you be home?

YASMINE

Not sure. After a walk, we're heading to see other things.

She doesn't define 'other things' and I want to ask, but I remain silent.

YASMINE

But yes, it'd be good to get to the gym later.

ME

Have Raj bring you to the gym when you're done. I'll meet you there.

YASMINE

Okay.

Some of the tightness eases from my chest and I slide the phone away. She doesn't completely hate me, is still willing to train, so that's something.

I stalk them for another few minutes, watching the guy

she's with more than her. Ensuring he doesn't put his hands on her.

When I'm satisfied, he'll keep his life—for now—I turn around and weave between people walking the path to return to my car. Most move out of my way. Maybe it's my expression threatening death if they annoy me.

Knowing Yasmine will be busy for a while, I first go home to change and shower and drop off my bag. To walk into my condo and be instantly swept up in the scent of jasmine. Of *her*.

The couch has a blanket messily strewn on it, the TV remote on top, obviously from her last use. I wonder which movie she chose to get lost in while I was gone, and then hate that I wasn't here with her. Hopefully she isn't mad enough to have continued "our" show alone. I've come to enjoy it, even if I don't completely understand the plot.

Home drags my mood even lower, so getting to the gym is relieving. To hop onto a treadmill and run from the tightness in my heart.

I nstead of the hours I expect to be waiting for her, only one goes by the time the door opens and shuts. When I spot the curtain of black hair rather than a soldier entering, I instantly press the power button on the treadmill and hop off before it comes to a stop.

"Earlier than expected," I admit. She's even changed, which means, at some point, she went home too. Based on the timeline, she didn't stay at the park very long, and they couldn't have possibly gone anywhere else.

I refuse to admit to myself why that fact makes me pleased.

She shrugs but her cheeks turn red. She's as eager as I am.

Letting her maintain her lies for now, I lead her toward the mats to first stretch, and then to begin training. The two guys grappling evacuate immediately, heading off to the side. We stretch, first loosening her muscles.

"Ready?"

32
YASMINE

Although I wanted to explore more of New York after Central Park, I thanked Oliver and explained my husband was home and I wanted to see him. Since Oliver doesn't know our situation, he merely winked and said he'd text, to make plans for another day.

The truth being, when Caladin's name popped up on my phone, I was both excited and angry. Anger should have been the *only* feeling, but my heart thumped a bit faster at reading he's returned. I hate myself for that. But I agreed to train with him because it'll be a great way to unleash three days of resentment.

Because that's what I'm feeling. He had me half-naked in our bed with an understanding—or so I thought. Sex. We both crave it, so what the hell is his deal? But then the asshole *left* while I was available and horny because the bliss that man brought my body with a mere ice cube wasn't enough. It was a taste; an appetizer and I desired more.

I want *everything*.

So yeah, I'll meet him at his gym to "train" so I have an excuse to hit him, to show him how fucking pissed I am.

My entire life, I've been quiet. Between Rozelyn and me, I was the shy sister. Dad never worried about me getting into trouble because I was the "good child." When Dad suddenly rushed me across the country, I only questioned him *after* we left.

No more. Not again. I'm fucking done.

I'll be making *noise*. And he'll be hearing me until he's deaf.

Or...that's what I thought.

But when Caladin knocks me to my back *again*, I wonder how I assumed this would go. That was, what, the eighth time? We only begun grappling a few minutes ago.

With a grunt, I shove to my feet, throwing my body at him, my movements messier than what he's taught me. Messy but focused as I dive for his knees, aiming to knock his balance off, but he side steps and practically jumps over me, nudging my back until I end up with my face in the mat.

"Fuck you."

I spin, getting to my feet and throwing my fist toward his face. He blocks with a palm, and twists my arm while I fight in discomfort to be freed. He releases me after a second but blocks my next hit, his leg stretching to trip me.

This time, while I'm lying on my stomach, I glare. My teeth press tightly together, biting down on the million and one curses threatening to unleash.

With his own cocky smirk, he stares down. His arms crossed, like he has all the time in the world to wait for me to get up. There's a hardness in his gaze not normally there. No humour. None of the Caladin I know.

This time when I lunge, it's not with a single move. It's with many. It's erratic. Fists thrown into his face, feet into his legs, my body using every bit of strength, every puff of breath, everything I have in me.

He blocks every single one but has to work at it, which makes me pleased. For a moment, his cockiness slips and I reach the true fighter beneath the surface. The one who must move quickly, block hits, and control their opponent. By the end, I'm pinned against his chest, my hands in both of his, our breaths heavy and mingling in the tense room.

His gaze lands on my lips and I turn my head and wrench my wrists away. Skin against skin burns, but he releases me.

"What the hell is your problem?" I demand, backing up a few steps to catch my breath. "This," I gesture between us, "isn't training. This is punishment. You're not giving me a fair shot."

"Not my fault your movements are messy. Three days passed and you've forgotten everything I taught you."

"Fight me properly," I dare, "and I'll show you what you've taught me. But that's not the issue, is it?" I approach again, hands shoving into his chest. He falters a step, which we both know he's allowed me to. A rumble runs through the few soldiers exercising in here, which I ignore and push again.

And again.

And again.

Him taking a step back every single time, not fighting back. Not until he reaches the edge of the mat and he takes a single stride into me, forcing me backwards.

I shove into his chest. A punch to his abs, which honestly, hurts me more than him. "Tell me what I've done to entice whatever bullshit whiny ass mood you're in."

He smirks. "Big words coming from you."

"What do you mean?"

No response. He looks away. Glances over the room.

I've never commanded one person, let alone a room full of

them, but inhaling a deep breath—a difficult feat considering how out of breath I am—and holding Caladin's gaze, I order, "Everyone out."

No one moves. *Of course, they won't. You're not their boss.*

Caladin's voice is firm, commanding in his own way. "Her orders are to be obeyed."

Everyone filters out, and within a minute, the door's shutting behind the final guy, giving us complete privacy. Caladin crosses his arms, erecting a firm stance. His head tips to the side, studying me as I work up the courage and breath to speak.

"What did I do, Caladin? This isn't training. This isn't fighting. This is a game to you, knocking me over every three seconds. What. Did. I. Do?" With every word, every verbal pinch, I step closer to him until we're toe-to-toe. "You have no fucking right to be angry when *you're* the one who walked out on me the other night!"

His crossed arms come between us, brushing the edges of my breasts as he glares down. "You're welcome. Gave you the space to move on rather quickly."

Move on? What is he...? It dawns on me; a click in my brain.

"Raj told you about Oliver."

"Oliver," he repeats with a sneer. "Thanks for that."

"Don't hurt him." I jam my nail into his abs. "He's my *friend.*"

Caladin rolls his eyes. "At least you picked well."

"Picked...were you watching us?"

His jaw ticks, but he admits, "In Central Park, yeah. He can't be that interesting, considering you answered my texts right away. And here's an intriguing fact—" He drops his arms to my waist and that's when I realize how utterly fucked I am. "You asked for a few hours. You got here one hour later. What changed?"

"Wanted to kick your ass for the other night."

Despite the banter, his next blink loosens some of the tightness in his eyes. But his hold on my hips remain. A threat, if anything. "I'm sorry. I thought it was for the best. Today proved it was, I guess."

I'll tell him the truth about Oliver soon, but for now, he deserves to feel that green emotion clinging to his back. The one I'm pleased to point out. "You're jealous." Because if he feels it maybe he'll stop denying what he wants.

"Nope. Simply protecting what's mine."

"Bull. Shit." I perch onto my toes, trying to get more in line with his gaze. "There is no other reason you would have stalked us through the city."

I know I've won because he drops my hips and walks away, wiping a hand through his hair. With that space, he loses everything. His fight. His tenseness. A deep sigh travels from him to me and when he finally speaks again, it's with his back to me, hands knotted in his strands.

"I don't know what's wrong with me, Yasmine. I don't know what to do!"

Because he's trying to keep a deal he made me in the beginning, even when so much has changed. Both our desires have unravelled and I'm done running. Done fighting the inevitable.

"Oliver's only a friend. He works at the coffee shop I've been spending my afternoons at. He and his boyfriend have been dating for three happy years."

Three...two...one...

Caladin spins. "He's gay?"

"Yeah. Awfully pleased to hear he's not trying to get in my pants."

"No, just—" The look in his eyes counters his lie though.

I walk by him, shaking my head. "Look, I can't do this, Caladin. We were finding a balance, or so I thought. I was up for taking this to the next level. I *want* to. But I refuse to deal with whatever miscommunication drama this was." I pause, chewing on my bottom lip before adding, "I'm done staying silent about certain things. It's all I've ever done and I'm sick of it. You included. This is confusing. Figure out what you want. Figure out how you want this marriage to go. When you do, you know where to find me."

I make it three more steps before a hand wraps my wrist and tugs me against his chest. Everything's a blur, but amidst it, I spot the colour of decisiveness.

His decision is made before his mouth crashes onto mine.

His hands are in my hair, and mine are in his. Our tongues battle for dominance. Our breaths matched as he walks me backwards. One step, two, and then—

"Oh!" I'm freefalling, but I've never been more protected than now, as Caladin's hold remains firm and he lowers me to the mat, coming down on top of me. "Here?" I ask, scanning the gym. No one's here, but anyone could walk in.

He busies himself by pulling up my shirt, tugging it over my head, and then my sports bra quickly follows. "We owe it to each other to not wait another minute, don't you think?" Warm hands cup my breasts, his thumb and forefinger pulling at my nipples until they shift into tight, little buds.

"Yes," I reply, breathless now for another reason as he pulls on my nipples before taking one in his mouth. While he sucks, his hands peel down my shorts and panties, and once again, I'm naked beneath him. "Your turn."

I've seen him shirtless a number of times. Have felt his erection against me. But god, with my mouth watering, and the knowledge I'm so close to seeing him fully, I reach for him. Only for his hands to come up over my wrists and pull them above my head.

"No touching until I've had my taste, *piccolo tigre*. I recall how sensitive you are. This won't take long."

He kisses down my chest, paying special attention on both my breasts until my thighs are rubbing together, the ache spreading from my chest to my core, to my entire body. I'm slick between my legs and he hasn't even touched me.

But as he works his way down, his pleased growl makes me instantly wetter. "Doesn't take long with you, does it?" He pauses, his eyes flashing up my body, and if that isn't the sexiest thing ever, I don't know what is. "I love that about you, Yasmine."

The way he says that—his words melted and soft, melding into my every nerve, ruining me.

Keeping eye contact, his tongue flicks out at my clit. And again, and again, every touch enticing another noise from me, another rock of my hips, all while his gaze remains steady. It's so erotic to watch him eat me, even when he eventually breaks eye contact. His mouth covers my entire core, his tongue slipping inside. I watch until the sensations build too strong, the heat expanding in my stomach, until my noises become cries and my eyes flutter shut, head tipping back, hands scraping at the blue mats beneath me.

"Fuck...Caladin...fuck!"

He alternates between fucking me with his tongue and licking my clit and then I explode, my orgasm moving my hips faster, chasing the feeling, praying it never ends. Never ends even as everything in my life becomes clear.

This. This is the moment. The *only* moment that makes genuine sense.

The second my breaths even out, his fingers are right there, two slipping in so easily, filling me. All I *feel* is him. All I *see* is him.

My hands make no purchase as they reach for him, my sounds borderline pathetic when he discovers the deepest place of me. He angles himself overtop me, his eyes scouring my expression, picking apart every sensation he uncovers in my weeks of hidden refusal. He smiles, and it's so natural, it makes me wonder why we haven't been doing this since the beginning.

"Come for me, *piccolo tigre.* Give this to me."

His fingers scrape the button that makes denying him impossible and I orgasm again. His mouth devours me, thumb circling my clit in tandem with his tongue. Fuck, it's so much— *he's* so much.

My core tightens around his fingers and I feel the gush of liquid pouring between his hand at the mat, wetting his clothes too. He swallows my moans, gives me some of his own back, and when he releases my mouth and slides his fingers from me, it's to lick my juices.

"Fuck," he whispers when he's finished. "I'm so fucked. You've just made me lose."

Fuckable lips pout. "Lose?"

Oh, I've lost. Lost everything. Myself by the end of the night.

Exactly like she's tired of being quiet, I'm tired of denying what I've known for days. This is going to crash and burn and my every concern will come true, but at this point, I can't even care.

When she nearly walked away from me, that was the ultimate deciding factor. I couldn't stomach it. Couldn't witness that being our ending. So I accepted the crash and fell alongside her.

I shake my head, telling her I won't be answering her question because it doesn't matter.

I could die in this very moment. Yasmine stretched on the mats beneath me, her lips swollen from my kisses, her skin pink from her two back-to-back orgasms, and her pussy drenched. Drenched and fucking waiting.

"Your turn." She grabs at my shirt and pulls it up my back. I help by discarding it to the side before starting at my pants. They're tough to remove, my cock hard and straining.

Once I'm freed, her gaze zeroes in on me. She shifts closer, reaching between us until her warm, small hands are cupping my balls, rolling them. For once, she looks shy, and when I tilt her head so I can see her face, the tips of her ears are pink, her cheeks a deep flush. My thumb strokes over the warmth, revelling in how both bashful and confident she can be.

"Fuck." It's my turn to curse as her fingers wrap my length, stroking me once, twice, until I'm seeing stars. Until I steal her mouth again, fisting her long hair, twisting and pulling on the strands until I'm in control again.

Her thumb strokes over my head, spreading precum. Her touch is firm, my cock sensitive and aching to be inside her. Keeping one hand in her hair, I reach between us, stroking my fingers through her wet core, using her desire to coat my cock. Then I wrap my hand around her wrist and force her strokes quicker, harder.

"Feel us together," I whisper against her lips. "Your orgasm is all over me."

She whimpers, pressing into me as her thighs inch apart.

"God, I want to take my time with you, Yasmine. I want to explore every inch, make you come undone in every way, but I need to finally feel your tight pussy around my cock."

Her strokes pause as her heated gaze turns upwards. She's never heard me speak so brazenly before, but I've never had a reason to. Forever keeping myself locked away, behind the agreed-upon barriers.

After this, I can't hold back. *Won't* hold back. I want to play with her. After the ice cube event, I crave all the other ways, the other tools I can bring her to the edge with. Even now, even while I'm desperate to be inside her, I scan the gym, searching for something.

But when her hands clutch my wrist, forcing my attention back onto her, she's as desperate as I am. Playing will be another time. For now, weeks of build-up, of lust, of denial dissipate the moment I lift her thigh.

"Like this?" she asks, a brow lifting in curiosity as I take my cock from her grip and stroke it over her core.

My answer is a slow plunge inside her. Slow, testing, stretching her without pain, but not so slow like I was fucking a virgin. I'm an asshole enough to wish she still was, that Gene didn't exist in her history because being the first to claim her pussy would be the equivalent to being the first man to walk on the moon.

Yes." I growl, seating myself all the way. "Exactly like this." I throw her other leg over my hip, my arms sliding beneath her until I have all her weight, kneeling on the mat as I thrust inside her.

Her legs tighten around my waist, but that's all the position allows for. I maintain a steady rhythm before flipping us over, my back to the mat this time, and her atop me. A fantasy I hadn't realized I had until now.

She makes a face, implying being impressed, as she lifts onto her knees and then slowly back down, taunting me.

"Don't think you're in charge because you're on top." To back my point, I grip her hips and thrust up at the same time I pull her down. She cries out with the new angle, my cock burying deeper than when I was on my knees. I do it again and again, before stating, "Like this, I get to see more of you. Your tight cunt swallowing my cock." My gaze drops between her thighs, the sight of me moving in and out of her enough to make me come. "Your breasts," I cup them, thumbs stroking over sensitive nipples, "bouncing in my face. Your expression when you realize what you did."

"What did I do?" she asks breathlessly, but I don't answer.

Instead, I bring my knees up, pushing her forward until she lands on her hands, her breasts in my face; the intention behind my actions. I take a nipple between my teeth, biting down, tongue flicking against the nub. She's sensitive, and one day, I want to test if she can come from nipple play alone.

I bounce her harder, using her as a body and nothing else. Trying to convince myself she's only a woman; a single fuck; no one that matters, but every attempt is useless. Every attempt *at an attempt* is useless with her every breathy moan, every cry, every thrust that reminds me who exactly she is. With her jasmine scent and dark hair, it's impossible to forget that this is my *wife*.

The woman who's become my addiction. The woman who'll be my downfall.

When her walls clamp around my cock, she's close, so I maintain the rhythm of my thrusts but switch to her other breast, sucking on that nipple. The change in focus does it and her head drops onto my shoulder, her neck muscles useless as she cries through her next orgasm. Her desire makes it slicker between us, and I don't slow. Don't give her a chance to come down from her orgasm while my thrusts speed up.

"Caladin," she gasps, arching her back. "It's too much." My arm binds her waist, forcing her down. Forcing her to *feel* this.

"Yes," I agree. "Consider this further punishment. You don't get to relax. You wanted this, so you're going to fucking *take it.*"

I roll until she's on her back again, and hike her leg up. She's a mess, her hair frazzled, skin a deeper colour, eyes unbridled. Her lips are an addictive shade of pink. She's a dream come true, and I'll remember her like this always.

"What did I do?" she repeats an earlier, unanswered question, which this time, I'll reply to.

"You ruined me. After this, I'm so fucked, Yasmine. You have no idea what you did when you—"

When you came into my life.

When you became my friend.

When you turned into my motherfucking addiction.

Her brows lower in confusion, but my next thrust wipes that away. Her head tips back into the mats, her nails scraping at my shoulders with her orgasm. She lights my skin on fire, pleasure from her painful scratches even while the pressure builds in my cock, my balls drawing tighter. The familiar tingle and I come with a final, impactful thrust.

Punishing and pleasurable.

Warmth spreads from me into her and eventually, my movements slow so I can study her like this. Remember her *exactly* like this.

Sexy. Serene.

Her eyes flutter shut and then a small smirk stretches her lips, eventually a giggle following.

I shift hair from her eyes, baring her face, but using it as a reason to touch her again. "What's funny?"

"That was a good cardio workout." She glances over my shoulder, twisting her head around the gym. "Huh. Good thing I kicked them all out."

"As if I'd let anyone else see you." My palm rubs over her soft thigh and down her leg, as far as I can reach. "You're all mine."

"I don't know," she says in a sing-song voice. "You might have to share me with Oliver. He's quite the lover, if you must know."

"Minx." Today was the prime example of what *not* to do. Trained as a mobster sometimes means act first, ask questions later, but typically, the best course of action is to examine all the evidence. Gather the facts and go from there without making assumptions. It prevents war.

Not this time. I threw that training right out the window with my jealousy and enticed a war between us that I ultimately lost. The war of my senses because after this, I'll be unsatisfied with this being our one and only time.

Like a drug, I will grow addicted to her. And like any other addiction, it'll be nearly insufferable to end it.

"Non voglio amarti ma mi sento già come se fossi sulla corsia preferenziale verso la mia lenta morte."

"What's that mean?"

"Nothing important," I lie, and then slip onto my knees, pulling my sated cock from her. "Go clean up. I'll grab our clothes and will bring them to you. Then we should go home because I plan on feeding you and fucking you again."

"Maybe in the opposite order." After a heated grin, she obeys, and I watch her ass as she goes, only moving into action when she disappears into the changing room. As I gather our clothes, I repeat my last statement in my head.

I don't want to love you but I already feel like I'm on a fast track to my slow death.

We don't end up fucking at home because once she eats, she passes out. Dead, even for it only being the mid-afternoon. After a walk in Central Park, a workout from hell, sex, and then food, her body needs the rest.

Instead of letting her sleep, I run us a hot bath and carry her from our kitchen to the bathroom, shedding our clothes before climbing in. Me first, to get into position, and then I lift her in, lowering us both into the steaming water, her back to my front.

"What's this?" She rolls her head until she's looking at me from upside down. "Massages the other day. Hot bath today. You're really good at this aftercare thing."

"I aim to please." I reach for the soap, lathering the bar with the water, before washing over her neck and shoulders. "You deserve this. I'm—" I stop, my next words making my throat dry and scratchy. "I'm sorry I was such a dick."

"You were," she agrees without thought. "But I also didn't go about this the best way. It's just—" This time, she's the one who pauses. Her fingers glide up my left leg as she thinks over her answer. "*This* wasn't supposed to happen, you know. I never wanted a husband. I wanted to go home to my sister, to Montreal, to *home*. The place I've always been. What Dad did, even before I knew the entire truth, it sucked to be yanked from one's life, and when you showed up, the only thing I dreamt of was getting back to it. So yeah, being shoved into a marriage was another straw. My determination to hate you stemmed from not wanting to be *here*."

"I understand." In her place, I'd act the same. In a short while, her life got turned around and she wanted normality again. Marriage to a *Famiglia* Consigliere wasn't her definition of normality.

"I wasn't done," she murmurs in an amused tone. "Obviously, I didn't want this. So when you offered independence, as much as you were able to grant me, it was appreciated. But then, you turned out to not be so bad, Caladin. Once we began actually spending time together."

I distract my thoughts by washing her, caring for her, instead of admitting my own path of how we got here. Putting it into words is too much.

So I switch topics altogether and wonder, "Central Park tours with new, random friends. How'd that come to be?"

She chuckles, the soft sound reverberating off the tiled wall, forever ensuring it's the sound I'll hear when I'm in here. "You moved me to New York and I've barely seen any of it."

My washing pauses, realization hitting me. She's right. Having been born and raised here, New York seems the same to me. Familiar. I've never had to think about what it's like for an outsider, and considering she was also from a large city, I didn't contemplate her interests in discovering the differences.

"Shit. I really am a horrible husband, aren't I?"

She twists slightly until I can see her broad grin, which softens the blow of her agreement. "Yes. But it's not all your fault. We did agree to be nothing more than roommates."

"Roommates still hang out."

"It's like you're trying to take the blame or something." Her nose scrunches in amusement and she twists back around, resting her head against my chest. "I also could have, and should have, asked. Apparently, we both suck at communication."

I rest the soap aside to instead use my hands, lightly massaging her shoulders and arms as I allow emotion to seep into my explanation. "I'd agree with that. You went along with your family since that's what was expected of you. In many ways, me too. My parents were great role models, but as a kid, I didn't think about how lessons were being imprinted onto me just from observation. When it mattered, when I was a teenager and could have used their example of love, communication—being a wedded couple—they weren't there. Erico's parents were the prime, typical model of a mafia arranged marriage. Joint only to preserve the family's bloodline, ensuring an heir and eventual leader for the *Famiglia*. Even Ariella made Erico realize what he was missing in life: the example of love and a good relationship. I didn't exactly have any lessons on how to be a husband, but I was okay with it." *Was* okay with it. "You know why I won't love you." An identical statement to every other time we've had a conversation about *us*, but this time feels more. "But I'm tired of running from you too."

Crash.

Burn.

An eruption of destruction.

That's my future.

I'm assuming, but I *feel* Yasmine will be unhealthy for me.

Like a drug, she'll be unhealthy and everything I need—everything I didn't know I was missing. My air, my breath, my hea—*No*. I cut the thought off before it formulates. Obviously, I'm growing as tired as she is.

We fall silent for a few moments, both of us lost to thought, as I continue to massage up her arms and over her shoulders, her back, until she's lightly moaning. My touch dips beneath the water, over her stomach, and around her hips until I'm hovering over her pussy.

"Sore?"

She shakes her head, so I slide a single finger over her clit, finding her slick and wet, and not from the water. A pleased rumble comes from my chest, knowing she got wet simply from my touch.

And this is why and how she'll break me.

"Want me to stop?"

Another head shake so I slip my finger inside her, curling until her back arches, her lips parting in a breathy, silent moan. A whimper as she bites her bottom lip, but with my free hand, I twist her head until I'm able to brush my lips over hers.

"Think you can come again?"

She nods, her secondary noises her agreement.

She does come. Quickly too, with little effort. A finger pumping her, a thumb stroking her swollen clit, and a moan I swallow with my mouth, kissing her through it, praising her with my whispers, enticing the nerves in her tight form to obey my every silent, physical command.

With heavy pants, she relaxes against me again. Her eyes shut, head curled on my chest. She rolls slightly, burrowing into me in the bathtub, and I wrap my arms around her, holding her tightly.

Enjoying the feeling of her resting on me entirely too much.

I'm so fucked.

Minutes later, when I think she's fallen asleep, she mumbles, "Can I make that third wish yet?"

"Of course." My heart beats just a bit faster, wondering what she'll ask for. If I can grant it for her. I'll do anything to make it possible.

"I wanted to return home because it's familiar to me, but deep down, I desire experiencing the world. My dad always had me bubble wrapped, demanding I *be* a certain way. For a hot second, I was actually excited when he dragged me to B.C. Confused and angry and lost, but it was somewhere new I'd get to explore. Similarly, here I was introduced to another part of the world. It's why I enjoy movies. Seeing fantasy lands created from writers' visions, experiencing real places within fictional stories. It's closer to some countries than I'll ever get. That's my wish. I want to see the world."

Done.

34
YASMINE

Two days later, I'm back in the coffee shop after classes, working through a textbook of notes for an upcoming exam. Raj is in his usual place by the door, sipping on a water bottle as he surveys the unusually busy café.

Oliver's at the counter, serving customers as they enter at a steady rate. We spoke briefly when I showed up and ordered, and I again apologized for Saturday but he brushed me aside.

My attention returns to my laptop when a black blob comes up on the other side, and I sigh, struck by how similar this is to the other day when what's-his-face introduced himself. Parker. Parker who didn't look twice at me in class today and even moved seats altogether to one across the lecture hall. I wasn't bothered by it though.

When I look up, it's into the grinning face of my husband, who's reclined against the chair's cushioned back, one leg crossed over the other. It's times like now, surrounded by college students, I realize how much Caladin stands out. How much he exudes death and danger, even if I see him in another light.

In his suit, his dark eyes surveying the shop, he stands out. A powerful confidence that even the business students, who often also wear suits to class, don't even have. A darkness surrounds him, making the students who do glance his way return to their own business just as quickly.

"How'd you know I was here?"

Caladin's eyes come back to me, rolling. "Don't insult me like that."

"Raj?"

"The tracker I have on your phone."

I glance at it sitting on the table beside my mug. "Psycho."

"You forget who I am, *piccolo tigre*. You might have sharp claws and pointed teeth, but they won't always guarantee your safety. I will."

Even my insides heat at that possessive statement. That was...hot.

It matches him. In the days I've gotten to know Caladin in *that* way, it's who he is. He woke me up yesterday morning with his mouth between my legs, and then took me to his favourite breakfast place in the city. Then on a tour of the Statue of Liberty. We spent supper at one of his favourite restaurants on the Upper East Side, and then returned home to watch a movie, which ended with me riding him on the couch.

Dare I say it, but I'm happy.

When I called Rozelyn on the drive this morning, she laughed, said "Told you!" and hung up, instructing me to "enjoy" Caladin.

"Why are you here?"

He reaches for my mug and brings the steaming glass to his mouth. With a smug smirk, he sips, before his face scrunches. "Ugh, I had come to check this place out but what *is* that?"

"A latte."

"It's too sweet to be considered caffeine. That's a disgrace to the coffee bean."

"Then ask before you steal. Lesson for you."

He returns my mug to my side and his hand slides from the hot ceramic onto mine, gripping my fingers. "You should know by now, I don't know how to share, or properly communicate."

A sharp whistle cuts into our conversation, and while I jump, Caladin doesn't release my hand, only slowly turns his head to look at the person standing above us. Oliver with his arms crossed, clearly freed from the ongoing rush he's been serving.

"You two are heating this place more than the coffee is." Then he drops his arms to slap Caladin on his shoulder, in a friendly guy manner. "Hey, man, you must be the husband. I'm Oliver. The friend from Saturday."

Caladin's sharp eyes land on Oliver's hand, and I'm seconds away from advising Oliver to remove it before he loses fingers. Once again, I've only seen Caladin in one light, but his fight proved how dangerous he can be.

"I am 'the husband' as you put it, yes." Caladin shifts, knocking away Oliver's hand to offer his own in a shake. "Caladin Rossi."

Oliver's mouth slips open and he doesn't quite manage the shake. "R-Rossi." His eyes flick over Caladin's suit. "You guys are real?"

Wait, why would Oliver know about the mafia? Shouldn't they be this underground organization or something?

Caladin chuckles, a sound of death and destruction. "As real as that sickeningly sweet coffee my wife somehow stomachs is."

"Wait." I lean forward, lowering my voice from anyone listening in. "How do *you* know about the mob?"

Oliver shrugs, his easy grin quickly replacing any previous

nerves. "One hears things when they grow up in this city. It explains him." He gestures toward Raj. "Good to know, Yasmine, you're clearly a woman to never piss off." He throws a wicked grin at me before shifting to Caladin. "So, if you're this scary dude who you know..." he mouths the next word: *kills*, "people, has she told you about Parker yet?"

"That's not sticking to your idea to not piss me off, dick," I curse at the precise second Caladin's sharp gaze cuts through the tension and onto me.

"My wife's left that name conveniently out of her mouth. Please, Oliver, enlighten me."

Another grin says Oliver's way too amused. "Oh, just some douche from one of her classes who tried to hook up with her the other day. Luckily, I saved her from him."

What is happening? My worlds are colliding.

"If you must know," I cut in before Caladin can respond, holding up my left hand, "this actually saved me. He saw my ring and took off. Even sat on the other side of the room today."

"Good." Caladin smirks. "Wouldn't want things to get messy now, would we?"

Oliver whistles at the exact second the door chimes again with another customer entering. "Damn, you two are cute in a weird way. Anyway, I gotta go. Good to meet you." With his departure, he slaps his hand down onto Caladin's shoulder again, clearly unbothered by who he truly is. "See ya."

Once he walks away, Caladin only shakes his head, amused. "Interesting character."

Leaning forward, mindful of my hair nearing my drink, I whisper, "How does he know about you guys? Aren't you a secret?"

"Not as much as you might think we are. Our name is known throughout the city, and depending which circles you run in would depend if you hear it or not. Your friend there probably knows people who know people. If he's attended any club or bar we own, which is likely, he could have overheard it. It's positive. Means we're feared. People know who controls the city. Speaking of," he pulls out his phone, "what's your friend's last name?"

"Not sure. Why?"

Pursing his lips, he shrugs. "I'll figure it out."

Figure it— "Wait. Are you looking Oliver up?"

"Yes. If he wishes to be friends with you, then I want his background to ensure he's safe."

"He's a student. He's fine."

Caladin gives me a hard look. "No offence, but you didn't know your own father was the villain. Didn't know your sister was working for him. Your sense of who is and isn't fine isn't exactly trustworthy. He won't be harmed. It's a simple background check. Unless I find something I don't like, of course."

And then you'll kill him. I glance from Caladin toward Oliver, hoping with everything in me he's simply what I've known him to be: a college student working at the coffee shop. Friendly, and in a solid relationship of his own. Not some underground villain.

On some level, I appreciate Caladin's protectiveness. His last statement is insulting, but correct. So many people in my life hid the truth of who they are, so yeah, I'm not exactly the best judge of character.

Once he lowers his phone, he asks, "When's your term end?"

"December."

"Hm, that won't do. I thought exams indicate the end. What have you been studying for?"

"Mid-terms. Which, by the way, you're interrupting." I gesture to the laptop and textbook spread on the table.

"Yes, well, you've interrupted me in worse ways. When's mid-terms over?"

"Two weeks."

"Good. In two weeks, I have a surprise."

I watch him. Wait. Nothing. "Gonna tell me?"

"Hm, no. Consider it incentive to get an A." Then he stands and sweeps close to me, tipping my head up and plasters an extremely heated and possessive kiss to my lips. He's grinning, carefree when he pulls away, and then his lips brush over my forehead in a parting touch. "Have a good day, *piccolo tigre*. I'll see you tonight."

He walks away, throwing a two-fingered salute toward Oliver and then nodding at Raj on his way out, and then he's gone.

But I feel his presence for hours more.

The two weeks fly by. Once I got studying underway and writing midterm papers, everything else sadly slowed down. Gym visits turned into every three days. I took one night off to go watch one of his fights again, and that was much needed for my brain before I returned to studying the next day.

All my classes had a visible energy of stress that I carried home every day. I'd be at the coffee shop for hours longer than normal because I'd get so lost in studying. Usually it was Caladin's text bringing me home, urging me to eat.

I've experienced another side of Caladin through this too. A supportive side. He's taken over cooking or ordering food. He's the first to run me a hot bath to pass out in. Is understanding when movie time consists of thirty minutes before my self-imposed bedtime. More than once, I've fallen asleep on the couch and woken to him carrying me to bed.

We haven't had much sex in the two weeks, not as much as either of us would like, simply because I'm *so* tired, and stressed. By the time my first midterm comes and goes, one-fifth of my stress goes away. But the very next day, I'm back at another exam, so the relief is short-lived.

A call to Rozelyn—a very brief one, one morning on my drive in—had her thrilled. Claimed this is how I've always been regarding my studies, but I don't really recall. She said if I'm like this, it means I've officially gotten fully into my new life, and that's positive.

By the time I exit the hall after my last exam, I feel *free*. Freed from midterms, and though the semester isn't over, it's a marker for the near two months that have somehow passed since Caladin found me in B.C. Only two months, but it feels like a lifetime.

Raj follows me out from his seat in the hall's farthest corner. A demand Caladin made to the school, that even if it's an exam, he must be present. Especially when he learned the exam I just completed was the same class Parker shares with me. Turns out, he looked in on him too.

He's possessive and I don't know how to feel about it. I should hate it, considering everything, but I'm secretly thrilled. Like these past few weeks have shown me how much of himself he truly tapered down in the beginning.

Raj opens the building's front doors, but I stop short at who's leaning against the SUV.

Caladin.

Caladin in his suit, glasses covering his eyes, a playful smirk lining his mouth. A few people study him as they pass and I'm thrilled to be able to walk right into his arms and kiss him. That he's mine.

"Well, hello." He grins, pushing up his sunglasses. "Finishing exams really puts you in a good mood."

"I'm free," I reply simply. "For now, anyway."

"For longer than that." He taps me on my nose before pushing off the vehicle and opening the back door. Once I'm inside, he follows me, and Raj takes his usual front seat.

Actions no different than every other day, except Raj and I being joined by him is unusual. "What are you doing here?"

"You'll see. Raj, what we spoke about this morning."

"You got it, sir."

"What's happening?" I ask, anxiety shredding at my nerves, but my smile is too freed, too large to be fully tapered. Whatever he's doing, it's making me excited and eager. Somehow, my hand ends up cupped in his, and it grounds me.

"You'll see," he repeats. "For now, sit back and enjoy knowing you've finished your exams, my studious, *moglie*."

Wife. He's taken to calling me that too. Often, it seems to slip out at the most random of times, when he barely realizes he's doing it, since there's always a flash of surprise in his expression afterwards. The ongoing reminder of what we are to one another is making this all seem more real.

Still don't know how to feel about it either.

Raj drives us away from the university, not in the usual direction of our condo, but into New Jersey. Eventually, we pull onto an airfield with only a few small, private jets parked over the large tarmac.

"Are we going somewhere?"

"There's a whole world out there for you to experience, and I'm going to make your wish come true."

The *Famiglia* plane, the very transportation that brought me here, grows larger as we approach. As Raj swings the car to a stop, Caladin immediately gets out with a wide grin, and heads for the back, retrieving a suitcase I hadn't noticed earlier.

This was all pre-planned. This is why he asked me two weeks ago about my exams.

I scramble to follow. "Wait, Caladin, we can't leave. I have school. Midterms are, well, it's in the name. Middle of the term. I still have more to go."

Caladin hands the bag off to Raj, who leaves us alone. "Yasmine, your dedication is amazing, but my mind won't be changed. I've worked it out with your school. Like it or not, I will be the one to open your eyes to all the wonders this world has."

My chest pangs in both longing and logic. This is *insane* to be taking off like this, but fuck if I don't want what he's offering.

He walks away, already knowing he's won—no he's *winning*.

"Wait." I jog to keep up with his fast steps. "You have to work."

"I told Erico this is our honeymoon, not that he'd ever tell me no." He pauses, glancing my way, his thumb brushing the underside of my neck. "Let me do this for you, Yasmine. You made a wish and I want to grant it. Want to be by your side as you see a whole world beyond North America. Visiting other countries, experiencing new cultures, it gives a point of view your movies are unable to." His touch strokes up my cheek, stopping by the corner of my eyes. "Let me open your eyes, *piccolo tigre*. That's my only wish for you."

How can I deny that? How can I deny *him*, but also myself?

I glance behind me, into the direction of the city. School. The gym. Home. Everything natural and a part of my routine. Then I study the massive plane on my other side. The gleaming, white paint, the wings that'll take flight soon, gliding through the harsh air above, connecting us from this continent to another.

It's the symbol of not only entrapment, being what brought me here, but freedom. It'll take me from here, let me experience places I've only ever dreamed about.

It's irrational and irresponsible.

But I agree with, "Okay," and the knowledge that denial was never possible.

And Caladin's responding grin makes my response worth it.

35
CALADIN

The itinerary is up to her. Our destinations, our timings, it's all on her. The plane's been stocked with fuel, and is easily refillable in every country. I've swung things with her school, and Erico basically sent me off with a cheery, "Fucking finally!" after telling him my plans for my wife.

Our trip's barely began and I know I'll be learning a lot about her in this time.

The Yasmine who first became my friend I'd found to be fun.

The Yasmine who I've witnessed be studious and focused I'd found to be downright admirable.

The Yasmine I uncover within the course of our trip so far is fucking *addictive*.

The Yasmine I currently have tied down, blindfold covering her eyes, her head thrown back in a silent scream as I trail a silk strip over her pussy, is my ultimate undoing.

We're two days into our trip—most of that has been in the air so far—as she directed us to Egypt for our first stop, claiming she wanted to tour the pyramids and all the evidence of the ancient ways before modernity tore it down. Sightseeing isn't really my thing, and while these trips are something always accessible, I've never bothered taking one, but today has been fun. Cool, even, seeing literal history.

I now have an appreciation for her desire to explore beyond North America.

But our hotel in Egypt is by far my favourite. The colours are rich, the people overly polite to obtain our money, and the flavours unique and delectable.

None better than the sweet flavour staining my tongue when I had it buried in her cunt, edging her before pulling away.

When I was initially planning this trip, I made two vows to myself: that she'll decide where we travel to, but I'd be showing her pleasure in every single place by teasing her senses in all the ways I crave to.

"Caladin," she whimpers, "I can't anymore."

"You can do it. Two more minutes. Hold on."

"I-I can't." Her hips rock, her body squirming despite the ties keeping her tight to the bed.

In her defence, I've had her on the edge for a while now. After removing her sight and access to touch, I had her spread out in an X on the bed. With the red silk strip in my hand, I've been teasing her body. Stroking it over her hard nipples, her stomach, between her legs, I tease her until she's desperate and soaked, and then I grant her pleasure with my fingers or mouth, but right before she can orgasm, I pull away.

We're three rounds in, and while I won't admit it to her, she'll be coming during the next round.

I trail the silk between her breasts again, paying special attention to the way her back arches into the material. It ends between her legs, getting darker with her desire, and I conclude the torture by trailing it down her legs, tickling the bottoms of her feet until her toes curl and push into the mattress, seeking reprieve.

"Caladin."

"Shh. Next time, I'll have to bind your mouth too." And eventually, I plan on removing her hearing as well. Sensory deprivation truly brings great pleasure. Orgasming without being able to see, hear, or touch, with only the feeling of what *I* grant, leaving her completely in my hands requires a lot of trust between partners, so it's something not frequently done in my causal sex experiences, but with her...*god*, I plan on doing as much as she allows me to.

She bites her bottom lip, obeying me as I toss the cloth away, and stroke my hands up her legs, my thumbs brushing her cunt lips. "Feel good?"

She nods, still remaining silent as per my latest instruction. In many ways, she's a natural submissive, and perhaps she would be in her personality too, if there wasn't so much fire within her.

"You're allowed to speak, to choose. My tongue or my fingers?"

"Your mouth."

While it waters with temptation of her offer, neither of the options I presented was a true option. Not right now because with me allowing this orgasm, I want to feel her. She'll be extra sensitive, extra taut from all her near-instances.

I kneel between her legs, my cock painfully hard, and in one hard thrust, enter her as deep as I can, her wetness a natural lubricant. I slide partially out, coating myself before settling in all the way. Her feet dig into the mattress, her muscles clenching as her next sound is a loud shout.

"Fuck," she pants. "Fuck, fuck, fuck, Caladin, this is so—" Her speech cuts up as I rock my hips into her. The angle pushes me against her swollen clit. "I feel fuller. More than usual."

"I know," I say darkly. "That was the intention. Now, you're going to come for me."

Some of her natural snark slips into her breathy reply. "Oh, I will, will I?"

"Mm. You will if you want to come again at all on this trip. Don't threaten me, Yasmine."

"Oh, please. The moment I lick your cock, I'll have you begging to be inside me."

She's not wrong.

Her pussy tightens, her orgasm nearly instant. Her head slams into the pillow and it's this vision right here, I'll one day take into the darkness.

"Fuck." She groans. "Fuck, fuck, this is so much." Her cunt squeezes the life out of my cock, pulling out any precum with her orgasm, her scream one the guests next door probably can hear. When she's finished and panting, she states, "You didn't come."

"Not yet." I pause. "You're probably pretty sensitive. We'll stop."

She shakes her head. "Yes, but don't."

I tug from her pussy, wiping a finger down her sated core. "No, I need you well for all my other plans." It'd be irresponsible to force her into more orgasms.

"Okay, but," she licks the corner of her mouth, "can we try something?"

"Such as?"

"Kneel over me."

"I am, but in case you need a reminder—" I thrust my hips against hers and my cock slides through her wetness.

She smirks. "No, I want you in my mouth."

Fucking Christ. I inch up the bed, my hand reaching for the ties around her wrists so she can gain control, but she shakes her head.

"No, leave them. I trust you."

This is the ultimate trust, and my insides burn with that knowledge. She's tied down and in a position where she could so easily choke, while being unable to speak her safe word. Yet, she's willing to let me remain in control.

"Your blindfold?" I'm torn between wanting to see her pretty eyes staring up at me while my cock's down her throat, and leaving her without her sight too.

"Leave it on."

I grasp my cock and bring it closer to her lips, pausing first to command, "If you need me to slow, or stop, or anything, knock your hand against the headboard." When she nods her agreement, I tap my cockhead against her bottom lip, inviting her to open.

She does, sucking deeply, her tongue stroking the base of my head, right over the sensitive part that makes me see white spots. Makes my hands tighten around the headboard for something to focus on so I don't slam my way down her throat

She lifts her head and takes me another inch before releasing me only to whisper, "Do it. I want you to. Do what you're thinking about right now."

"Yasmine—"

"Do it."

Fucking Christ, this girl.

"Only if I can see your eyes." Without waiting for permission, I rip her blindfold off, needing to see her eyes as she sucks me, but more importantly, to use them as an indicator of discomfort. I pet her hair, thumb brushing close to her eyes, holding her gaze as her lips take my cock again and I thrust once, shoving myself deep into her.

She swallows me easily, even fucking grinning around my cock, her lips curling upwards as her tongue wraps my head.

"Remember to knock if you need to," I remind her before fisting the hair beneath my palm and doing what I dreamed of. I thrust deeper, my grip ensuring she swallows all of me.

She chokes, and I pull back slightly, but she shakes her head, staring up at me with clear eyes. Eyes that don't indicate pain or discomfort. That she's okay with this. She's enjoying it.

"Fuck, Yasmine, you look so fucking pretty right now."

Of course, she is. Because this woman is fucking *mine*. Made for me, I swear to fuck. Every second I spend by her side, I think I understand why my parents were so obsessed with one another. When you find the person that makes you smile through anything, that makes your heart beat faster with excitement and slower with ultimate trust, it's impossible to ignore those truths.

Her eyes flash to mine, and that's when the heat in my spine builds. When every nerve in my body tightens with the impending orgasm. I stroke a finger down her throat, feeling the exact spot my cock reaches. That alone makes me harder, causes the heat to increase.

I fuck her face. With my wife tied up, after her own orgasms brought on by silk, I come down her throat, harder than ever before. The moment I catch my breath and my soul returns to my body, I'm shifting down her body, pulling my cock from her mouth and checking her well-being.

She licks the corner of her lips, catching stray drops of escaping cum and that makes me want to do it all again. To keep fucking her until we both die. "Bit pent-up there," she teases.

"Sorry if seeing my wife tied up with my cock down her throat wasn't the hottest thing ever."

"Hm. Well, if that was the hottest thing, then I vote we continue trying to one-up ourselves on this trip."

See? Im-fucking-possible not to fall for her.

Something I'm terrified to even be thinking.

Something I'm finding more and more difficult to deny.

In Greece, we explored the ancient ruins while Yasmine walked around with a Bluetooth-controlled vibrator buried in her pussy. Her adamant refusal to fuck by the ruins was the only reason I waited until we returned to the hotel room that night. It was okay because after the tours, we ate at a waterfront restaurant and I had the thrill switching the toy on every time the waiter came by to speak with us.

In Italy, I personally had a lot of fun, being able to speak the language I've grown up learning. Yasmine continued to give me heated glances with every conversation, and later admitted thinking me speaking Italian was hot. So that night, I didn't use anything extra. Just her, me, and my words, as I talked her through her orgasm using the entire Italian language, telling her things—admitting truths—I'll never even admit to myself.

In Paris, she sucked me off atop the Eiffel Tower after I paid an insane amount of money for a completely private tour. So private, the tour guide also wasn't allowed with us. It's become my favourite place in the world, but not because she was on her knees for me. No, up there, her expression when she stared at all of Paris was so liberating, so joyful, so infectious. She of course, got me back for Italy, and lorded over the fact that she was able to speak her broken Quebecoise French in France. The two dialects are quite different, but she did better than my every pointless attempt.

In Spain, I introduced nipple clamps to her and she wore them as I ate her pussy for three consecutive orgasms before I released her tight nubs and fucked her into her fourth orgasm.

There's a lot of history in Spain, which she knows quite a bit about after once watching an entire docuseries about Madrid.

In London, she requested trying hot wax. Turns out, all the plane rides between the countries, she's been researching, and I was only too pleased to grant her that wish as well.

Every wish she wants will be granted or I'll die trying.

A fucking terrifying truth, but it's the reality that quickly hits me. The truth of my avoidance. Her smile, her happiness, her pleasure in every shape and form...it's everything.

She did wonderful through the wax, her safe word not even a near whisper at any point. Since it's her first time, I chose a massage candle, which burns at a low heat for such instances, and I avoided dripping wax on any overly sensitive areas. I created circles on her stomach and lines on her arms, getting close to her core but not quite touching.

She came so hard.

The entire trip, I've been very cautious, always having a weapon a hand away, even though we've ran into no issues. Somehow, it's made me more on edge, like I'm waiting for *something* to happen.

With her by my side, it's only a matter of time before someone sparks a war on earth and tries to take her from me.

I fucking dare anyone who wants to try.

Having been to numerous countries now, I can accurately say, it'd be a shame to watch the world burn if someone ever succeeded.

36
YASMINE

Thoughts of school, responsibilities, and *life* are so easily forgettable being in Europe. Hell, pretty sure both Ariella and Rozelyn are waiting on return texts, but unless I'm photographing the sights, my phone holds none of my focus.

After Europe, we spend days in a private villa in the Cayman Islands. One of those over-the-water ones with a floor that sees into the ocean, so when Caladin fucked me on my hands and knees, I orgasmed while fish swam by.

At one point, he fucked me into the white sandy beach, with people down the stretch. No care for them or if they could see us when he sprinkled sand over my breasts as I came.

In the two weeks we've so far been gone on this vacation, I've learned Caladin is kinky. He offered to "tease my senses" one day, in ways similar to the ice cubes, and how we could both receive pleasure from it. Given how satisfying the ice cubes were, my agreement was instant. Since then, sex has been more than only our bodies, and Caladin's toolbox of treasures seems never ending. One of my favourites is and will remain our first night in Egypt when he teased me with silk strips.

Not to say, I haven't explored him either. I know the precise way my tongue can cause him to lose his mind. Where on his body he's most sensitive. What he looks like beneath me when I'm riding him.

After the Caribbean, we tour the United States, where Caladin brings me to some of the major places within his country. We end up completing at least two states in a day, but don't visit each one.

Orlando, Florida, to explore the major amusement parks.

Las Vegas, Nevada, where a lot of *Famiglia* business is ran from.

Keystone, South Dakota, to see Mount Rushmore.

Washington, DC, to drop by the country's capital.

Alcatraz Island, California, because Caladin felt my horror-movie loving heart would get a thrill out of it.

It did. Might be my favourite destination, second to Egypt.

And then up to Canada, after speaking with Nico Corsetti, because Caladin felt it criminal I haven't even toured my entire country. Until Dad dragged us across the country, I'd never been outside Montreal. The cross-country trip didn't count since stops were minimal and only to refuel.

We avoid British Columbia to keep a wide berth from the Seven, but explore the mountains of Banff, Alberta, even making plans to return one winter. Caladin says he'd like to see the Canadian Rockies in all its frosty glory, and then to fuck me in front of a fireplace while watching the falling snow through the massive chalet's window. Man has dreams, but I'm not complaining.

We drop by Grasslands National Park on our way through Saskatchewan, only because Caladin was determined to drive through the province once I made the argument of how flat and boring it is. Once we reached the edge, his consensus: *"Wow, you were right."*

We tour everything in Toronto, Ontario, a massive city and have lunch inside the CN Tower. Then Ottawa, Ontario, the country's capital. Since we saw the White House, it only made sense to visit Parliament Hill as well.

And then toward the east coast, where we ate the best fish and chips ever and spent an entire afternoon on a boat, floating around Nova Scotia's harbour.

As we board the plane to return to New York, I glance over the small space of Prince Edward Island, a province I hadn't initially wanted to visit, but Caladin did, simply for its unbelievably tiny size.

"That's a deep sigh." Caladin leads me to the couches inside the plane and away from the door so the stewardess and pilot can prepare for takeoff. They must be eager to go home and return to their families, since they've been carting us around. Caladin claims they were well compensated, but it's not the same.

"Yeah, it sucks to go home, but we have to. I should get back to school, and you work. We can't live abroad forever but, no offence, New York is such a letdown after everything we've seen."

Caladin takes the space beside me and tugs me on his lap when the engines fire up. He's been doing this more and more —touching me. Having me sit on him.

With his head buried in my hair—I've learned he enjoys the jasmine flower scent of my shampoo—he mumbles, "Oh, but we're not going home. Not yet, at least."

I turn so fast, my hair whips him in the face. "Where are we going then?"

His mouth opens, about to answer me, but then with an

evil grin, he shakes his head. "Ah, I think I'll hold off on telling you for now. You'll see soon."

~

Less than two hours later, a familiar skyline comes into view, stealing my attention from the movie I put on a while ago. Caladin's been passed out since takeoff, his head on my lap while I've pet his hair in a way that's calming for both of us.

That is, until my screech makes him nearly tumble from my lap as I rush to stand. "Montreal! You brought me back!"

He drops a kiss to my forehead as he rights himself. "I'd be an ass to take you on a world-wide adventure and not even visit your sister. When I spoke with Nico about entering Canada, I requested a day trip here." He pauses, his finger coming up, which tells me he's about to be serious. "We'll be here until tomorrow night. That gives you time to see Rozelyn and Della, if you're comfortable. Plus, time for you to show me all your old haunts."

I want that too. I didn't realize I did, but to show him a piece of me and the city I was raised in feels like something a husband should know about his wife.

"Only if you finish giving me the New York tour, including everything you did as a child."

"You got it," he agrees.

~

And that's how I run into my sister's arms on the front steps of the Corsetti mansion, sounding like an absolute maniac with my screech. She might have come to New York in the beginning of my union, but this feels different and not because I'm on familiar soil. But because *I'm* different.

"You have no idea how excited I was to hear you were coming!" she yells, slowly pulling me back but not releasing.

"Um, you and me both." I toss an amused look over my shoulder toward where Caladin hangs back, beside the car Nico sent to pick us up. "It was only when the plane began its descent into Montreal that I recognized the skyline."

Rozelyn glances between the two of us. "Yeah, speaking of, you never messaged me back the other day. Where have you been? Ariella mentioned to Della you two took off for some honeymoon?" Her statement is a question, but through her meaningful look, there's another one: *What changed since the last time I saw you?*

I smile and shrug, uncertain how to respond to her question because I barely understand.

The door behind her opens and Flynn steps down, tipping his head in greeting as he walks up behind my sister, his hand affectionately brushing her back.

"Yasmine!" Della quickly comes to Rozelyn's side, her arms lifting and dropping in this awkward motion with her internal battle.

I get it. The last time we'd seen each other was when Della was going undercover for Dad and I helped her get ready for the Corsetti party. I was bitchy that day, maintaining the guise my sister demanded I do.

But a hug seems too...too something.

Instead, Della makes the decision to reach for my hand. "I'm sorry about everything. Especially your dad."

I jerk back. "You're sorry? I feel like we," with my head, I indicate Rozelyn, "should be the ones apologizing. Dad really fucked us all up, didn't he?"

Rozelyn agrees with a murmur, but Della simply stares,

humming lightly in debate. "I'd argue against that. Do you remember when Ariella and I moved in, what our parents said to all of us?"

I snort. "Vividly. 'You're a family now. Act like it.'"

"We didn't. We were catty for all the wrong reasons," Della continues. "Finally, we did right by them. At this point, we're all past the point of apologies because there'd never be an end to the list. In the weirdest, most unexpected ways, we are *literally* family now. Your husband is my sister's husband's cousin. Rozelyn is dating my husband's enforcer, who's like a cousin to him and his brothers. You have my sister in your city and I have yours." She shares a fond glance with Rozelyn, suggesting a deeper relationship than I'd ever believe they could form. "By pure fate, we're connected. Us to each other, to the very family your father spent years convincing us was the enemy. Two mob families connected by my sister's union. We're more stepsisters now than when we were actually stepsisters."

Then the purpose for many of those listed connections approaches behind Della. While I'm aware he wouldn't harm me, I still take a subtle step toward Caladin as I come face-to-face with Nico Corsetti for the first time *ever*.

Seen in images, heard about from Dad, but never having met before, he's terrifying in the same way that Caladin can be under the right light. A pressed suit, expressionless face as he stares at me, a guise of death while he decides if I'm worthy to be around or not.

And then he breaks, his hand stretching toward me. "Yasmine. Heard a lot about you. As in," his eyes slide to Rozelyn, rolling, "a *lot*."

Rozelyn sticks her tongue out at him, an action if I wasn't witnessing for myself, I'd believe I imagined the whole thing. "Yeah, yeah, Corsetti."

Caladin approaches, his hand jutted for Nico. "Long time

no see. Not since Ariella's wedding." I assume he adds that last part for me. Ariella mentioned their wedding took place here, with only the Corsetti family and Caladin in attendance. He signed their marriage certificate alongside Della as a witness.

"Welcome," Nico greets, his mask falling back on in front of the *Famiglia* Consigliere. "Thank you for finding Yasmine."

"Did it for Ariella." He grunts. "But all the information and support you offered was invaluable, so thank you."

So many *thank you's...*

Like Della was thinking the same thing, she laughs. "See what I mean? Family, in the most fucked-up way. But still," she reaches for Nico's arm, looping hers around his, "we'll leave you and Rozelyn alone. I know she's the true reason you're here."

She turns away, but before she makes it even a step, I throw my arms around her. Not entirely sure why; maybe it's all her statements about family. I've never felt particularly close to Della. Nor Ariella, because that connection only came when she was hospitalized. But still...to heal some old wounds, I hug her, burying my face in her neck, so she can hear my whispers without anyone else overhearing.

"I want us to all be okay after this. After everything. Thank you, Della, for offering that."

Her arms tighten around me once and she nods, silently saying *You're Welcome.* Before tugging away entirely, she wraps me tighter again, and explains, "That one's for Ariella, if you don't mind delivering it."

She leads Nico away, who glances at Caladin. "I have drinks, if you'd like. Yasmine will be safe."

Caladin looks toward me, seeking permission, and I give it with a wave. "I'll be fine. Go. I'll find you when I'm done."

Still, he pauses, his gaze dropping to my lips. In the weeks, there's never been hesitation between us, but he does now, and I assume it has to do with the group observing. In our travels, we were around so many strangers, but this crowd knows us. Rozelyn's aware of the details of our union, so to kiss me, especially in front of another mob family, shows Caladin's true colours.

I'm not even sure which path I want him to take, but his ultimate decision is to touch the back of my hand as he passes, mouthing, *Have fun*, before trailing after Della and Nico.

Flynn, without hesitation, gives my sister a kiss before following the three of them into the mansion, leaving Rozelyn and me outside alone.

"Figured we could walk." She steps around me, tipping her head toward the massive property. "It'd take hours to lap the land once. Probably get lost before we do. That way, there's no one to overhear."

"Works for me."

The second we reach the grass, she glances behind her, ensuring we are indeed alone before swinging us both to a stop. "Something's changed with you." She scans my face, which is growing redder with every pass. "You're happy, and based on the chemistry radiating between you and your husband, I assume it has to do with that."

I take a step, forcing her to follow, so we're not remaining in one place. "Yeah. We became friends, I guess. It grew from there. Emotions, jealousy, shit communication—that's our story."

"Uh huh. And how'd you get here?"

"By plane."

She knocks into my shoulder. "Smartass. You know what I'm asking."

"We're concluding a world-wide trip."

I launch into stories of everything we've seen, the places we've been, and retrieve my phone to show her all the pictures

I'd taken. Scattered between the ruins, museums, and landmarks are pictures of Caladin and me, and though I try to swipe past them quickly, my sister snatches the phone to examine them in more detail.

"Huh. So in front of the pyramids, he kissed you. Then you two look so fucking blissful on top of the Eiffel Tower." If only she knew where his smile had come from. "Every photo," she swipes faster, "you two look so pleased. You're happy. You look in lo—"

"Don't say it." The mood immediately turns sour, the breeze blowing harsher, and I steal the phone, sliding it into my back pocket. "No, we're just...we're being."

"Mhm."

"Will you stop?" I snap, rounding on her. "It's not like that."

She grabs my shoulders, leaning closer, staring at me in the way only an older sister manages. "What's it like then? Define it for me, Yasmine, because I'm seeing evidence of a married couple *enjoying themselves* and hate to tell you, sis, but that concept isn't illegal. Look at Ariella and Erico. They found happiness in their arrangement and I've said from the beginning, you need to as well. Looks like you have."

"You have no idea what you're talking about."

Her lips fold down at the edges, like she's in deep contemplation. "All right. Pretend I don't. Again: define it for me."

I can't.

I rip from her hold and walk away, forcing her to trail behind. "There's nothing I can say, Roz. Nothing. We're just being, that's all. I asked to see the world and he made it happen. Once we're back in New York, this bubble we've been wrapped up in might pop for all I know."

After a long pause, she grabs my hand. "You'll figure it out. I have faith."

I hope so.

Genuinely hope so because I don't know how to go back now.

We ended up spending most of the evening with the Corsettis, even joining them for the most fucked-up family dinner ever. Nico invited his sister, Aurora, and her boyfriend and Corsettis' Captain, Rosen, along with his younger brother, Rafael, and his girlfriend, Isabelle, for dinner too.

Needless to say, we got a photo taken and I sent it to Erico, who roared with laughter over the fact I somehow found myself seated at a table with a whole lot of people who would have happily once used this opportunity to gain an edge over the *Famiglia*.

The dinner went so late that there wasn't a chance to explore Montreal, so we retreated to a hotel for the night, turning down Nico's offer of a room. In truth, I was terrified that being around her sister for so long would make Yasmine spiteful again, when I'd have to bring her home. I couldn't handle if we'd go backwards in whatever progress we somehow made.

The next day, Yasmine takes me around the city with all the expertise of someone who did indeed spend her entire life here.

Breakfast at a famous Montreal bagel restaurant in which we decide, though both cities are known for the bagels, New York does them better.

We walk around Old Montreal and she explains the dark humour surrounding the Lachine Canal, which is the body of water in the Old Port. Apparently, it's where a lot of dead bodies get dropped off, but knowing Nico, it's probably less than a joke than she realizes.

We climb Mount Royal, which in some ways, is her city's equivalent to Central Park. Huge, grassy, touristy. Difference is, it's a random, giant mountain in a city. I had so many questions about that.

We explore the Biodôme, an indoor ecosystem facility, which leads into plans to visit Central Park Zoo when we're back in New York.

Then we ended the day by eating poutine, which is a weird combination of fries, cheese, and gravy. When she ordered, I almost had it tossed in the garbage, considering it looked like something that had come from a dump.

Until I took a bite.

"Oh, my god," I groan, "how is this so good?"

Grinning, she lifts her arm, the rubbery curd cheese on her fork stretching until eventually snapping. Then she twirls the fork in the air, wrapping the cheese alongside a fry onto it, and pops the whole thing in her mouth. "Told you."

"Canada." I shake my head. "Don't forget about that red cup takeout place you mentioned. After catching way too many White Rock residents with them, I'm very concerned for your country."

She laughs and using her fork, points to someone walking

by the outdoor patio we're seated on. I follow the line of her utensil, spotting the very same red cup in someone's hand.

"Yes, that! I swear those motherfuckers are gonna haunt me at this point."

She's giggling so hard, I'm hit with another wave of the emotion I still won't even admit to myself. Her hair's free around her face, falling nearly into her food with her constant laughing.

"Before we leave, I'm gonna need to try one and see what the fuss is."

Her laughs slow until she can talk again. "Sure, but before we head to the plane and you return to your American ways, there's one more thing you need to experience. Eating a BeaverTail."

Did she just say...? "You eat beaver's tails? Isn't that your national animal? That's barbaric!"

~

Turns out, it's a deep-fried dough pastry that's only shaped like a beaver's tail.

And it's very, very, very delicious.

That red-cupped coffee place isn't so bad either.

Canada's an interesting place. Growing on me the longer we're here. After all, it did produce Yasmine.

Which makes the country priceless in my mind.

I still can't get over the amount of times "eh" is used in casual dialogue, but I suppose, every country has its faults.

~

"Caladin."

"Hm." I glance at my cousin, where he's seated on the edge of his desk, both of us facing the window behind. Outside, Ariella and Yasmine are lounging by the pool. The bikini Yasmine's wearing should be criminal, but it reminds me of the one she wore on the beach in the Caribbean too, so I can't mind that much.

"Caladin."

"What?"

"I'm losing you again."

I turn my head away from the window. "What?"

Erico smirks and crosses his arms. "Well, considering I asked you the same question three times. Your head's clearly still in Europe. Or was it the rest of the U.S.? Oh, or Canada?"

"Funny." I shove off the window, even as the urge to look outside again grows, but I won't give him the satisfaction. Instead, I stalk toward the bar he keeps on the far side of his office, giving my hands something to do.

"I don't want one, no thanks," he says sarcastically, making a point that I hadn't offered him one. "Ariella won the bet obviously."

"It's not over. Don't count your losses yet. I'm not in love with her." My eyes drift to the window, wondering what they're talking about.

He slaps his desk once, hard, jerking my attention. "Ha. Good one. You went from begging me to put you on a job and get you away from here to abandoning your role to spend an extended honeymoon with her. You know, I still haven't gone on one with Ariella."

"Maybe you should get on that. Clearly, I'm a better husband than you." The irony there is disturbing.

"Point *is*," he says, growing exasperated, "do you see my point?"

Sadly, yes. "Nope."

"Liar. You're lying to yourself, but I can't wait to see you crash and burn when the truth catches up."

Too late.

"Look," he sighs, "be careful. You either admit what you're pretending you're not aware of, and be happy with your wife. Or you hide it, even from yourself, and you'll eventually end up pushing her away out of obligation or guilt. Then she'll hate you, and you'll lose her either way. Depends how you want it to go down."

"Any updates on Gene?"

Erico sighs again at my obvious avoidance of the subject.

There's no point in talking about her.

I down another chug, my gaze finding the window again. No point at all.

Later that evening, a text comes through with an offer too good. Not for the money but because it'll work out this feeling within me. I can't punch Erico, but I can and will whoever the fucker is believing he'll beat me.

"You wanted to see another one of my fights, right?"

I'm struck in the gut when Yasmine looks at me. She's fucking stunning—always—but more so like this. Naked in our bed, her skin flushed from the orgasms she just rode from my mouth. The sheet pools at the base of her back from where she's stretched out on her stomach, scrolling social media on her phone.

"Yes. Did another one come up?"

I flip the phone around so she can read the message. "Starts in two hours. Enough time for another workout, and then to drive over."

She squeals as I drag her over my lap and settle her atop my cock.

~

Like last time, I lead Yasmine to one of the VIP balconies. The same soldiers as last time are there, nodding their greeting before shifting their attention to the pit below, giving us privacy.

There's a lot of differences this time from the last, and I'd be lying if I said I didn't love every single one of them.

The last time I left her here, it was with a sense of longing. We joked about a prize for winning, but now, I steal a kiss immediately and without question. Last time, I wasn't certain how she'd react to the violence involved, but this time, her hands stroke over my pecs and around my shoulders, the depths of her eyes getting brighter when she wishes me luck.

In the pit, once my name's called, I immediately look up. Having her here, watching me, knowing she's cheering me on... fuck, it makes it all worth it. A woman at my side.

I get it, Father, I do. You always wanting Mother around.

I understand him because I want Yasmine around too. Always. Every fight. I won't agree to one if I'm unable to kiss her beforehand, or look up and see her there for me.

She gives a subtle wave before pointing at the announcer, telling me in her own way to pay attention. I wink and obey as my contestant enters the pit. Doesn't seem too bad. He's a muscular fucker, but still smaller than me. One of those bodies with large biceps and a wide chest but skinny waist, so he's not proportionate at all. He grins, walking to where the announcer points to.

The crowd erupts in a yell with the impending fight. My

competitor meets my eyes, a mean grin stretching his face, looking entirely too wrong.

Why's he look familiar? Like I'd seen him in the past.

When the announcer drops his hand, he doesn't attack. I do, because there's never room for doubt. I leap on him, immediately taking him to the cement ground, one leg on either side of his waist. But I don't punch because something's wrong. Every instinct trained into me deems it so. He's not fighting back.

With a fist formed, I lean closer to him so I can speak over the noise. Normally, I wouldn't hesitate, and for all I know, this is some sick game to get me to lose, but I have to know. Have to respond to the incomprehensible twist in my gut.

His grin expands and he utters, "The Seven says hi."

Ice numbs my nerves. My fist lowers, mind racing.

He pushes into a sitting position until I'm crouched over his lap. "You didn't really think they'd free her, did you?"

Her. Yasmine.

Fuck.

In that second, gunshots ring out. Screams. Lights flicker. The crowd scatters.

Fuck. No.

It's happening. The very thing I avoided—every reason I ran from what Yasmine and I could be—it's happening. My father and mother were so in love, exactly like the obsession Yasmine and I feel for one another. It's led her to my fights. To here.

To where the gunshots are firing.

My gaze immediately finds the balcony, my feet pushing me off whoever the asshole is. I must get to her. As fast as I see a flash of colour from her dress, my body connects with the cement flooring, the fucker shoving me down.

I roll on pure instinct, barely missing the elbow that

follows. He misses me and hits the cement instead, the asshole roaring in pain. Good. Fuck, I don't have time to fight him, but it's obvious this is a giant setup. He's here to distract me.

It's fucking working. Every step I try to take toward the exit, he's right there, slamming into me, pushing me to the ground.

My men better be getting her the fuck out. She *better* be okay. Gunshots continue ringing, the underground space rampaging with the crowd screaming as they clear out.

From far away, I hear her. *"Caladin!"* But the second I try to look up, he's clawing at me.

I whirl, slamming my fist into his face. Once to get him down, and then another to knock him out, so he's no longer a barrier. Before I connect the second hit, he asks, "How's her pussy? Still as tight as I remember?"

"Gene, I assume."

He smiles, his teeth tinged pink with the blood I've already ripped from him. "In the flesh."

So many reasons to kill this fucker, and how I fucking wish I had my Glock or a weapon of any sort, but these fights are hand-to-hand, which means my weapons are locked away until after the fight.

Lifting my leg, I slam my entire body weight onto his face, my foot connecting with a loud crack. I don't check if he's dead or not; no time for that.

I take off.

And that's when smoke and heat devours the room.

When the doorway is sealed by flames.

38

YASMINE

When Caladin's opponent comes out, I lean over the railing, trying to get a better look at the man. The height we're at puts us at such a distance it's challenging and the room's lighting is very dim, only making it worse.

"Careful, Mrs. Rossi," one of the soldiers murmurs, moving closer, his hand inching in preparation to catch me. I won't be leaning over that far.

When the announcer lowers his hand and the fight commences, Caladin attacks first. Usually people fight back, but this guy goes down right away, Caladin climbing atop of him.

Then everything pauses. They're talking? Whatever he says has Caladin lowering his hand.

Something's wrong. I feel it. A sick sensation slithers over my skin, making me itchy and chilled at the same time.

"What is he doing?" one of the soldiers murmurs, confirming this isn't normal.

And then—a scream. A shout.

Someone fills the entrance to the VIP area and before I have

338

a chance to make them out, I'm being yanked to the ground by my arm.

Bang, bang!

Two gunshots. Two men. Two bodies that immediately fall around me.

Lights flicker overheard, cutting off my vision of the approaching gunman. I'm frozen with fear, clinging to both the cement floor and the pole closest to me. My eyes bounce through the flickering lights over the approaching man, the dead soldiers, my heart panging at their losses, and down to the chaos breaking out. People are running everywhere, screaming, and I can't make out Caladin amidst it all.

"Caladin!"

An arm grabs the edge of my dress, lurching me to my feet and right into the slimy face of Jasper.

"What the fuck?" I breathe. I should be more panicked, but it's all replaced by complete and utter fear. My body is numb and unresponsive, every fighting instinct crushed by the memory of his heavy hand slapping me, his slimy touch inching up my thighs.

"Hello again, Yasmine. You didn't think we'd truly let you go, did you?"

"Yes." I shove a palm into his chest, trying to recall all Caladin's lessons. "Yeah, I did because you gained an alliance with the *Famiglia*. You won, Jasper. You fucking won."

"Oh, that doesn't go away," he says darkly, bringing me closer to his body. I gag, a vague and uncomfortable recollection of the last time we stood like this. When he hit me and I was powerless to fight back.

I'm not powerless this time.

With a screech, I slam my fist into his cheek, trying to throw my entire body's weight into the hit, to maximize the pain. He doesn't even flinch, instead slamming me against the railing. He leans close, tipping me back until my hair is pulled toward the floor below, gravity weighing the strands down.

"Cute attempt. Seems you've been learning. As I was saying, we'll still have the connection with your new family. They probably should have read the contract better. Deal stands even with your death."

Clink.

Weight pulls against my right wrist. Cool, metal cuffs are wrapped around my wrist and linked to the railing.

"No, please!" I jiggle them, already knowing that's useless.

Jasper backs up, the smile of someone who's won. "This is to send a message to your family—both the Corsettis and the Rossis. No one comes into the Seven's territory and thinks they can bend the rules. *We* set them. Turns out, De Falco, you've been a better asset than we believed." He backs away, his phone held up. He flashes it briefly, letting me see he's already on a call, and my stomach drops because this can't be good. Eyes on mine, he gives a command that guarantees my death. "Light it up."

"Wait, Jasper, no!"

He chuckles, walking backwards, pausing at the doorway. "See you in Hell, Yasmine. But hey, good news, you'll be reunited with dear ol' dad sooner than you believed."

Then he leaves me at the precise second smoke fills the massive room below.

The pit!

I stand, the metal of the cuffs dragging along the railing as I peer into the dim downstairs.

"Caladin!"

He better still be alive. He *must* be alive. He—

A figure comes into view. Caladin's staring at me, relief etched all over his face. "I'm here, Yasmine. I'm coming!"

I wiggle my hand. "I'm cuffed. It's Jasper. He's here."

"They lit the motherfucking building on fire!"

That's when I see it. The fire creeping through the main entrance—the only entrance in this stupid place. This was all planned. Every second of it. Caladin being trapped by fire down there, me locked away from him in cuffs. Both of us meant to watch one another die.

I won't die. *We* won't die.

People are done controlling my future.

"*Piccola tigre,*" he yells up. Fear paints every syllable, anxiety climbing his throat. "Do what you can to get out of those cuffs. You must. Break your hand if you have to. Smash the chain against the pole. Anything. Get free and don't look back."

He's asking me to leave him? That won't happen, but the getting free part will.

I meet his gaze for only a second before a cloud of smoke makes it impossible. I curl my hand, trying to make it as small as possible, to squeeze out of the cuffs. Metal digs in; Jasper obviously pre-tightened these to my size.

"I can't do this. I can't...I can't." Still I try. I yank, the skin of my hand ripping with every attempt. I slam the chain against the metal, aware there's no way my strength will win against these cuffs. "I can't, Caladin...I can't." A murmur I know he can't hear, but it feels like I'm talking to him and that's enough for now.

More smoke's filled the room now, clogging my lungs. I cough through it, the scent of fire immediately going to my brain.

I won't die like this.

The bottom of the pit is completely filled with smoke, the doorway pure orange with flames.

"Caladin!"

No answer.

He can't be dead. He fucking can't be. He's coming.

He's coming and I'll be ready for him.

There has to be something...

The two dead bodies of Caladin's men are near me. They'd have weapons. Knives. Something.

"Fuck, I'm sorry." I reach for the closest one, finding his gun in his holster. I take the heavy metal in my hand, staring at it, realizing I have no idea how to use it. I'd more likely shoot my hand off than manage to break apart the cuffs, so that'll be plan B. I reach into his pockets, thanking my lucky stars when finding a switchblade.

It's heavy in my hand, and I flick it open, staring at the pointed edge and the cuffs. Fuck, I'm going to end up slicing off my hand, but here we go...

"Yasmine!"

I must already be dead. The smoke burned away my life because I'm hearing his voice.

Caladin appears from the shadows and smoke. His bare chest is red, inflamed, his right arm worse. His hair's dishevelled and the way he drops to his knees in front of me has me wondering how numb he is to not have flinched in pain.

"Fucking Christ, baby, you're okay." Relief paints his hands as he cups my face and takes me in a quick, heated kiss. "We have to get out of here. The entire building's on fire."

"I found this." I all but throw the knife at him and he immediately works at the lock, some-fucking-how managing within seconds to unlock it. The cuffs fall from my wrist, sliding the rest of the way down the pole.

He stands, yanking me with him, pocketing the knife and grabbing the gun I managed to unlatch from his soldier. He throws the two fallen a sorrowful look, curses, and then wraps his arm around me and drags me to his side, hissing when I brush against the redness on his body.

"Are you okay?" I demand, leaning away to grant him the space he doesn't allow.

"I am now. You're alive. Let's go."

The fire obviously began in the hallways because the moment Caladin drags me into one, my eyes are itchy, throat filling with smoke I try to cough out. It's worse here than the pit, and definitely more than the VIP balcony.

"Use your dress to cover your nose. Breathe in as little as possible. I'll get you out alive."

"I know." Luckily, it seems like most of the fire is down the other way, and the path to the door is mostly clear. But it'll only be for so long if we don't get out of here quickly. I wonder if everyone else escaped.

His arm tightens around my waist and he expertly leads us toward the entrance. I recognize the stairs we're ascending. There's a door at the top. That's the main exit. We're so close to freedom.

We're there.

Even he breathes out a heavy sigh, releasing me on the third step from the top as he goes for the door. He yanks on the handle.

Nothing.

"Fuck." I don't know which one of us says it, but it fills the room, right alongside the smoke.

It's hot. It's foggy. Fuzzy. Difficult to stay awake, but I'm trying, even as I fall against the wall, my head losing the strength to remain upright.

I think I'm sitting.

I do manage to look back down the way we came. The thick smoke. Black. The dim lighting.

And then a flash of light. Orange.

Fire.

We're fucked.

We're dead.

I watch Caladin who's jerking on the door with every muscle in his body. The gun's in his hand—a bang. It does nothing, locked from the outside. Blocked, perhaps because that's who Jasper is.

Power and fury mix. His noises are an animalistic rage, his fists banging against the metal door. I think he's yelling, but it sounds so far away. Kicks, a body thrown at it.

He'll save me.

I love you.

I should let him know. Not sure when or how it happened, but I think I've known for a while now. At some point during our world trip, it dawned on me how much I didn't *not* want to love him anymore. He might have his reasons for not wanting to love me—ironically, we're in the middle of his reason—but I can't stop my heart.

"I..."

Somehow, he must hear me. He must because his next growl is specific: "Yasmine, stay awake. Do *not* shut your eyes."

"I..."

"*Piccola tigre, non prendere la mano della morte. Ti salverò.*"

I've always enjoyed his language, even when I have no idea what he's telling me.

"I...love..."

Smoke consumes me.

Death puts things into perspective.

I wonder, in the moments before my parents were killed, what went through my father's mind. Fear, certainly, but if I'm anything like him, it wasn't fear for his own life. It was fear for Mother's. The stress of trying to get her out alive. Of his mind running through every possible scenario, every outcome, every potential escape until it all blurs into a jumbled mess.

Between them, I hope Father died first. If he had then he wouldn't have to live a second longer with the ultimate horrific realization that he *failed*.

I failed the moment Yasmine sat on the step and stopped coughing. Her body gave up trying to expel the smoke, but rather, accepted it into her.

Fuck, I failed the moment I brought her with me. If only we kept our distance from one another, she wouldn't be here. She'd be home safe, studying. Perhaps I could have left her in Montreal with her sister, keeping her far away from me.

But I was selfish. I allowed her to come. *Revelled* in her

being by my side, at my fight, witnessing me beat the fucker who challenged me.

Therefore, I'm at fault for her death.

And if Father didn't get shot first, did he feel the very burst of life inside him that I do now? Because while a large part of me wants to take her in my arms and hold her until the afterlife comes for us both, where I will cling to her for eternity, another feeling bursts.

Not protectiveness. Not fear.

But the ultimate taste of determination.

I once said I'd raze this earth if she was taken from me, and it's that emotion I tug on. That emotion that makes me drop the useless gun because it's not doing anything to help, and I high kick where the handle is. The Seven likely strapped something to the outside; because that's what I'd do in their position. Which means, it's not impossible to get out.

Just a challenging bitch that requires every muscle, every kick I can manage in rapid succession. I cough through the smoke, glancing behind to ensure the fire hasn't travelled up the stairs yet. Somehow, this old warehouse is still standing, but for how long, I don't want to be here to find out.

I kick and kick and kick and—

The door budges an inch. Light from outdoors seeps in the tiniest bit.

But it's not light from the outdoors. It's the light of *hope*.

"I'm getting us out, Yasmine. You'll be okay."

She *will* be okay or else someone will fucking pay with their life.

Another half-inch.

"C'mon, motherfucker."

Kick, kick, kick—

Metal falls away. Crashes as the barrier is broken. The door opens and the outdoors rushes in as a welcoming fresh breath, while fire and smoke mingle with nature.

Blinking through the immense smog, I trip down the two steps and pick up the woman who officially owns all of me. My legs wobble, the burn on my side stinging. I ran through the fire that trapped me inside the pit, having no other option. It was either be confined down there or burn to get to Yasmine, and the choice was simple and one I'd make time and time again. The burn will heal.

And so will she.

"You'll be okay." With every step I take, I repeat it. I'll continue doing so until it becomes true. "You'll be okay because you're not allowed to leave me. Not after I've just found you."

Once outside, my lungs suck in fresh air. It isn't enough; not for how much I swallowed, but it's a start. I shakily walk us as far as I can from the warehouse, every step pained so it's not very far at all. The fire roars louder behind us, telling me pure luck managed to save us.

"You're okay." I stroke a hand over her soot-smudged face. Her wrist is red from the cuffs the asshole chained her with. "You'll be okay."

My energy snaps like elastic and I drop to my knees, keeping her cradled against my body. I fall onto the cement lot beside the warehouse, an arm wrapped around her, right as the sound of sirens come from the distance. With all the jostling, she still isn't awake.

"You're okay. You're okay because I love you. I saved you. You're okay. You'll wake up."

I brush her hair off her face and sweep my hand to her neck, checking for her pulse. She's okay. She'll be alive. There will be a beat—

Nothing thumps beneath my fingers.

My responding roar is drowned out by the numerous sirens fast approaching.

I must stay awake. They must fix her. I saved her. She *will* live...she...will...

Black consumes me, my smoke-filled lungs making roaring impossible and I drop my head onto her shoulder.

~

Beep...beep...beep...

The annoyingly bright light implies Hell, which means I failed. That, or the sirens got to us in time and I'm in a hospital.

"Morning, sunshine."

Nope, it's Hell, or else my cousin wouldn't be here.

Groaning, I find him leaning against the nearest wall. My eyes continue over Erico, surveying the rest of the room. It's a hospital. Not much to say beyond that. Beeping machines are on either side of me, a tray on wheels to my right, a shut curtain past it.

"We run this city and you didn't even get me a private room?"

Erico smirks and pushes off the wall to bring over a cup from the tray. He angles the straw at me, but with a glare, I snatch it to drink myself.

"Not totally broken."

"No, just badly bruised, burned, exhausted, and filled with smoke."

I groan, everything coming back. There's one fact more important above all else and I sit up to find her, my side screeching in discomfort. I lift the hospital blankets, spotting the white bandages taped to my side, where the burn is.

"Yasmine."

"Two minutes and I'll bring you to her. That's all I'm asking for."

I level him with a sharp look. "Fuckin' serious right now?"

"Deadly. She's not awake yet."

"She's alive?" Relief whooshes out of me. "The last thing I recall...before the darkness. I checked her pulse. She didn't have one."

Erico smiles almost sadly. "She did. It was very faint. You saved her, Caladin."

"Fuck," I say, my spine decompressing. Waking up to find her dead, I—the thought cuts off. "I didn't think..."

"I know. That's why I'm asking for two minutes, to catch you up before you go rushing off."

"How many days has it been?"

He holds up a hand. "Stop asking questions. I promise, I'll answer everything." When I fall against the pillows with an exaggerated huff, he says, "*Last night*, I got a call from the NYPD about the warehouse fire. Immediately rushed over. Got there the same time they did and we found you two passed out on the cement. Ambulance took you both right away. Yasmine's alive, Caladin. Heavy smoke inhalation. They have her resting and on antibiotics. When she wakes and they clear her, she'll be on bed rest at home. Dr. Rancott is already on standby to support. You also had a lot of smoke in your lungs, but less than her. The side of your torso is burned, and your leg muscles are bruised." He pauses, glancing at my side. "Caladin, they showed me the wreckage of the door. I don't know how you did it, but you shouldn't be alive right now."

"Gee, thanks, love you too."

"No, you misunderstand. I saw the pole they had wrapped around the door's handle. The strength it would have taken you to get that open..." His gaze shifts to the curtain and back. "That was some fucking insane adrenaline you used. It's the only explanation the doctors have for how you managed it."

"Yeah." I shut my eyes, nearly not telling him the next part, not willing to relive the horror. The single moment I'll see in every nightmare for the rest of my life. "When she shut her eyes —when I knew I was minutes away from losing her…I lost it, Erico. I went ballistic on that door because I had to. For her."

With a gentle smile I hadn't known him capable of making, he rests his hand on my shoulder in a supportive manner that says *good job*. "The burns?"

"Ran through fire. Fuck, Erico," I jerk my head, eyes squeezing as I return to the beginning of last night. "It was a setup. The fucker signed up to fight me was goddamn Gene. Obviously a distraction while Jasper attacked Yasmine. He shot Thomas and Jonas and cuffed her to a pole. Then the place was on fire. The pit's entranceway was filling, and it was then or never. I knew I'd be injured, but it was that or death. Once I escaped the pit, it was getting to her, and then to the door. It was fucking strapped shut."

Erico's hands tighten around the bedrail. This whole time I've been worrying about Yasmine, but his own brotherly love for me had him concerned.

"Glad you're both okay. Seriously, I grew a few grey hairs when I found you on the ground."

"I need to see her," I tell him with conviction. "When I'm healed, I'm flying to B.C. Jasper's days are numbered for what he's done." But before he dies, I'll be learning the exact reason he wanted her killed.

Erico's concern melts away and he reaches for his phone, tapping on it. "Yes, that's the best part. It was obviously arson so the NYPD searched the area for anything suspecting. Tracked a SUV fleeing the city with stolen plates." He turns the phone, showing me the video feed of the warehouse we torture captives in. Bolted in chains in the centre is the very fucker who's about to greet the underworld.

"He's mine."

"Figured he would be." Erico slides his phone away. "Consider that incentive to get better."

"I'm fine. The burn will heal. Resting won't change shit, but that," I point to his phone, "that's ending the second Yasmine's home." I slide my legs to the edge of the bed, readying to stand. "Take me to her before I have to hunt her down myself."

He holds up a hand, coming around the bed to stop me from advancing. He's seconds away from getting a punch too, but for a moment, I entertain him since he's so far been useful. "See, when they brought you both in, I asked myself, if this was me and Ariella and I woke without her, what would I do? The answer: I'd tear this place apart until I found her. So I saved the medical staff the stress of trying to contain you and slipped them a bit to make this happen."

He grasps the edge of the curtain and pushes it the opposite direction. The design manages to make it slide quickly, revealing my life.

Yasmine.

Her skin is cleaner than I last saw, obviously wiped up from the soot. She looks okay. Asleep.

I stagger to her bedside, clutching the railing, breathing through my emotions before touching her and wrecking her more than I already have.

Erico passes us, heading for the door, but I don't look away from her. "Ariella's in the waiting room. She'll want to stop in to say hi. Rozelyn and Flynn are on a flight. They land soon."

I nod but my throat is too full to answer. It makes sense her sister's on her way here after everything. Fuck, if it didn't gut me so much, I'd send Yasmine to Montreal to keep her safe. Unfortunately for her, I'm a selfish fucker, so I can't.

Without looking up, I tell Erico, "By the way, your wife won the bet."

His laughter echoes through the room long after he goes, signifying something very similar to that sliver of light from the warehouse's door last night.

Hope.

It's with hope I touch Yasmine's cheek, cupping her face as I lean down to breathe in the scent of jasmine. Even through everything, it clings to her.

"Wake up, *piccolo tigre*, it's all over. Wake up so I can tell you how much I love you."

40

YASMINE

"*Wake up, piccolo tigre, it's all over. Wake up so I can tell you how much I love you.*"

Well, I'm officially dead. I must be. Only in my dreams would Caladin say that.

There's pressure on my hands, and then another voice. Gentler, familiar. "How much longer 'til she wakes?" My sister? Yep, dead.

An even softer whisper: "Erico, where are you two going?"

Ariella? She doesn't talk. She *can't* talk.

Yep, it's a dream.

A weight lifts off my chest. I *breathe*. Air that isn't tainted or clogged with smoke. Clean air.

Air that opens my eyes to the world.

To the bright overhead lights and the two faces that suddenly appear. Rozelyn and Ariella, both of whom look pleased.

Not dead then?

I groan. "What happened?" Did that come out normal? My throat is as dry as a desert.

My sister bring a straw to my lips and I suck in as much as I can. The tepid water feels colder than it should. How many days has it been since I drank? Because while I try to release the straw, instincts have my lips clamping tighter, continuing to chug until she pulls it away with a murmured warning.

"What happened?" I try again, stronger this time. With effort, I manage to get halfway sitting to scan the room around me.

A hospital room with my sister and Ariella each claiming a side of the bed. Flynn's leaning against the wall across from the bed. But that's it.

Caladin.

"Is he okay? He was—" What was he doing? What was *I* doing?

Smoke. Fire. A door. He was throwing his body at it. I was useless to help. I passed out instead.

"Oh my god, is he—" Did I imagine what he told me? Was that my brain bringing him back to life to speak the words he'll never tell me?

"He's fine." Rozelyn touches my arm. "He's okay. You're both okay. He got you out, Yasmine." Her voice cracks, as does her expression. "Fuck, Yasmine, when Erico called us...I thought I lost the only true family member I had left."

"I'm okay because of him. Where is he?" I stare at Flynn this time, insisting he answer me if they won't.

Rozelyn strokes my hair. "You've been asleep for nearly three days. You took in a lot of smoke. They had you on IVs for a while. Caladin woke up less than a day after the accident and discharged himself the same evening. He remained by your bedside until, oh," she glances at the time on the wall's clock, "four hours ago. He and Erico left to do something." She huffs her laughter. "He'll be so pissed because he was determined to wait until you woke before going, but after so many days, his agitation only grew more and more."

Flynn shoves off the wall, walking toward the door. "I'll go call the Rossis and let them know you're awake."

Ariella reaches for my left hand, squeezing it in a supportive manner, and mouths, *You scared me.*

Her and me both. Focusing on my sister again, I demand, "Where'd he go?"

Rozelyn shares a look with Ariella, and whatever silent conversation they have has her shrugging. "How much do you remember?"

"All of it. The Seven was behind the attack."

She nods. "Well, they caught him. That's what's Caladin's up to."

Oh. I don't need a definition for that. "Gene was involved."

Her brows dip before her eyes widen, nose scrunching. "Gene. Like, our Gene? Ugh, I hated that guy. Never knew what you saw in him."

"Me neither."

"Well, they didn't find him so he must be beneath the rubble. The warehouse is gone. Erico mentioned it burning down maybe five minutes after they found you, which means, it was a very close call."

I replay what I remember. Caladin coming for me, uncuffing me, his side— "He's injured. Burned."

She nods, her mouth pulling into a partial frown. "He doesn't seem too concerned about that. Withstood the smoke better than you. No one could get him to rest for long."

Flynn returns then. "Spoke with Erico. Guess Caladin's right in the middle of it. It's...messy apparently." Excitement lights up his eyes, a look appropriate for a man's who's a career enforcer. "Anyway, he didn't want to interrupt him, so it'll probably be a few more hours."

I take his words in like a deep breath. That's good. As much as I want to see him, Jasper deserves death.

"They're about to start a war with the Seven when they kill him, if it's traced back here." Jasper's arrival into the New York was likely a known plan, so when he doesn't return to B.C., it'll be obvious. "The Seven won't stand for one of their own getting slaughtered."

It's Flynn who answers. "Well, Nico already guessed it might come to that and is ready when you need us."

"Like Della said," I murmur. "Family. United through marriage."

Both Ariella and Rozelyn squeeze my hands.

~

Hours later, a loud commotion comes through the hospital halls, interrupting all the updates Rozelyn's been sharing. A "fucking move!" a crash, and then bangs.

"Jesus, he's not subtle." Rozelyn smirks. "Seems your worries from our visit are pointless."

I hope so. After what happened, who knows how he'll be? His every concern came true last night. The very thing that happened to his parents, happened with us. He might push me away after this and that—that I won't handle.

The door bursts open and the explosion that is Caladin rushes in. His entire focus locks on the bed, on me. A breath shudders out of him and whatever the chaos seconds ago, a flip has been switched and he's calm.

"We'll leave you two be." Rozelyn hugs me briefly and then leads the way out, followed by Flynn and Ariella, who meet Erico at the doorway before the door's shut behind them.

He doesn't come closer.

He stares.

His hair is wet, likely fresh from a shower. I could only imagine what he looked like previously and showing up to a public hospital covered in a murderer's blood would have created more chaos.

"Caladin."

He drops to his knees.

I scramble from the bed, practically getting to mine in my rush to be by him.

He curses, reaches for me, but then his hands fall to the ground. "Fuck, you need to be in bed."

"I need *you*." I cup his face since he won't touch me, inching closer on my knees, uncaring how ridiculous this looks. "Are you okay?"

His eyes search mine. Commits every inch of me to memory before scanning the rest of me. And then I'm in his arms, his mouth claiming mine with an intensity, and he's nodding into the kiss, reassuring me *we're* all right.

When we're both breathing heavy, not that it takes me long, he drops his forehead to mine. "I didn't comprehend the complete and utter relief I'd have at seeing you awake until I did. I...fuck, *piccolo tigre*, you terrified me. Every single second. I-I couldn't find your pulse."

His voice breaks.

His expression follows.

And then *he* does.

His head buries in my shoulder, and then there's dampness. He's crying. He holds me tighter than he ever has before, like we can never get close enough to one another. Like it'll never *be* enough.

He sniffles and pulls away an inch, tilting his face to breathe. "The last time I cried," his whispered admittance paints my skin, "was at my parents' funeral. Nothing's mattered so much since them. Nothing since you, Yasmine." He lifts his head, showing me his tears. The evidence of his feelings. His fears and his happiness. "Something snapped in me when you shut your eyes in the warehouse. For the first time since learning about my parents' deaths, I felt something. My entire focus was on saving you, and then I did, and you—" *Breathes in.* "I-I thought you were dead. And while I've spent the past three days watching you very clearly alive, breathing as you slept, it's not the same as *seeing* you awake."

I cup his cheek, thumb stroking over his skin. "You saved me, Caladin. I'm here because of you. But I have to know one thing because I won't survive life by going backwards. Does this change anything? What happened was everything you were worried about, why you didn't want a relationship. So did this change anything?"

His eyes shut and my heart shatters. I feel his answer even before he gives it. He's denying me. Denying *us.*

He pushes to his feet, cradling me and walks us back to my bed. Instead of releasing me, he climbs in too, keeping me over his lap. This feels positive.

"When I left you on the VIP balcony and went down to fight, when you were on the balcony cheering for me, I understood why Father always allowed my mother to accompany him to places. If felt so fuckin' *right* having you with me. Just having you present gave me energy and willpower. A new drive." He pauses and if he had a near-smile, it's gone now. "When everything was going down, when your eyes shut, I wondered how my father felt. If Mother was killed first and his final seconds were spent in agony, feeling like a failure. Or if he went before her and didn't witness her death. In some ways, for him, that'd be better. Because, baby, when I thought you were taken from me...it's something I've never felt before and never want to again. It's the sign I needed to not shove you away. So, no, to answer your question: what happened won't separate us. I'm done hiding from the truth, from hiding from what could be." He cups my neck, keeping my gaze steady on him, as though it'd be anywhere else. "I love you, Yasmine. Despite my hardest not to, you wormed your way into my locked-up heart."

"I think I heard you tell me that. I assumed it was a dream."

"No more dreams." His lips trace an invisible line over my cheek. "No more wishes. Just hard facts. Realities we're about to make come true." His lips freeze over my skin. "If you want. You also had your reservations..."

"I think those reservations died long ago. I've been terrified that one day you'd wake up and remember your own boundaries and my heart would break. When we were in there, right before my eyes shut, I tried to tell you how I felt but the smoke prevented me."

"Fucking fire." He growls. "I think I've known for a while."

We fall silent, both of us committing one another to memory until I eventually curl up into his chest, wondering at what point will the nice nurse from earlier return and demand him to get out of my bed. It's an argument she'll likely lose.

"Flynn mentioned you caught Jasper." I reach up to play with the damp strands of his hair. "He's gone for good?"

"All those jokes I'm not mobster enough for you; Erico has pictures of the evidence of tonight, if you'd like."

I shudder, imagining the slaughter. As nice as it'd be to see the evidence of vengeance, the visual depiction is too much. "Knowing he's gone is enough. And Gene? Rozelyn said no one was found at the wreckage."

"Fucker better hope his soul burned right alongside his body so I don't have to hunt him down too. He kept trying to keep me down, but a rough kick to the face knocked him out. After that, I ran to get you so I'm assuming he burned with the building."

Shame what happened to the man who'd once been kind to me, but clearly, once the mask came off, he's as psycho as everyone else my father was associated with.

My hand rubs down Caladin's side. "You ran through literal fire to get to me."

"Nothing's safe if I'm kept apart from you. Now," he cups my head and rests it over his heart, "I'm tired, and you need rest. Sleep, and let me hold you. Let me know you're all right."

"As long as you're holding me, I will be."

And then I do sleep with the peace of knowing that while Jasper may have almost kept us apart, he's the ultimate reason we're together.

After Yasmine passes out, I simply hold her. Shut my eyes and hug her and recall everything that's happened today.

After two days waiting for her to wake, I couldn't wait another second knowing the reason for her injuries was still alive and breathing, so I dragged Erico away from the hospital and we had ourselves a visit with our friend.

"You know that war you didn't want to occur? I think it's occurring."

Erico slaps my back. *"Back then, she was a Corsetti problem. Now, she's family. We protect our own. The Famiglia stands with you. Do what you must."*

So I did. Jasper, for all his big words, didn't last as long as I would have liked. He released a few facts but nothing overly important. Already stuff the Corsettis mentioned about the Seven and their purpose. He believed working with me would save him, but I already had his gravestone marked for death.

Nothing on this planet would save him at that point. Not

even the consequences that'll likely befall us in the coming months over killing one of the Seven.

Since I didn't get the fight I needed the other day, I started with that. While still hung in chains, I beat him to a fucking pulp, every hit, every kick, a warm-up for what was coming.

Then the weapons. He lost his fingers, gained some stab wounds, and I had been tempted to leave him sore, abused, and hanging there until tomorrow, but ultimately, his life had already ran its course. Was sure to take a lighter to various parts of his body, burning away flesh in the same places my injuries are.

Then Jasper was no more.

Which also means the contract to the Seven is done. They might be pissed about that, or more that we killed one of their own, but they fucked with the *Famiglia*; therefore, they pay.

A nurse pops her head in, spots me on the bed with Yasmine, but then thinks better and simply shakes her head. "She okay?"

I nod, not speaking to avoid possibly waking her. She needs sleep, not only so she can heal, but so I can hold her for longer. Once the nurse leaves again, I shut my eyes, tighten my hold, and sleep.

I t's another day later before I allow Yasmine out of the hospital. Yeah, allow. She was adamant to be discharged right away, claiming I had worse injuries than her and didn't stick around, but I care about her more, so there's that.

The morning of her discharge, Rozelyn and Flynn headed back to Montreal after Yasmine said there's nothing more that can be done.

Instead of heading to our condo, I drive in a direction I

haven't been in a long time. Two years, to be exact. At some point, I stopped visiting because nothing I said or did changed anything, and it became easier to bury them.

"A cemetery. Oh." She puts it together as quick as her question formulates.

I get out of the driver's side and then unlatch her from hers, keeping her hand tight in mine as I lead us toward the Rossi section, pre-owned by the organization for decades. I pass grandparents, and other older, long deceased relatives, heading for the large, double stone at the very back. Tucked way over here by Erico's parents to give the grieving orphan space to cry without being seen. They explained it as that, but in a kinder way.

With my wife's hand in mine, both of us fresh from a hospital, I lead her to formally meet my parents.

The tombstone hits the same it always does: with a dull ache in my sternum. Two years might have passed, and in some ways, it feels like hardly any time, but in others, too long.

Releasing her, I crouch, uncaring as the grass stains my clothing. My hand brushes over each of their inscriptions, picturing this moment under different circumstances. Returning from B.C. with Yasmine, like how I had, but being able to introduce her *in person* to the greatest parents. They'd love her. Mother would have taken Yasmine under her wing and taught her how to deal with my bullshit.

Would I have even tried to gain the distance I had if they were alive? I'd have no fears of losing Yasmine. And now that I nearly did, those fears have grown exponentially. Grown larger, but not ones I'll think about either because the bigger fear is not having her by my side.

She crouches beside me, studying the tombs.

"So, this is them." How does one introduce their wife of months to their deceased parents? "This is the outcome of after cops were called to the scene of the shooting. Each had a wound to their hearts, so at least their deaths were instant. It's always calmed me, knowing they weren't in pain. And they were together.

"For a long time, I hated them for it too. If they didn't love one another so much, perhaps I would have had lost only one of them. Then I met you, and now I'm mad at myself for feeling like that for all these years. My hate wasn't fair to them, or me."

She rests her head on my shoulder. "No, but living in the past also isn't the way to go about it. When Mom died, her loss wrecked Rozelyn and me for a long time. Dad certainly wasn't paying for counselling, so I started researching ways to get over the grief. There's a lot online about losing someone, but one piece of advice that always stuck with me was that at some point, accepting it doesn't mean forgetting. It means moving forward. Your parents wouldn't want you to be stuck in the past, grieving their deaths, skipping relationships out of fear."

"You're right. They'd want this. You. Us. This is why I've brought you here. What happened to them was a tragedy, and what happened to us was also one. Two sad starts, two different endings. Like I said this morning, I'm done pretending I don't have feelings for you. So I'm vowing to you, Yasmine Rossi, with my parents as witnesses, to love you until the Earth stops rotating and the end wipes away existence. Because death, death won't end my feelings for you."

I seal that vow with a kiss, and then sit cross-legged in front of the tombstone, like how I did when I was ten and during all the years following. Only this time, teenage me would be impressed by the girl seated on my lap as we regale my parents with tales of our travels.

And plans for the future.

Wishes and dreams we both have.

Including a final one of her own, as we head back to the car much later. "So you taught me to fight, except I think I still need more practice. Can you teach me to use weapons too?"

I laugh. "Not that I plan on you *ever* needing to protect yourself like that again...yeah, I think it'd be best. Although, now I'm thinking it's a bad idea. What happens when I piss you off, and not only are you able to effectively punch me, you'll shoot me in the exact area you'll know won't kill me?"

"Guess you'll have to take a chance."

Always. I'll never bet against her.

When the doctor examines her lungs for the fourth time this week, he declares them clear of smoke.

"You know what this means, right?" I ask, swinging her inside the condo, walking her backwards down the hall.

Her cheeks get pink, admitting she very much is aware. "Means you're about to fuck me."

"Means I'm about to show you the ultimate experience. I want to take away *all* your senses. Leave you with absolutely nothing but what I give you."

She shivers. Her pupils dilate. Her head bob is quick and eager, biting down on her bottom lip as I release her, gesturing for her to go ahead to the bed. She undresses quickly and lies in the centre, head on the pillows, and watches me from where I stand by the end.

"You sure you want to do this?" It's something we've spoken in detail about the past couple days because I want to ensure she's completely comfortable and willing. She's given me her limits. "Don't do this to appease me."

"I want to," she reassures me in a firm tone.

I approach the bed, skirting a single finger down the inside of her arm, enticing a shiver from her. "Safe word?"

"Egypt."

"If you can't talk?"

"Three knocks to the headboard."

"*Mia buona, piccola tigre.*"

She shivers at the praise but replies, *"Je t'aime, Caladin, mais je suis prête pour ça."*

"I know you are." Yeah, I've been trying to learn the language. Parts of it anyway. Not understanding everything she tells me adds to the lure of her.

I head for the closet and return with a box of items I'd selected for this moment and ones she'd already agreed to. I lay it on the floor so she can't see which order it'll be used in. As I stand, I grip the silky black blindfold and rest it over her chest, covering both nipples.

"Ready to begin?"

She meets my gaze, a naked, raw look when she nods, handing every part of her over to me.

I tie the blindfold around her head, shielding her beautiful eyes. Shame, but it'll be well worth it. Once it's on, she readjusts it slightly.

"Good?"

"Mhm."

"Can't see anything?"

"Nothing but black."

Then I bring out a thin, red rope for her wrists. We'd spoken about Shibari but her limit was anything too restricting and having rope around her torso, but she asked for her wrists and ankles so that, I can grant her.

With the rope, I do her ankles first, having her pull on them both to test, and then her wrists. One to each bedpost, but only after she reassures me she's okay.

Then, from my bedside table rather than the box, I retrieve the item I'm most eager for: my headphones. I place one in her ear, adjusting, and then the other, before switching on a soft melody to fill her ears.

With her sight gone, her arms bound, and unable to hear me, she'll never know what's coming.

As much as it fucking pains me, I walk away.

Fuck with her sense of time too. Not for long, of course; only a few minutes. But long enough, she'll wonder why I'm not beginning right away.

42

YASMINE

My wrists and ankles are bound, I'm listening to a random, slow song, unable to hear anything beyond the noise cancellation headphones, and the blindfold over my eyes robs me of sight. I'm excited though. Anticipating the first touch.

Once Caladin started the song, I expected him to touch me since, when we spoke in more detail about this, I asked for nothing beyond these three senses. Which means, in terms of preparation, he's done.

But nothing's happened yet.

I swear I'm getting wet from waiting alone, the expectation of what's to come building. A year ago, if someone had told me I'd be willingly allowing my husband to play with my body in such ways, I'd have laughed. Sex with Gene was basic and Caladin's icy experience was the most adventurous I'd been. Our worldwide trip, where he teased me with anything he managed to find, was thrilling. And I craved more.

But he's waiting. Why is he waiting? How much time has passed since this song began? More than three minutes, surely, but it's not slowing. If he's put it on a loop, then it's a useless indication.

"Caladin," I whisper. Not that I can hear his reply if he gives it, but no touch follows.

I wait and wait and wait and when my mind's about to fray, lost to this insanity, my body jolts.

One, two, three hot drops to the stomach. Nothing that'll burn me, but not expected. Drops that make me hiss and roll my stomach until the drops slide down my sides.

Hot water.

He drips three more drops and the bed dips.

Icy cold replaces the heat. A ball of pure chill—an ice cube —follows the path the hot water took. The temperature difference is striking, but feels *so fucking good*. Like unbelievably erotic. Water in two different forms: liquid and solid, and yet, it's enough to drive me insane.

"Caladin," I murmur, unable to hear my own words, but knowing he can.

The ice disappears for a second and cool lips trace over my ribs, kissing over the water to paint his statement against my skin. *I love you.*

"I love you too."

He smiles and I get the point of this. *Feeling* everything because it's my only sense.

He pulls away and more water drops follow, this time over the hood of my clit. The area is very sensitive to the heat, but I trust he wouldn't do anything to harm me, so although my heels dig into the bed, I don't stop him.

The bed shifts again. Anticipation builds. He follows the heat with ice, and if he's near my pussy, that means—

With my next inhale, nothing happens. Nothing at fucking all. The bed moves again, and then he's gone. Off the bed?

"Caladin," I whimper. "Don't do this to me."

More water drops. One with each hike in the soft melody, like his actions are aligning with the song.

No movement, but suddenly his hands are on my thighs and he's wrenching them wider. I realize, he's likely at the end of the bed, standing over me.

A cold tongue licks up the hot water, first on my hood, and then trailing down to my clit. My feet push into the bed, but his weight comes down on me, forcing me open for him. He licks one side of my pussy, where my thigh meets, and then the other, framing me with his icy licks.

His mouth disappears for a second, and then he's back and I'm jolting at having more than just a cold tongue touch me. An ice cube trails right over my core and with some carefully placed flicks of his tongue, it disappears.

Inside me.

"Fuck," I curse. "Fuck, fuck, fuck..."

I feel it all. His smile against my thigh, his tongue dragging slowly over my clit, teasing, and my heated pussy melting the ice cube inside me. It melts slowly, dripping freezing water down between my ass.

How can this feel so good? It doesn't even make sense how an ice cube can bring me this much pleasure.

And then his mouth covers my core and the water never makes it to the bed, instead being greedily drunken up. The heat from his mouth causes the ice to melt even quicker but every flick of his tongue, every lick, I feel it all.

My thighs tighten around his head as the elastic band stretches inside me. Every pass of his mouth is another inch gained. And by the time the ice is completely melted, Caladin dips his tongue inside me. The intrusion is the final snap of that elastic and I come.

It's strange to feel my own moan in my throat but not be able to hear it over the soft melody. He does; I know he does, because he whispers something against the inside of my thigh. Quickly, his lips in a poetic caress and I have no idea how I made his motions correctly out, but I do.

Beautiful.

My insides are coming down, my thighs falling to the side. Caladin promised me a few orgasms, but now that I've had one, I'm not entirely sure how I'll manage another.

His mouth pulls away. My core is a sloppy mess of cum, saliva, and water, but I don't care.

I turn my head as though to follow his steps, except he could leave the room for all I can hear. My thighs rub together again, waiting and waiting for what's next. I have some idea what's in the box, but not the order he'll be using everything.

Something soft strokes over my nipples and I arch into the feeling of rubber. He trails them over my nipples, once, twice, and then—*vvvvvvv.*

The rubber vibrator glides down my stomach and toward the mess. I hope he won't tease me as long as he did in Egypt; not sure I can manage being edged that many times tonight.

He drags it over my core and the rope means being unable to clamp my thighs together and keep him there. I'm good, though, and allow him to work as it continues over my thighs and down my legs, right to my feet and back up. Over my hips, my stomach, and my breasts again. Every tease brings a moan.

In their bindings, my fingers curl. It's ticklish in a pleasurable way that confuses my body. Like it doesn't know how to react. He completes another pass before the rubber disappears altogether and the bed dips again.

A leg on either side of mine and his weight possessively presses me into the bed. He cups my neck, angling my head in way convenient for him, and then his mouth slashes against mine, kissing me roughly. Like fire we walk through together with no way out. A burn I throw myself into, wanting him to consume me.

His mouth moves possessively, dominating and claiming, his hard cock pressing against my core. I rock my hips into his, thankful to have enough rope to do so. With every press of my hips, his hold on my face tightens, almost angrily.

He pulls away with a harsh breath I feel against my skin and, jaw still between his fingers, he licks my lips. Down my throat, over my collarbone, pausing at each nipple to tease them. His kisses a trail down, his mouth moving against my skin, but I can't make out everything he tells me. His whispered promises, his praise, his wishes are in a rapid succession, but I *feel* them. Not the individual words, but the impact behind them.

The truths.

The future.

And then his fingers follow and he traces every word he's painted to my skin, imprinting them further. His hair trails along my stomach when I feel two fingers stroke my wet core once, twice, and then he sinks inside deeply.

"Caladin..."

His fingers curl.

"Caladin."

They pump.

"Caladin."

His thumb moves over my clit.

"Caladin."

The elastic stretches. The fiery heat returns. I'm too sensitive to last long. Not that I ever do with him.

"Caladin."

A punishing thrust.

"Caladin!"

I come, my pussy clamping down on his fingers, and he

smiles against my stomach. They greedily keep him in place until my cries quiet and I wonder what's next.

He pulls his hand from my core and moves my legs aside, kneeling between them. His cock bounces against me, bracing, and then—

My back arches, toes curl, moan rips up my throat, arms thrash in their bindings as Caladin enters me. He grips my hips, slamming into me all the way.

I can't see him, can't hear him, can only anticipate his thrusts by his body against mine and it's fucking everything. He's *everything.*

And then the earbuds are tugged from my ears, my ankles and hands undone, and the blindfold removed between his third and fourth stroke. I go from deprivation to overwhelmed instantly, every sense returning to me at once.

He falls on me, one hand on my neck, the other on my shoulder to thrust harder. His thick growl coasts over my chest when his head drops into my neck, teeth nipping at the sensitive skin.

"Fuckin' hate how fantastic you feel. I had plans. So many plans to make this go on for longer. So many more tools to use on you, but I can't wait." He hikes my leg over one of his arms, his thrusts punishingly hard, but he knows I can handle him. His free hand loops between mine and he holds it above our heads, still keeping me captive while giving me back my senses. "You looked so fuckin' perfect, but I wanted you to see who's inside you. Wanted you to hear us together."

His mouth takes mine again in a rough, breathless kiss. I try to move with his thrusts, but he's too quick, too controlling and I allow him to be. Release my entire self into his hands.

I'm freed beneath the pass of his mouth, the thrust of his cock hitting deep inside me, the clench of his hand around mine as our orgasms build together.

"Why are you my every addiction?" He growls against my mouth. He nips down my throat, whispering words against my skin. This time, I hear them. Hear them, feel them, but can't understand them.

"Sei perfetto per me."

"La mia piccola tigre. Tutto mio. Sempre e per sempre."

"Tu verrai e non ci separeremo mai."

"Vieni per me, piccola."

That final one is an order. The translation is lost to me, and I'm not completely certain, but I feel it. Feel it in his final thrusts, his sounds, so when I arch into him again, the blinding white light consumes me, the elastic snapping, the fire burning through my form as my pussy milks his own orgasm from him and we come together, with him still mumbling promises into my skin.

He releases my hand, my leg, cupping my face as his thrusts slowly. His thumbs stroke my cheeks beneath my eyes and he smiles. Simple and beautiful. A smile of love. Devotion. And adoration.

"You're the greatest deal I've ever made, Yasmine. On my soul, I promise I'd do it all again for this outcome."

"I love you too, Caladin."

When Raj exits the lecture hall, I know my reason for being is close behind. She comes out in her Canada Goose winter coat—it was her insistence to purchase the huge, puffy thing—and knee-high leather boots, hair flouncing as she runs from the building and straight into my arms. I'll never tire of the rush having her in my arms brings to my soul.

"I'm fucking done! One more semester, starting January, and this degree is over! It's the program that kept on going, from school to school to school."

I kiss her deeply, sweeping her up to place her inside the vehicle. "Good. Because I'm giving you a graduation present, and then next week, we're headed to Montreal."

Her mouth drops open. "We are? Why?"

I gesture toward the city decked in string lights as Raj takes us toward the airfield. A Caribbean trip is a great way for my wife to celebrate freedom from school once more. Travelling with her is slowly becoming a compulsion.

"Christmas, duh. We'll spend Christmas Eve with Erico and

Ariella here, and then we're all headed up on Christmas morning to the Corsettis'. Nico called Erico this morning and invited us to their holiday party." I knock against her shoulder. "Guess Della was correct. We're all a giant, weird-ass mobster family now. Della wouldn't dare spend a holiday without her sister, and we all know you and Rozelyn would enjoy being together."

"God, yes," she gushes. "That's amazing, and already, I can't wait, but where are we going now? Don't lie, because this route is becoming familiar."

She causes even Raj to chuckle from the front.

"Somewhere I can fuck you without anyone overhearing."

Her eyes narrow. "That can be so many places."

"Next time, be more specific in your questions."

"You suck."

"No, *you* suck." My gaze drops to her lips and her ears tinge pink with embarrassment.

She leans forward and whispers, "Maybe when we arrive at whatever mysterious place we're headed, I will. Depends how much you piss me off between now and then."

Arriving to the same over-the-water villa we stayed in last time should bring only excitement, but the moment I carry her over the threshold, I'm fucking terrified. I shouldn't be. We've essentially already said the words. But this feels more permanent.

I lower her to her feet on top of the window in the floor, which reveals the water below. She was on her hands and knees the last time we were here, being fucked from behind. Yeah, that was a good memory and one I will be replicating.

"Wow, food and wine already laid out." She heads for the

table, which was prepared only when we were checking in. "Quite the end-semester gift. A bit much, don't you think? I'd have been happy with pizza and watching movies all night."

"I know." I come up behind her, cupping her shoulders. "But I'd like to think of this as our honeymoon."

She turns in my arms, a smirk lining her mouth. "We already had one of those. The worldwide one, in case you've forgotten."

"That was for our first wedding. I'm hoping this will be for our second."

"Our second...?"

After pulling the ring box from my pocket, I drop onto one knee and click it open, showing her the custom-made ring I had done weeks ago. The turquoise and diamond setting that reminds me, in many ways, of her eyes.

"Your first wish was to be happy. To be free to make your own choices. I prevented that from coming true at every turn, but I'm making up for it now. With every fibre of my being, I'm wishing you allow me to be the man who'll do that for you." I reach for her left hand, prematurely sliding the first ring off her finger. "This one represents a marriage forced upon us both. One we didn't want. But this, the question I'm asking you now, is of my own accord. My own heart literally in my palm. I love you, Yasmine. Let me marry you right this time. Let me show you the world. *Give* you the world. Make you *my* world."

"I made that first wish before I fully understood what I wanted or needed. There is nothing for you to make up for because you've done so, and continue to, time and time again. I'd be honoured to marry you again, Caladin. This time with our family surrounding us, while we speak vows and truly mean them. But," she crouches and takes back her first ring, "this might be a symbol of a rough start, but I see it as a start. Period.

It brought us together, and I can't hate it for that. I want to keep this ring, not to wear, but to cherish."

I remove the new ring from the box and slide it on the bare spot on her left hand before standing and sweeping her up in my arms, taking her mouth in a heated kiss.

"We'll do things a bit out of order this time. Honeymoon first, then the wedding."

As I carry her to the bed, she shoots me a mischievous smile. "If we have a new marriage starting, do I get three more wishes?"

With her spread out on the bed, looking at me how she is, my wish already came true; therefore, she can have as many as she wants. "Anything for you, *piccolo tigre*."

"In that case, I wish for you to come fuck your wife. Hard."

"That I can make come true, over and over." I lower my head, whispering against her lips, "And over." Then her neck. "And over." Her collarbone. "And over. Until you're limp and all mine."

"Too late. I'm already yours."

Good thing wishes can't be taken back.

Thank you for reading! Finish the series with The Bonds in Christmas (Fractured Ever Afters #6.5), a holiday novella featuring all your favourite couples and what's next for them.

Shop signed books by scanning the code below:

ALSO BY M.L. PHILPITT

Fractured Ever Afters

A 6-book (& 2 novellas) mafia romance series of interconnected standalones based on fairytales, featuring the Montreal mafia and the New York Famiglia.

The Desire in Deception (Prequel Novella)

The Hunt in Elusion

The Craving in Slumber

The Beauty in Scars

The Freedom in Captivity

The Sound in Silencea

The Obscurity in Wishing

The Bonds in Christmas (Epilogue Novella)

The Bratva's Elite

A 4-book mafia series of interconnected standalones featuring the Russian Bratva.

Merciless Queen

Deadly Knight

Defensive Rook

Violent Pawn

Captive Writings

A new adult suspenseful romance series that progressively gets darker with each book

Ruthless Letters

Obsessive Messages

Vicious Texts

Burning Notes

Twisted Holidays

A series of dark romance holiday novellas

Silent Night

Egg Hunt

Fright Night

Be Mine

Midnight Kiss

Lucky Clover

Black Magick

A 5-book paranormal romance series of interconnected standalones featuring witches, vampires, shifters, mortals, and demons.

Dark Flame

Dark Mist

Dark Storm

Standalones

A Vampire for Christmas

Audiobooks

Silent Night

ACKNOWLEDGMENTS

Honestly, this series has been life changing for me and most of that has been due to all you wonderful readers so thank you so much for sticking it out with me. Whether you've been with me since a prior series, book 1, or discovered this series partway through. I appreciate you all so much.

My betas: Megan & Colleen - thank you for being so valuable through this book, and all the others.

Thank you to my editor Rebecca Barney from Fairest Reviews Editing Services. Another series down! Can't wait to send you future books...

To Megan, my PA, who keeps me on track. The shit she's dealt with through this series.

Thank you to The Next Step PR. Colleen, Megan, Anna, and of course, Kiki - you're all amazing. Thank you for everything you do. You're the best team to have!

Thank you to Cat Imb of TRC Designs for Yasmine's cover, and for giving this series such a beautiful image!

Thank you to Karina (@id_rather.be.the.moon) for double checking my French in this one and the entire series.

Thank you to all the bloggers, booktokers, and bookstagrammers who helped with the release of this book. Your help doesn't go unnoticed!

ABOUT THE AUTHOR

USA Today Bestselling author M.L. Philpitt writes both dark romance and paranormal romance. When she's not writing made up realities, she's reading them. She lives in Canada with her four pets and survives life with coffee and an obsession with fictional characters, especially the morally grey kind. By day, she masks as a therapist.

WARNINGS

- Explicit sexual content
- Abuse (not by MMC)
- Captivity
- Physical violence (not by MMC)
- Suicidal ideation (brief mention)
- Orgasm denial/edging
- Murder
- Forced marriage
- Death
- Stalking
- Recollection of parental death
- Bondage
- Sensation play & deprivation